As Above, So Below
A Dægbrecan Publishing Book / 2023

Published by Dægbrecan Publishing

Book design and editing by Nicholas Edward
Cover design and internal artwork by Nicholas Edward

ᚾ

Library of Congress Control Number: 2023944985

Hargrave, Ingram A.

ISBN 978-1-955810-22-7 (Paperback)

Praise for As Above, So Below: A Hermann Horst Mystery

"Oh my goodness—*As Above, So Below: A Hermann Horst Mystery* is a fantastic read! Ingram Hargrave has produced a masterful historical mystery with his debut novel. ... This is fast-paced with a lot of action, plenty of creepy castle, and a great balance of really good storyline. ... The author took considerable effort to make this an historically precise, and culturally accurate for the times, novel with a literary feel to the writing and presentation of the story. I have no doubt that the Hermann Horst mysteries will be a huge hit with a new generation of mystery lovers, much like Agatha Christie's beloved detectives were when they hit the book scene in the twentieth century. I am very much looking forward to this series!"

—Abigail Darby, Author of *Merryhearth Manor & Me*

"I love a book with great characters, a deeply atmospheric setting, and a plot that keeps me guessing to the very end. Ingram Hargrave achieved that, and then some, with *As Below, So Below: A Hermann Horst Mystery*. From the moment Hermann stepped onto the night train that took him deep into the Hungarian countryside—I was there! This book sucks you right into the pages and you become an invisible participant in the action. ... If you like historical fiction, love whodunit mysteries, find haunted castles irresistible, and adore unpredictable characters and complex plots—you'll love this book too!"

— C. S. Leonard, Author of the McBee Magic series.

"Ingram Hargrave weaves a suspenseful tale of murder, mystery, and the occult against the backdrop of a Neo-Gothic estate with a dark past, taking familiar tropes from different genres but offering them from a unique and vividly described new point of view. The interplay between philosophy, psychology, and the supernatural added depth to the narrative, and the exploration of morality and forgiveness made for a thought-provoking read that really stayed with me. The novel's well-crafted atmosphere and intricate plot have a lot to offer fans of gothic styling and Hermann's blend of logic and the occult added a unique layer to the story that creates a wonderful juxtaposition for modern readers to relate to. Overall, *As Above, So Below* was an immersive reading experience that combined historical drama with intricate characters and a gripping mystery, and I wouldn't hesitate to recommend it to fans of suspense and intrigue everywhere."

— K.C. Finn, Reviewer with Readers' Favorite

Praise for As Above, So Below: A Hermann Horst Mystery

"I hardly put the book down until it was finished. Ingram Hargrave is extremely detailed and descriptive in his writing, which really helps to pull you into the story—at least it did for me. I felt like I was there with Hermann as he helped Géza to investigate and solve the murder. The world is more than black and white and this story helps to reiterate that."

—Lauren, Advanced Reviewer

"This was fun! I read a lot of Agatha Christie growing up so this was a bit nostalgic and comforting to read. Hermann Horst reminded me somewhat of Hercule Poirot, in the sense that he is observant, underestimated, and can get to the center of a problem and solve it. I can't say enough about how much I like the way Horst - and the story itself- is written. The descriptions of the estate grounds, gardens, castle interior, and the details given made it very easy to picture what the setting looked like. And Horst is wonderfully written—knowledgeable, amiable, well-spoken, witty, and handsome. While reading I felt like he was someone I wanted to meet in real life, to pick his brain or just hang out and chat about whatever. I enjoyed the evolution of Horst and Geza's relationship during the story from two awkward strangers to two professionals who respect each other's expertise and abilities and who are almost friends. Murder is always an intriguing element, especially when possible conflicts like affairs, blackmail, general scheming, a questionable inheritance and a touch of the occult are involved. The book has an interesting cast of characters—the grumpy patriarch, the spoiled son who no one keeps in check, the daughter who can be flirtatious one moment and abrasive the next, the butler, the gardener, and so on. . . and almost everyone is more than what they seem. I thought the story was well put together, and the red herrings were well done. I did not correctly predict who the real killer was, but I had an enjoyable time trying to do so!"

—Ellen, Advanced Reviewer

Ingram Hargrave

As Above, So Below

A Hermann Horst Mystery

Dægbrecan  Publishing

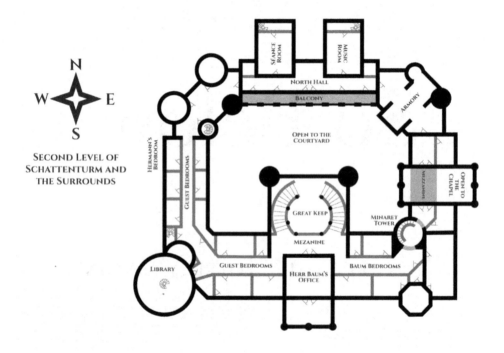

N
W · E
S

**SECOND LEVEL OF
SCHATTENTURM AND
THE SURROUNDS**

SÉANCE ROOM

MUSIC ROOM

NORTH HALL

BALCONY

ARMORY

HERMANN'S BEDROOM

GUEST BEDROOMS

OPEN TO THE COURTYARD

MEZZANINE

OPEN TO THE CHAPEL

GREAT KEEP

MEZANINE

MINARET TOWER

LIBRARY

GUEST BEDROOMS

HERR BAUM'S OFFICE

BAUM BEDROOMS

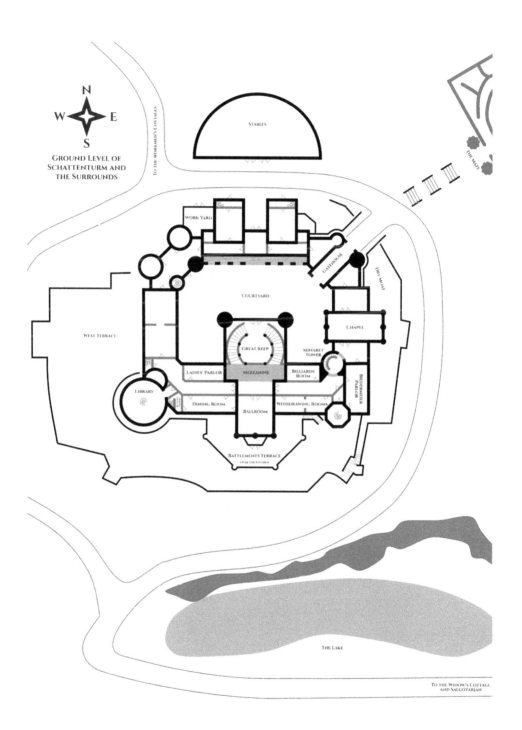

N
W · E
S

GROUND LEVEL OF
SCHATTENTURM AND
THE SURROUNDS

STABLES

TO THE WORKMEN'S COTTAGES

THE MAZE

WORK YARD

COURTYARD

GATEHOUSE

DRY MOAT

CHAPEL

WEST TERRACE

GREAT KEEP

MINARET
TOWER

LADIES' PARLOR   MEZZANINE   BILLIARDS
ROOM

BIEDERMEIER
PARLOR

LIBRARY

DINING ROOM   WITHDRAWING ROOMS

BALLROOM

BATTLEMENTS TERRACE
OVER THE KITCHEN

THE LAKE

TO THE WIDOW'S COTTAGE
AND SALGOTARJAN

As Above, So Below

Chapter 1

Grandeur, the word that best captured what the lecture hall was meant to convey. Rich oak paneling lined the walls through which the tall, arched windows admitted the blue-grey sky that permeated every nook and cranny of Vienna in the spring. Hovering above the expansive space were geometric, gold-filigree designs set artfully into the intricate frames of the coffered ceiling. Rows of seating steeply descended from the back of the room towards the sprawling chalkboard. A substantial oak desk provided a point of balance at the center of this universe of knowledge, perfectly positioned below the ornately carved seal of the University of Vienna.

Hermann Horst presided over this opulent academic setting when his class on comparative mythology was in session. He managed, with some effort, to have his lectures feel close, conversational, despite the room's omnipresence and inconvenient echo. The architect had probably not intended this—more likely the opposite—the perception of prestige, of stateliness amongst the student body, the lucky few who could study there at the center of political and educational power.

The students were much the same as they always were, a sea of expensive suits of nearly identical black, brown, and grey wool with the latest cuts and detailing. They were differentiated mostly by their fathers' professions, likely the same professions they would pursue—future aristocrats, financiers, diplomats, attorneys, and historians—all of them the flower of Austro-Hungarian society. The exception being one of the only female students admitted to the university that year, on a tenuous part-time basis, of course.

Hermann had a fondness for assessing the people around him at a glance. The second-year in the third row, for instance, used a pencil for taking his notes rather than a pen which gave the impression he often changed his mind about the key points of the lecture, or that he was a bad speller. A young man with sun-streaked hair, who chose to sit at the back of every class in an aisle seat, began a rhythmic metronome with the bounce of his knee towards the end of Hermann's lectures, suggesting strongly that he was a member of a rowing club and feared being late for practice. A small-framed student in a black suit near the front of the class had recently tried to grow a beard, with very mixed results. He usually kept his head of curly black hair down whenever Hermann focused on Teutonic or Medieval topics, but seemed bright and focused when the ancient Greeks were mentioned, as he was for the current lecture, so perhaps he was of partial Greek extraction himself. Hermann made a mental note to engage him in conversation during the next Department of Philosophy social event for the students.

As Hermann wrote the Greek word on the blackboard that was to be the focus of the rest of the lecture, he practiced the same mental trick on himself. If an outsider tried to summarize him at a glance, what would they conclude? The professor wore a brown suit of moderate quality with a blue tie that highlighted his steel-blue eyes and athletic build. The suit said that he either didn't come from a wealthy family, or else he was intentionally thrifty, preferring his accolades in the form of professional accomplishments, achieved in a prestigious academic world that didn't rely entirely on one's status in society. He was extremely young to be a professor, looking every bit his twenty-eight years, but no older. If any of the students thought it was odd that their professor looked more like a fellow member of their fraternities or sports teams, none showed it. His sandy-blond hair was neatly styled around his rectangular face, except for one strand or other that he was always having to brush back after it fell out of position. His age and middle-class background must mean he was highly sought after for his academic abilities, or that he had a powerful benefactor who helped him achieve his career. Considering Hermann taught courses within the Department of Philosophy, the latter would be more likely. People had told him there was something in his expression, a warmth about his eyes that made him approachable, so he didn't come across as arrogant or elitist, for which he was thankful. He smiled to himself as he finished the last stroke of chalk because the unruly strand of hair had just fallen down over his right eye.

Hermann turned to face the class, dusting a bit of chalk off his hands as he spoke.

"The Areopagus, a hill named after the god Ares in Athens, where it was called the Areios Pagos. The Areopagus served as the judicial seat of Classical Athens, the place where trials for sacrilege and murder were held for centuries. The scholar Apollodorus tells us that the origins of the Areopagus lie in myth, like so much of Greek culture. After the son of Poseidon assaulted the maidenhood of Ares's daughter, Ares sought retribution and killed his daughter's attacker. When Poseidon found out, he demanded a trial be held, presided over by the rest of the Olympian gods. The gods convened on the Areopagus and found Ares innocent of murder." Hermann walked around to the front of the oak desk to sit on its edge, then folded his arms. "The victim was avenged, the villain disposed of, and the loving father left free from punishment. What was the meaning of this myth?"

He looked across the lecture hall where every pen was poised, ready for the results of his usual line of Socratic questioning. Hermann signaled to a student on the right who'd raised his hand. "Yes, Herr Spahn?"

"Justice? That even the gods aren't above the law?"

"But was the law determined by the other Olympians? Would it have been their opinions on the matter that set the precedent?" Hermann moved on and signaled to a man in the center of the third row. "Herr Draxler, what do you think?"

"Perhaps the myth was meant to establish a hierarchy of offenses. That rape should be treated worse than murder."

"Indeed," Hermann said with a nod. "One does get that impression. But is there another facet to the tale?"

The next hand that Hermann noticed came from the first row on the left, the only female student. "Fraulein Althofen?"

"The myth is meant to give legitimacy to the court of Athens. If the Areopagus is the place where the gods held trial, and where the gods abided by the rulings, then Athenian court rulings over men must have had at least as much legitimacy as the gods' rulings did."

"We have our answer," he said as he walked back around to the board. "This myth is an example of etiology, from the Greek, aitiología." He swept the chalk over the board in large strokes. "It means, to give a reason for." He turned back to face the class. "Legends often serve the purpose of explaining why things are the way they are. In this case, that not all killing can be considered murder. That it's often complex, messy."

Hermann noticed the door at the back of the lecture hall open; the bearish form of his department head entered. Doctor Kießling was a large man with an equally large, but well-kept, brown beard. The old man shut the door quietly, then leaned against the back wall, clasping an envelope from one end. He watched as Hermann called on a fourth-year who was slouched in his seat, casually supporting his chin from an armrest.

"Herr von Stadl, you have a question?"

"So, what's the origin of the Greek oracles and augers. You, especially, must have a theory, Professor Horst."

"Do you mean, what purpose did the occult serve in legal rulings in Ancient Greece, or is your question more broadly posed, Herr von Stadl?"

"Both, I suppose."

Hermann crossed his arms and paced slowly in front of the old oak desk. His students, particularly those who'd had him for other classes, liked to hear his thoughts when he waxed esoteric.

"Oracles, like the one at Delphi, delved into symbols and signs sent, they believed, from the beyond. The curling of smoke from a holy brazier, the flight patterns of birds, or the condition of an animal's entrails. From temples charged with the energy of prayer and devotion, they gave warnings and advice to almost everyone who wanted to know the future or learn the opinions of their ancestors. They tapped into a well of experience and understanding latent within the human psyche and collective spirit, or so the histories tell us."

He paused in thought, thumb and forefinger resting on the edge of his angular jawline, then continued in a low tone, drawing their attention and keeping them focused, even the usual skeptics.

"The occult was then, as it is now, a broad term to refer to everything secret and potentially knowledgeable. Usually only to be accessed by a gifted few who could tap into an ineffable power. These same founts of knowledge and intuition may still be at work today, for those who master the methods of accessing them. The ancients fell into mystery cults and numerology. The medieval courts into alchemy. The renaissance vanguard into secret societies. And today, we understand how the psyche may tap into the abyssal world of unconscious knowledge. Some today seek signs from the deep recesses of the mind through secret rituals and scrying into messages from the dead. Who can say if our interests now are any more, or any less, valid than those of the past?"

He might have continued, but Hermann saw one of Doctor Kießling's eyebrows raise and could half hear the man's grumbling protests from across the room. Occultism was not a course on offer at the university, but Hermann did have a knack for allowing it to bleed into class discussions. It may have been to give the students an added interest in the otherwise dry coursework of comparative mythology. Or, strictly subconsciously, it may have been a means of enhancing his relevance to a student body of his own generation. During his time as a student at the University of Vienna, Hermann had devoted himself to his studies more than his aristocratic peers. He had begun with an advanced placement in architecture at the Academy of Fine Arts where he'd planned to continue, but a change of interest convinced him to switch tracks to the liberal arts. By the age of twenty-two, he'd earned a doctorate in philosophy from the University of Vienna, and garnered a position on the university's junior faculty two years after that—in no small part because of Doctor Kießling.

"Let's move on from the Greeks and come back home, to Germania Antiqua. Does anyone recall the fate of Balder?"

A lanky, blond student on the right with round brass spectacles raised a hand. Hermann nodded to him.

"Balder was the Teutonic god of light and purity, son of Wuotan and Frija. He was killed by Hadu with an arrow made of mistletoe."

Hermann nodded. "Yes, and why was he killed, Herr Uhlmann?"

"The god Loki was jealous of Balder receiving affection from the other gods. Loki knew that mistletoe was the only thing that could hurt Balder, so he tricked the blind god, Hadu, into firing a mistletoe arrow at him."

Hermann continued off that point. "Loki is the trickster and chaos god, the one who betrays many of the fair gods throughout the myths. Grimm proposes that his name stems from an Old Teutonic word meaning to bend, or to lie. Balder's name, in contrast, means bold or brave and has connotations to daytime and shining light, hence his position as a god of purity. Loki was sentenced for his crimes. He was chained to a rock in Naustrant, a realm in the underworld, where all murderers, adulterers, and oath breakers go to be punished in the afterlife. A nasty place, with poison dripping from walls made of snakes, where the corpses of the dead will be gnawed on by the dragon Nidhouwari."

He paused for effect. "So, what can we infer about our ancestors? They had no fine stone temples or generations worth of scrolls stored in libraries. At least not at that time," he said as he held up his arms and looked to either side of the opulent room, which elicited a few chuckles. "What do our simple, barbarian forefathers have in common with the Greeks?"

The young woman in the front row seemed eager to respond and raised her hand again. Hermann obliged.

"Yes, Fraulein Althofen?"

"They viewed murder as a complex act, as did the Classical Greeks. Loki was responsible for Balder's death by using Hadu, who didn't know what he was doing. That was dishonorable, like many other things Loki had done to the gods. The punishment was meant to fit the crime of subversion and cold-blooded murder. The other occupants of Naustrant are an example to the living. Adulterers who'd violated the marriage bond and oath breakers who'd foresworn their friends and masters. It was an etiological tale to establish a part of Teutonic culture, just like the Greeks did with the Areopagus."

Everyone in the hall was watching her with rapt attention, most with curiosity, but one or two with disquiet.

"The punishment of Loki parallels the trial of Ares," she continued. "Murder wasn't a cut and dry issue. Loki used trickery to kill Balder, whereas Ares was acting out of passion to right a wrong. There was enough evidence in both cases to establish the intent of the killers. It wasn't that our ancestors weren't civilized, it's just that they lived in a world where some kinds of killing were justifiable and others weren't. Namely, pre-meditated murder."

Once finished, she realized that she'd become the center of attention and retracted in her seat, more than a little embarrassed for stepping out of her expected lane.

Hermann smiled. "I couldn't have said it better myself, fraulein. I hope the rest of you were taking notes." He clapped his hands together. "Now, I want you all to have read the first half of Tacitus' *Germania* by next week's class. We'll start on our next subject, Interpretatio Romana, the study of foreign cultures through a Roman lens. Enjoy the weekend, everyone."

Doctor Kießling waited until the throng of students had thinned before making his way down to Hermann. The old man had a penchant for dressing well, as he did that day in a dark-grey suit that matched his tie and the whisps of grey scattered throughout his beard.

"Did you enjoy the brush up on mythic tribunals?" Hermann asked as the head of the philosophy department made his way over.

"I was impressed by the fraulein's display. I had reservations about admitting a female student, even part-time, but it seems they were unwarranted."

"Maybe you'll convince the board to change their rules on admittance, to allow the other half in?" Hermann offered with a wry smile.

"Oh ... well, let's not get too hasty," said Doctor Kießling.

The prospect seemed to have surprised the old academic, as Hermann expected. A bit of good-natured banter on egalitarianism might have been fun for the young professor, but his former mentor would have been preoccupied with how a change in admission rules might affect fundraising and donations from the alumni, or if it would upset the student organizers. As usual, Hermann needed a bit of reigning in before he let his interests run too wild. Kießling had maintained a fatherly disposition towards the young man since Hermann's own time as a student; he still was his mentor in many ways.

"Anyway, I received a very strange visit from a most impertinent courier just a few minutes ago. He insisted I give you this letter as soon as possible. It says it's from the Hungarian police."

Hermann could see that clearly enough from the return address as the doctor handed him the envelope. It was from an Inspector Orczy Géza, Budapest Gendarme. He recognized the Hungarian placement of the surname before the given name, a holdover from their ancestors' time on the Eurasian Steppe, he remembered. He tore open the envelope and pored over the contents of the letter. Kießling's face elongated as he peered over the top of the letter a few times, testing his skill at reading upside down.

"It seems I'm to assist in a murder investigation, Doctor." He folded the letter and slid it back into its envelope. "And I'm to leave at once."

"Why?—I mean, why did they call for you?"

"Apparently they're in desperate need of a bona fide specialist in parapsychology and occult practices. Something about a curse that's impeded their investigation."

Those were interests of Hermann's that he'd let run wild. So wild that he'd written two volumes on parapsychology over the last few years. A benefit of his standing as a junior professor was that he was spared many of the dull administrative duties, like serving on committees and organizing conferences, that his full-fledged counterparts spent much of their time on. It gave him room to devote to his own unsanctioned research. Few but the most eccentric really cared to study the science of the paranormal, and those that did were more often than not already biased by their own amateur secret societies and mystery cults serving as after-dinner entertainment. The host of well-known charlatans and con artists scattered around Europe also did nothing to uplift the field in old academia.

He loved teaching mythology and history, but Hermann's preferred fields of parapsychology and the science of the occult were still either scoffed at or frowned upon, even by the veteran liberals of 1848 amongst the faculty and alumni. His age probably had a lot to do with the attitude of the old white beards. They may have thought he needed more time to mature in his interests since it wasn't that long ago they had been teaching him themselves. After all, one's star could fall quite far if it was let to.

He'd only needed to read the letter once to decide that an excursion from academia, into the events that make history, was exactly what he needed. He loved Vienna and the university, but it had a constraining feel at times. You could only push the material so far, help draw only so many conclusions for the student body, before the board or other faculty took issue. There was always something in the old epics, Minnesänge, and the legends to inspire the next generation of aristocrats and middle-class men, practically every student was ready to learn about the greatness of their ancestors. However, getting to the underlying truth—education without bias—was Hermann's goal for his students, and spirits did dampen somewhat with his more realist attitude of the material. He hadn't quite gotten around to lecturing about the politicization of religious authority over the eons.

"Hermann, do you really think that's wise? You took up all this paranormal miscellany with more than a little gusto after what happened to your sister. We all thought it could help you work through your grief, but now you're talking about it in what, a professional capacity? And at the expense of your students' curricula at that."

Hermann ignored the reference to his sister and pressed on. "Don't worry Doctor, I'll ask Wilhelm to present what I already have on the schedule, and I won't be gone for more than a few days. The police in Budapest have set a deadline for the whole thing to be wrapped up by the end of the week, according to this letter."

He did not add that his teaching assistant, Wilhelm, would also need to continue their combined research into seventeenth-century witch and werewolf trials during his absence.

"What about your reputation?"

"No one will know besides the family that owns the estate and the police. Plus, it could provide a very valid example for my research on mass paranoia. How else throughout history can whole towns claim to see ghosts and demons around every corner?"

Kießling shook his head and rubbed his eyes. "Fine, fine. Go ahead. I'll tell the others ... that you're out on official business, to lend some historical context to a police investigation in Hungary. Yes." Then he laid a hand on Hermann's shoulder. "But please, my boy, take care of yourself, and try to keep your eye on the right road."

Hermann smiled as he thought about the murmuring that would ensue later amongst the board members as they sipped brandy at the Rudolph Club.

Chapter 2

After running through his office to get Wilhelm up to speed, Hermann made one more stop before he headed home to pack: the library in the new Ringstraße Universitätspalast. The letter he received from Inspector Orczy stated that the estate he would be traveling to was called Schattenturm, located in Nógrád county. The library, he knew, would have a wealth of information to help him get acquainted with the area and hopefully the house as well. He didn't want to arrive a complete outsider.

The building made an excellent improvement to the university, though the old library hadn't been expanded upon so much as collected into the new space. Still, its three levels of storage allowed for at least 60,000 volumes, the largest in the empire and the whole German-speaking world. The magnificent glass-skylight ceiling made lamps mostly unnecessary, outside of the winter months. Hermann checked out three books: *The Chronicle of Ottoman Hungary*, an outdated copy of *The Great Houses of the Empire*, and *The Sigils and Hereditary History of Austrian Aristocracy* reprinted with an addendum in 1872 to clarify and expand upon the new titles of the dual monarchy.

With two suits and enough shirts for a week, a change of formal evening wear, the library books, shaving kit, and his note satchel, all tucked neatly into two cases, Hermann took a last look around his apartment. He exhaled the breath he'd forgotten he'd been holding, then made his way down to the street and hailed a cab for the Raaber Bahnhof. The humid spring air in Vienna never smelled like wildflowers or icy winds rolling down the Alps as it had back home in Salzburg. It was more like the myriad of bakeries on a good day, and horse droppings and factory emissions on a bad day. He arrived at the bustling station just in time for the afternoon train to Budapest, via Preßburg.

Hermann stowed his cases in the bachelor's cabin assigned to him and made his way to the dining car. He took an isolated seat at a small side table at the far end of the car, facing out and ahead in the direction of the train's movement. The other passengers, fortunately, teamed up or joined with their own companions, and none of the loners asked to join him. Hermann needed the time to himself, to learn all he could about Schattenturm before he arrived, and to mentally prepare himself for the scene he was about to encounter—one that could manifest haunting memories of the last time he'd seen his sister. He carefully positioned the three volumes he'd brought to the dining car in front of him on the table, beyond the reach of his rotkraut's vaguely disgusting vibrations.

As the slanted light of the Vienna sunset dipped out of view and the train rolled beyond the city's limits, Hermann read over the letter from Inspector Orczy again to absorb as much detail as possible.

April 4, 1886
Salgótarján, Nógrád County

Dear Professor Horst,

I am writing to you on behalf of His Majesty's Budapest Gendarme Police Force to request your assistance in an ongoing investigation of a murder which, I am ashamed to say, His Majesty's Police has been unable to solve thus far.

I will spare you a sentimental prelude and get straight to the point. Twelve days ago, the Nógrád county police were dispatched to the estate of one Johan Baum to investigate the murder of his chief gardener, Andrej Fehér, who was found dead in the cypress maze outside of the old mausoleum. Herr Baum is an industrialist from Budapest who bought his home and lands a little over a year ago. The estate is close enough to the town and mines of Salgótarján to manage his business affairs there without much issue. In truth, his estate is a castle, though its medieval fortifications were renovated into a kind of palace by the previous owner, a late Freiherr von Voitsberg. Schattenturm has over one hundred rooms surrounded by more than one thousand acres of gardens, hunting woods, and tenant farms. However, make no mistake, the splendor it once enjoyed has been slowly falling into decline since the end of the von Voitsberg dynasty.

The gardener was discovered with a hammer lodged in the back of his skull. The cause of death was obvious homicide, but the perpetrator remains unknown. The body of Andrej Fehér was found by his apprentice, Pavol Soták, a boy of eighteen, around midmorning. He reported the death directly to the estate's butler, who sent for the county police. The police searched the grounds and surrounding woods for three days, but found no trace of the assailant. Thereafter, they sent for aid from the Budapest Royal Gendarme, which is where I entered the drama.

Within the day of the request, I arrived at Schattenturm and began my investigation. I had a hunch that there was more to the story than a simple murder by some roving cutpurse or Gypsy as was first believed. The hammer that killed Andrej had come from a decorative placement in the armory hall of the gatehouse, part of a large collection that Herr Baum personally negotiated to retain in the acquisition of the estate. The butler assured me that the weapon, and everything else, was in perfect order when he finished his rounds of the house the night prior. This suggests the weapon was taken sometime after the butler fin-ished his parlor service around ten o'clock in the evening, and completed his rounds of the castle thereafter. What exactly the gardener was doing in the maze near the mausoleum, in the middle of the night, has still not been determined. I highly doubt that Andrej Fehér was inspecting the hedge trimming by the light of the waning gibbous.

So far, I have relayed to you the simple facts of the case as it stands, but there is another aspect which has impeded my progress and affected the sanity of all involved. The household and town are in a state of subdued hysteria due to some old legend that Schattenturm is the focus of a curse, laid out by the original patron of the founding family, Gustav Freiherr von Voitsberg. When von Voitsberg conquered the castle from the Turks in the late 1600s, he allegedly swore that if his family were ever to be driven from their home, his spirit would rise from the grave with the power of the devil to drive the interloper out. It's hogwash that the staff and townspeople have taken up with gusto.

Stranger though, is the effect that this legend and the murder have had on the Baum family, the present owners. Frau Kam, Herr Baum's mother-in-law, who has apparently always dabbled in the occult, has begun trying to raise the von Voitsberg spirits through card readings, seances, and the scrying of her family Bible. She's determined to know whether the spirits of the castle are bent on removing them from their new home. Herr Baum is dismissive of her beliefs, but others in the household fear or respect the old widow. Erzsébet Baum, Johan Baum's wife, prays daily for an end to the whole thing.

Unfortunately, the superstition and occult activity has cre-ated an obstacle to my traditional investigative practices. Few are willing to speak to me in any way, beyond retelling the same basic facts over and over. I believe that nearly everyone involved in the case knows more than they are willing to reveal, and I have good reason to believe the curse is a smoke screen that benefits the murderer.

Frau Kam informed me that you, Professor Horst, have quite a background in the occult and a predilection for studying such things from a scientific perspective. I have briefly reviewed Frau Kam's copy of your book, The Paranormal Psychological Polemics of the Modern Mind, and found your methods to be sound and, dare I say, logical. Your view of the supernatural as a kind of mental projection may help me. Your unique specialization and empathetic grasp of the occult could be the only route to expose the murderer. If you can appeal to the nature of the staff and the family, to speak their language on ghosts and curses, then I am hopeful they will open up to you, if not me, and reveal enough information for this investigation to be concluded.

To be fair, I must admit to you that I am not accustomed to the paranormal or to superstition. I am skeptical about all this occultism, but I can see no way to the end of this case without taking it seriously. Simply put, I need your help. I am nearing the end of my time here as my commanding officer has cut my window to the end of the week to wrap up the investigation. After that, the murderer will escape the law, and Andrej Fehér will never know justice.

If you are willing to drop everything to assist His Majesty's Gendarme and give service to your country, send word as soon as possible via telegraph. There is daily rail service to the station in Salgótarján on the northbound line from Budapest. If you should accept, I will be waiting for you at the rail and mining station with transport to Schattenturm where one of my men and I have been stationed, and where accommodations have been provided, courtesy of Herr Baum.

Sincerely,
First Lieutenant, Senior Inspector Orczy Géza

P.S. Pack appropriate outdoor boots.

Hermann set the letter down and released a deep sigh. It wasn't every day that one was called upon to help solve a grisly murder, much less one steeped in enough superstition to hamper the police. He wondered what he was getting himself into. It was no matter though, he was on the night train now and had sent the telegraph from the station in Vienna. For whatever might come of his involvement with Schattenturm, Hermann intended to be ready—hence the collection of books he'd brought with him, the contents of which he began to study in earnest as the hours slipped by.

The first he cracked open was *The Great Houses of the Empire* which featured a lengthy section on Schattenturm. The house was constructed between 1850 and 1863 by a Georg Friederich Freiherr von Voitsberg. The interesting point was that while the house was remodeled in the Neo-Gothic style, parts of it encased a preexisting thirteenth-century Hungarian castle complex, including the keep, main hall, inner bailey, towers, and curtain wall. In the seventeenth century, the Ottoman occupant of the castle had added a minaret which was kept by the von Voitsbergs, cloaked under a new spiral tower and lookout room nearly double the minaret's original height. The gatehouse and armory featured prominently as the collection space for a grand assortment of medieval and early modern weaponry that the Freiherr had inherited through the work of his ancestors. The majority of the book's description of the house focused on the newer additions, such as the ballroom, dining room, and the grounds which Inspector Orczy had mentioned in his letter.

The section on Schattenturm also contained a condensed biography on the owner, Georg Friederich Freiherr von Voitsberg, who was still living at the time of publication. It seemed he was the center of the imperial party circuit, famous for his massive masquerades, elaborately themed parties, and for hosting acrobatic performances in the house which drew guests from as far away as Venice, Königsberg, Leipzig, St. Petersburg, and Paris. Hundreds would descend on Schattenturm and the local area, at times too much for the whole county of Nógrád to accommodate. On those occasions, the freiherr would charter a private train to and from Budapest to ferry his guests for days of hunting, partying, and gambling. Commonplace at his parties were towers of French champagne, party gifts of small jewels, token silk handkerchiefs blazoned with the von Voitsberg crest, and the most delectable cuisine. The freiherr's hospitality extended to every corner of his once-vast estate of tens of thousands of acres, and guests were encouraged to admire his priceless artwork and tapestries, fine furniture, imported carpets, sculptures, paintings, books, and the extensive grounds and gardens surrounding the house. The author had stated it was, "To be sure, a regular Versailles in its heyday." Hermann sensed the author's references to the ridiculous level of decadence, and the comparison to Versailles, were not necessarily a compliment.

The other two books, *The Chronicle of Ottoman Hungary*, and *The Sigils and Hereditary History of Austrian Aristocracy*, proved to be far less exciting. *The Chronicle* described the Ottoman Empire's conquest of Nógrád, Hungary, and the castle with it, following the defeat of Louis II at the Battle of Mohács in 1526. Schattenturm changed ownership again when it was seized in the 1690s as the Holy League countered the Turks and pushed them out of Central Europe. That was when the von Voitsbergs had entered the picture. The progenitor, Gustav von Voitsberg, was little more than a mercenary in the Habsburgs' service during the war. However, with the support of a few men, he took the castle in a single night. After scaling the walls, they orchestrated a gruesome spectacle that *The Chronicle* refused to elaborate on, and declared victory for the Holy Roman Emperor. The Emperor, in return, bequeathed the rank of reichsfreiherr to Gustav and all of his descendants, along with the castle and vast land holdings.

The Sigils and Hereditary History showed the lineage of the von Voitsberg title down through the centuries to Georg Friederich Freiherr von Voitsberg who, at the time of the book's publication in 1872, had no legitimate issue; so, the title and lands would pass to his brother or his brother's children. The family crest appeared at the top of the entry and drew Hermann's closer inspection: a pale arm holding a war hammer on a grey background with ermine trim girdling the frame, accompanied by the motto "Sanguis Aeterna," *Blood Eternal* in Latin.

There was no mention in any of the books of the family curse cast by the original freiherr, Gustav von Voitsberg. Hermann realized he would have to dig further to learn about the curse and why everyone was taking it so seriously. The hammer was an interesting feature relating to the old family, but that alone wouldn't explain why the inspector had sent for him. He had planned to read on, but dawn began to stream through the windows as the train rounded a turn and blew its whistle.

An attendant approached him, "Pardon me sir, you'll need to return to your cabin now as we're approaching the station at Salgótarján."

Hermann returned to his cabin and sunk back into the red cushions of his seat as the cadence of the railcar jostled him slightly, rolling over the undulating hills of the Hungarian plains. He rubbed his eyes for lack of sleep and watched the train's advance on the village from his window. The approach was marked by two lines of hills, steadily narrowing and rising into small mountains as the train travelled inwards. The first thing Hermann noticed when the train slowed were several mining depots cluttered with sooty coal cars and an assortment of storage buildings that were labeled *Iron Ore* in both German and Hungarian. Dominating the scene were cranes and a large conveyor-belt mechanism that hoisted thousands of tons of coal rock, all overseen by the watchman's tower. The dusky haze hanging suspended over everything in sight revealed the purpose of this newly built shanty town. It reminded Hermann of his visit to the salt mines in Salzburg when he was a boy, though the bitter taste in the air here wasn't mineral dust, it was coal ash. If anyone wondered who was responsible for this industrial cataclysm, they need only read the patron's name emblazoned with great red stenciled letters—from railcars and the little peaked-roof train station to the pay office, and on half the signs that could be seen from the train's window. His name was everywhere in this company town, in Baum's town.

Chapter 3

Hermann disembarked onto the platform with his two cases. It was early morning and he looked around to get a proper read of the town and the kinds of people dashing about in their daily routine. The dirt of the town's streets mixed with the coal ash had created scattered puddles of oil, explaining Inspector Orczy's advice to bring a pair of boots. He grimaced when he realized he'd forgotten to pack a pair and was left instead with his standard black loafers, more suited to the halls of the university back in Vienna.

Once most of the passengers had cleared, Hermann watched as an impressively tall man appeared from a swirl of engine steam at the front of the platform. As he came nearer, Hermann noted that he was at least 190 centimeters tall, with wavy dark-brown hair, emerald-green eyes, and a square jawline set off by a neatly trimmed short beard. Hermann thought he looked like a statue of Árpád come to life, save for the modern attire. The man was wearing a first lieutenant's uniform of the Hungarian Gendarme: a dark-green, placket-tab jacket with a matching shirt beneath. His neckline was framed by a collar band with a matching set of gold stars, vertically aligned on each end of the band. All of this was topped by his black kepi hat, adorned with a gold button and soutache trim. Hermann noted, with a frown, that the man was wearing a pair of sturdy black boots with his dark-grey trousers.

"Professor Horst, I presume?" the man said in German, with only a trace of a Hungarian accent. He assessed Hermann apprehensively for a moment.

"Indeed, and you must be Senior Inspector Orczy Géza?"

Géza nodded and took one of Hermann's cases, freeing his other hand which allowed the men to shake.

"I was very glad to receive your telegram last night, Professor Horst. Your journey was quick on the heels of my letter it seems."

"I was anxious not to waste a moment. You indicated that there was a very short window remaining for the investigation."

"Just so." Géza motioned, ushering the professor off the platform. The two walked down the street, past some dingy yellow houses, in the direction of an ornate black carriage hitched to two matching horses, equally dark in color. Géza waved to the coachman who strapped and secured the cases to the carriage's rear boot. He said something further to the man in Hungarian which Hermann was unable to make out.

Once they were off the road and into the carriage, they set out northwards as the sights slowly passed outside the windows.

"Salgótarján is mostly quiet if you tune out the sounds of the mines and the rattle of the coal-railcars," said Géza. "There's a general store that doubles as the post office." He pointed to a flat-fronted, clapboard building across the moat of mud that served as the main street. "A few shops for specialty items, a butcher, the bank will cash a cheque from most other branches, and there is the antiques store that Frau Astrid von Voitsberg runs toward the north end."

"Von Voitsberg? Is she a relative of the late freiherr then?"

"She's the sister of the current freiherr ..." He pulled a small notebook out of his placket-tab pocket and flipped through it quickly. "Friederich is her brother's name.

Though it was their uncle, Georg, who was the last freiherr to live at Schattenturm."

Hermann nodded, connecting the details from *The Sigils and Hereditary History*.

"That's close to everything this place has to offer, but don't worry, Herr Baum has assured me that you won't have to rent a space in the workmen's bunkhouse. The butler, Herr Fürth, will have made a room ready for you at the estate. Probably in the castle's western hall where Officer Erdei and I have been quartered. We can get started straightaway. I have the evidence gathered in the spare livery room downstairs."

"That would be ideal. Could you tell me about the family? How are they handling the situation?" asked Hermann.

"Herr Baum has been incensed by the coverage in the papers coming out of Budapest. They don't present him or the castle in a good light. Otherwise, they seem to be reacting as one would expect, calm on the surface, but shaken up."

Hermann nodded. "I'm new to murder investigations, but in conducting my research on the parapsychological, I've become a sort of specialist in studying and interpreting behavior. Have any of the family exhibited signs of behavior that seem ... well, off? Has anyone been caught in a lie, even a small one? Any moodiness that seems uncharacteristic for the situation?"

"Well, we've come to part of the reason I agreed to bring you out here. I've never been one for subterfuge. I'm afraid I may have missed something with these people, the staff too."

Hermann noted the implication behind Géza's use of *agreed* but decided against reacting to it. "Yes, I can well imagine the social distance between the family of a landed estate and the staff, the gardener specifically, is considerable. You must have a short list of suspects though?"

Géza sighed. "I won't play coy, Professor. I've treated Herr Baum as a suspect since I first arrived, but we can get into that once we have the evidence in front of us, so I'm not speaking blindly to your frame of reference. Baum is cagey with me and acts more like I'm an agent for one of his competitors' companies than an officer of the law."

"I wonder if that's due to the nature of his business? Your letter said that he relocated here to manage the mines."

"So he says. I haven't heard him speak about his business directly since I arrived. He's close-mouthed about it, but it would have to be very demanding, considering the hours he's kept."

"What about the investigation? Will we be, or have you already been, confined in its scope?"

"I still have the authority to investigate as I will, thank god. No one is off-limits, and no place is out-of-bounds, yet. The Baums don't have the number of staff that the house was built for, so we'll be left alone the further we get from the kitchen and the few rooms on the southern side of the main level that the family frequents. Only the children venture outside to the grounds. Herr Baum has been locked in his study for most of the time that I've been here."

The inspector's deep voice trailed off and he grumbled something that Hermann couldn't hear. This left a wake in the flow of conversation which Hermann used to look out the window as the carriage passed by two churches on the northern end of town. One was Catholic, in the Baroque style, and painted the same yellow as the houses he had seen earlier. The second, a Lutheran church, was built in a Neo-Gothic fashion and painted with a matching shade of yellow, situated across the street and up a small rise from the first. Hermann half smiled; the Greco-Roman and the Teutonic were battling it out again, though now in architecture and congregational tithes rather than with halberds and stake fires. Both churches had small signs in Slovak, probably trying to draw in the migrant workers coming down from the Tatras for work.

In place of clapboarded structures, the houses on this end of Salgótarján were made of brick and stone, washed in painted stucco with red-tile roofs, many with windows in the peaks of their shallow gables. The ruins of a small tower were visible on a high hill above the town, overgrown with scrub, and surrounded by thick woods. The pleasant scenery was punctuated somewhat by the slanted glares a few of the women, in their gardens or drying their laundry, shot toward the black carriage as it passed.

"Inspector, is there any ill will borne toward Herr Baum, or to Schattenturm at large? Would it relate to the curse and its effect on everyone as you mentioned in your letter?"

"The staff at Schattenturm are hard to read. None of them told me much of their personal feelings about the house or Baum. Nor did they reveal if they knew anyone with a grudge toward the victim, Andrej. They were more open with me the first day I arrived and began my investigation, but the day after, this curse nonsense was all anyone would talk about. That's one of the reasons I took Frau Kam's advice and sent for you."

"So, it was Frau Kam who named me directly?"

"Yes," the inspector said matter-of-factly. "She has two of your books and went on about your most recent, the something-something of the modern mind."

"*The Paranormal Psychological Polemics of the Modern Mind*," Hermann offered.

"Yes, that's the one," Géza said as his index figure shot up. "I looked through it a bit myself. While I can't speak to the paranormal topics, I did like that you grounded all of the sightings and supernatural events in categories based on the participant's character and mental state. I was hesitant at first to entertain Frau Kam's recommendation ... well, her insistence really, but your methods seem sound, and if they can help solve the case, I'd like to put them to use."

"I always try to find the most logical answer to explain the kinds of torment my subjects and clients experience. The mind plays tricks on us, Inspector, and makes us prisoners of our own beliefs and assumptions. Rarely is there an unexplainable occurrence. The simplest answer is usually the right one."

Géza nodded. "That much is sure."

The inspector regarded Hermann. Not unlike Hermann, it was the inspector's habit to assess and take in as much as possible about a person at a glance. His professional success depended on an accurate estimation in an instant. Hermann was a few years younger than Géza, but not so young as to look boyish. He had a firm jaw, and there was something in his face, the lines across his brow that said he'd lived more than you'd expect for a man his age. His loosely combed blond hair, streaked with lighter tones, indicated he spent a fair amount of time outdoors in the sunlight, clearly not a typical academic. His build was that of a man who was accustomed to regular physical activity. His fair complexation was set off against the dark grey of his suit and black tie, making him appear paler than he was. Hermann held his posture tight and tall, like an officer or an aristocrat, which intrigued Géza, based on his own background. Overall, this Professor Horst seemed sharper and more commanding than the effete scholar he'd expected.

"Forgive me, but you seem a bit young to be a professor."

Hermann smiled. "It's true that most of my peers are older than I am. However, I teach history and mythology for the most part, and the Board of Philosophy is of the opinion that a younger perspective keeps the students more engaged on their material. Based on my enrollment rosters, it seems to be true. Though, my work on the parapsychological has not been endorsed, despite an adherence to logic in my cases."

"Could you give me an example of a case where there was no logical answer?"

Hermann hesitated a moment, feeling that there could be a hidden motive in the question, maybe to test him, see if he was just a crackpot.

"Well, there was one experiment I conducted with four fortune tellers that turned toward the inexplicable. I had made a study of some of the more well-known psychic practitioners nearby to Vienna. It was really very simple to deduce their methods once you removed the superstition or hope of reaching the dearly departed. I went in disguise with my research assistant, posing as an established businessman and his friend. He and I had agreed on a few key elements of our backstories and the clues that we would divulge along the way. I dressed in tweed and carried a locket with an English engraving on it which would point to my character spending a lot of his time, or youth, abroad. The brands of our clothing pointing particularly toward Scotland. My assistant went in a suit more typical of a shopkeeper, with very sturdy and well-kept shoes which might indicate a cobbler. Three of the fortune tellers proved to be charlatans and fell for the bait and our contrived backstories, thereby revealing their tricks to those in attendance whom I debriefed afterwards on the setup and how the psychics could read our tells, so to speak."

"And what was the character or nature of the clientele to these places?" asked Géza.

"Really anyone who was desperate to reach the dearly departed, or who wanted closure and had been denied it in life ... from the bourgeoise to the wife of a factory worker," Hermann answered.

"It's sad to see people be misled and swindled due to grief. Better to let the dead rest and get on with the living." Géza paused for a moment, running his hand over his beard. "And the fourth fortune teller?"

"The fourth was a bit more curious ..."

The professor paused as he assessed the inspector and how much detail he should go into with the story. They'd only just met and Inspector Orczy seemed very determined to dismiss the uncanny. Both passengers braced themselves as the carriage rolled over a particularly large rut in the trail. The driver yelled back his apologies.

"Átkozott," Géza muttered through gritted teeth. "Baum can afford to build half a town, but not a new road to his own house. Never mind, you didn't hear me say that."

Hermann smiled a little. "So, the fourth psychic was a Gypsy woman, operating on the outskirts of Preßburg, who would entertain all manner of folk in her very ornate traveler's caravan. Her tribe never acted in a criminal way and so steered clear of the authorities, only ever running afoul of a landowner when they camped on Church property. They'd winter in the hills to the north when business slowed, and that's where I first met Frau Vadona. I'd gone by myself on that occasion, considering the singular acceptance of the woman's appointments. I'm not sure how she did it exactly, but I believe her powers of perception must have been very great. She never let on that she had done so, but she saw through my disguise. In her fortune telling, she told me accurately of my past in Salzburg as a boy, saying that the air tasted of salt and—," he stopped himself before telling the painful part, "—and of my faith."

Géza drummed his fingers on his knee as Hermann continued.

"I was actually quite spiritual in my youth. My parents worried that I might become a minister at one point and give up my scientific studies. I was always chasing the root of divinity in nature ... but I digress, that was a long time ago. Frau Vadona told me how I sought the truth in all things, 'A rare quality for a simple businessman,' she'd said. 'Perhaps you seek to know more about your competitors and how to thwart them? No ... what *you* seek is deeper. I think, like me, you wish to know about the land of the dead.'"

Géza's brows furrowed. He looked like he was starting to lose faith in his narrator's objective credence. Hermann thought it best to give a more sanitized version of the story's ending, to keep the inspector on his side.

"She then provided a premonition of the usual vague type ... to be on the lookout and how danger would soon find me. She ended the session by drawing upon the memory of my late parents and how they were proud, but worried about me. I suspected the fortune, and the sentiment from the beyond, were meant to draw me back for more readings and, of course, to dole out more money. I categorized her case in my book as an example of the failure of my controlled disguise, but not as an overt case of charlatan fraud. I believe she must have heard something in my accent or a dialectal word of Bairisch, though I had tried to sound as Viennese as possible. With a keen enough eye, my disguise could very well have been seen through, leaving me to give away my true tells."

Géza visibly lightened by the end. "You certainly did your best with the Gypsy woman, and the other fortune tellers were exposed for frauds. Well done."

"The true frauds usually turn over."

Géza relaxed and reached for a small stack of envelopes from the seat beside him. "Would you mind if I go through my mail? I wouldn't ask, except that I've received three letters today and the one is quite thick."

"Go right ahead."

"I don't want to hold you up once we're up to the ... house? castle? I'm not sure want to call it exactly. The scenery is beautiful from here. This all belongs to the estate." He motioned out of the window as he said the last.

As the inspector fiddled with his envelopes, Hermann shifted in his seat to get a better look from the side window of the carriage. The black-velvet curtains obstructed the view somewhat, though the thick oak and beech woodland could be clearly seen. They had reached a series of gently rolling plateaus that stretched up and over the side of the glen that Salgótarján rested within. The landscape was filled with elder-growth forest that hadn't been timbered in centuries. The understory was kept clear of everything but a few bushes, mostly blanketed by large, deep-green ferns and short grasses in places where the sunlight streamed down in bright rays. It was beautiful and serene, and no doubt game was abundant. Hermann wondered if the locals had been able to freely poach during the years between the last freiherr's death and Herr Baum's arrival. As the carriage rolled on, Hermann relaxed his head back onto the black cushions, a perfect match to the curtains, the headliner, and sidewall covering. The vague notion that this ride felt a little like a hearse's delivery to the crypt seeped into his thoughts.

Inspector Orczy sighed deeply as he bundled his letters and looked out the window of the carriage before placing them inside his coat pocket.

"Bad news? If you don't mind my asking."

"No, just tedious, regarding the last one. It was the critique I was expecting from my commander. Nine days I've been here, with little to show for it. The other two were more promising. A report I was expecting on the remaining von Voitsbergs' finances from the tax office in Budapest. And a letter from my fiancé, Kornelia."

"Anything of interest in the report?"

"Indeed, it gives more detail than Frau Astrid was willing to divulge. The situation between the two families is somewhat strained, from what little I've heard from Herr Baum. Of course, he tells a different story than the one I wrested from the manager at the local bank. Apparently the von Voitsbergs felt cheated of their inheritance, but there was nothing to be done on that account unless they could've come up with several thousand forintok. Frau Astrid took up the mantel for the family and negotiated their continued ownership for a time, but obviously it came to naught, and the estate was sold. According to this," he patted his breast pocket, "her brother, Herr Friederich, purchased a commission in the army and is stationed somewhere around the Banat-Belgrade border. We're about to pass the widow's cottage now where Frau Astrid and her mother live." The inspector pulled back the black curtains to his left.

The carriage was passing by a wide drive that led toward a Baroque two-storied house, painted a shade of golden honey. It was at least twice the size of any in the town and far from a proper cottage.

"Are we far from Schattenturm, now?" Hermann asked.

"Not at all, only another five or so minutes by carriage."

"Being so close to her lost inheritance would be a painful reminder of what she and her brother should have had."

Géza frowned. "I hadn't thought of it that way before. These places are a far cry from what I'm used to dealing with, Professor. Family trees longer than I can reckon, cottages the size of palaces, and connections to everyone imaginable in government. Things are a lot simpler when a drunk shoves his friend under an oncoming carriage."

Hermann raised an eyebrow.

"I digress," Géza said in a grumble.

"I know what the aristocracy can be like, Inspector. I want to help, and if that means putting aside rank or censor, then around me please do so, by all means."

"A cél szentesíti az eszközt." Géza said in a kind of recitation.

"And what does that mean?"

"Just that I think we'll get on well."

Chapter 4

T he carriage slowed as they emerged from the woodland, and the forest gave way to fields of green winter
wheat dotted with large oaks. A series of three vast terraces,
culminating with a castle on the uppermost level, stood in
full view. At the lowest level, a serene, opaque lake abutted
an outcropping of rock that jutted jaggedly from the sloping lawn of the terrace above. Across the lawn rose dark,
weathered crenelations that gave way in places to shrubs
and bushes where the foundations had deteriorated. The
castle itself seemed to have been pulled directly from the
pages of a medieval poem. It rose above faux battlements
on the uppermost terrace, topped by shingled roofs,
framed by towers at each corner, with a high octagonal
keep shooting toward the sky behind the main façade. The
spires made the castle look like it was holding up massive
spearpoints ready to do battle, crowned with a wreath of
daggers at the top of the keep.

Hermann was stunned by the sight, even after so much
sensory overload from years surrounded by the beauty of
Vienna. What stood out most to him was the stonework. It
was composed of a dark rock that manifested across the
castle in varying shades of deep beige, dark grey, and charcoal, with the decorative pieces of stonework around the
windows and doors appearing completely black. The
house was true to its name. Schattenturm was indeed a

shadow tower—magnificent in its effect to inspire both awe and dread at the same time.

Géza broke Hermann's momentary trance. "It's really something, isn't it?"

"It is the best example of Burgenromantik I've ever seen."

The carriage turned on the path around the edge of the lake to begin its rise, skirting the eastern edge of the castle towards the gatehouse.

"I'll take your word on that. It always gives me a chill coming up the drive. The maze is just over there, Professor."

Géza pointed to the opposite side of the carriage from the castle, down a series of further terraces, to a low spot where several acres were filled with twisting and riling snakes of cypress hedging. A stark building was visible in a narrow clearing in the center of it all. The misty, early morning fog still clung to this depression below the castle. It appeared to defy the brilliant rays of penetrating sunlight and maintained its cool cloak of grey gloom. Hermann pressed closer to the glass as the carriage turned to the left to cross a short bridge toward the gatehouse; it loomed like a gaping mouth, ready to engulf them, full of razor-sharp teeth from the portcullis. The horses slowed and solemnly navigated the entrance through the gate, bringing the carriage and its passengers to a stop in an enclosed courtyard. They were encircled by tall windowed walls, towers, and decorative façades on all sides. The keep, which competed for height with an ivy-clad, spiraling stone tower with large windows at its pinnacle, stood beside them.

Two young footmen were fidgeting with their livery as an older man watched the carriage, much like a hawk eyeing a mouse. One of the footmen opened the door for the passengers as the other went to the carriage's rear and began off-loading Hermann's luggage. The courtyard was covered in white pea gravel, picking up the light from the bright sky and reflecting it back onto the castle walls, to little effect as the light was dulled and repelled by the dark stone. Hermann stepped from the carriage after the inspector.

The old butler raised his chin, looking at Hermann over the point of his nose. His stark white curls were combed back, threatening to burst loose should the sticky mold of his hair wax fail. They framed his heart-shaped face and set off his blue-green eyes under thick eyebrows that matched his Van Dyke goatee.

"Welcome to Schattenturm, Professor Horst. My name is Fürth. If you would follow me, I will show you to your room."

The old man turned before Hermann could respond and made his way through the great keep's pointed-arch doorway, past a set of carved-oak doors. Hermann and Géza followed. It took Hermann a moment to adjust to the bright light and color inside the entryway, after the muted greys and blacks of the carriage and the courtyard. Two staircases curved along the walls of the keep around eight columns that rose to the pointed arches of the blue-and-gold ceiling, like the stems of a collective flower. The interior was entirely white, cut stone with intricate floating buttressing and railings between the pillars that made the interior space feel paradoxically awe-inspiring and welcoming.

Fürth stopped and turned on his heel near the opposite side of the expansive space. He was framed by a central arch leading to the room beyond, and above him hovered a balcony on the mezzanine. He studied the professor as Hermann paused to look around the room. Fürth could tell by the stitching that his suit wasn't new, and his shoes were well-worn, perhaps due to his salary? However, the gold ring on his middle left finger, with intricate engraved writing, seemed to dissuade the assumption that he struggled for money.

"You will be staying in the western hall, Herr Horst. Herr Baum would like to speak with you once you are settled. He will be in the library. You are invited to dinner this evening, white tie of course. You will be expected in the east parlor at eight o'clock." His icy gaze turned to Géza. "The invitation has been extended to you as well, Inspector Orczy."

The two footmen came bumbling in behind Hermann and started to stomp up the stairs to the right, carrying the cases with them. Fürth's eyes grew wide in horror as he stepped past Hermann and Géza to confront them.

Géza took the opportunity to coordinate his next steps with Hermann. "I need to answer these letters, Professor. I'll meet you below stairs, by the kitchen, in about an hour. It's just to the left here and down the servants' stair. We can start in the evidence room and move on from there."

"That would be good. I'll try not to get lost," Hermann said, craning his neck to look through the doorways beyond the underside of the stairs and up on either side of the mezzanine.

When Hermann turned back toward the butler, he was berating the footmen, barely keeping his voice inside the realm of a whisper. "Never bring trunks or packages through the keep. You take them directly downstairs and then up through one of the access stairs to the guest rooms. Weren't you taught anything? Never mind, give me those before you scuff up the walls."

Hermann had to pick up his pace to keep up with Fürth who was trudging up the stairs with his cases at a furious pace. Hermann stopped him upon reaching the landing, "Fürth, would you have time to give me a tour of the house? The architecture is marvelous from what I've seen,"

"Indeed, it is marvelous." The butler's eyes brightened. "The renovations were carried out at the personal instructions of the late Freiherr von Voitsberg. He brought in the finest craftsmen from across the empire and even several artisans from France." His chest deflated, then he continued, "But I don't have the time today. I'm kept far too busy with my duties to provide a discourse on our history, herr.

You may ask Frau or Herr Baum. Frau Baum may be found in one of the rooms on the main level. She is drawing up plans for new decorations and furnishings. Though, I expect you will see plenty enough of Schattenturm during your investigation. This way ... please."

Hermann followed, and as he ran his hand along the banister of the mezzanine, he felt a layer of dust come away. They continued through the archway to the right. Hermann glanced at the large double doors in the center of the mezzanine as he passed, noticing the polishing effect of heavy use of the brass handles. They entered a hall lit by only two of six gas lamps. An open doorway was set off at an angle to a turn at the end of the hallway. Inside was a large, well-lit library with a narrow circular stair of its own with wrought-iron handrails spiraling up and down toward opposing floors. Fürth paused to shut the library door, eliminating all of the natural light that had been let into the hallway, casting them into a pocket of dancing shadows from the low-lit gas lamps. After the turn, they came to one end of another long hallway with a further five doors visible. All were closed like the hall before, but there was an obvious air of mustiness and dust here. It was very dark with no windows to illuminate the path. Only one lamp here was lit, and that one only on a low flicker inside a shiny metal sconce to reflect as much light as possible, for as little expenditure. Hermann wondered if the state of the house was a reflection of a lack of funds, or just an unwillingness by Herr Baum to loosen the purse strings.

Fürth entered the last door on the left and stood at the threshold as Hermann passed. "This will be your bedroom, herr. I hope you find it ... comfortable."

He had hesitated on the last word; it didn't take Hermann long to guess the reason why. Hanging above the bed was a life-sized portrait in oil. Pictured was a tall man, painted in the Baroque style, with long, wavy ashen-blond hair and light-grey eyes, almost silver. He was featured in armored black plate with yellow detailing. In one hand he held a black-and-grey war hammer while his other hand pointed passively at the shape beneath his left boot. His boot was perched on the neck of a dead Turk, turban askew, and mouth hanging open with a lolling tongue and rolled eyes. Behind the lord, at a distance in the background, was the medieval version of Schattenturm, encased in a haze of smoke and dust, the remnants of a battle that had waged all around. The old minaret was visible as were some of the fortress curtain walls, but instead of grand halls and the keep, there were stout towers with roofs of red tile and some lower buildings set into the walls themselves. All was built of the same dark stone as the modern reimagining, showing that the name, at least, was original. A brass plaque at the base of the ornate picture frame identified the man simply as Gustav Freiherr von Voitsberg.

"Breakfast is in the dining room from eight to nine o'clock."

"Thank you, Fürth. Tell me, why is such a grand portrait of the progenitor of Schattenturm displayed in a guest bedroom instead of somewhere more prominent?"

Fürth never let his eyes drift to the portrait as he responded. "Herr Baum felt that the portrait was more suited to a private quarter where one could ... *admire it* on special occasions." He gave a slight nod to Hermann as he shut the door behind him.

Hermann turned toward the two large, triple-pointed windows which framed an unlit fireplace. Beyond them was the view of the western rise. It sank away in the thick scrub below the battlements and rock formations under his window. There were some nice pieces of furniture in the room and the bed was large, but a dusty smell permeated the expanse like it had in the hall. The painting exuded no sense of ease or relaxation. The silver-grey eyes of Gustav Freiherr von Voitsberg shone with an intensity that the artist must have worked diligently to capture. Hermann was in their continuous focus as he unpacked his clothes and hung his dinner jacket in the wardrobe. He briefly considered throwing the folded dust cover placed on top of his armoire over the portrait, but reconsidered when Gustav glared more intently as though he was reading Hermann's thoughts.

———————◆———————

Hermann stepped from his room into the gloom of the dimly lit hallway and headed for the library. Intuitively, he knew Schattenturm was as much a player in this murder as the people who passed through its great gate. The house felt eerily sentient as he strode slowly down the length of the hall. Devoid of wallpaper, showcasing only the dark stone that made up the whole castle, accentuated by dark wood paneling rising to waist height, it was apparent the house was in a state of decline. The lamp at the end of the hallway had gone out, leaving the archway into the curved section around the library tower in bleak gloominess. Hermann pressed on, undeterred. He entered the curve of the hall and knocked once on the carved library door, then entered into the capacious space.

A large window opposite the door cast a wall of grey spring light that nearly blinded him in the transition from the dark entrails of the castle. To his right was a large unlit fireplace made of intricately veined, green marble with ornate carvings of men in battle. They were garbed in old Teutonic clothing and armor, rather than the Greco-Roman style you might expect. There were curved bookcases filled with antiques and leather volumes all around, following the shape of the tower walls, with a ladder on rails that circulated the whole perimeter. Near the fireplace was a set of wingback leather chairs and a Persian rug with a garden design in cream, green, and blue. In the center of the room was a guardrail around the opening where a spiral wrought-iron staircase wound up and down to at least two more levels in the tower. Hermann could hear a fire crackling, though from where he stood he couldn't see it. He walked over to the guardrail and looked up through the opening in the spiral, seeing a glimpse of a domed ceiling painted dark blue with stars, then he looked down and saw orange light mixed with the grey glow from more windows.

"Herr Baum?" he called out.

"Yes. Down here," came a deep reply.

Hermann descended the spiral staircase to the lower level which matched the one above, but was filled with map books and chart decks. There were several large tables arranged around the room, each with maps open and sprawling over one another. By the fireplace stood a thickly set man with dark, oiled hair in a brown day suit, only the middle button of his jacket was fastened. The fireplace behind him was made of an earth-colored stone decorated with fallen heroes, the three Norns examining threads at a spinning wheel, and veiled women speaking to one another.

As Hermann entered, the man at the center of the room regarded him with small, practically black eyes.

Johan Baum cleared his throat. "You must be the professor I've been hearing so much about," he said, more in the form of a statement than a question.

"I am, herr. How do you do?"

"Fine. Fine. Though I'd be better if I knew the killer prowling around the county was locked up." Baum was clearly not a man for trivial small talk. "My mother-in-law tells me that you commune with ghosts and goblins. She thinks that'll help quiet the vengeful spirits roaming these halls." He chuckled.

Hermann forced a smile. "I study the reasons why people feel they have had contact with the supernatural, rather than making a study of the ghosts or *goblins* directly. It's a fine distinction, but an important one."

"Hmm." Baum began to fiddle with a large-faced ring on his finger, turning it over and under again. "I'm a practical man, Herr Horst. I know what I can see and touch, what has value and what people want. My mother-in-law has stirred up the household with this talk of spirits. The papers in Budapest have caught on and have been running free with the whole spectacle for the better part of two weeks now. I'm sure you've seen the headlines already."

"As it happens, no. I didn't have a chance to look at the papers on the train, and my Hungarian is essentially non-existent."

"Wealthy industrialist still searching for the ghostly killer stalking his household. That was the headline on page two this morning!" He groaned. "Any embarrassment is a great embarrassment. In my world, competitors will pick a man apart for the smallest thing if it means taking over his contracts. I'd do the same to them and they know it. You can't look weak, and a man who can't keep his servants in line and his household under control looks like a weak mark. That's why I need this nasty business done for."

"Inspector Orczy and I will do our best."

"Inspector Orczy," he said with a sneer. "You need to know that Inspector Orczy isn't up to the task. If there's a killer still here, and I doubt that, then it'll be you that finds him if anyone will. Inspector Orczy has fumbled this investigation since his arrival. He's been looking in all the wrong places."

"He informed me that there was a belief at first that a Gypsy or some other vagrant had killed Andrej, but that he's discovered evidence that the killer must have been closer to home," said Hermann.

Baum straightened and noticeably stiffened. "It seemed perfectly reasonable that Andrej was killed by some cutpurse or other. The man always had a penchant for wallowing in low circles. That's why I suggested it to the Nógrád police." He began fidgeting with his ring again.

Hermann thought it odd that Baum would know the personal habits of his gardener. "I admired some of his handiwork coming through the grounds on my approach this morning. He seemed quite talented. It's a shame he may have been of poor character."

Baum turned and made his way over to a decanter and glasses along a wall. He lifted the crystal topper and poured himself at least a finger of the amber liquid. "The man was a degenerate gambler, and he lacked respect." Baum sighed, then drank. "He's been as annoying in death as he was in life."

"Surely one gardener's death couldn't have that much of an impact on you?"

"It's not just him, Professor Horst. It's this whole house and everything that goes with it. I bought this place as a way to fend off my rivals' games and impress some of the court in Budapest. I remember from my younger days how alive this place was, the center of attention for half of the empire. When it became available, I knew I had to have it, for the reputation and the opportunity it promised. Instead, I was cheated." He took another drink.

"How were you cheated?"

"In the contract, everything was supposed to be included. The furniture, the art, the decorations, the staff. It was supposed to be turnkey. I expected to swoop in, make a few repairs and let my wife, Erzsébet, update some of the décor here and there to be ready for the season in a few months. But when we arrived last year, the house had been stripped, or nearly so. Almost all of the art ... that which could be carried out ... was gone, furniture too. I have only enough left to furnish a few of the rooms properly, but nothing near what I'd need to make use of the place as I had intended. Fürth told me the staff had been reduced to a skeleton crew for years. No one from town will take a job here, so I've had to send as far as boys' homes in Budapest to find footmen."

"That's quite the turnabout. Do you know what happened?"

"It was the bank. They said that old von Voitsberg's debts hadn't been paid and the personal assets of his inheritance had to be considered separate from the real estate."

He finished the glass and set it down hard on the silver tray, jarring the crystal decanter.

"Did the bank's agents tell you why they reneged so suddenly? There would have been several years since the late freiherr's death to work out the debt payments."

"Five. Five years," Baum replied. "The sale was a trick to get me up here and trap me. But never mind that," he said with a wave of his meaty hand. "I want you to cut through all this curse nonsense and find the killer. It'll be someone connected to Andrej's debts, I'm sure of it. I tried to have him curtailed a few times because he'd disrupted the staff and gossiped to the locals about the household."

"Do you know much about his character, herr? If I can understand more about the man himself, I can work faster."

Baum paused before replying. "He and I only spoke a few times since I purchased Schattenturm. Andrej had a reputation for thinking himself above the other servants, even the footmen. He was lazy. Slow to start and finish any project."

While Baum went to get another drink, Hermann glanced around the room. On the far wall was a table with large maps spread across it. They looked like topographical reliefs, though what they focused on, he couldn't say. One looked quite antiquated, some kind of vellum with old quillwork and blotchy ink forming shapes and connected lines. It was half obscured by one of the newer maps laying over it.

"What of the servants, Herr Baum? Do you suspect one of them might have wanted to kill Andrej?"

"Not that I could tell you. They're a tight-lipped bunch." Baum followed Hermann's wandering eye to the maps, then frowned. "Keep me informed of anything of note, Professor. Otherwise, we're done here."

Chapter 5

Hermann checked his watch before heading to the kitchens to meet Géza. He had time to explore and see what he could of the castle. He needed to get a feel for it—its energy as much as its floor plan. To his right, the length of the main hall stretched out before him, crimson wallpaper rising out of dark wood paneling, interspersed with inset-shelving nooks, mostly empty of the artistic curiosities they were designed to display. The vaulted hall ceiling was painted blue to match the ceiling in the great keep. The buttressing of the series of arches shot down the walls on the right and left, ending in points above the paneling, reminiscent of the ribcage of a dragon. Von Voitsberg had clearly spared no expense during the remodel.

Hermann spotted the entrance to a servants' stair to his left, at the end of the main hall. The door was nearly imperceptible, but it was a sight he well recognized from his youth: faint seams in the wood paneling and a very subdued handle at waist height. None of it was meant to be properly noticed by the upstairs inhabitants. He stepped into the cramped space with steep stairs and only a little natural light from some windows made to look like arrow slits. He followed the stair up to the second floor. Then he took the hall back the way he'd come, past his bedchamber, beyond the faint glow of the last lamp, to the end. Here, the hall curved to the right and ended in an unlocked door. After stepping through, he found himself in complete darkness. He stood motionless, allowing his eyes to adjust while he attempted to get his bearings. Any idea he may have had of the house being easy to navigate was quickly dispelled. It was proving to be a maze all its own, this one of stone and wood rather than cypress.

The shuttered hall was wide, with half a dozen or more doors stretching out on his right and two doors and a curtained window on his left, a reception hall he presumed. It was draftier here than in the rest of the house. The cobwebs and dust on everything were plain evidence of its abandonment. With only two footmen, and maybe a few more housemaids and scullery maids, it wasn't surprising to him. Hermann thought it strange that a man of Baum's fortune wouldn't have hired more staff and simply bought more furniture to make up for what wasn't included in the sale. That Baum had made little investment in the house was becoming evident as Hermann explored. Was the estate so expensive that its purchase had strained the tycoon's budget?

Hermann felt cool air on his fingertips when he tried the righthand doorknob on a pair of doors that he figured must lead onto a balcony overlooking the courtyard; it was unlocked but he decided against stepping out. Making his way through the gloom, he noticed the first door on the left had seen traffic, the dust on the hardwood floor was disturbed. When he tried to open it, he found it was locked.

He continued toward the center of the hall and past the thick curtains that may have once been rich, royal-blue sateen, but now were hardly distinguishable from the cobwebs and moth spinning that covered them. He opened them, illuminating the hall with a shaft of grey light. The ghostlike appearance of large vacant squares and rectangles on the walls gave away the location of what once had been displayed: paintings and tapestries. Notches in the floors provided clues as to where heavy curios once stood.

The space reminded him of the last time he'd seen his home in Salzburg. Everything had been sold, except what would fit within his new apartment in Vienna. Black crepe hung from the windows and over the transom above the door, even as the last family furnishings were carted off. The entry-hall staircase and honey-colored oak floors would no longer welcome him home. When he had looked back, before closing the elegantly carved front door forever, the house seemed sad to him, a longing not to be abandoned by the last family member to have loved and enjoyed it.

The next door was unlocked when Hermann tried it. Inside were mounds of white linen draped over furniture and other items. Light, fortunately, was more abundant here due to large windows with curtains that were partially open. He made his way to an oddly shaped, large covered object along the left edge of the room and felt through the linen to the object below. He carefully lifted the cover so as not to shake the dust off onto himself and realized he was looking at an exquisite gilt floor harp, engraved with floral and ivy designs. He found more instruments beneath the dust covers. A cello, several cases of violins, horns, even drums. Herr Georg von Voitsberg had had nearly a complete orchestra at his disposal. Likely they had once played to guests during the many soirees hosted at Schattenturm.

The sound of voices from outside the windows brought Hermann back to the present. He edged his way to the nearest music room window and saw a girl with long, braided black hair in a grey riding skirt and jacket. She was talking to a much taller boy who was wearing drab trousers and a dirty shirt, clutching his cap in his hand. He couldn't make out what they were saying exactly, but the boy was stressed. He shook his head and grasped her left wrist, leaning his face close to hers.

"I can't do it. I won't do it!" the boy said, loudly enough for Hermann to hear.

The girl wrenched her wrist free of him and stepped back, her long skirt billowing with the movement. The boy straightened and put his cap back onto his ruffled, ginger-colored hair. The girl said something that Hermann couldn't hear, turned, and made off out of view. The boy walked off rigidly in the other direction.

Hermann turned back to the music room and made his way to the opposite end where an inconspicuous door was situated. Behind it he found the top of another steep servants' stair. He carefully made his way down, cautious not to lose his step. At the bottom was a door leading into a room with another door switch-backed behind him. Through this last door he stepped out into the daylight that had greeted him on his arrival in the courtyard. Breathing deeply of the fresh springtime air, Hermann realized the house was truly a maze. The killer, if he knew the house, could enter and move from one room to another, between halls, and through towers, using the servants' stairs and passing through rooms no one had cared about in years. With adequate familiarity of the estate's layout, anyone who wanted to could come and go at will, undetected.

In front of Hermann was a short thoroughfare, across from which was a stable complex with wide-planked siding and large double doors that swung outward. Stalls spanned the interior, arranged in a fan shape. Only a few of the stalls were occupied. Several large workhorses were situated to the left, followed next by the black horses that had pulled the carriage, and then a long absence of occupants before Hermann scanned all the way around to the other side and saw the girl in the grey riding habit, stroking the muzzle of a grey horse with black eyes that matched those of its master. She was watching Hermann from below the brim of a stylish black top hat, pulled low over her dark eyebrows. Hermann crossed the space between them. She was young, maybe sixteen or seventeen, but she held her head aloft, confident, petting the horse's neck in slow, deliberate strokes.

"You must be the professor that Grandmama invited. You'll be the absolute center of attention tonight," she said, looking him up and down through her long dark eyelashes.

Hermann noted the black gloves that matched her polished saddle, positioned for her on the back of her color-coordinated horse. He straightened and gave a slight nod. "How do you do? I'm Herr Horst, professor and one-time investigative aid."

"And which of those three personas should I use to refer to you? No … let me see. Professor … yes, I shall call you Professor. I like the image that comes to mind with that address." She giggled and covered her smile with her gloved hand, studying Hermann's appearance over her fingertips. She flipped the reins over the horse's head as she spoke. "My name is Rachel, and you can address me as Rachel. My brother Josef is probably skulking around out here as well. And this is Sternenlicht, my favorite mare. My only mare, now that Papa has moved us out here."

"Pleased to make your acquaintance." Hermann then nodded toward the horse, "And did you have many horses before the move, *fraulein*?"

A wide smile spread across her face. "Oh yes. I had three mares and a gelding. His angsty temperament made him an excellent jumper." Her face drooped and she took on a pouty expression. "That was before Papa sold him and the other two. It was a terrible fight to let me keep Sternenlicht. He probably turned the others into glue. If only we were still in Budapest." She sighed.

"It can't be all that bad. You must have much more room to roam and ride with her now that you have an entire estate at your disposal."

"It doesn't compare to riding through the parks or with my friends. There's no one here worth seeing." She dropped her chin and looked up at Hermann through her eyelashes, "But maybe that's about to change."

"But you must have more liberty to explore the vast gardens and grounds here, no?"

"Oh, I see what you mean. Of course, the space does grant one certain … freedoms, at least from Mama's watch." She smirked, then met Hermann's eyes.

Something in the intensity of her gaze, and the white contrast to the black pupils, waxed sinister to Hermann. He squinted a little, off put off by the innuendo. He would need to be careful in his dealings with this one.

She read his body language and looked annoyed. "Ah well, Csordás will be waiting by now. He gets very cross with me when I'm late." She raised one eyebrow. "Was there something you needed Professor, or were you just taking an impromptu tour?"

"As it happens, I was looking for a way down to the kitchens. I promised Inspector Orczy that I would meet him there." He looked around. "Maybe a stable hand could help me find them? I recall seeing a lad with red hair being about on my arrival this morning."

"Oh, Pavol? Don't pay that stupid boy any mind. He's useless. Though nothing is very hard to find here ... once you know your way around."

As they stepped back onto the small thoroughfare, Hermann saw a groomsman already kitted out and waiting beside a lean brown gelding.

"From here," she said, "you go west around the wall to the work yard. Just inside a small courtyard, there's a door next to the well pump." Sternenlicht whinnied and bobbed her head. "Wait your turn, you'll be out in a minute. She gets fussy when she doesn't get her way ... as do I." Rachel smiled from beneath the brim of her riding hat.

"Thank you, fraulein. I commend your sense of direction. You certainly do know your way around. Most ladies in Vienna loathe the idea of ever stepping out of a parlor, much less navigating the work yards."

She squinted. "We're made of sterner stuff than that in this family, *Herr* Horst. I can assure you of that." Once Rachel was mounted on her side saddle, she asked, "Which room have they put you in? The lamps are turned off at night and I would hate for you to get lost in the dark."

Hermann hesitated. "I've been set up in a room on the western side, fraulein. It's nearby to the inspector and his assistant, so I shouldn't have much trouble."

"Well, you have nothing to worry about then, apart from old Gustav. Though, if you ever get lost just take every right you come to, and you'll eventually make your way out onto the courtyard."

She kicked her mare into a trot. Hermann watched as the raven-black braid of hair formed a visual parting line down the back of her coat as she ventured onto the trail with her trainer.

The kitchen was just where Rachel had said it would be, though the path was more complex below ground, inside the belly of the beast. The hallway resembled a cave tunnel with its dark-green paint from the floor to chair rail height, set against a shade of dull grey above and on the ceilings, as if moss had crept up the damp surface over the years. Hermann observed half a dozen unused rooms for storage, doors left open to let in light to the hallway through their small windows set just above ground level outside. He was glad to hear the clattering of pans and orders being doled out as he made his way deeper into the work zone where the dismal space sprung to life.

Off to the right was a framed opening that led into a large kitchen where several maids were going anxiously about their work: kneading bread, tending a stock pot on one of the line of induction stoves, and one busily cutting and peeling a mountain of different vegetables on the center table, near a long egg stand. Hermann saw a short, stout woman with her hair bundled under a white cap standing with her back to the doorway. She wore a white apron knotted around the small of her back, over her practical dress.

"I can't have any mistakes tonight, Tímea. No eggshells. No extra salt. And for heaven's sake don't forget to whip the crème before the pudding goes up."

"Yes, Frau Kovács," the one at the stock pot responded, straining the words out.

Hermann watched the cook turn to the woman next to her who he had not noticed at first. She wore a long black dress, crisply starched, with a large ring of keys hooked to her belt line. She had greying hair braided and pinned into a tight bun.

"We'll need to have fish for tonight, and some fresh coriander," said the cook. "I would ask Pavol to go to town myself ... but I haven't been able to look at the boy since ... since ..."

The words caught in her throat and she began to cry, then she plopped down into a chair at the end of the table and pulled a frayed handkerchief from a pocket in her apron.

"There, there," said the other woman. "You'll be alright. Is there anything you'd like me to get you? How about a cup of coffee or some of those biscuits you like so much?"

The two maids chopping vegetables and kneading bread exchanged a look.

"Oh, if only we had some fresh strawberries." Kovács dabbed her eyes with the handkerchief, voice breaking. "Do you remember how he would pick me the little wild ones he'd find? He loved when I would make him a parfait. Sweet soul ... he never did any wrong by nobody. What kind of world are we living in? Now he's a cursed soul. We're all cursed."

She began to sob, her worn face scrunching up and her chest heaving in erratic motions. Emotional as she was, she tried to hide her face from the maids as she got up and hurried out a door at the far end of the room. The woman she had been talking to watched her go, worry and grief plainly visible on her face. The maids too had all stopped what they were doing, leaving the room draped in silence, save for the rolling broth in the stock pot.

Hermann stepped in to introduce himself before his unintentionally timely eavesdropping was noticed.

"Good morning," he said.

The woman with the key ring turned, a little surprised. She regained her composure, defaulting to a straight line of incredibly thin lips firmly locked together.

"Hello. You must be the professor, Herr Horst."

Hermann gave a nod.

"How can I help you?" she said.

"First, may I ask if she's going to be alright?" Hermann raised a finger, pointing in the direction the cook had fled. "She seemed very upset. Was she referring to Andrej Fehér?"

The woman's lips pressed tighter before she responded. "Frau Kovács will be alright. She was very fond of Andrej. Mostly what she needs is an answer as to why anyone would want to hurt him." She hesitated. "And why it would take so long to find his killer." She had her hands clasped together, her left thumb rapidly rubbing the side of her right wrist.

"I expect everyone here needs an answer to that." Hermann noticed the maid stirring the stock pot and those at the table had not continued their work, remaining still to watch and listen. "Inspector Orczy told me that he had readied an evidence room, Frau … ?"

"Schrode. I'm head housekeeper here." She raised her chin during her pronouncement and let her hands fall lightly down to her sides, erasing the tension that had been evident before.

"If you'll follow me, I'll take you there now. It's around a bit of a dip and a bend."

She led Hermann down the green-grey hall and to the left at the end, then into an off-the-beaten-track area of the downstairs level. Just like the hall he had explored upstairs, everywhere out of sight of the normal operating areas seemed to be neglected. Dark and damp, with just the barest amount of light to be spared from an open door and the small windows.

"Frau Schrode, I should like to speak with some of the servants, including Frau Kovács. Would she be up for it today or tomorrow?"

She paused midstride and turned around, eyes downcast and a frown furrowing.

"No, herr. Frau Kovács has been in a delicate state since the murder ... since Andrej's death that is. She's a woman of few secrets, but deep emotion. If you need anything from her, you can ask me." Her right cheek twitched as her eyes rose to meet Hermann's.

Hermann thought to himself that it might be good to have Frau Schrode's perspective first. It would be the first below-stairs impression of the gardener, something to compare against later testimony.

"Very well. I must warn you that I may be a bit blunt in my questioning. I have a habit of forgetting sentimentalities when I'm focused on a task." He smiled.

She nodded curtly and continued toward the end of the hall. Once there, she opened a door on the right and held it as Hermann entered the small repository.

"Officer Erdei, this is Hermann Horst, the professor from Vienna," announced Frau Schrode.

Hermann found himself in the presence of a young man in a plain green-grey uniform that matched the color coding of the downstairs halls and rooms. The man looked up from a ledger he had been writing in.

"Oh hello, I am Erdei, helper to Ellenőr Orczy," he said with a very thick Hungarian accent. "Mein Deutsch ist nein gut."

"Nicht gut." Hermann replied. "But that shouldn't matter much. It's good to meet you."

Erdei was young, and he clenched his teeth together as Hermann spoke, nervous acting.

"The inspector said that he had gathered all the evidence, so far, here?" Hermann gestured toward a large table in the center of the room.

"Um ... the ellenőr, he put all the ... um, bizonyíték ... on the table." He motioned to the sideboard, the center table, and a makeshift table made from two sawhorses and a long plank against the far wall.

Frau Schrode spoke, "If that's all, Herr Horst, then I'll get back to my duties. Should you need anything, just ask one of the maids or myself and we'll fetch it for you."

"Thank you," Hermann said as he turned to face her.

Before backing carefully out of the door, she crossed herself, then headed hurriedly down the hall. He could tell that her eyes had been locked on something on the center table. Turning through the direction of their gaze, he spotted what had taken her attention. Lying in the middle of the large center table, the area surrounding it void of objects, was a blood-smeared, spiked war hammer—the weapon that had been lodged in the back of Andrej's skull.

Chapter 6

Hermann stepped closer to the table. There was no mistaking the murder weapon as it lay, center stage, in the display of evidence. The hammer wasn't exactly what Hermann had imagined. Given the house and the extravagance the late freiherr had enjoyed, the hammer was plain. In fact, it was terribly plain by comparison. The war hammer had a smooth, unadorned wooden shaft, approximately seventy-five centimeters long. The lower one-third was wrapped in black-leather gripping to the base. Its heavy iron head was made of a blunt nose in front, balanced by a twelve-centimeter curved spike on the opposite end. Unlike decorative medieval instruments of war that Hermann had seen, this one lacked cut channel decorations or exotic polished wood. What wasn't plain about the war hammer, however, was the blood. The hammer's spike was stained red from the sharp-tipped end to the fitting where it was secured to the handle shaft. It had sunken as far into Andrej's skull as it could go. The shaft also had blood spatter on it. Hermann leaned over the center of the table to look closer.

"There's almost no blood on the leather grip. The killer's hands must have blocked the spray," he said.

"Az ellenőr azt mondja, hogy ne takarítsunk semmit, mert az zavarhatja a vizsgálatot," Erdei quickly put in.

"Officer Erdei, my Hungarian is worse than your German, forgive me."

Erdei furrowed his brows a little, straining to see perhaps whether the translation would become apparent, then let out a little sigh of relief as Géza entered the room.

"I see that you found your way all right, Professor."

"Yes, with a little help from Rachel Baum and the housekeeper, Frau Schrode, to get through the labyrinth. I saw Frau Kovács as well. If it's possible, Inspector, this place is bigger inside than it looks from the outside."

Géza nodded. "It has that effect. I see you need no introduction to the murder weapon then." He made his way around the table, facing Hermann. "Andrej's skull was broken-in completely on the back left side. It would have been an instantaneous death, or near enough to it, thank god."

Hermann raised his palm to cup the same spot on his own head. "Andrej probably didn't see the blow coming. It's a blind spot. The killer must have hit him with great strength. Look at the blood spatter all along the shaft," he said.

"Very good. Yes, it's not normal for head wounds to splatter this much without effort. A musket ball or small impact point will puncture the skull and cause some blood spray, but in this case," Géza pointed up and down the hammer, "the murderer hit hard and struck deep, causing a rupture and flow of blood and brain matter. However, Professor, great strength as you put it, may not necessarily have been needed."

"How so?" asked Hermann, motioning toward the hammer. "May I?"

"Yes, please. Pick it up and note the weight of the hammer," replied the inspector.

"About three kilograms."

"Precisely. We know the killer held the hammer near the end of the grip, due to the lack of blood in this area. By holding the hammer so near the base, even a weaker person would have achieved great force. The further the fulcrum point from the head of the hammer, the more force is achieved from the swing."

"I see. You know a great deal about this, Inspector. Have you investigated many brutal murders?"

Géza's expression stiffened. He stood a little straighter and fixed his eyes ahead. "I've had my fair share of exposure to violence with the Hussars in Bosnia."

Hermann didn't prod. "Could the killer have been holding the hammer with both hands, considering how little blood there is here?" He imitated the motion with his fists closed together around the leather grip. Erdei chuckled uneasily at the gruesome gesture. Géza sent him a stern sideways look in response which Erdei tried desperately to avoid.

"You have a keen eye," said Géza. "I thought much the same."

"Was blood found anywhere else?"

"We looked. The murderer would have been covered in blood, spray on the face, hands, shirt, et cetera. But no blood was found anywhere, other than at the site of impact, no bloody clothing or shoes were discovered, and not even a hand or footprint was found anywhere," said Géza.

"So, the murderer must not have been concerned about being seen when returning to where they had come from, or they had a spare set of clothes nearby."

"Yes, another reason I ruled out that it was a Gypsy robbery or a random act. To escape without leaving a trail of evidence indicates the killer likely has knowledge of the estate."

Hermann added, "And, since Andrej was ambushed from behind, the killer knew how to approach him undetected."

Géza motioned to the makeshift table behind him. "These items were found with Andrej's body, inside the larger of two packs. What do you make of them, Professor?"

Hermann made his way over to the table where a long coil of thick rope was set alongside a grappling hook, the broken pieces of a lantern, a thick belt with several picks and clasps, and a pair of calf-high boots. Hermann examined the items and picked up one of the boots which he turned over to face sole up. They were studded with nails for traction.

"These are hallmarks of a miner or someone working from heights, such as on the outside of a building."

"How do you mean?" asked Géza.

"I grew up in Salzburg. Our city was named after the salt mines that made our bishops wealthy, and our citizens comfortable with climbing. My parents used to take my sister and me to visit the salt mines sometimes as a kind of field trip, to add to our geology and geography lessons at home. We hiked often in the hills and learned to rock climb. I've also seen men wearing equipment like this to refurbish the exteriors of some of the historical buildings in Vienna, or to help in the construction of new ones."

Hermann loved the outdoors of his childhood. Memories brought on the scent of the crisp air high above Salzburg and the sensation of the fir trees brushing against his skin. Things had been simpler then, for everyone, especially for Ingfrid. She loved gazing over the white stones of the Hohensalzburg fortress, imagining it was a secret realm of princesses and chivalric knights ringed by the mountains like a hidden kingdom to keep it safe from the outside world. She had been too sheltered, he thought.

Erdei asked something of Géza in Hungarian which the inspector answered. The officer had something else to say in return. Hermann remained confounded by the language, sure he'd never be able to pull much out of it, being neither Teutonic, nor Latin, nor Slavic.

"What you say supports Officer Erdei's theory that these items belonged to the murderer. That he must have been trying to climb into the castle with the equipment and was apprehended by Andrej. The murderer may have been forced to leave the items when he fled."

Hermann rubbed his chin. "But why climb in? That is, the place is full of unlocked entry points ... doors and windows at ground level. I found a number of them myself, in just the short while I've been here. And why visit the maze with the equipment? That's nowhere near the castle's entry points. Was there anything else on or near the body, Inspector?"

"Just this other pack made of soft canvas. It looked like Andrej dropped it when he was hit. But there was nothing inside and it was clean, so it hadn't been used for gardening from what the officers on the scene could see."

"So then, we're back to this." Hermann turned to the hammer. "A prominent symbol within the von Voitsberg crest. A message to someone who understood its context?" He leaned in again, looking at the hammer that was now back in its place of exaltation in the center of the table. "The hammer was taken down from its place in the armory, in the upper level of the gatehouse, and arrived in the maze. Its singular purpose for being there ... a sneak attack from behind, with obvious intent to kill. How did the murderer come to possess it?"

"That is one of many questions I have been unable to resolve."

"Inspector, I need to see where the body was found."

Géza shook his head a little. "There's nothing left down there by way of evidence, Professor."

"I'm more interested in the mindset of the killer in the time leading to the attack and the moment of execution. I need to discern what the killer was thinking and how he felt when he achieved the end."

"We'll go to the maze then. I'd like an opportunity to see your psychoanalysis at work. I'll send Erdei to Salgótar-ján to ask the shopkeepers and mine operators if they remember someone purchasing the specialized equipment, and if so, who and why."

Géza led Hermann up the servants' stair and into the main hall beside the keep. The two took the same route as the one they had used that morning, out through the courtyard and beneath the armory gatehouse. Once they crossed the short bridge, Hermann and Géza had vantage over the northeastern surrounds of the castle. They were atop a long series of terraces set into the hillside with stone steps and landings connecting them. The morning had nearly ended, and the mist that had hung low over the maze had gone with it, leaving behind a snaking webwork of green on green, hemmed in by a rectangular border of the same cypress variety as the interior. Located in the center of the maze, Hermann spotted the top of a singular structure, an ornate dome of some sort supported by a bird's nest of dark stone. Beyond the maze, the forest stretched in all directions, the underbrush deeply shaded by the angle of the sun over the treetop canopy.

"Andrej's body was found in the opening at the center of the maze," Géza said. He pulled out a piece of paper from his lapel pocket. "One of the county officers drew a map of the route which I've kept. It's more or less a straight shot, so long as we don't miss the right turns, just right turns mind you."

"Are there any other entrances to the maze besides this one?" Hermann pointed at the break in the wall of foliage at the bottom of the terraces below.

"No. And I had my men check and double check the perimeter for gaps or a hidden opening. We found nothing. This is the only way in or out, unless the perpetrator punched through more than a meter of dense hedges which would have left a mark."

Hermann nodded and they proceeded down the steps, beyond two tall, narrow hollies that served as entry spires on either side of the access point. The pathways between the cypress hedges were wide enough, but the angles of the maze created a growing sense of claustrophobia and confusion. The soft walls of greenery were too thick to see through, not that there was anything more than pathways on the other side, and instead of breaking at right angles, the maze danced and swirled on its course. Each alley bent and moved around like a snake in its winter hollow, interspersed with subtle breaks to the sides, or as forks that led into more dizzying courses. None of it seemed to lead anywhere.

After what seemed like an eternity of twisting and doubling back on their own direction, the duo emerged from the maze. Their exit point from the cypress hedges brought them to an expansive, rectangular-shaped formal garden. From where they stood, the mausoleum rose from the far end of the space, drawing the eye of the onlooker to its crown, the dome Hermann had been subconsciously using as a guidepost while they navigated the maze. Up close, it was the shape of an inverted tulip wrapped in weathered, metallic-green copper. An alley made from tall, columnar cypress trees ran the length of the garden. Each carefully shaped cypress was separated by a stone bench, giving the peculiar impression of an aisle leading the traveler to the gates of the afterlife. The massive, detailed cast-iron doors, set in the dark stone of the ornate building, abruptly truncated the green pathway, creating the effect of an end to one life and the beginning of the next, should you care to enter.

"The body was found here—," said Géza, he had stopped between the third and fourth columns, "—about two-thirds of the way up the alley, toward the mausoleum. Andrej was lying face down in the grass with the hammer lodged in the back of his skull. He would have been facing the building at the moment of impact. The intensity of the hammer's blow required two officers to dislodge it."

Hermann looked at the area where no trace of the grisly scene now remained, no bloodstained blades of grass or depression in the earth.

"Where were the items found, Inspector?"

"The rope, pick, and boots were here inside the large pack, in the grass ... near the body. The smaller, canvas pack was here ..." Géza pointed to the foot of the bench nearest. "And the lantern was shattered in front of him. Likely he'd been carrying it and it broke in the fall."

"Was the larger pack disorganized, or orderly?"

"I couldn't say. It was in the same condition as you saw it in the evidence room."

Hermann crossed his left arm over his chest, supporting his chin with his right thumb and forefinger. "Odd that if the gear belonged to the killer, he didn't remember to retrieve it. And what was the point of the smaller pack?" He looked around, imagining the body lying as Géza described. "To which side did the handle protrude from the skull?"

"Excuse me?"

"Was the hammer's handle angled toward Andrej's left or his right?" Hermann clarified.

"I'm not sure. There was no mention of it in the notes from the county officers."

"Hmm."

"But there was a drawing done of the body's arrangement that one of the men did. I still have it here." Géza pulled out a small leather-wrapped notebook from his lapel pocket and leafed through the pages before producing a small piece of paper with a rough outline of a body.

Hermann took it and studied the shape's position. "I'm sorry Inspector, but I'm going to have to ask you to allow me some liberty with this."

"Pardon?"

"Go ahead and lie down there, in front of the bench," said Hermann.

Géza produced a reluctant, if not annoyed expression, only somewhat shielded by his beard. "I'd really rather not, Professor Horst."

"Why not? It'll only be for a moment."

"My uniform is freshly pressed." He seemed to be searching for a more convincing argument. "And it's disrespectful to the dead ... you know, bad luck to step into a dead man's shoes."

Hermann smiled in reply. "Come now, Inspector. I'm the one who would know about the supernatural. I can assure you that there's no harm in it. I only need to know how the killer might have struck Andrej. You can see for yourself that there's no blood to stain your uniform and it looks quite dry otherwise."

Géza grumbled something in Hungarian and laid down with his belly along the grass. Hermann carefully directed and adjusted the position of Géza's limbs and head to match the sketched notebook outline. He then stood back and looked over the mock corpse. The right leg was bent, with the hip pushed to the left, the head angled left, the right arm crumpled beneath the body, and the left arm stretched out, presumably from having held the lantern that broke in the fall. Hermann looked around and studied the scene from several vantage points, moving this way and that.

"Professor?" Géza asked, angling to try and see where the man had gone. "Have you seen enough?" There was no response. "Professor Horst?"

Hermann swung out from behind the cypress column behind the inspector and mimed a strike with both hands over the area of the feigned corpse, watching as an invisible Andrej fell and landed in the place that Géza now occupied.

"Isten!" Géza exclaimed, tracking Hermann's sudden appearance from his peripheral vision.

"Did you hear the rustling, Inspector?" said Hermann, imaginary hammer still in his hands.

"I heard something, yes."

"Interesting," Hermann replied. "I apologize, you can get up now." He made his way around to Géza's front and offered him a hand, clean of any imaginary murder victim's blood.

"Did you notice anything significant?" Géza asked.

"I believe the killer struck from Andrej's right side, from around the back of the cypress here, but there's an incongruity in the ambush. How did he mask his footfalls on the grass? It was quite loud from my perspective, and I assume any man with his wits about him, on a dark night in the middle of a maze headed toward a mausoleum, would have been attuned to the sounds around him."

"Unless his attention was otherwise focused," said Géza. "And you could tell all that by a drawing?"

"The drawing and the surroundings. I agree with your assessment that Andrej was killed instantaneously. Given his bent right leg, he was likely stepping forward with that foot in the moment of his death." He paused. "Inspector, were there any marks on Andrej's face or body, besides the death blow?"

Géza frowned as he thought for a moment. "Yes, there were some scratches on his face, caused from brush probably, the result of his working in the gardens. But apart from that, no."

"Hmm," said Hermann. He then walked toward the mausoleum's entrance, studying the stylizations and the ground around the structure. "And there was no evidence that anyone had entered or exited the mausoleum?"

"None. The county officers all swore that the place was locked when they arrived. I also examined the area with the few officers I had at the beginning. We all looked around the building and inside. We found no trace of tampering with the locks or the foundation. Fürth confirmed that we were the first to enter it since Georg von Voitsberg's death."

"Did Andrej have a key to the mausoleum?"

"There were no keys whatsoever on Andrej's body. According to Fürth, only he and Herr Baum possess keys to the mausoleum. Frau Schrode said the same, only the master and the butler had ever had a key over the years.

The gardener's assistant, Pavol, said he didn't know if Andrej had a key which supports what the others said."

Hermann turned to look down the alley, imagining the body of Andrej lying with his head smashed in and his killer drenched in blood standing over him. The tops of the maze's point-of-entry holly spires were just visible over the distance of the tall cypress hedges, with the stairs rising up beyond them to the maw of the gatehouse and its windowed towers above. Further still was the keep's jagged crown and the pinnacle of the spiraled tower, the former minaret. Half-a-hundred windows stared down at him where he stood by the entrance to the mausoleum, but only three bore real significance in the immediate scene—the three looking out from the armory hall, positioned above the gate.

"Do you see it, Inspector?" said Hermann.

"See what?"

"Those three windows are the only ones above the gate, so that's the armory room?"

"That's right."

"It would not have been hard to spot someone in the night, here in the opening at the center of the maze, provided the moon was bright or they had their lantern lit. The killer could have clearly seen Andrej from the armory where the hammer was as good as handed to him."

"True, but you know how long it took us to get through the maze and to this spot from the castle. If the killer saw Andrej entering the maze, by the time he made it here from the castle, Andrej would have been gone," said Géza.

"Did the gardener come here often? Was it his regular routine?"

"I don't have an answer to that, but Pavol said the maze only needed trimmed a few times a year, and don't forget, it was the middle of the night."

"Do you know where his assistant, Pavol, would be at this time of day?"

"He'll be back at the staff cottages if I'm not mistaken. Though I must warn you, he was quite difficult to interview the few times that I tried."

Hermann nodded then looked back to the castle. The light of the midday sun cast deep shadows over the windowpanes, positioned under their black stone lintels, making each look like a multitude of dark cells beyond which anything perched, or waited, or watched.

Chapter 7

Hermann and Géza worked their way back through the maze to the entrance where they had entered, and headed for the thick woodlands beyond the manicured gardens. The path they took was little more than a game trail through the dense ferns and undergrowth. After a few hundred meters, the beginnings of the groundkeepers' cottages came into view. Six single-storied, half-timbered houses with thatched roofing, and a large barn that doubled as the coach house, were visible along the side of a wide trail. Each one's wattle and daub was painted an earthy shade of coral while the timbers were darkly stained. The collection of cottages was more its own village than a string of lodges. The quaintest one of the lot stood at the end of the collection with a well-trimmed hedge backing a short fence running along its front. Beyond this were a few bean poles and rows of nestled cabbages while a planter box under each window bore soft white flowers with speckles on their petals.

Géza stopped a short distance away from this well-tended cottage. "Before we enter, you should know that the boy's been unusually quiet, would say nearly nothing about the murder to the police or myself. In fact, he's barely spoken at all, except to Frau Kovács and Frau Schrode. He was the one who found the body."

"Is there any reason why he'd be close with Frau Kovács and Frau Schrode in particular?" asked Hermann.

"Kovács had been very fond of Andrej, he ran errands for her and did her special favors, so Pavol knew her. And Schrode ... well, I haven't heard much from her, so I can't really say. Maybe she has a soft spot for the boy."

The two entered through the gate, and Géza knocked on the cottage's door. Soon after, a thin boy, only a little shorter than Géza, appeared in the doorframe. He didn't say a word, just nodded and motioned for them to enter the first room which was being used to store a few closed trunks and not much else.

"Pavol, this is Professor Horst, from the University of Vienna. He is visiting the estate to help solve Andrej's murder."

"Good day," Hermann said, scanning Pavol's features. It was the same lad that he had seen in a heated encounter with Rachel Baum outside the stables earlier. Ginger-colored hair, light hazel eyes, skin tanned from work outdoors, and dirtied shirt and trousers held up by suspenders.

The boy only nodded, his eyes downcast beyond the tip of his long nose to stare at the floor.

"I'm here to help however I can with the police investigation, Pavol," Hermann said. "I want to know who killed Andrej and why. You were likely the last person to see him alive ... and the first to see him dead ... other than the killer."

Pavol raised his eyes and looked blankly at him.

"Is there somewhere we might sit? I'd like to go over the details with you and ask you a few questions."

"Yes, through here," Pavol said. His voice carried a thick Slovak accent.

He led them into the second room which served as a kitchen, dining room, and living room all within a few square meters. Pavol ushered them toward two high-backed picket chairs, near a small stove in the fireplace. He poured water into a kettle from a pitcher near the sink, lit the fire in the stove with a match, and set the kettle to boil. He positioned himself on a picketed bench, with a red and white embroidered quilt folded over the back, facing Géza and Hermann. Hermann thought the boy looked a lot like the bean sprouts outside the cottage. Overly long arms and lanky legs that left his trousers slack like flagpoles, his face was angular and pointed.

Pavol rubbed his knees a little, until he noticed his own motion and sat back, forcibly still, hazel eyes locked toward the floor.

"Pavol, why don't you tell the professor what you told me about that morning when you found Andrej's body?" Géza said.

Pavol didn't look up to answer. "I woke at dawn, like every day. I saw Andrej was gone, so I thought he was at work. I went to get some tools and I saw the shed was unlocked. That was odd. Andrej always locked the shed at night so the tools didn't get stolen. So I knew then he wasn't working and I thought he might be passed out somewhere, so I went looking for him. I found him in the maze."

"Yes, that's exactly what you've told me for nearly two weeks, and nothing more," said Géza. "What else do you have?"

Pavol didn't answer. He kept his eyes locked on the floorboards.

"Speak up, boy," Géza pressed.

Hermann flinched slightly. "I realize that this must be difficult for you, Pavol," he interjected. "You were Andrej's apprentice. You saw him day in and day out. That kind of close quarters forms a bond. I'm sorry for your loss."

Pavol's brows tensed, and his left leg bounced on the ball of his foot. He didn't acknowledge Hermann's condolence.

"You two shared this cottage?" asked Hermann.

Pavol looked up at him and nodded.

"It can be hard to lose those who we're close to. Do you have any other family? Someone who you could rely on?"

"My mother lives in Poprad. We write to each other."

"Poprad, where is that?"

"To the north, in the mountains. The Germans there call it Deutschendorf."

"That sounds far. How did you come to live at Schattenturm?"

Pavol looked at Hermann again, before replying. "My parents had eleven children. Some older than me, most not. When my father died, my mother became a laundress. She couldn't afford to feed all of us, so she told me I had to go and find work. I came south, and tried, but there was nothing but the mines. Andrej found me and got me a job here as his apprentice. That was seven years ago."

"It sounds fortunate that you met Andrej, then. Did he teach you gardening?"

"Yes, he convinced the old herr that I had potential. I have my own ideas, but it doesn't matter. It's not my place to give suggestions."

Hermann wondered how Freiherr von Voitsberg had been convinced, just a few years before his death and supposedly in financial turmoil, to take on an apprentice gardener.

"Oh? Do you mean you have designs for the gardens? I'd love to see some. I've been admiring the work on the grounds since I arrived."

Pavol's eyes lightened. "Do you mean so, herr?"

Hermann nodded kindly.

Pavol rose to retrieve a tall book standing between a few titled volumes of different sizes on the top shelf of a glass-doored secretary across the room. He opened the book and flicked through a few pages before turning around and handing it to Hermann. On the page were detailed landscape designs for a French garden with plants and materials written in German. The designs on the following pages matched the precise metrics of the first, with straight lines and very good proportionality.

"These are very impressive," said Hermann. "They're yours?"

Pavol nodded.

"They look as good as what I've seen at the university in Vienna. How old are you? Have you had any formal training on architecture or landscape design?"

The faintest impression of a smile came over Pavol's face before it dissipated. "No, I just drew them myself. And I'm eighteen. I wanted to show them to Herr Baum, but Andrej said they weren't good enough for that."

Hermann wasn't lying to the boy, but Andrej obviously had. Pavol's sloping shoulders and near-permanent frown made him look like a beaten dog on two legs.

"And are the rest of these books your drawings as well?"

"No. Just this one. The others are books I bought or Andrej's ledgers for expenses and receipts."

"Pavol," Hermann leaned forward, "what were the typical daily duties you and Andrej got up to on the estate? Can you tell me what your duties were?"

"Sure." Pavol sat back on the bench. "I manage the forests, the rocks around the foundation of the house, the cottages here, I rake the gravel in the drives, clear the horse manure on the drives and around the coach house, trim the maze a few times a year, manage the gardens around the far edge of the castle, and I tend the fences."

"That sounds like quite a lot. What did Andrej do?"

"He trimmed the plants around the outside of the house, watered the ones in the courtyard, raked the pea gravel in the courtyard, cleared away the vines, and washed the stones if they needed it. I took over those duties since Andrej died."

Hermann furrowed his brow a little. "That hardly seems like a fair division of labor. What did Andrej have to say about that?"

Pavol frowned. "He said that it was best to let the people in the big house see what you were doing so they value you. He didn't need to work that much, so I did the rest. It was always worst for the couple of weeks after he got paid when he started to slack, but at the end of the month

70

he was always around the house." Pavol noticed that Géza had started to take notes in his notebook and cast his eyes down again. "There's nothing to really say. I told the police everything I know about Andrej's death."

"I know, Pavol, but you were the closest one to him. We really need to know more. What kind of man was he?"

Pavol began to rub his knees, back and forth, keeping his eyes cast down. "Andrej was good to take me in. I had nowhere to go and no one who cared for me. He gave me a place to sleep, food to eat, and in exchange I worked." He stopped rubbing his knees. "He used to remind me of that a lot. Said I should be grateful to him ... and I was. He was lazy though. He liked to drink a lot and gamble at cards in town, or to try flirting with the girls there."

Hermann sat back in his chair and interlaced his fingers. "Do you think he had any enemies, Pavol? Someone who'd lost a wager to him, maybe?"

Pavol's eyes shot up to meet Hermann's, then darted over to Géza, then they lowered again. "No. He only cheated Slovaks at cards. Mostly the ones on migrant work. None of the Hungarians trusted him. He was liked here by the cook, Frau Kovács, and he'd bring her things I'd grown in the garden or found in the woods, you know like berries and stuff."

The kettle began to bubble and whine so Pavol took it away and retrieved a coffee pot from above the sink. He scooped out some ground coffee from a can, then poured the water from the kettle into the pot and took down two cups and a small strainer.

"That information was helpful, Pavol. Did he have good rapport with anyone else at Schattenturm? Another member of staff, or the family?"

"He would cut flowers for the frau to have in her ladies' parlor and the dining room sometimes. She liked his flowers a lot. He was very good at that. And he used to speak a lot with the old Freiherr von Voitsberg before he died. He used to show him around the gardens we tended or make arrangements of the flowers for the halls and the library. He liked being in the library."

Pavol poured the coffee through the strainer into the two cups and brought them over to Géza and Hermann before taking his seat again.

"The freiherr used to let him borrow books from the library and I think they used to talk about them when he would finish. He liked the freiherr and was sour after he died. He didn't get on so much with the new owner, Herr Baum. But Herr Baum let him come back."

"What do you mean come back?" asked Hermann.

"After the old freiherr's funeral, Herr Fürth wouldn't let Andrej enter the castle or grounds no more. He hated Andrej."

Géza scratched loudly with his pen and paper, causing Pavol to study the motion for a time.

"Why do you think it was that Herr Fürth should dislike Andrej?" asked Hermann.

"Herr Fürth thought Andrej was getting above himself, forgetting where he came from. Andrej used to call him an eel to his face. Nothing ever came of it though because Andrej was protected in the freiherr's will, to stay on with a wage. That's what he told me. He went away to Budapest for a few years. Maybe to work. He never said why, but things were very quiet in those years, so it didn't matter much. Just after the castle was sold to Herr Baum though, Andrej came back and was kept on as the head gardener like before."

"Did Andrej continue to receive a wage even though he didn't live and work here?"

Pavol shrugged. "I don't really know, but most of the other servants were sacked after the freiherr died. The maids are mostly laundresses in town now, and the footmen went to Budapest and wherever else they could. Frau Schrode used to give us their news when they would send letters back."

"There is something I don't understand," said Hermann. "What led you to the maze that morning, Pavol?"

Pavol swallowed hard.

Géza stopped scribbling notes and looked intently at the boy.

"Andrej used to talk when he was drunk about how the old freiherr had told him that he still had some money stored away. He said it was Turkish coins, solid gold ones. He said the old freiherr told him that part of the money belonged to him, to Andrej, but that the freiherr had forgotten where he'd put it. Andrej said the freiherr had wanted to ask his brother where they'd left it, but his brother had been dead for a long time. Andrej thought the money must have been in the brother's tomb in the mausoleum."

Géza all but exploded. "Why didn't you tell me any of this when the police and I questioned you days ago?"

Pavol started to look antsy again. "He said that a long time ago and I didn't think it was important. I never believed him. Besides, you would've just thought he was a grave robber." A sharpness had slipped into his tone. "I don't know if that's why he was there that night, but in the morning when I was searching for him, what he said came back to me, and I thought it was worth a look."

Géza tapped his pencil on his notepad and straightened his posture, but said nothing more.

"Do you think he was meeting someone there that night?" asked Hermann. "Maybe they were going to look for the money together. It's a brave thing to try and enter a crypt by yourself at night."

Pavol shook his head. "Andrej didn't have any real friends, except maybe Frau Baum and Frau Kovács."

Hermann and Géza exchanged a look.

"He never would have split something like that anyway. Andrej would barely give me a wage. Herr Fürth paid him on my behalf and Andrej wouldn't part with a cent of it if he felt he was owed the money instead of me. I think that's why he stayed here for so long after Herr Baum had it out with him. He felt like he was owed a place here."

Géza scratched out another line, then asked "What do you mean, that Herr Baum had it out with Andrej?"

Pavol looked down and began rubbing his knees. "I ... I don't know. It was just talk. It wasn't for me to ask him. Only they had ... that is, Andrej had upset Herr Baum and he had wanted Andrej to do something for him or leave. I don't know, I'm sorry." He looked at a small cuckoo clock over the mantel. "I really need to get back to my work." His eyes returned to Hermann, almost pleading to be let go.

"Pavol," Hermann said. "Grief can be a terrible state to be in. Is there anyone here that you can talk to? Maybe someone closer to your own age than old Frau Kovács? Are you friends with any of the young people?"

Pavol's eyes flicked around Hermann's face and then back down again, hands still rubbing his knees. For a lad of eighteen, he had all the jitters of a much younger boy. Hermann thought that whatever the financial arrangement had been between Andrej and him, it was certainly not to Pavol's benefit, but there must have been more to it.

"There's no one else. I ... I don't need to speak to no one. Is that everything you wanted to know?"

"One more thing, then you may go," said Hermann. "Did Andrej own rope, a grappling hook, or studded boots?"

Pavol practically shot up from the bench to retrieve his gloves from the tabletop behind him.

"Pavol?" asked Hermann.

"Yes, he kept them in the shed. That's why he was so careful about keeping the shed locked. That's how I knew something was wrong that morning. The shed was unlocked and those things were missing. May I go now?"

"Yes, but if you don't mind, I would like to stick around for a moment and look through Andrej's ledgers. If that's alright with you?"

Pavol nodded, placed a cap over his ruffled red hair, and ducked back through the first room and out the front door.

Géza turned toward Hermann and raised an eyebrow. "The boy is a bundle of nerves, and he certainly has plenty of motive, not to mention opportunity, for wanting Andrej dead," said Géza. "And mystery solved regarding whose equipment it was. But what I'm most interested to know is what happened between Baum and Andrej? It sounds like they had a serious argument."

Hermann rose from his chair and approached the secretary. He ran his fingers along the spines of the brown-and-black speckled ledgers, looking at the dates written on them.

"He suggested that Andrej wasn't on good terms with Herr Baum, Herr Fürth, with many of the Slovaks, or anyone in town, really. Ah ...," said Hermann as he pulled out the most recently dated ledger. "April 1886."

"I've already looked through those, Professor. I didn't see anything of note," Géza added.

"Sometimes men tell us about the important things in what they *don't* say." Hermann scanned the entries, reading a few aloud to Géza as he went. There were notes for the purchase of replacement shovels and hoes, a budget for seeds based on some of the plants that had not survived the previous winter, and some other minor things.

"I don't see where this is going," said Géza.

"There's no mention of a purchase for rope, grappling hook, or studded boots, Inspector." He then opened and scanned through the ledger for March, then February. There was no mention of the gear in those either. "Andrej didn't want those purchases to be on record. It seems that Pavol has kept up with the bookkeeping, given the different handwriting after this point in April." Hermann scanned the shelves again and stopped at an irregularity. "However, there's an empty space on the shelf here where several as-yet unused ledgers are. Do you see?"

Hermann pointed to an empty space that had caused most of the books on the left-hand side of the lowest shelf to fall over.

"Maybe there was never anything there. The boy said Andrej was lazy, so why should he care if the books fall over?"

"Because there are three empty ink wells here and a few pens that are all ink stained. I can see at the beginning of April, Andrej recorded their purchase here, but there's hardly enough writing in this volume to suggest all three wells would be used by this point."

"The boy must have used them for his drawings."

"No, he used a lead pencil for those. Which was smart because he could make changes to the designs without wasting the more expensive paper."

Géza rose and inspected the secretary for himself, frowning over the line of ledgers and the small portfolio books with loose paper that Pavol had stowed away on the top shelf. He turned back to Hermann. "So, you think Andrej was keeping a secret diary and making purchases for some reason. With enough ink to fill up practically a whole book?"

"Perhaps, Inspector. And I think this collection of Turkish coins has something to do with it. There's been no motive up to this point. A man from a background like Andrej's isn't concerned with hard work and progress. I've known his type over the years. They'll work until they have enough saved to become louts, and once the money runs out along with the drink, they go back on the gang to start the cycle over again. Andrej was lucky to have been pro-tected here for so long, though the old-time servants proba-bly knew well what he was."

"And Baum?" said Géza.

"I'm not sure. It could be any number of things that caused their alleged argument. I'll have to know more."

Hermann replaced the ledgers on the shelf, placing them back into chronological order. He then started to put

Pavol's portfolio back when a piece of paper caught, sticking out of the top, forcing him to stop. He opened the portfolio to the page. It was a rough design of the grounds of Schattenturm, including the lake, the maze, the workers' cottages, and the footprint of the house in solid, dark lines. Some small images, resembling little half-moons, drawn around the grounds caught his attention. In the makeshift key, they were labeled *openings in the rock*.

"Inspector, what do you make of this?"

Géza approached and looked where Hermann was pointing. "I'm not sure, but I think we need to find those spots on the property."

"But what kind of openings would he mean?" Hermann said, more to himself than to Géza. Hermann studied it for another moment, then took the drawing, folded it, and put it inside his jacket.

"I'm glad the case is coming back into the realm of reality," Géza said as he tucked his notepad back into his pocket. "I was worried for a few days that I might lose my job because of a ghost story."

"Coming back, yes, there's still the question of who started the rumor about the curse, and whether that's related to whatever Andrej was up to."

Géza frowned deeply with an intense look. "To that, Professor, I believe I now have a theory."

Chapter 8

Géza remained guarded about what he knew while the two were still in earshot of the groundskeepers' cottages. It wasn't until they were walking on the lane, back toward the stables, that he opened up. "I can think of one man who would have a good reason for spreading that rumor. And if he's tied to some kind of fight with Andrej, then things are going to take a very bad turn."

They trudged on, with Géza watching the tree line and the dark silhouette of the castle.

"I'll start at the beginning," he said. "I arrived here with three extra officers, junior investigators like Erdei. We examined the crime scene. There wasn't much that we could make out that was different from what you saw this morning. However, there was one thing found, not near the murder site, but a distance away, under a hedge halfway through the maze. It was a single gold coin with Moslem writing on it, like the Turks use. It was far under the hedge, and my man only saw it thanks to the glimmer it made in the reflection of the sunlight."

"That's more than a coincidence, then," said Hermann.

"Indeed, though I didn't think so at the time. When I interviewed Baum, he confirmed that he had told the local authorities that he thought Andrej had been killed by a Gypsy or some other criminal type. He alluded to Andrej's reputation with these kinds of people, saying that he often gambled and was a known card sharp in the town. The local police weren't able to find anyone who'd recently been badly conned by Andrej, though. The Gypsies were mostly out of town, just a few here and there, with the big troops elsewhere at the time of Andrej's death. The Slovaks said they hadn't seen Andrej for several days, and the last time they did, he'd lost a round of cards to a trio of them. Baum told me that he'd sent for more experienced men from Budapest in order to move the investigation along and quell the papers which were anything but complimentary."

"That fits with what he told me this morning in the library."

Géza sighed. "But with the knowledge we've gained from questioning Pavol, I'm thinking about what happened when I showed the coin to Baum. He'd looked surprised at first, fondling the coin and turning it over. Then he said it was his, that he had dropped it when walking the grounds some time ago and he was thankful for its return. He slid it into his pocket. I asked what it was, and that's when he became defensive and said that it was what was rightfully his, from the old collection of the house. I didn't know what that meant but wrote it off as being unrelated to Andrej."

"Hmm, anything else that, with what we know now, seems relevant?"

"Yes. Prior to my interview with Baum ... and the hand-off of the coin, he was hot to have the crime solved and the investigation given every resource needed. But that changed quickly. That evening was the last that I was invited to dine with the Baums. I was sequestered down-stairs. The next afternoon, I received word that two of my men, but not Erdei, had been recalled and my superior told me that I needed to treat Herr Baum with the respect he deserved as a leading figure in the kingdom. That's also about the time I learned of the legend of the curse and that it had spread to all the staff and many of the townspeople. After that, no one would speak to me properly. They would cross themselves and clam up at the very mention of Andrej, or of Schattenturm."

They came around the edge of the stables on the lane leading to the front of the castle. Sunlight shone on both their faces as their eyes adjusted to the brightness.

"So, you think that Herr Baum spread the rumor in order to impede your progress?" said Hermann.

"The curse came on incredibly quickly. Sure, there was a bit of superstition here and there regarding the murder, but nothing you wouldn't expect. Then all of a sudden, no one would speak to me." Géza shook his head. "There seems to be bad blood in this town toward the police anyway, besides Baum's influence. I'm not sure why. I'm shocked at how quickly Pavol started to speak with you. I'd be days ahead if he'd been willing to share that information with me when I first interviewed him."

Hermann half-smiled. "I doubt it's anything special about me. I've found in my work that everyone has a story, and they jump at the chance to tell it. I just keep asking questions, patiently prodding, until I stumble onto something."

Hermann looked up at the castle. The sunlight cast deep shadows over the windows, shrouding them in tones that matched the dark stones.

"Fürth mentioned we were both expected for dinner tonight."

Géza scoffed. "Yes, he left a message for me."

Hermann continued, "It'll be a good opportunity to try to work out more about Herr Baum and the others. As a dinner guest, I'll be able to steer the course of the conversation somewhat. There's another thing, Inspector," he stopped and turned to face Géza, "I saw Pavol earlier today when I was working my way down to the kitchens. He and Rachel Baum appeared to be having a heated encounter. Pavol had ahold of her wrist. I couldn't hear most of it, but at one point the boy raised his voice and said, 'No, I won't do it,' or something along those lines. When I asked Pavol just now if he was close to anyone at Schattenturm or in Salgótarján, he said no. Why would he lie?"

Géza shook his head. "This place has more layers to it than an onion." He kicked some gravel with his right foot then chuckled. "You can't go back to the castle with shoes like that."

Hermann's brown shoes were caked in dust, mud, and maybe a little manure from all their trekking throughout the grounds over the course of the morning and midday.

Hermann groaned. "In my rush out of Vienna, I forgot to pack the boots you suggested."

"The general store in town sells boots and shoes. If we head there now, we can probably catch Erdei. It's only about five kilometers back to Salgótarján if we take a few shortcuts."

They headed in the direction of town, taking several foot paths to come out on the road the carriage had traveled. As they neared Salgótarján, Hermann noticed the sideways looks cast in his direction from the townsfolk were now more curious than hostile, unlike earlier when he was observed from the window of the hearse-like carriage. Since that morning, Salgótarján appeared to have depopulated. There were no more fast-rolling carts filled with supplies, or lines of workmen coming and going. Hermann guessed that the mines' scheduled work shifts were responsible, there'd be no time to spare a worker in the middle of the day, because of the mine boss's haul quotas and the workmen's need for steady income to support their families.

Once they reached the center of town, Géza directed the way to the doorstep of a newly built storefront. Inside, everything was labelled in German and Hungarian. One price in the Hungarian Forint and one in company currency. It seemed that Herr Baum preferred to control the exchange rate of his employees' labor at a nearly two-to-one ratio. Géza pointed Hermann to the back of the store where some shelves were set up with a variety of footwear, while he approached the shopkeeper with a number of envelopes pulled from his breast pocket. Hermann tried on a suitable pair of boots and wore them to the front counter where dozens of products from cigarettes to butter were blazoned with the same red lettering he'd seen from the train that morning; Baum's name was in every frame of view. Hermann paid as Géza watched the clerk place the stamps on his envelopes.

"He's actually run a tele-phone wire all the way here from his steel mill in Budapest?" Géza asked the clerk as he pointed to a sign in Hungarian.

The clerk looked over the rim of his glasses at the two men. "Yeah, it was quite the thing," he said in a thick Hungarian accent. "A technician arrived a few days ago and ran all sorts of wires in and out of the back room. Herr Baum had already run a telegraph wire up to the castle, but I guess that wasn't enough. I'm now the county's mail officer, tele-phone operator, and its best salesclerk," he said with a laugh. "Not that anyone can use the thing. It's strictly for emergencies and Herr Baum's business in Budapest. It rings day and night though, and the installer told me someone has to be here at all times to patch through the line, otherwise the signal will be too weak."

"What a world we live in, to be able to talk to someone across the country," Géza said.

"Indeed," Hermann chimed in. "What could be so pressing about his business that he'd need to install a faster communiqué than a telegraph?"

"Maybe it's his curse," the clerk said with a chuckle, before he deposited Hermann's payment into the register and wrote a small receipt.

Hermann thought that might be true, but not from a tangible perspective.

"Which way is Frau von Voitsberg's antiques shop?" Hermann asked Géza, once they were back outside.

"It's just down this lane on the right. A nice enough little place, though the prices are more than anyone here besides Herr Baum can afford."

"And does the frau mind unannounced visitors to her shop?"

"She's pleasant enough, but if you want to avoid any haughtiness, don't mention Herr Baum. When I questioned her, she may as well have been an archduchess."

"Hmm ... Inspector, would you mind if I spoke to her alone? If she's predisposed to put up her armor around the police and the Baums, I may get further with her posing as an intrigued client or tourist."

Géza frowned. "Well, I don't think there's much to gather from her. She hasn't had much to do with Schattenturm since its sale ... but let me know if she has a story to tell if you stumble onto it." He chuckled good-naturedly. "Meet up ... say, in about an hour? I'll find Erdei and see what he has to report about where Andrej acquired the gear."

Hermann found the antiques store right where Géza said it would be, though it took a minute to ascertain that it actually was a store. There was no sign over the front door, nor anything else to indicate the cream-colored stucco house with a red-tiled roof, and painted shutters, was any different from the other homes on the street. Hermann had to discretely peer through several windows before determining that this one, with far more furniture than was normal, all arranged far too close together, was the one he was looking for. A little bell chimed to announce his arrival as he entered through the front door. There was no one in sight. Three rooms, including the hall, were packed to the brim with incredibly ornate furniture. Finely carved sideboards, tables, chairs, and a drawing room set of Rococo sofas and lounges, were crammed against each other with small alleyways spaced between, just wide enough to squeeze by.

Many pieces were draped in dust covers to protect them, and large crates and trunks were stacked around the interior walls. It functioned more like a warehouse than a shop to Hermann's eye.

After a moment of assessing a large, fine oil painting hanging on a wall in the hall, a woman appeared from a doorway at the other end. Hermann was immediately struck by her beauty. She was tall, her height accentuated by the vertical lines of her muted-blue dress with white lace around the bodice. She had a long neck and heart-shaped face, enhanced by high cheekbones.

"Good day, fraulein," he said turning to face her. "My name is Hermann Horst."

She approached Hermann with the cool poise that only an aristocratic upbringing would afford. Her bright, silver-grey eyes studied him intently before the first word was uttered.

"Charmed," the woman replied coolly.

The transom window over the front door caught the color play in her ash-blond hair with golden undertones, braided and bundled above the creamy silk skin of her cheeks and forehead.

Hermann filled the gap left by her lack of introduction. "I was admiring this painting. It's Baroque, no?"

The silver eyes finally detached from Hermann's face and glided to the painting. "Indeed. It was commissioned by my ancestor, the third Freiherr von Voitsberg. The scene is Odysseus' return to Ithaca. It's by Julius Strasser of the studio of Anton Mengs, from 1774. Early Neoclassical, rather than true Baroque. It once hung in the Antiquities Room at Schattenturm ..." She paused, waiting for a look of recognition to cross Hermann's face. When none appeared, she continued. "Schattenturm is the castle a few kilometers from here."

"Oh yes, of course," Hermann responded. "It's remarkable. The dynamic aspect of the figures is very advanced for the period. You must feel honored to be able to offer such a painting. I know a few colleagues of art history in Vienna who would love to host it in the university's gallery, or at the new Kunsthistorisches Museum, once it's finished."

"That *would* be an honor," she said. A warmth crept into her tone of voice at the mention of his credentials. "However, this piece has been reserved for a private collection. This is merely its temporary home. It represents one of my favorite subjects. A family rightly restored, and harmony set back on the scene of the Aegean after so much conflict." She turned back to face Hermann. "I apologize for forgetting to introduce myself. My name is Frau Astrid von Voitsberg."

Hermann gave a short bow from the neck.

"I don't have many pieces for sale, but if you're an art enthusiast, there are several that you may enjoy viewing," Astrid said as she motioned toward the room on Hermann's right.

"You have quite a fine collection I see. I'm certainly an enthusiast, though no art historian myself."

"Many of these pieces represent a portion of my inheritance from my late uncle, the sixth freiherr. I treasured them at Schattenturm for many years before his death. It seems right that they should be in my care, even if they are only in a place such as this." She twirled a petite hand around in a wave.

"Such as this, frau? Your establishment is well-positioned in town to catch the eye of a traveler, just down the road from the train station and near the center of town. I'm sure you will profit here."

Astrid paused in mid-stride on her way to the right-hand room. "True, though they must go to the right kind of buyer, and my sense of *the right kind of buyer* is particular. I'm not a shopkeeper, despite what this studio might imply. Think of me more as the preservationist of a homeless collection." She turned to face him. "Are you a visitor to Salgó-tarján for any particular purpose, Herr Horst? We don't have much in the way of entertainment since the death of my uncle. The town has lost most of its charm since these mines opened recently."

Hermann regarded her gaze again—sharp, her eyes molten silver ready to be cast.

"I was called by a local resident to assist with mounting fears regarding a curse that plagues the town, according to an old legend."

"How intriguing," she said slowly. "The only curse in town that I know of concerns poor Herr Baum and his manufacturing business." She practically sneered the trade description.

"I'm not here at the behest of Herr Baum, frau, but it does concern him in a wider sense." A case of fine pocket watches caught Hermann's eye. "Ah, these are quite something. This one tells not just the hour, but the phase of the moon, no?"

Astrid drifted around a large glass case to come to his side. "Yes, it does. My father, Albert von Voitsberg, bought it in a shop in Freiburg, during his time at the university."

"I would have thought the son of a freiherr would choose Vienna? Though, maybe I'm biased."

She smiled. "My father wanted to experience more than just the empire. He said it was important to know how other Germans lived, spoke, and felt about everything. He loved history and folklore. Freiburg was the perfect place for that, so near the Rhine and independent enough to not be entirely Prussian-dominated, nor overly Catholic." She sighed. "I do miss him often."

"I'm sorry for your loss, frau. He sounds like a man after my own heart."

"Really? What is it that you do, Herr Horst? You said you were from Vienna, and you are here for what purpose, something to do with the superstitions of the country folk?"

"I'm a professor at the University of Vienna. I specialize in history, mythology, and folklore, through the Department of Philosophy."

"How delightful," she said. "We're so bereft of quality company here. Much less anyone interested in anything German over Magyar these days. But I'm afraid I couldn't part with any of these," she said as she looked over the case of watches. "They're far too dear to me, and the memory of my father, to let them go."

"I understand. Loss can be all consuming." Hermann's brow creased and he shifted his gaze toward the window for a moment. "The slightest reminder of someone we've lost can resurface so many memories. An inanimate object can become the embodiment of the last bit of their essence. Even when it is only a shadow of what they once were to us."

Somewhat surprised at the slight change in the tone of his voice, and the fleeting expression of pain that crossed his face, she looked at him more thoughtfully. He had not been forthright with her in his reasons for being in Salgótarján, nor for entering her shop, that was clear. However, there was a genuineness about him, a thing born from personal hardship.

Hermann studied her expression, trying not to be distracted by the delicate, floral scent of her hair ... was it ... jasmine, no honeysuckle. He cleared his throat. She was melancholy, yes, but there was a curiosity there, too.

"I have something else, from the Schwarzwald, that I think you might enjoy," she said. "Though I can't part with it either, it was a gift to me from my father." She led him back through to the hall and turned to focus on a very large, incredibly detailed clock, hanging halfway up the wall beyond the stair. "See if you can guess the story being told around the hütte."

Hermann crossed his arms and studied the clock. It featured a multi-story chalet with balconies containing intricately carved figures. It didn't take Hermann long to realize the figures depicted one of his favorite epics of German history. He smiled and turned to face Astrid who had been studying him while he'd been studying the clock. "Is it the tragedy of Arminius?"

She smiled modestly. "I've never heard it called a tragedy before, but yes. Father loved the story. A boy, taken from his home and raised amongst his enemies, returns to his people and frees them from imperial dominion, with the help of his wife, the seeress Thusnelda, of course."

"It is a fine piece of work, and it captures all the main elements." Hermann paused. "But after Arminius' victory, Thusnelda was taken and held hostage for the rest of her life in Rome. Arminius was driven mad by the act, ultimately causing the other German tribes to turn on him." His eyes dropped. "A brief and shining display, made moot by national disunity."

"Though ... we aren't speaking Latin today, are we?" she said.

"No," he said with a chuckle.

Astrid glided to the next room. "There's more in here you may like, though most of it is boxed away. You said you were a professor, but I fail to see how a professor of history and folklore would be of help in dealing with a curse."

"In truth, frau, I'm here to assist at Schattenturm. There was a murder there some weeks ago, the gardener as you must have heard by now."

She turned in liquid motion, folding her hands over one another at the end of her bodice. "I have," she said. "It was a dreadful business, taking place somewhere on the grounds. My maid told me that the police had already identified a suspect, that he must have fled in a troop or by coach to Budapest."

"Not quite, I'm afraid. The police are of the opinion that the killer is still at large, hidden in plain sight."

Astrid reached up to touch the charm dangling on end of her necklace. "That's horrible. Why hasn't anything been done sooner?"

"The evidence, so far, is circumstantial. However, someone has been spreading the tale of a curse that will fall upon all those connected with the house, including the townsfolk. The lead inspector believes this was done to hamper the investigation. So far, it has worked. Hardly anyone will speak to the police openly now."

Astrid's brows knitted together as she turned, necklace in hand. "What is the nature of the curse? I haven't heard of anything specific before, Herr Horst. Though, the townsfolk aren't likely to tell me such things to my face."

"That may be, but its effect is profound. The curse foretells of the day when Gustav Freiherr von Voitsberg will rise from the grave with the power of the devil to drive away any interloper, and by association, those who would support the interloper in dislodging his own family from their rightful home in Schattenturm. There are some who believe this time has come and Andrej Fehér is the first of his victims."

"The townsfolk are superstitious, Herr Horst. I don't doubt that a curse like this would keep them silenced," she said with a shake of her head.

"That's where I come into play. As it stands, I've spent the last several years as an authority on the parapsychological."

Astrid didn't register an understanding of the subject.

"The study of why people feel they have encountered the supernatural and what that says about them and the world around them. I'm to help in the investigation by finding the root of the sentiment around the curse which supposedly dooms the Baum family of Schattenturm for their interloping against the founder's family ... your family, as it were."

Astrid smiled. "While the Baums are not *of* Schattenturm, I can assure you that my family has had nothing to do with Andrej's death. There have been legends in this town for centuries, since Schattenturm was taken from the Turks. What's left of the von Voitsbergs want nothing to do with Herr Baum or his family." Astrid frowned and moved to look from the exterior window where she had a view of the road.

Hermann studied her expression. It looked like grief, deep-seated grief.

"My father, Albert, was a good man, Herr Horst, but he wasn't the heir to the freiherrschaft. That honor fell to my uncle, Georg. He was older by two years, but my father was always the elder of them where it mattered."

Hermann watched as her head dropped.

"My uncle was in debt. He loved his fabulous parties, rich gifts, but he could never balance his checkbook. My father kept him in order as much as he could while he lived. At first it wasn't hard, especially while Schattenturm was still being renovated, but by the time I was old enough to notice, things had soured. My father died, and soon after, the money was gone. Much of it lost in the crash of '73, I believe. After that, things ... deteriorated. Servants were dismissed, repairs ignored, some artwork and furniture sold off in secret. Somehow, my uncle left enough for my mother, my brother, and me to live, but only enough to support us in the dowager's cottage on the grounds of the castle."

When Astrid turned back to face Hermann, a hint of tears obscured her silver-grey eyes, like ice over window-panes.

"He lost Schattenturm, our home, and my brother's inheritance as the seventh Freiherr von Voitsberg. What we have now is a landless title and what was explicitly left in my uncle Georg's will ... what I was able to convince the bank to allow us to keep. I gave up my dowry fund for my brother's purchase of a commission into the army. At least *he* may yet have a future."

Hermann felt uncomfortable, empathetic to her plight, as he shifted slightly.

"So no, Herr Horst," she continued, "my family has had nothing to do with any murder or with Schattenturm as it is. And the last thing any of us want is to start some feud with the Baums."

"I apologize if I have upset you, frau. That was not my intent."

She smiled and wiped away a tear. "Don't worry. I'm stronger than the girls who need their smelling salts." There was an awkward pause before she continued. "Do you think you'll be able to catch the killer?"

Hermann looked up, relieved at the turn back to the case. "I hope so. The Baum family has been quite disturbed by the ordeal, and even though I'm just a professor, I find there's something oddly poetic about the course of justice."

She raised an eyebrow. "Perhaps you could write a thesis on us when you've finished?"

"To do that, I'll have to be able to interview people properly without a curse getting in the way. Do you think a word from one of the von Voitsberg family would help set things at ease in the town?"

"Well ... I'm not sure that I can really help that—"

"I'm sure it will speed up the police's work," interjected Hermann. "The inspector wrote to me saying that the curse was keeping the staff at the castle and some of the towns-folk from giving satisfactory statements. The interviews are necessary to close the case, even if many of them are just a formality. The inspector has all but determined the iden-tity of the murderer. A victim of Andrej's card tricks."

"I'll see what I can do. The right word to the right people and all that."

Astrid walked back toward the hall, and Hermann felt his visit coming to an end.

"Do give my regards to Frau Baum, Herr Horst. She seems a gentle soul, from the few times we've met."

"I will give her your regards. May I call on you again, Frau Astrid? I was actually interested in some of your pieces, and my apartment in Vienna has been quite bare of the artistic touch."

Astrid smiled back at him. "Certainly. I think you would be exactly the right kind of buyer. Though next time, perhaps we can speak about history or literature, and not murder?"

"I will try my best."

Hermann gave a short bow and parted from Astrid who watched him for another minute as he made his way up the street and away from her not-so-antiques-shop gallery.

Chapter 9

Hermann spoke in a low undertone as he and Géza walked back to the castle. "Frau Astrid seemed distraught at the loss of her birthright, and the standard of luxury that came with it, not to mention her dowry and opportunity for a good marriage. She knew the gardener's name, though she probably knew many of the servants' names when she lived at Schattenturm. Nothing else really stood out to me."

What Hermann didn't say was how much he and Astrid von Voitsberg had in common, including her father's and his own interest in history and folklore.

Géza grumbled. "It sounds like you got more from her than I did when I questioned her."

"I admired her art collection and her philosophy behind some of the pieces."

"How's that?" asked Géza.

"My parents placed a lot of importance on understanding our history, not just as Salzburgers, but as Germans. I think they would have rather Austria joined with the rest of the states back in '48. We weren't nobility like the von Voitsbergs, but we weren't poor either. It gave us a level of freedom, with one foot in each social circle, bourgeois and upper crust."

"Yes, I can see where that would be helpful. My parents struggled as farmers most of their lives. They owned their own land which is more than many, but their work left only a little breathing room for a comfortable living. I was lucky to make it into the military as a teenager. From there I had a chance at a career. Frau Astrid seems more downcast than she ought to be."

"She does have a fair dose of pride, I'll admit. I'd like to learn more about her uncle, Georg von Voitsberg. She appears to take after her father, an academic I'd say." Hermann paused. "What about your time in the military?"

"I made it into the Hussars. I always had a knack with horses and I'm a good shot. There's not much to say, really. I went as high as an enlisted man can go, then I hit a road-block with the officer corp. I was never going to be allowed to rub shoulders with the sons of dukes and viscounts."

"So, you decided to transition to the police?"

"I found an opening in Budapest and I took the chance. Until now, until this case, I've been pretty good at my job. The way this town has closed ranks against me though ... well, I'm not sure how long I'll be employed if we can't crack this soon."

"About that ... I asked Frau Astrid if she would use her influence to improve our chances by dispelling some of the curse's effect."

"And how do you think she can do that?"

"She's the highest-ranking noblewoman in the town, even with her family's fall from grace. My guess is that she has more sway here than one would realize. By the way, when did you question Frau Astrid? How long after the murder I mean?"

"About two or three days after I arrived."

"And that was after the curse had spread?"

"Yes, why? Do you think she's involved?"

"She may be," said Hermann. "At first, she claimed no knowledge of the curse which isn't likely. And she was hesitant to help until I told her that you'd already made a determination, but just needed to collect some statements to close things up."

Géza frowned. "I see. Was there anything else I should know about her?"

"She's still tied to the past. I've seen it in my work often enough. Frau Astrid seems possessed by the life that she ought to have continued, she hasn't let go and moved on. She told me about her uncle's debts and the ruination of the family just before and after his death."

"Andrej was also part of that world, not her world exactly, but maybe they had a connection?" said Géza. "Andrej didn't seem the type to leave a favorable impression on a woman like Frau Astrid. Though, Frau Kovács would have had him canonized as a saint." Géza shook his head.

"True. A gambling card sharp would hardly be fit company for a frau. And she certainly has reason enough to loathe the Baums, since they're the cuckoos in her nest," said Hermann.

"Hold on," Géza said, stopping and turning to halt Hermann with a hand. "What do you mean? Did she say something about Herr Baum?"

"Not particularly. It's natural, Inspector, to hate those who've come into your home after you, especially if you've been forced out by circumstance."

"But nothing directly about Baum?"

"No."

Géza's jaw clenched. "There's something about him. Like a man on the brink, but I can't figure it out. Men like that are dangerous. If he's guilty of murder, I won't look by and let him get away with it."

Hermann noted Géza's intensity. His statement had been more than a little out of place. The inspector might have a point though, Baum was difficult to read and he was very edgy, that much was clear.

The sight of Schattenturm did nothing to put them at ease. The shadows of the spring afternoon, exaggerated by the setting sun, caught and lingered on the spires and crags of the dark stonework. Each window cast back the glare of the light to act as a hundred mirrors. Hermann couldn't shake the sense of isolation the place gave off, a palace with almost no one to care for it. There were no guests to fill its rooms, and no stately events to give it purpose.

Their footsteps echoed off the walls of the courtyard, crunching through the pea gravel as they made their way back to the great keep's doors. Despite the creak of the old hinges, a sort of hushed conference was being carried on in the hall beyond the entryway. Hermann and Géza passed a look between themselves and made their way carefully, quietly, to the edge of the room where they could hear more clearly.

"I've told you how many times to stop speaking nonsense?" came a woman's strained voice. "You will dress for dinner and comport yourself with dignity. Do you hear me?"

"Don't talk to me about dignity," said a younger sounding woman. "You know as well as I do that I'm not the one Papa will throw out on her ear when he learns about what's been going on under his nose for months."

"You don't know what you're talking about. Whatever you think you saw that day, you didn't."

"That's not what Andrej had to say about it. Don't deny it, mother. I already know. He told me you wanted him, were so lonely that you couldn't see straight. That he knew a way to cheer you up."

The sound of a slap echoed down the hall.

"Get out of my sight. I don't want to see you before dinner, and don't you dare embarrass me or your father."

"Or what? Another scandal? Another move? Maybe this time Papa will send me somewhere I actually have a chance."

"Your actions have consequences, Rachel. Everything we do is watched and acted on. I won't let you bring down this family over some trifle."

"You wouldn't know anything about it!"

Rachel Baum's footsteps could be heard stamping down the hallway just as her mother's footsteps clapped quickly back toward the eavesdroppers and faded away into one of the rooms.

Hermann and Géza moved back from the edge of where they'd been listening.

"This is the first I'm hearing of any scandal involving Frau Baum and Andrej," said Géza.

Hermann repeated Rachel's statement, "Whatever you think you saw that day, you didn't. Did she have some sort of liaison with Andrej?"

"Not that I've heard. Not that they would fess up to it."

"I haven't been introduced to her yet. I could try and learn more if I were able to speak with her."

Géza frowned and traced the edge of his beard. "She'll probably have gone to her parlor, it's down the hall, along the inner wall. Go alone, Professor. You seem to be able to pull honey from a spigot."

"Alright. I'll let you know what she says."

"I'll go up and get changed for dinner then. Those little medals never seem to stick on properly. And give me that box with your muddy shoes. I'll drop it in your room," Géza said with a chuckle.

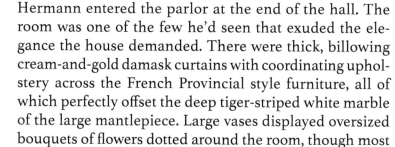

Hermann entered the parlor at the end of the hall. The room was one of the few he'd seen that exuded the elegance the house demanded. There were thick, billowing cream-and-gold damask curtains with coordinating upholstery across the French Provincial style furniture, all of which perfectly offset the deep tiger-striped white marble of the large mantlepiece. Large vases displayed oversized bouquets of flowers dotted around the room, though most were wilting badly and dropping debris around their bases. Clearly, they'd enjoyed an extended stay, with no replacements.

Frau Baum was tending to one bouquet against the far wall between two of the room's windows. Her back was to Hermann as he entered. She was a blue silhouette with dark hair, so thin as to look almost childlike, and the fashionable bustle of her dress set her out of proportion. She was fondling one of the long strands of brittle greenery, watching it crumble from decay under the pressure of her fingertips.

Hermann made to clear his throat to avoid startling the woman more than she may already have been by his arrival. She turned round, dropping a petal from the bouquet as she held her hand aloft. Hermann caught a glimpse of a deep blue mark as she twisted her neck, nearly the same shade as her dress collar, barely visible above her collarbone. Her white skin matched the tone of the marble mantlepiece, and that of her daughter, Rachel. Though clearly over forty, she retained a calm grace and only slight creases in her brow above her full eyebrows, and in the smile lines beneath her dark eyes.

"Good afternoon, frau. I am Professor Horst. Inspector Orczy sent for me from Vienna to aid in the investigation of Andrej Fehér's murder."

She inhaled sharply. "Oh, of course. Welcome to Schattenturm. I wish it had been under more pleasant circumstances. Have you found everything to meet your needs?"

"Yes, in fact I believe the inspector and I have made a good start to my first day."

"Excellent. Johan will be so pleased. He's been fretting terribly for the last few weeks over this ... awfulness."

"I certainly don't wish to prolong any discomfort on Herr Baum's part. His mind should be set at rest by the time we're finished."

"That's good to hear." She gave a weak impression of a smile. "This whole ordeal has dragged on and on for what seems like an eternity. I'm not sure my nerves can tolerate much more." She motioned to the set of opposing sofas and coffee table. "Please, sit for a moment. We'll have to change for dinner shortly."

"Thank you," he said, choosing the sofa facing the windows. "I've just walked up from town, and I had the opportunity to enjoy the beautiful setting here."

She nodded. "This estate is so grand, almost overbearingly so. I remember it from my time as a girl when Father and Mama would visit for one of the many balls or galas."

"The house and grounds are truly remarkable."

"They are, but tedious to maintain." She looked off for a moment before her gaze settled back to her fingertips where a slight stain had been left by the decaying foliage. "Though, I thought you arrived this morning? I hope you didn't miss your train just to traipse all the way here this afternoon."

Hermann smiled. "Oh no, fortunately I took the overnight from Vienna. I had to return to town to find some appropriate walking shoes. While I was there, I took the opportunity to meet Frau Astrid von Voitsberg at her gallery. Do you know her?"

"Ah, Frau Astrid. What a charming young woman. She has had such strength to deal with her fall. It's a pity, what happened to this place."

"How do you mean?"

"That this place sat almost empty for several years before Johan purchased it. It was in quite the state of disrepair, no doubt from old Freiherr von Voitsberg's unfortunate financial situation in the years before he died. Several of the staff were retained after his death, and that may be all that kept this place from being ruined."

"And that must have partially been thanks to the late gardener?" He nodded in the direction of the bouquet between the windows. "Have you had any ideas about his replacement yet?"

She curled her fingers into a folded fist, hiding away the green mark she had been studying. "No. Unfortunately, Andrej was one that you don't find often. Schattenturm will never be the same without his guidance and artistic expression."

"Artistic expression? I've heard little of his talent thus far. You say he was an artist?"

She gave a little laugh. "Hardly. No, not an artist in the sense of an academy trained maestro. Though, he had such a knack for flower arranging and seasonal variations. This house was always full of his bouquets."

"Did you have plans with Andrej?"

"Plans?" she said, looking up suddenly. "What do you mean? No, I never had plans with him."

"I've seen several remarkable landscape drawings for French-inspired gardens that would be quite nice if ever there was the opportunity. A shame that they may never come to fruition."

She relaxed. "Oh. Yes, I have seen those drawings once or twice. I had a few improvements that I suggested, but Andrej ... Andrej, took great pride in his designs. I don't think he would have been the best person to try and implement my vision for this place."

"His assistant seemed quite the protégé from what I could tell. Very talented."

"His assistant? You mean the Slovak boy. What's his name?"

"Pavol Soták, frau."

"Pavol," she repeated flatly. "I'm not sure we'll be able to keep the boy on. This estate needs to be brought back to its former glory. I will need the best for that. He doesn't fit with my vision."

Hermann sat back against the sofa. "A pity. To witness such horror."

Frau Baum adjusted on the edge of her sofa, ruffling the fabric of her skirt. "Horror?"

"Yes, to come upon one's mentor in such a state. I believe it must have been an act of terrible passion. How else could that hammer have been so thoroughly lodged in Andrej's skull?"

The color drained from Frau Baum's face which was a marvel to Hermann, given her already pale complexion.

"Fortunately, he didn't suffer long ... from what I've heard," she said, looking again toward the decomposing flower arrangement.

"Inspector Orczy believes it must have been quick, nearly instantaneous. The hammer would have shattered his brains upon impact. If he struggled with his assailant beforehand, who could say but the murderer?" Hermann watched Frau Baum for any sign of discomfort that could convey a clue. She made no comment, only tensed her shoulders in a kind of reflexive shudder.

"Were those some of his last arrangements, frau?" Hermann said, looking between Frau Baum and the rotting bouquets.

"Yes, indeed they are. I've not had the heart to dispose of them yet, but they'll have to be let go soon now."

She rose, not noticing that Hermann rose simultaneously, in curtesy. She walked to the nearest bouquet, her back to him now. "Ignore what you've wanted, but couldn't have," she practically whispered.

"What was that, frau?"

She twirled back around to face him. "I said that it's time we departed to change for dinner. The cook has had an opportunity to prepare something splendid this evening. Shall we continue this conversation later, after dinner? Mama will be delighted to meet you. She's been a fan of your work, and she's been terribly excited about this whole ordeal. Your presence will be the cherry on her cake."

———————————◆———————————

Hermann looked himself over in the mirror, straightened the tails of his dinner jacket, and smoothed the board-like, stark-white shirt beneath. It had been a whirlwind twenty-four hours, he thought to himself. Yesterday afternoon he had been carrying out his droll routine at the university.

Now, he was neck-deep in a web of intrigue surrounding a vicious murder. He looked at the painting above the bed: Gustav von Voitsberg, denizen of the clan whose memory shadowed everything to do with Schattenturm. Hermann mused to himself about the potential of the old freiherr's ghost visiting him in the night. What connection his spirit may have to the estate's centuries worth of inhabitants. The history here was rich and tumultuous as Hungarians, Germans, and Turks all left their marks. Would they communicate in the afterworld, or would the language barriers prevent it? Maybe the problem had been resolved by incorporeality? He checked himself as was his habit of doing; the downfall of an ancient family was no laughing matter, especially one that had been instrumental in freeing their country from occupation and tyranny, and which brought so much beauty into the world with this house.

"I doubt you'd give up any secrets about this place, would you?" he asked the painting.

The portrait gave no reply, but Gustav's eyes followed Hermann to the door. A trick of the light and the painter's exceptional skill.

"Herr Hermann Horst and Inspector Orczy Géza," Fürth, sounding very formal, announced the two men as they entered the parlor. The Baum clan was arrayed across multiple pieces of honey-colored Biedermeier furniture with matching striped upholstery. Johan Baum was fixing himself a drink from the tiger-oak table, set between the two windows at the back. Rachel Baum was seated to one side of a tall clock with her hands folded over the dark-grey folds of her dress, while her plump brother, Josef, slouched in his dinner ensemble on the opposite side. The very thin Frau Baum sat on a sofa in front of the fireplace. She looked elegant in a deep-blue satin bodice and over skirt, a white-carnation-patterned under skirt, and a neat bustle showing off the extravagance of excess fabric required to create a flowing short train. Hermann noticed the bruise he'd seen earlier was now no longer in view, hidden beneath her high collar.

A figure in an ostentatious, all black gown approached Hermann from his side. She wore multiple layers of black satin skirts and an intricate bodice with long sleeves and a high neck trimmed in black lace. She donned a black bonnet with a thick black veil thrown back over the top, trailing over her shoulders like a cape. The woman underneath was old, with sharp cheekbones and bright, amber eyes that shone out beyond the wrinkles and crow's feet lining her face.

"Professor Horst, welcome to Schattenturm," the woman in black said. Her voice scraped over the words like she needed a glass of water. "I am Frau Kam. This is my daughter Erzsébet Baum, and my two grandchildren Josef and Rachel."

She swept her black-gloved hand around the room fluidly with the palm facing up, like they were delicacies on order. Hermann gave a short bow to each, despite having already been acquainted with all but Josef.

"We are so pleased to make your acquaintance, Professor. How was your journey? You must have already seen much of the house and grounds by now. What do you think of our den of shadows?" She smiled, revealing striking ivory dentures.

"I'm pleased to meet you, Frau Kam, though I wish it could have been under less macabre circumstances. I arrived this morning, and I've been at work since. Schattenturm is marvelous. Such craftsmanship and attention to detail in every room I've seen."

"Splendid," said Frau Kam. "Tell us, have you found the fiend who buried a hatchet in the gardener's skull?" She moved in closer, looking expectantly at Hermann, as was everyone in the room.

"Unfortunately, not yet. However, Inspector Orczy and I have a good idea as to how the killer must have ambushed

Andrej with the hammer. Most brutal," Hermann replied. He'd made a point of mentioning Géza.

Frau Baum's lavish skirts rustled. "Professor, while we are thankful for your help, let's not get into too much detail about the ... incident. I don't want to fray the nerves of the children."

"Oh come now, Erzsébet. They're old enough to understand murder and death ... and what comes after," Frau Kam retorted, a wide smile growing in her wrinkles.

"It's still too early in the case to reveal details of the investigation," said Géza.

"And it wouldn't be suitable at dinner, certainly," said Hermann.

"You're quite right, Herr Horst," said Erzsébet, giving her mother a cautionary sideways glance. "We only pray that this nightmare will be over soon."

"Nightmares don't come into it, dear," said Frau Kam. "What we're dealing with are spirits, active, vengeful spirits. You know as well as I that when Johan bought this place, he didn't make any effort to put them at ease, and after centuries of dynastic habitation at that. It's no wonder they'd want to punish us," she said, before sitting on the other end of the sofa from Erzsébet.

Herr Baum stepped forward, drink in hand. "Hmph," he muttered, but said nothing more, preferring the comfort of his crystal tumbler's contents.

"So, have you encountered the shades yet, Professor?" Frau Kam asked.

"I can't say that I have, but the supernatural does have many people here, and in the village, on edge. I aim to peel back the curtain and lay out the facts of what we're dealing with."

"I hope you do, Professor. The spirits are very active in this house. I've heard them in the walls, whispering things the living aren't meant to hear. And they play the pianoforte in the old, closed up music room, longing for happier times and their lost loves," Frau Kam added, with a laugh and clapping of her gloved hands.

Fürth interrupted the scene with his reentry.

"Are you ready for us?" Erzsébet's question was more of a plea than a query.

The butler gave a stiff, one-way nod as he held open the door to the hall.

Erzsébet rose and held out an elbow on a willowy arm. "You will escort me, Professor. Johan will follow with Mama. Inspector Orczy will escort Rachel, and Josef ... will follow."

Chapter 10

Hermann followed Erzsébet's guidance to the head of the long, oval-shaped table, opposite where her husband would sit. He pushed in her chair as she sat down, careful not to overdo or underdo the move, then he made his way to the seat on her right where a small card with his name had been placed. He saw that Fürth and the footmen had done well, with freshly polished silver urns of simple, long-stemmed white tulips, fine china and crystal place settings, silver flatware for each course of the meal, and all of it underscored by an embroidered-lace tablecloth. Hermann noted that the table could be substantially lengthened by additional sections which were currently acting as discrete side tables placed around the periphery of the room. The shortened length gave a more intimate and friendly feel to the gathering. Two tapestries hung on the wall behind Hermann, flanking the great fireplace that was crackling and emanating warmth from the ornate fireback. There were several large portraits hung around the walls, fine landscapes that looked vivid in the Quattrocento fashion. There were also smaller empty spaces on the walls that must have once displayed paintings, but which now displayed slightly less faded sections of silk wallpaper. Hermann wondered how many of the missing masterpieces were awaiting the *right kind of buyer* in Frau Astrid's antiques gallery.

Once the ladies had been seated by their escorts, Géza and Johan took their seats, with Josef following behind.

Frau Kam was across from Hermann, to Johan Baum's left, directly to the right of Géza who was seated at the foot of the table. Rachel and Josef were at the other end of the table to their father and mother's sides, well away from the thick of the adults' conversation. Twin candelabras illuminated the fine crème of leek soup placed in front of them which they sampled as Fürth and the more senior of the two footmen circled with white wine.

Once Frau Kam had finished her soup, she wasted no time in locking Hermann into conversation.

"I must say, Professor Horst, I was quite impressed by your *Paranormal Psychological Polemics of the Modern Mind*. You highlighted exactly my own theories regarding communion with the spirits. That they can be reached if you just have the right mindset. You don't write like someone who mediums for a living, though. You sound philosophical, even scientific."

"I try to look at the afterlife and the departed as a kind of energy that we can tap into, that we can channel and read like a telegraph message, establishing an actual connection. Understanding the sort of Morse Code that is being relayed is the more difficult part of the whole field. There are a plethora of frauds out there who aren't looking at the realities of death and after-death, but who just want fame or an income."

"So, what are you saying?" Johan Baum interjected. "That we all float around in space waiting for a message signal after we die?"

"No, more like our residual energy, from a lifetime of living, is left over on this world after we die, and those who know how, can interact with that energy."

"You mean our souls?" asked Frau Kam.

The footmen cleared the soup bowls.

"In a way," Hermann replied. "Though not exactly. I firmly believe in the notion of the human soul, a part of our being separate from our bodies that leaves us after we die. Where our souls go exactly, I don't have a theory on, and it probably varies greatly on your profession of faith. That kind of presence leaves a mark in its wake. We feel it when our loved ones pass, like their presence in a house or when we sit down to write them a letter years later and forget for a moment what's happened. I think we feel it even when we get gooseflesh as though they've passed right next to us, though we're nowhere near where they've lived."

"Would that not relate more to someone's mental state rather than a spirit? How can you gauge an experience like that?" asked Géza.

"By measuring against a control variable of their emotional nature and character at large," Hermann replied. "A baseline of how they interact with others and the notion of the supernatural. The more a person is consumed with their emotions, or supernatural themes, as a hobby, the less reliable they usually are."

Erzsébet fidgeted and interrupted them as the footmen brought in two platters from the butler's pantry. "We'll be dining as service à la Russe, Herr Horst. The style had not caught on the last time we visited Paris, but then they would want to keep service à la Française."

Erzsébet smiled, enthused by her well-rehearsed joke. Her enthusiasm quickly started to fade as she noticed the silence from the other diners. The more senior footman led, carrying the platter with the carp to Frau Kam, the second followed with the sauce accompaniment. Rachel snickered softly behind her hand.

"I've wondered why we don't have our own service à la Autrichien or service à la Hongroise. Maybe the customs of other nations couldn't keep up with our würstel and knödel," Hermann said, in an attempt to lighten the discomfort of his hostess.

Frau Kam let out a laugh and Géza and Johan both chuckled. Erzsébet gave a small smile in gratitude. The carp with lemon dill sauce and asparagus tips kept the party contained for a time after that.

Rachel eventually broke the silence, speaking down the length of the table, far out of turn of the flow of conversation intended by the placements. "Professor Horst, what you said earlier about a person's connection to the afterlife and the dead ... if someone can contact them, does that prove the existence of God?"

Erzsébet shot her daughter a cold look. "Rachel, dear, that really isn't a topic fit for a young lady," she said. "How have your riding lessons come? You may have something in common with Inspector Orczy. He was a dragoon, you know."

"A hussar, actually. The dragoons are attached to the Landwehr. I served under the Honved in Bosnia," Géza said.

Erzsébet looked worried that the conversation might lead back toward the concept of death. "Oh," she said, and took a sip of her wine.

"You never told me that," Johan put in. "I had a contract for the manufacture of the new artillery around that time. How did they perform?"

Géza grimaced and looked like maybe he'd suddenly developed a case of indigestion. "I would rather not say."

"So you weren't near the front then? What was your role? Courier?" Johan said with a chuckle.

"A description of your guns' capacity for carnage isn't suitable for dinner conversation, nor for ladies ... herr."

The table remained silent for a few moments.

"Well, Professor, let me ask, does the existence of the soul prove the existence of God, like it's told in the Bible?" asked Frau Kam.

"So many religions have their own ideas on god, divinity, and the nature of the afterlife. I'm not sure that I have enough information to make such a declaration. Let's look at the Buddhists of the Orient for example, they believe our souls are trapped in an ongoing process of life, death, and rebirth until we come to an understanding that all of existence is a kind of illusion. After one has achieved enlight-

enment, the soul leaves the cycle and becomes pure existence."

"That's nonsense. How can you fight to leave existence
and also become existence?" said Baum.

"I think you'd have to ask one of their monks or gurus,
and I doubt we'll find one of those in the empire. However,
the same concept applied to our own ancestors when they
first encountered Christianity. For the Teutons, the Mag-
yars, the Slavs, life was cyclical and the living were a contin-
uation of the work and deeds of their ancestors, whether
they lived honorably or dishonorably, healthily or
unhealthily. One couldn't escape the tribe and the blood
that flowed through one's veins. So, they had an immense
difficulty in being convinced of the individuality of the
Christian mission towards personal salvation, that we are
born sinful and require cleansing. Such a thought was
alien to them and was unnatural based on their own role in
life and nature."

A footman rounded the table bearing sweetbreads
with plum chutney.

"So does that mean God, Yahweh, Adonai, Elohim,"
Frau Kam twirled her wrist as she relayed the names, "isn't
any more special than any of those other false idols?"

"Now we're delving into philosophy, and more like into
religious debate, which is never a good combination with
dinner." He smiled. "Personally, I think Yahweh, Jesus,
Brahma, Buddha, are like these sweetbreads. Each are
made from different offal: some liver, some kidney, some
heart, some a mince of several, but in the end they're all
served on the same platter, and we like the best of what
we're offered. We each have our favorites and some of our
constitutions can only tolerate one, but none of them inter-
fere with our understanding of the world as it exists and the
forces that act upon it, like electricity, the tides, and the
shifting of the Earth in space."

Silence fell again across the room. Géza hid his half
smile behind his napkin before reaching for his glass of

wine. That seemed to trigger a chain reaction as each of the diners drank from their glasses of red while the sweetbreads went mostly untouched, apart from those on Josef's plate which disappeared, leaving behind pink smears on the white china and his large lips.

Fürth refilled Herr Baum's glass of red while Frau Baum turned the conversation toward the latest fashion in Vienna. She had taken Rachel and stayed there with a cousin the year prior, before the purchase of Schattenturm. She barely touched her serving of grouse, focusing on the new names in the catalogues and the presentations to the younger archduchesses as they appeared in exhibitions later in the season.

Over dessert, Herr Baum finished his glass of golden Vouvray Moelleux before the serving plates of cheeses, strawberries, and cherries had been fully arrayed. "What I don't understand about all this, Herr Horst, is why it's necessary to let in a mystic of the great beyond to a murder investigation." He looked at the inspector. "It can't be that hard to put all the pieces together and come to a conclusion."

Géza returned the comment by meeting Baum's stare with a steely gaze of his own, unbroken, as the inspector lifted his glass to drink.

"Now then," said Frau Kam. "Johan, you forget yourself. It was I who invited the professor here, and the inspector obliged me."

Géza nodded slightly in Frau Kam's direction before speaking. "As we have seen, once the staff and the residents of Salgótarján learned that Andrej was murdered by a weapon that eerily, if not intentionally, matched the von Voitsberg crest, they lost their inclination to speak to the police. I was glad to consider an unconventional approach to getting at the truth which has evaded us thus far."

"Superstition can be a powerful inhibitor," added Hermann.

"As can Father's checkbook," said Rachel, smiling at no one in particular.

Erzsébet rose quickly, not waiting for Hermann or a footman to pull back her chair. The gentlemen scrambled to rise as well.

"Shall we go through to the drawing room? There's a marvelous Erard on which Rachel has been practicing her Chopin." With that, she turned and rounded the table toward the door, shooting daggers at Rachel as she went, who rose to follow her mother in tandem.

———————◆———————

The drawing room was richly furnished with large sofas and intricate wallpaper, showcasing a chinoiserie design. Hermann surmised the Baum's must have had, or had purchased, furniture enough to elegantly outfit the few formal rooms he'd already seen. An adjoining room was visible through open pocket doors, revealing a card table and a piano made of rich, dark mahogany. Josef sat to play solitaire at the card table while Rachel and Erzsébet Baum whispered quickly in the drawing room, before Rachel departed for the piano. A footman offered Frau Kam a snifter of brandy as she settled into a chair by the fire. The trill of Rachel's opening keys reverberated through the two rooms as Hermann fixed himself a brandy and took a seat on a long sofa opposite Frau Kam. The sound of a more simplified piece by Chopin splendidly distracted everyone for a few minutes until Frau Kam grew bored.

"I never liked that man, Andrej," the old widow said. "He was such a lout. Never where you needed him to be, except when it was nearly time to pay him for the month. And he was sneaky, thought the family didn't know how he shirked his duties and gambled his earnings." She took a sip of her brandy.

"Sneaky, frau?" asked Hermann.

"Yes, quite. Before the maze became the scene of a murder, I walked there nearly every day. The spirits are so active in the alley leading to the mausoleum." She leaned her head back, taking in a deep breath. "Like they're in the air all around you. There must've been great spiritual power in the von Voitsberg family, to leave such a trace."

"And Andrej?"

"Oh yes. When I would sit to commune with the spirits, someone often spied on me. Little glimpses here and there. I'm sure it was Andrej. Plus, there was my antler-handled knife that went missing."

"You lost Father's hunting knife?" Erzsébet cut in.

"Not lost dear, taken, stolen. It was very valuable to me, Professor. Silver detailing, carved from the antler of a red deer my late husband stalked. He made an anniversary gift of it. It was a powerful stag in life, so the knife helped to direct the flow of spirit energy when I communed."

"And it's gone now? Because of Andrej?" Géza pressed.

"Just so. One day I had it with me in the maze, directing the energy of the interred to me. Oh I had great messages come to me that day ... but I got up to check a suspicious noise and when I came back, it was gone."

"That's hardly convincing, Mama."

"Don't let your rose hip fingers become rose tinted glasses, Erzsébet," Frau Kam jabbed.

Erzsébet shifted away from Hermann and her mother to speak more exclusively with Géza, to which Johan gave a muted chuff. Rachel's tempo and force in the Chopin piece intensified.

"Erzsébet had a soft spot for him, as did most of the old von Voitsberg servants," said Frau Kam. "He was wily, that gardener. A very smooth talker if ever you'd met one, but he never fooled me. I spotted his rotten aura from the start, it wasn't good." She leaned toward Hermann. "And he wasn't good. In league with the Devil," she said. "Why else would he steal my knife, but to warp its powers? I tell you, the fearsome spirit of Gustav von Voitsberg rose up and took the fool's soul down to Hell with him as punishment."

"Ha!" Johan let out from over Hermann's shoulder. "That's a new explanation. What do you think of that, Inspector? Think you can make an arrest after that vital clue, or weren't you paying attention?"

Géza and Erzsébet had stopped talking. Agitation played over Erzsébet's face.

"Hush now," said Frau Kam. "As I was saying, Professor, the Devil is at work here in some way ... which makes so much sense. The energy of the spirits is palpable. I've met six already that I can name. Professor, we must have your help in a séance."

Rachel's piece began to draw to its close.

"Please, Mama, no more of that," Erzsébet said as she rose.

"You haven't told us *your* theory yet, dear," Johan sneered, giving his wife a nasty look.

Erzsébet drew her left hand up to cover her throat and neck, what little was exposed, just as Rachel's piece ended. Erzsébet immediately gave a subdued clap and a broad smile which Hermann and Géza took up as well.

"Thank you, Rachel, for such a lovely piece," her mother said. "If you will all excuse me, I'm very tired and I'm feeling ill. I wish you all a good night." She gave a little nod to Hermann and Géza, then finished with a cool, short stare at her husband who went back to refill his drink from the side table as she left the drawing room.

Rachel wandered back into their side of the room to stand near Frau Kam.

"Ah Rachel, you play so well. Will you let us hear something else tonight?"

"Perhaps in a little while, Grandmama. First, I want to hear more about what Herr Horst has to say about the spirits. Mama wouldn't let me at dinner."

Rachel drifted over to sit on the sofa where her mother had been a minute before. She twisted her position to angle the tips of her knees barely a few inches away from Hermann's thigh. He shifted in turn onto the furthest edge of his cushion.

"There really isn't much to say, fraulein. Most people think they're dealing with spirits when often it's their own energy that manifests to interact with the mind."

"What about when that's not the case?" she asked.

"Then it can be a serious matter." Hermann looked toward Frau Kam. "Your knife, for example, has been imbued with your own psychic focus. You believe it will channel the voices and will of the spirits, so in a sense it will do just that."

Frau Kam had her eyes locked on Hermann in contemplation. She reminded him of some of his more committed students from Vienna.

"And that energy is strengthened through ritual?" Rachel asked.

"It can be. Many cultures believe that there must be an initiation into any serious social, political, or religious matter. It's the focus that is the key point. They may be communing with powerful gods or the impetus of the state, but what's more important is that a group of people are powerfully connecting their psychic will together for a common end. That has a certain amount of power in the corporeal world."

"Sounds like the first night at the Gentlemen's Salon in Budapest," Johan put it. No one laughed. "What about reality, Herr Horst? How does any of that psychic conjecture relate?"

Hermann spoke without turning to face Herr Baum. "Well, if a few dozen, or hundreds, or thousands of people believe in the power of something, work to achieve its will, and form their lives around the precepts in the ritual or imposed culture, then by extent that ritual has had its intended effect. The participants and those they interact with will act out the necessary function of the rite."

"Fascinating," Frau Kam rasped.

"What about for darker forces? Rachel leaned ever so slightly toward Hermann, her perfume overtaking him in a cloud of scent. She almost whispered, "Could this work as well to achieve ... ?" she let the question trail off.

Géza furrowed his brows and subtly looked between Rachel and her father who was swaying slightly.

"The formula, as it were, remains the same," Hermann continued. "I've seen people do terrible things to win the favor of the force they think they're conjuring, or to impress and initiate themselves into a society."

"That must have been terrible to learn about. Do you have an example?" asked Rachel.

Hermann was about to answer when Josef spoke out, apparently no longer playing solitaire. His eyes were bright and he had an odd smile on his face. "Is that what those folks in Mexico were doing, with their pyramids? I saw a picture book where a priest took out a man's heart. There was blood everywhere."

"Hush, Josef. That's pagan nonsense, not at all what Professor Horst meant," said Frau Kam as all eyes turned back to Hermann.

"I don't have any examples that could top the Aztecs, sorry. Just a word of caution that everything we do has an effect, whether we realize it or not."

Hermann stood as Johan stumbled and caught himself on the sofa table, causing some of the glasses to tumble over.

"It's been a long day and there's more to be done if Inspector Orczy and I are to find Andrej's killer. So, I wish you all a good night. Herr Baum, Frau Kam, fraulein, Josef."

Géza put in much the same reason to retire, more than a little glad to be done with the entire evening.

Chapter 11

Despite the gloominess of his room and the lack of moonlight, or perhaps because of it, Hermann did not manage to achieve any level of sleep. He tried very hard to forget that he was sharing the room with Gustav von Voitsberg, avoiding the portrait as he'd changed out of his dinner attire and prepared for bed. Not knowing if a murderer was about was another unpleasant thought. He had checked every nook and cranny of his room for anything out of place before settling in, besides making sure his door was locked. The feeling of unease grew as the hours passed, building with each toss and turn. There was an almost imperceptible tone in the air, like someone had struck a tuning fork and the resonance had lasted far longer than it should have, always on an uneasy decibel. After hours of sleeplessness, he sat up and grabbed hold of the lamp on the bedside table and lit it from the box of matches in the drawer beneath. Once a sheen of orange rose to fill the space around him, he tilted back the small clock on the table to read the time: three twenty-four. At least he hadn't turned the whole night over, he thought to himself.

Hermann got out of bed and wrapped the dark robe he had brought with him over his night clothes, then he slipped on a pair of indoor loafers. The resonance continued, like a ringing in the inner ear. Hermann turned down the flame on the lamp, in case it was the hissing of kerosine, but the tone continued, sending gooseflesh up his arms and the back of his neck. He went around the room, searching for anything out of place, something causing the sound. When he reached the area near the bedroom door, he detected a different sound—faint whispering.

He gently braced his hands on the door to support himself as he pressed his ear and cheek near the doorframe to listen. There was at least one voice, maybe two, speaking hurriedly. He couldn't make anything out before the whispering began to subside and pass. He turned back to the room, contemplating taking the lamp with him into the hall to follow the voices, then thought better of it. Gustav was looking at him, his eyes gleaming red by the glow from the lamp. The background of the portrait seemed alive with the flickering of the lamp's flame, battle and rising smoke swirled behind the freiherr as the dead Turk beneath his boot wheezed out his last breath.

Hermann stepped into the hall and quietly shut the door to his room behind him, thankful that the low light of the hall's gas lamps had remained lit and masked the glow that would otherwise have been visible from under his door. He made his way to the end of the hall near the library door which was open to the dark, quiet space. No sound nor light came through the further hall out to the keep, only stillness. He turned back the way he'd come, past his bedroom, and walked through the halls he'd explored the previous morning. He entered into the narrow passage at the end, beyond the archway and the faint glow of the last lamp. He followed the passageway to the right and made his way into the now familiar shuttered and neglected reception hall. It was wholly pitch black except for a thin trail of orange-yellow light streaming from underneath the door of the first room on the left.

Hermann carefully positioned himself near the door, then reached for the cold metal of the brass knob. He paused as he heard voices within. One was clearly female, but he couldn't make out what any of them were saying. He slowly turned the knob, but it caught halfway through and wouldn't turn any further. He carefully returned the knob to its starting position, a faint scrape of the mechanism made his heart pound inside his ears. He made his way past the window that looked onto the courtyard, where he'd earlier witnessed the heated exchange between Rachel Baum and Pavol, to the second door on the left which led to the old music room; it was still unlocked. From there, he hoped to spy the interior of the first room across the span of the courtyard. He crept around the draped instruments and furniture to the middle window and looked out, thick black curtains obscured all but a narrow space in the window of the wing directly opposite him. Within, he saw a table, illuminated by a single lit taper, with several things laid out upon it. He could make out at least two pairs of hands, clasped together around an object in the center of the table. His view of the people was obscured beyond the wrist by long sleeves that trailed toward the floor.

From this vantage point, Hermann saw nothing of any real use. It was critical that he learn the identities of the people sitting around the table. Resolved to get into the room before the party separated, he made his way down the narrow servants' stair at the end of the room, feeling for every step carefully in the blind darkness, then to the switch-backed door, and made his way out onto the open space in front of the stables. He quickly crossed the courtyard to the opposite wing from the one he'd just departed and found the doorway identical to the one he'd just exited. He tried the handle and was relieved when it opened, a low creak at the twist of the hinge forced him to pause momentarily and listen. Nothing. He felt his way up an identical set of servants' stairs to those he'd just descended. The voices in the room beyond grew louder, the higher he climbed. He stopped at the top of the servants' stair at the door into the room. The voices just beyond where he stood were clearly audible.

"We'll begin again," came the raspy voice he recognized as Frau Kam's. "Don't slouch or they'll be offended ..."

She spoke deeply. "Great spirits. We call upon you to join us in this circle of three, joined by blood, one kindred to another. You have taken a life on these grounds, spilled the blood of one you deemed *unworthy*. Use the power of that vengeful act and reveal yourselves to us. We seek to understand your wrath and settle you."

Hermann listened, but no spirit voice came forth. Then another voice, higher, younger, began.

"If you be not spirits, then you are dark forces beyond our world. Take this blood, given up to you in offering, and present yourselves to us." Hermann recognized Rachel's voice.

She then chanted something, low and rhythmic in a language that Hermann did not recognize. The chant was taken up by Frau Kam and then a third voice joined, more clumsy than the other two. The chant rose in speed and intensity, iteration after iteration, until suddenly it stopped. Silence.

Hermann turned the door handle and entered the room. The slow, prolonged screeching of the door's hinges announced his arrival. Frau Kam, Rachel, and Josef looked toward the shadow moving toward them, from the nearly imperceptible service door. Each appeared to be holding their breath, eyes wide, hands clenching tighter in each other's grasps, folds of their long, hooded robes trembling.

"Good evening," Hermann said, in a deep, steady tone as he strode into the room.

Frau Kam let out the breath that she had been holding and began to breathe rapidly. "God have mercy, Professor. You nearly scared us half to death."

"Ah, you may have been better equipped to contact the spirits in that state," he replied.

Rachel Baum pulled her hands from her brother's and grandmother's grasps and poised herself, expression composed and genteel, like she had been at dinner. Josef squinted at Hermann and gave an involuntary shudder.

The room was bedecked with black drapery and deep-colored furniture with dark cushions. The three were seated at a small round table with several matching chairs, additional chairs were set away against the walls. An ornate, oriental throw covered the table and hung low while a scrying board and planchet were situated directly in the center. The board was circular with the letters of the alphabet arranged around the outer rim, and Arabic numerals formed an inner ring around a sun and moon. An eye, radiating beams with hands that grasped Egyptian ankhs, was positioned at the core. The single candle cast low, yellow-orange light over the room. It sat next to a bell suspended from a metal spring bar. One of the empty chairs contained a small, white, rabbit doll in a flowing red dress made of velvet.

"I do apologize for interrupting your séance, frau. The energies may now be improperly tuned."

Frau Kam looked from Hermann to the board and back at Hermann, a more relaxed expression coming over her.

"Oh no, Professor. I think you were meant to find our circle," she replied. "Surely, it's not for *us* that the secrets of Schattenturm should be revealed, but for *you*, so you can find the murderer ... if he is a flesh and blood man, of course. Please, bring a chair and sit."

Rachel turned to look at her grandmother and narrowed her eyes for a moment before turning back to Hermann. Hermann made his way around the trio at the table and approached the chair with the bunny in the red dress. The stitched smile and grey glass eyes stared up at him.

As he went to move the bunny, Rachel spoke out, "Not that chair, Herr Horst. That one is reserved for Odette."

"Was Odette your doll as a child, fraulein?" he said as he walked toward another chair.

"No. She was here when we moved into this place. She can be very naughty." The corners of Rachel's mouth drew up in a closed smile.

Hermann placed his chair in the wider space between Frau Kam and Josef at the table. "Naughty? How so?"

"Well, she never stays put. Any time I try to move her to my room or let her read in the library, she always finds her way back to that chair. She doesn't want to leave it."

"It's true, Professor. I've seen so myself," added Frau Kam. "I once placed the doll in a cabinet in my bedroom and by morning the doll had gone right back to that chair. I believe it's a conduit for the spirits ... possessed."

Hermann looked across the table at the rabbit. It's smile and posture gave no sign of any ill-contented spirit. "That would be remarkable. Have any of you locked the doll in a trunk and kept the key on your person?"

"That wouldn't hold Odette back," said Rachel. "She led us to this room, and this is where she wants to stay. She's said so herself."

A cool breeze spread through the room, making the gooseflesh return to Hermann's neck. Frau Kam noticed it too and looked around the room. Rachel smiled, her black eyes like almond-shaped pieces of jet.

"You must have discerned that through your seances then? Did you take them up when you moved here?" asked Hermann.

"I've had some experience," Frau Kam answered. "When my husband died six years ago, I felt his spirit all the time, so I sought out mystics to help me commune with him. Over the years I learned much from them. The tarot, crystal ball, and eventually how to become a medium myself." She reached up to her neckline and drew out a circular locket on a long silver chain. "I keep his hair with me. The strands tie his spirit to mine, and he serves as my guide into the beyond. I've been able to commune with many spirits since then, but none so powerful as those that dwell here."

"What do you mean, Frau Kam?"

"Since nearly the day we moved in they've made themselves known. You can hear them in the very walls of the house, Professor, whispering and pacing to and fro. You can't see them of course, but they're here, all around us."

"Do you think the spirits are trying to drive you out of Schattenturm?" Hermann looked at each of the three before him, an open question.

"Despite my best efforts, I haven't been able to figure out exactly what they want," said Frau Kam.

"They're not evil," Rachel added. "I used to follow their sounds all around the castle. They've led us to all sorts of ... interesting places."

Josef looked like he wanted to pitch in, but Rachel shot a look at her brother that quickly shut his mouth.

The idea drew Hermann back to the map he and Géza had found in Pavol's book of sketches. He didn't mention it to them, and quickly changed the subject. "I assume you purposefully chose the witching hour, after three in the morning, for speaking with the spirits?"

"That was my idea," said Rachel. "I've read in some of Grandmama's books that spirits are the most active at this time. All kinds of darker energies feel free to roam."

"And was the scrying board your idea too, then?"

"Yes." She looked down, frowning. "Though we haven't had much success with it. The planchet won't move."

"I encouraged her to seek out any channels possible, Professor. I haven't been able to contact the spirits directly, so we thought trying something new might help," said Frau Kam.

"That was a good idea, frau. However, all of the participants have to touch the planchet in order for the energy of the spirits to be properly channeled. If you please ..."

He gestured to the planchet in the center of the board before placing the tips of his index and middle finger from both hands on the triangular piece of wood containing a clear crystal suspended in its center. Each of the other three followed suit and placed their fingertips on the planchet.

"I've studied the art of mediumship across the continent, from the perspective of metapsychics. I think I can help channel the energy and compliment your experience, Frau Kam ... leading us to some form of contact. Would you be all right with that?"

"Oh yes," she said.

"You will be the channeling rod for the group, frau. We'll concentrate our energies onto you, so that the planchet will be guided by your hand at the direction of the spirit that comes forth."

Frau Kam removed her fingertips from the planchet and drew the netting of a black veil from beneath her hood to cover her face. Then she took a deep breath, closed her eyes, and returned her fingertips to the planchet. Hermann looked from her to Rachel who was gazing into the crystal below, to Josef who kept looking between his grandmother, his sister, the board, and Hermann every so often.

"Frau Kam," Hermann began. "I want you to concentrate on your spirit guide. Draw him to you without speaking. Concentrate on his face and invite him to the table with us. This member of the dearly departed will help to show us the way to the spirits of this house and protect us from any ill-intentions."

She stirred for a minute or two, eyes closed and head hung low beneath the black veil. "I have him, Professor."

"Good. Everyone, close your eyes. Breathe in and out deeply. Find a rhythm to your thoughts like the ticking of a clock. In and out. In ... and ... out. In ... and ... out. Draw forth the spirit energy around you. This board will serve as the mouthpiece of any who may wish to speak to us tonight. Breathe in ... and ... breathe out. Frau Kam, I will begin to ask the spirits questions. Focus our energy and their intent, and they will speak through the board."

He focused on the breathing and body language of the trio around him. All three were relaxed, eyes closed, no tension in their wrists or forearms.

"We welcome the spirits of Schattenturm tonight. The four of us gathered around this board are in tune to the spirit world, and we seek to commune with any beings that may have knowledge of the murder of Andrej Fehér. Use our energy to gather your strength and speak through our medium, Frau Kam, with her spirit guide who will show you the way."

The cool breeze returned. Frau Kam stirred, her head moving slightly as though she was looking or listening for someone.

"If you are present, tell Frau Kam who you are."

Another breeze. The spirit bell on the spring arm tingled softly.

"I can sense them," said Frau Kam. "There is a man here. I can't see his face."

"Spirit," said Hermann, "show yourself to us at this table. Tell us what message you wish to impart."

The planchet began to move slowly. First it pushed right, then left, and then it glided to the letter H. It continued, O—M—E, then it returned to the eye at the center of the board.

"Spirit, do you mean to tell us that this is your home?"

"Herr Horst … the spirit … he tells me yes. He tells me that he used to live here."

"Good, frau. Spirit, we wish to understand why Andrej was killed, can you help us understand?"

The planchet glided sideways to the sun.

"He says yes," offered Frau Kam.

"Spirit, it will be easier to channel your energy if we know your name. Can you tell us your name?"

The planchet didn't move at first, but after a few moments, it glided around the periphery of the board, crossing and then resting on one letter after another.

"F—R—I—D—O—L—I—N." Hermann said the letters aloud as the planchet passed, before resting again on the eye. "Does the name Fridolin mean anything to any of you?"

In turn, they each declined knowing a Fridolin.

"Professor ... the spirit is very grief stricken. There's so much loss here," Frau Kam said, emotion thick on her voice.

"Fridolin, tell us, did you know Andrej?"

The planchet moved to the sun.

"Yes. Were you close to Andrej?"

The planchet moved to the sun again.

"Yes. Fridolin, can you tell us about Andrej's killer?"

The planchet didn't move.

"Fridolin," Hermann said, "we're trying to solve Andrej's murder. Someone killed him and we don't know why. Will you tell us?"

The planchet glided back and forth across the center of the board. Hermann looked at each of the three participants before him. Each seemed to have their eyes fully closed and Frau Kam's head was tilted back, veil laying slack over her face. The planchet landed on the moon.

"No. Why can't you help us, Fridolin?"

"Herr ... he is upset. He wants to leave us now."

"Fridolin, it is very important that we find out who killed Andrej. I must insist that you answer us. Everyone, I need you to focus very intently. It's not an easy task to compel a spirit. Focus your energy. Breathe in and out. Breathe in ... and out. Breathe in ... and ... breathe out. In ... and ... out."

Hermann let another few moments pass before continuing.

"Fridolin, is there someone in our group that you are connected to? Someone whom you care for?"

The planchet glided smoothly to the moon.

"No. Then, is there someone else here at Schattenturm whom you care deeply for? Someone you would protect?"

The planchet circled the board, before sliding over the edge.

"Keep your fingers on the planchet, everyone. I will move it back onto the board. Don't lose your concentration."

"Herr Horst, the spirit is upset. He's sad, lonely. My guide and I are trying to keep him here, but I don't know how much longer it can last."

"You're doing well, Frau Kam. Just a little while longer. Fridolin, please, tell us about the murderer. Where are they?"

Hermann looked at them again. Rachel seemed strained, her brows furrowed together, though her eyes were shut tight. Josef was still relaxed. Frau Kam lolled her head from side to side, her veil billowing back and forth at its ends. The planchet began to move in spirals out from the eye, circling the picture over and over. A strong, cold breeze circulated through the room and the candle diminished as the light died down. The planchet circled again and again before landing.

"H."

It circled round the board.

"E."

Another pass.

"R."

It circled again, slowed, and stopped.

"E," Hermann said. "*Here.*"

A cold breeze gusted across the séance table. The servants' door, through which Hermann had entered, swung shut with a screech and a bang as the candle nearly flickered out, throwing shadows across the room. Hermann looked up. Behind Rachel was the door out to the shuttered hall which had been locked. It now stood slightly ajar, and a figure was barely visible in the doorway. Gloom against pitch black. Hermann rose in a flash, sending his chair clattering to the floor. The figure ducked away from the doorway and Hermann made a mad dash across the room as the candle returned to normal. He threw the door fully open and charged into the hall.

Footsteps echoed faintly to the left, rapidly outpacing him. He followed them, running past the central windows and the music room door, then further, till he reached the end of the hall. He threw open the wooden door and was presented with the archway of the armory. He stopped and listened carefully. The footsteps were barely audible over his own heavy breathing and racing heartbeat. He turned back to the hall and pulled hard on a door opposite those leading to the séance room and music room. It opened to a balcony in a stone colonnade overlooking the castle's inner courtyard. He braced himself against the cold night air and leaned over the balustrade. Below him was the white gravel and across from him was the doorway to the great keep which rose higher and higher to its spiked crown crenelations.

Crunch. Crunch. Crunch. Crunch.

Rapid footsteps below drew Hermann's gaze to the left. A figure in a long dark cloak, face hidden within a billowing hood, made its way in long bounds to the steps of the chapel, then it ascended the few stairs and halted in the shadow of the overhang, dark on dark in the gloom of the moonless night. The figure turned and raised its hooded head to look at Hermann standing at the balustrade. For the briefest moment they surveyed one another. A silent stream of consciousness joined the two players, lasting hardly more than a heartbeat, before the figure turned again and glided through the great door into the chapel. The animalistic groan of the heavy door, pivoting on its hinges, echoed across the courtyard and reverberated off the dark castle's stones.

Hermann caught his breath, then waited for a while to listen and regain his composure. He stepped back into the shadow of the hall to make his way back to the others.

"What happened, Professor? Why did you run out of the room?" Frau Kam asked as Hermann reentered the séance room.

He paused, taking in each of them before answering. "Our séance attracted the entity who may have killed Andrej."

Frau Kam drew in a breath and clapped her hands together, a smile spreading over her face. The Baum children both looked at each other, their skin was white as sheets. Rachel's eye's narrowed to a squint.

"The spirits were drawn out. Whichever one has done the deed has been brought forth. Surely, you'll be able to uncover them soon," said Frau Kam.

"I think the killer is more flesh and blood than they'd like us to believe, frau. Ghosts don't need to run if they don't want to. And whoever it is, they are quite familiar with the castle and its layout."

The cold air from the hall sent the group into faint shudders.

"I suggest we all get to bed now," said Hermann. "Make an effort to secure your rooms from entry. I'll discuss this with Inspector Orczy in the morning, and we'll focus on keeping the house more contained."

Hermann's gaze was drawn to Odette whose posture had turned to face the action.

"Oh, and don't forget to say goodbye to the scrying board. We don't want to keep the portal open indefinitely. You never know what might come through."

Chapter 12

B efore descending to breakfast, Hermann locked his room and placed the key in his suit jacket pocket. He stopped at Géza's room, just down the hall from his own, and knocked.

"Yes?" replied Géza.

"It's Hermann, may I come in?"

"By all means."

Hermann entered as Géza pulled on his dark green jacket. He looked rested and put together. His room a perfect reflection of crisp—if no longer military—organization.

The inspector gave Hermann a once over and frowned. Have you slept, Professor? You look, well, a little haggard.

"It was a busy night. I couldn't sleep and laid awake until around three o'clock when I heard voices from somewhere near my room. I decided to investigate and encountered the Baum children, with their grandmother, set up in a room where they apparently have been holding séances and communing with the spirit world. It took quite a bit of navigating throughout the abandoned part of the castle to find an open door into their spirit sanctuary.

"How interesting," said Géza.

"I took the opportunity to try and find out what they know about Andrej. They were well versed in medium lore and took it rather seriously, given their cloaks and focal objects."

Géza finished buttoning his jacket. "I knew the old woman was involved in some kind of psychic pomp, but I didn't realize she had a whole setup. What did you learn, anything useful?"

"Maybe. Does the name Fridolin mean anything to you?"

Géza ran his hand over his neatly trimmed beard. "No. But we can ask around today. What else?"

"The planchet at one point spelled *here* in response to our question regarding the whereabouts of the murderer. At the same time, a cross draft from the hall caused me to look up. Inspector ...," Hermann locked eyes with Géza, "there was a cloaked figure in the doorway leading from the hall. The same door that had been locked when I'd tried to open it just a short time before. I chased him, but he shook me somewhere in the north halls, and eventually made his escape through the chapel, on the other side of the courtyard, a full story below where he'd been just a moment before. I spotted him from a balcony I went out onto."

"God in heaven," said Géza. He rubbed his forehead and paced for a minute, polished black boots tapping mutely against the thick carpet over the hardwood floor. Then he turned back, smiling.

"Inspector?" Hermann asked.

"You know what this means? That I haven't been a fool this entire time. The bastard is still here! Right here in the castle! I'd half thought I was chasing ghosts this whole time."

"I agree. Someone can roam freely throughout the castle, unimpeded by locked doors. They may be the murderer, or are involved with the murderer. They went to great lengths to avoid being unmasked.

Géza's look shifted back to calculation, his smile evaporating. Then a kind of wry expression came over him.

"Let's see how breakfast with the family is coming along, shall we?"

———————————◆———————————

Breakfast was arranged in the dining room with platters of sausages, butterflied steamed vegetables, and hardboiled eggs in stands, laid out on the sideboard, buffet style. Toast, honey, jams, and butter were arrayed in personal serving vessels beside each placement at the table, with the plates stowed separately on the sideboard. Rachel and Josef were already seated across from each other at the far end of the table. Rachel was wearing a pale violet dress with buttoned cuffs. Herr Baum was fixing his plate very slowly at the sideboard. Fürth was on standby to the right, outlined in the indirect glow of the morning light. All of the floral arrangements from the night before were gone, not replaced by any new morning arrangements. Hermann hoped to himself that the tulips hadn't been wasted on only one dinner.

Fürth noticed Hermann and Géza's entry and motioned them to chairs on either side of the table, one beside each of the Baum offspring. Josef watched them approach over the top of a magazine he'd been reading. His eyes, from this vantage point, resembled exactly his father's: dark and beady.

"Good morning," Hermann broke the silence.

Rachel suavely lowered her turned tines, and Baum looked over his shoulder before returning to his serving tongs.

"How did you sleep on your first night at Schattenturm, Professor Horst?" asked Rachel.

"Well enough. Fortunately, I wasn't disturbed by any wandering spirits past four this morning."

"Splendid," she said. "Though some of us have woken up on rather the wrong side." She cast a frown toward her father's back.

Johan finished serving himself and set his plate down on the table before sitting, as Hermann and Géza each took a plate from the sideboard. "So, do you two have an idea on where to start today? I'd rather this whole episode be over sooner rather than later," he said.

"We'll continue to explore every aspect of Andrej's death," Géza said.

"And might I be informed of what that will entail, exactly? Given that it's occurring on my own property."

"Herr Baum, we can't risk any detail about the identity of the killer being lost. Revealing too much to too many eyes and ears is the surest way to never find the culprit," Géza said with a tone of finality.

"Hmm." Johan growled, before plucking a piece of toast from the stand between the settings.

Hermann placed an egg stand on his plate alongside a steaming sausage, before taking the place beside Josef. He had no desire to be the object of Rachel's play this morning.

"Josef, have you had much time to take to the grounds?" asked Hermann

"To what?" the boy said, squinting at him.

"Based on your stalking magazine I assumed you had an interest."

"The boy's a crack shot," Johan said, through a bite of toast. The crumbs fell onto his vest beneath the links of his watch chain and fob.

"I am," said Josef. "I once downed a stag at nearly 300 meters."

"Impressive. You're lucky your father taught you so well," Géza said as he approached the table.

"Me? Ha," said Herr Baum. "I had the best sport shooters in the country teach him as soon as he could walk properly. I never wanted him to be even half a step behind the other lads."

"My own father was the same way," said Hermann. "I learnt the sport very young at his knee. We'd trek the mountains for hours."

Baum and Géza both seemed a little surprised.

"What was your game of choice?" asked Géza.

"I enjoyed grouse shooting, more challenging due to their size and ability to scale a mountain in a matter of minutes."

"Josef only plays at shooting. But you, Inspector Orczy, you must have real experience with shooting," Rachel said as she shifted to face her neighbor.

"I've been in shooting competitions," Josef protested.

"My position has sometimes necessitated a shot, yes, but it's not something I relish, fraulein."

"Oh, certainly not. To take a life is such a serious thing. I've often told my brother to respect those beautiful creatures he cuts down. Though they do provide the most succulent cuts."

Hermann noticed she hid her lack of sleep well. She had powdered beneath her almond-shaped dark eyes which set them off like gleaming obsidian quartz crystals against the glare coming through the windows.

"What's your favorite firearm?" Josef asked.

"I haven't had much use for them besides my service pistol. And, I often don't wear it when I'm not expecting trouble."

Josef didn't seem to have heard him. "Father just bought me a new smokeless rifle, imported from America. It hasn't even been released in Budapest yet. They say it can fire over 700 meters." He was practically squirming in his chair recounting the details.

"A smokeless rifle. How ingenious," Hermann said. "Though that kind of technology will make its way onto the battlefield, I'm sure. A sniper would be thrilled to get off a shot without leaving a trace."

Rachel was studying Géza's profile. She seemed transfixed on the movement of his biceps as he lifted his fork.

"I'd love to try it out, but Father won't stop working to go stalking with me, and there's no scout here that'll take me. Father won't get one for me." Josef's pouting had swollen his rotund face even further than it was already.

Rachel lolled her head to the side to look at Josef, exposing an expanse of her neck and what Hermann presumed to be the wrong angle to preserve her modesty, under her day dress, from Géza's perspective. Unfortunately, Géza—caught off guard by her movement—followed the visual line for a heartbeat, before correcting himself and clenching his jaw. Hermann eyed Johan Baum's body language. He had not missed his daughter's trick, or Géza's eye. Baum's thick lips popped open for a second and then pursed.

"I'll take you when I have the time, boy, and not a minute earlier. Where'd you think you got that shiny gun from, eh?" said Johan.

"What about a scout? I know you can afford one of those," Josef replied.

"What? Of course I can afford a bloody scout." There was a different tone in his voice.

"Then–" started Josef.

"Enough of this or you won't have a new gun. You'll learn some manners first," Johan said, raising a meaty finger to point at his son. "And you," his focus shifted to Géza. "I want you to get this whole thing done for. My patience has its limits as does your supervisor's." Herr Baum rose and tossed his napkin beside his plate.

"My supervisor is aware of my progress, and how close I am to finally bagging this killer. He won't walk amongst us free for much longer." Géza's green eyes practically glowed as he locked into a stare with Johan Baum.

The room was silent in the wake of the tension. Only Rachel seemed nonplussed, a closed smile spreading on her expression. Baum broke first and stormed out of the dining room. Fürth very calmly collected his napkin, plate, and setting without so much as an eyebrow out of place.

"Now that we've finished our breakfast, Inspector, I think we can make off," said Hermann. "Oh, and fraulein?"

"Yes?" said Rachel.

"What are your plans for today?"

She straightened and folded her hands on her lap. "I thought I might explore here and there, but mostly I'll be painting on the eastern shore of the lake." She leaned forward slightly. "There's such a lovely little spot under a willow tree there. Very serene."

"I'm sure that will aid in your concentration then." He rose. "Until later. Josef, fraulein."

Once they were out of earshot of the dining room, Hermann stopped Géza. "So, what did you get out of breakfast? You wanted to see who was there."

Géza stepped a foot closer to Hermann and spoke in a near whisper. "I wanted to see if Baum was feeling the effects of a stroll around the castle in the small hours of the night. Given the bags under his eyes and his temper, I'd say it's a strong possibility."

"He could have been irritated because you let the girl catch you in her game which he didn't miss. Her look of the cat that ate the canary said everything."

"Damn, I hoped no one caught that. Are you saying that she wanted to antagonize her father through me?"

"It's been no secret that you and Baum haven't gotten along. It's probably just teenage rebellion on her part. Testing the limits of her spoiling. She and her mother don't seem to have a strong bond, either."

Géza closed his eyes and shook his head. "That doesn't explain the tiredness, though."

"No, but we can't know that it was because he was running around the castle like a wraith in the night. Inspector, the figure that I chased was fast and nimble. He crossed the entirety of the castle complex in just a minute or two. Do you really think Herr Baum could manage such a feat with his digestive proportions?"

Géza gave a muted chuff. "I suppose not." Then he let out with a sigh. "But they could be accomplices, although it doesn't seem likely. I'm no further than when I started."

"That's not true. We know far more than we did yesterday morning, but how it all fits together is the catch, and if any of it points the finger to Andrej's killer." Hermann ran a hand through his sandy blond hair. "Now, we should get going. I want to start in the armory this morning."

Géza nodded.

The two made their way past the servants' stair nearest the great keep. The paneling on the walls was still in good order, but the curios, artwork, and many of the plaques and displays had been cleared while squares in the dust on the stone walls above marked where paintings had once hung. The craftsmanship in the castle was of exceptional quality as expected in a place designed to welcome and entertain prestigious guests. Finely cut stone everywhere and intricate carpentry in the floral-and-ivy crown molding. However, it was empty of all the little objects d'art and showpieces that would say to a visitor that this was a place of wealth and power—that the owner wasn't afraid to spend. Now, the opposite impression was given.

"Inspector, do you think Herr Baum is struggling financially to maintain the estate and the house?"

"He owns it outright as far as I know."

"There's scant artwork and furniture in the house. He told me he was cheated out of the contents in the sales contract, but why hasn't he replaced the missing pieces? He's had plenty of time."

"He wouldn't discuss his finances or his business in Salgótarján when I interviewed him. He pushed back hard when I pressed. I've had a nagging feeling from the start that Andrej's death may have been related to Baum or his business. The papers back in the capitol are calling him out every day. Of course, they're all owned by his competitors. The papers that Baum doesn't own himself, that is. He's well-connected in Budapest. My commander has received personal complaints from his friends in the government about this investigation."

"It seems odd that a man like him would relocate to the country and buy this old party palace without putting it back into use. He told me he wanted it to impress his competitors and shareholders. But here it is, too empty and too run down to use as he intended. Why?"

"My mother had this saying, Professor, *Ha van pénzed, kidobod a pénzt*. It means something like, *If you have money, you waste money*. Maybe he finally ran out of money?" Géza turned and continued to lead them toward the armory.

They came to the end of the hall and turned left, up through a wide tower hosting a formal stair with large-paned windows cutting so regularly into the stone it made the exterior walls appear to float on the panes themselves. Ahead of them was a set of tall and intricately carved double doors, furnished with a motif of a knight being presented with a chalice by a woman. The righthand door was slightly ajar.

"That's curious," said Géza. "These doors lead to the chapel."

"Why curious? The family doesn't use the chapel?" asked Hermann.

"That's my understanding. Fürth told me that no one had used this area since before the Baums moved in." Géza opened the righthand door and passed through.

Inside, they were able to look over the entire space from a mezzanine with a stone balustrade. From the splendid stained-glass in the rose window behind them, and in the apse ahead, the chapel was illuminated in bright light tinged with reds, blues, greens, and yellows that cast their colors onto the dusty, patterned tile floor. There were crates, boxes, and several trunks arrayed and stacked on the floor. Wooden benches were set into intricately roofed alcoves of dark wood, all encased in as much thick dust as the floor, evidenced through the reflection of the grey grime in the light.

"It doesn't look like anyone's in here," said Hermann. "However ... do you see there?" He pointed to a disturbance in the otherwise uniform grime of the floor below, leading toward the alter.

Géza squinted slightly. "I do. Come on, we can get down there from the lower level."

They doubled back the way they'd come, then down the stair in the tower, and through another large, intricate door into the main floor of the chapel. From there, the pathway leading to the altar was clearer. Between the boxes and several half-open crates, filled with straw, there was a makeshift opening that made a poor aisle. Hermann made his way forward, then knelt beside what appeared to be a wide shoe print. Elsewhere, the dust was scuffed and pushed around in larger sweeps.

"It looks like the staff was moving something in here," Géza said.

"Did someone come to take something out of one of the crates, you think?"

"I can't tell, but they must have pushed or dragged something down that way." Géza traced the direction with his forefinger, toward the altar.

At the end of the makeshift aisle, the altar was perched atop a dais over three steps. Its white marble shone brightly from the light of the apse above. To the left was a pulpit of matching marble, and a permanent triptych backdrop was positioned behind it all to form a screen from the rear-most holy sepulcher, though the painted panels had been removed along with the gold or other precious crowning that had once adorned the centerpiece. Hermann approached and noticed an ivory and silver chalice with four blue stones set at equidistant points around the lip. It lay on its side on the floor as though it had fallen off of the altar.

"Forgotten from the last mass?" asked Géza.

"Not going by the absence of the artwork," Hermann replied. "Whoever was responsible for removing the art wouldn't have left this behind. The Baums must have brought it here themselves, or else it was hidden away and missed when the valuables were removed. But what's it doing here now?" He picked it up and turned it over, studying it. The silver wasn't tarnished and there was no grime on its surface, besides from where it had lain, and the old Latin inscriptions were still legible. It was then that the scenes on the altar caught Hermann's eye.

"What did you find?" asked Géza.

"I'm not sure ... river spirits on a church altar?" He ran his hand over the images, revealing more details as some of the grime was disturbed. Maidens with long hair, their nakedness strategically covered as they reclined in reeds and under the branches of willows.

"There is a German inscription here, in an old dialect." He read it aloud.

> "Uns ist in alten mæren wunders vil geseit
> von helden lobebæren, von grozer arebeit,
> von fröuden, hochgeziten, von weinen
> und von klagen,
> von küener recken striten muget ir nu
> wunder hœren sagen."

Hermann smiled. "It's a passage from the Nibelungen. The medieval poem about Siegfried, the gods, and the adventures of our heroes. It translates as:

> 'In ancient tales many marvels are told us:
> of renowned heroes worthy of praise, of
> great hardship,
> of joys, festivities, of weeping and lamenting,
> of bold warriors' battles—now you may
> hear such marvels told.'"

"It doesn't seem to have much to do with church verses," said Géza.

"I'm not sure why it's on an altar in a chapel. I can't imagine a priest would be too happy giving the sacrament over nature spirits and our Heathen ancestors," said Hermann.

He rose and placed the chalice onto the middle of the altar's top. The grime there was already disturbed.

Géza noticed it too. "Ah, that must've been what was going on here. Someone got the cup out of storage, maybe one of these crates, and put it up as a decoration, only to have it fall at some point."

As Hermann stepped around the other side of the altar, he noticed that the sweeps and swirls in the dust ended abruptly at the altar's base.

"Perhaps," he replied.

Chapter 13

Eager to examine the armory, the two men made their way back to the second floor and proceeded into another hall, striped of all valuables, the same as those they'd already come through. Ornate blue wallpaper, with floral and ivy patterns, was all that remained of the former grandeur.

"Are the Baums living only in the southern and western wings?" asked Hermann.

"That's my understanding. I've seen the widow, Frau Kam, coming and going to the library and other rooms. Frau Baum doesn't leave her sitting room much, except to eat, sleep, or dress it seems. Baum stays in his office or is elsewhere in the town. The children keep to the grounds, riding or walking through the forest when they're not with the tutor who comes by every few days."

After following the leftward curve of the hall, they came to a large archway with a matching entry on the opposite side of the room which Hermann had briefly seen the night before in his chase. The armory was centered around multiple standing display cases at waist height, with two great circular fan arrangements on the flanking walls. One was made from more modern rifles and muskets, and the other was made of spears, halberds, and pikes.

Three windows on either end provided ample light to the cream-colored walls and cream-and-scarlet oriental rug, stretching the length and breadth of most of the room.

Hermann looked up and saw that the ceiling was positioned another three or four meters above the windows and the fanned display of weapons, thus providing room for a presentation of flags representing many states and battalions from across the centuries. Many of them appeared Turkish in origin, while one clearly showed the white-horsed knight and the crossed eagle of old Poland and Lithuania, and several more were distinctly Habsburg.

There was a display case under the farther bank of windows, on the exterior wall, with its glass lid propped open. Géza led the way toward the display case, past several of the cases in the center where Hermann saw very ornate knives, pistols, pin broaches, and other collectables. The case under the window displayed some very antique pieces from the Middle Ages like a pair of dirks, the broken blade and pommel of a longsword, one bracer with reinforcing metal, and what appeared to be the empty spot in the middle of the case where the war hammer had once lain. Its imprint left a weighted pattern in the red velvet fabric of the interior.

"This is where the murderer took the weapon. The case was found open as it is now," said Géza.

Hermann looked above the case, through the window. Down below, past the bridge, the stairs, and the terraces, was the maze. It stretched out in a neatly rectangular shape for what seemed like hundreds of meters of dark green, snaking lines. Roughly two-thirds toward the rear end of the maze was the mausoleum. Its dark stone like a miniature Gothic basilica, square in shape with its tulip dome wreathed in floral pinnacles rising from the corners and over the central axes. The alley of columnar cypresses was visible as well.

Hermann spoke aloud as much to himself as Géza, "None of the cases were locked, they don't have any locking mechanisms. Why this one ... why the war hammer?"

"How do you mean, Professor?"

"Well, the killer didn't grab any of the many available weapons. He grabbed the hammer, with its obvious relation to the von Voitsberg family crest."

"Yes, because of the symbolism," said Géza, "That much is not a mystery."

"Exactly. And because this wasn't a random choice of weapon, the killer has knowledge of this room and everything in it. But it's unclear if the weapon used on Andrej was meant to send a message to the Baums ... or if it was a message from the Baums to those that would get in their way."

"That means we're dealing with someone very close to Andrej or the Baums," said Géza.

"And, someone who knows how to manipulate the death to invoke the von Voitsberg legacy. Whether they were legitimately invoking the curse or not," added Hermann.

Géza rubbed the back of his neck and stretched his jaw muscles. "What we know for certain at this point is the killer had access to the house and knew it intimately. They knew where this weapon was and chose it specifically out of the dozens of others available in this room because of its significance. And, the killer likely knew the murder could be used to spread the rumor that the curse had been realized, unleashed as it were ... on Andrej. But for what reason doesn't seem clear."

Hermann nodded. "And we know from Fürth's testimony, unless he was lying, the hammer was in its proper place that night when the house was shut down for the evening. The murderer would have had to come to this room, retrieve the hammer, make his way down to the garden maze, and ambush Andrej who was in an unlikely location at an unusual time."

Hermann turned to look through the window again, down the hill and the cut terraces to where the edge of the maze closest to them was obscured. The wind picked up, rustling the leaves of the hedges, making the lines and angles twist and ungulate like pulsing veins full of blood. A slight whistle caught Hermann's attention from somewhere inside the room.

"But how would the killer have been able to travel such a distance from this room to the maze and then navigate it well enough to reach Andrej, unaware, in front of the mausoleum? It would be nearly impossible, surely?" said Géza.

"It should be impossible, unless ...," Hermann patted the garden sketch he was carrying in his pocket, "unless the killer knew of a passage from here to there."

He looked back toward the left side of the room where a small, circular alcove was positioned. It was likely the space made by one of the two small corner towers on the outside of the gatehouse he'd seen the day prior. The right-hand side of the room lacked a matching alcove.

The wind continued outside and shook the panes in the windows. The whistle sounded again. Hermann walked toward the other side of the room where an impressive mahogany cabinet with classically styled carving and a large glass door displayed close to a dozen plated and engraved double-barreled shotguns, bolt action rifles, and one repeating rifle with a lever action. Some of Herr Baum and Josef's collection no doubt, thought Hermann.

"Professor, are you all right? What are you looking at?"

Hermann didn't answer. He ran his hand around the edge of the cabinet, in the space between it and the wall.

"There's a draft. And there are scratch marks on the floor here, curved back to the feet."

He began tapping and pressing on various parts of the cabinet and pushed his weight hard onto the front corners.

"Professor, I'm on thin ice already. I'd rather not scuff up his furniture. What are you doing?"

Hermann continued to push, and a faint click sounded from somewhere within or behind the cabinet. He pulled on the left side of the cabinet which was fixed to a hinged piece of false wall. As he pulled, a narrow doorway opened, releasing a draft of cool air.

Géza smiled and stroked his beard thoughtfully. Beyond the cabinet and the doorway lay the space where an alcove would have been, but in its place was a set of stone stairs anchored on a floor-to-ceiling column of cut stone that wound down and out of sight, illuminated by the windows that mirrored its twin faux tower. There was a small crack and piece of a lower windowpane missing, causing the wind to whistle through the opening.

"This place is more than it seems, Inspector, and the killer knows it. We're going to have to catch up quickly."

◆

Géza returned to the armory equipped with portable lanterns, and he and Hermann slipped into the secret spiral stair hidden behind the trap cabinet door. Beyond the initial three arrow-slit windows, the stair shaft grew dimmer until the men were surrounded by inky pitch darkness. Were it not for the glow of the lanterns, they'd be stumbling blind down the smooth stone stairs. After twisting around and around the central pillar, they finally reached a portal into a larger space. Hermann went to the edge of the nearest wall and ran his hand over it.

"The stone down here is rougher. It's flaked and jagged, not smooth and polished like that on the higher levels." He examined more stonework further on in the passage.

"What do you see, Professor?" asked Géza.

"I think we're in the old part of the castle now. I read on the train out from Vienna that what we see above ground was built a few decades ago around the original medieval castle. The original curtain walls, towers, and even the minaret were all absorbed and turned into the skeletal structure of the Burgenromantik palace that Georg von Voitsberg built."

"So, we are in the *real* castle, now? Fascinating," said Géza.

The two continued through a more narrow passage, coming out into a larger space. There was natural stone to one side, faintly illuminated by the lantern light, like a grotto angling up and out into the chamber. They moved toward it, bringing large stone columns in front of them into the light. Géza raised his lamp and followed their line upward to barely visible vaulting that held up the ceiling. In front of them were arrayed dozens of similar columns, hoisting up vaults of their own, joining together like a massive spider's web of cut stone.

"This must be below the courtyard," said Géza. "Over there is the keep, I think." He pointed into the gloom to their left, at the murky outline of a very large wall with massive stones forming its foundation. In the center was a small, dark portal to a space beyond.

The darkness all around them, that gave way only temporarily to the light of their lanterns, was unnerving.

"Should the flames die, we could be trapped here, like blind mice in a maze," Hermann mused. "This space must lead into many of the old castle's buildings and walls. What we just came through was the medieval curtain wall, so this is the old bailey. The keep, the servant's hall, the north hall, almost everything must have a connection here, and to each other. If the killer knew about this, he could go almost anywhere twice as fast as any of us trying to navigate all the halls and stairwells above."

"Isten oltalmazzon minket," Géza said under his breath. "We need to find which path leads to the maze. Wait ... is that water?"

"I hear it too. It's coming from over here." Hermann turned them to the right, then through a narrow doorway cut through the natural stone that may once have supported a door, given its large iron hinges. Now, nothing of that remained, only the darkness to be pushed away in front of them.

They continued on, following a growing gurgle up ahead. At the end of the passage, they came to a mostly intact door that was slightly ajar. Géza tried to push it open, but it only barely budged. He handed his lantern to Hermann and proceeded to shove the door, using his weight to push the wood further along the stone floor. Each jolt onto the old wood sent out a reverberating boom into the small passage, echoing back to Hermann after a second or two from the undercroft of the bailey beyond. Once he had forced a large enough opening, Géza took his lantern back, illuminating the dirt covering his shoulder which turned his green jacket into a muted moss color.

Inside, Hermann was able see the enclosed space that was moderately lit by light from a long, angled shaft partially obscured by ruble and debris. Against the left-hand wall was an ornate mosaic pattern set by hundreds of painted pieces of tile, obscured by a layer of grime. They appeared to show geometric patterns in blue and green, all centered on a small basin and fountainhead that was pulsing a low stream of water into an algae-filled bowl that subsequently overflowed and cascaded to a trough and channel in the floor.

The waterway led to a square pool that encompassed most of the room's floorspace. It was mostly green, and very dark with algae. Neither man was able to see the bottom. Around the room were stone benches or ledges set into the stonework at even intervals. To the righthand side of the room was another waterway, leading away from the pool as it overflowed, to a wooden door with an archway cut into the bottom of it to allow the water to pass through unobstructed.

Hermann approached the door and attempted to open it using its dangling iron-ring handle, but it wouldn't budge. There was a large keyhole just above the handle that may have explained its immobility. Hermann set his lantern on the floor and crouched down toward the cutout. He angled his left arm to support his weight while he craned his head to peer through the hole.

"There's a tunnel beyond. It looks like a drainage chute for the pool. It's too dark to see how far it goes."

"I think this was once a bathhouse, Professor. We have them in Budapest. It makes sense that the builders would have controlled a hot spring on the site. Can you see if anyone may have come or gone through that tunnel?"

"Unless they had a key or could shrink to the size of a rat, I'd say it was unlikely anyone's gone this way in a long time."

"Let's move on then."

Hermann rose, then clapped his hands on the knees of his pantlegs to shake loose the dirt. He looked at the beam of sunlight streaming in, like a tether to the outside world. As he stepped forward, he thought that the beam shone into the main chamber's semi-open doorway, though sunlight wasn't usually yellow-orange and flickering.

Hermann moved back away from the doorway and against the wall, motioning for Géza to get back as well. Then he covered his mouth, staring at Géza, hoping he would understand. Géza looked like he was about to speak, confusion flooding his expression. Géza shut his mouth, eyebrows furrowing as he took a glance at the floor just inside the edge of the door. He must have seen the unnatural light because he looked back to Hermann, nodded, and stepped back around the half-opened door.

Tap. Tap. Tap. Steady footfalls, trying hard to stay muffled, sounded down the hall and echoed off the mosaics behind the two men. Hermann caught his breath, holding it before he realized he had stopped breathing. Géza slowly shifted his lantern to his left hand before reaching down to his right boot. He began to draw out a short rod from its back side. The light in the hallway grew stronger, reflecting down the wall. Géza angled the tip to his left hand, used a finger to latch on, and drew back with the right hand, extending the rod three times its original length. He gripped the rod tightly and drew it up in his fist to chest height. Hermann looked at him, locked eyes, and nodded.

Hermann raised his hand to begin a countdown. First the thumb. One. Then the index. Two. Hermann raised his chin slightly and readied for the third. Géza's muscles tightened in his arm as he braced.

Tap! Tap! Tap! Tap! Tap!

The sound thundered down the hall. Géza darted forward to the side of the door and used his angled stance to spring into the hall. Hermann followed just after. There was now a cacophony of noise thundering in the hall, light dancing wildly on the walls as the three runners dashed for the doorway. Hermann couldn't see anything of their prey, just the green of Géza's jacket and his black kepi which refused to budge.

"Bastard!" Géza turned to shout over his shoulder. "He's in the chamber now, keep up!"

Hermann was right on Géza's heels as they passed through the doorway into the open colonnaded undercroft. The light from the three lanterns danced wildly, each swaying back and forth with their holder's gait, casting long and hideous shadows on the walls and columns. Now the columns looked more like an illusion than a work of engineering, falling in and out of light as three bright spots twirled in the darkness. Hermann got round to Géza's left as they continued to chase the fleeing figure.

He was well ahead of them now by at least ten meters. Neither man could make out any of the fleeing figure's details, except a long dark cloak billowing out behind, with dark shoes or boots clipping furiously beneath. There was a hood pulled up over his head, fanning back widely in the catching air. The figure cut to the left, and a pale hand came up to grab hold of the hood in the turn, preventing it from flying back. The figure continued to run, but Géza was beginning to close the distance, right arm pumping through the air as his left was bogged down with the lantern.

Suddenly, the light and the figure shifted, turned back to the right and charged beyond another set of tall columns. The light shifted again and shot off fast to the left, air catching the flame inside the glass, causing the shadows around it to grow as its light flickered. The two turned to follow it again at a moment's switchback as the lantern light in front of them rose through the air. Then the light began to drop. Not drop ... fall.

It clattered to the stone floor, smashing the glass, and momentarily igniting the kerosene that spilled out into the flame. The men took two or three large strides, trying to slow as they were illuminated in a wash of bright orange. The figure was not there.

"Where is the bastard?" Géza exclaimed.

Hermann turned, blind beyond the reach of his light. Géza began to wheel around. Left, then right. Hermann paused, listening.

Tap. Tap. Tap. Tap.

In the distance, the footsteps were falling rapidly away from the duo. They echoed in the chamber, but Hermann focused on the bursts of noise. They were down and off to the left of their position. "This way, Inspector," he called back as he began to run.

Hermann weaved around several columns, tracking a diagonal path to the figure. They weren't moving as fast as before, but they were directing to a specific point in the darkness. He was thankful for the years of hiking in the mountains above Salzburg with his father and later his friends. His strong legs, endurance, and thin-air training had come in handy for the first time since his self-induced exile to Vienna. As he drew closer, Hermann made out the vague form of the lower portion of the keep that they had seen earlier, a large black maw of a doorway looming before him. The footsteps from the figure were no longer echoing in the open space.

"They've gone through, into the keep," he shouted over his shoulder to Géza.

Hermann continued on, but Géza had caught up by now, reaching out to grab Hermann's shoulder before he could make it through the arch.

"Let me, Professor. We don't know if he's armed."

Géza didn't wait for a reply and pressed past Hermann and under the archway into the space beyond. There were no white columns and Gothic finery here as the room above them had. Here, there was only a large and empty room with several doorways off to the sides, and in the gloom beyond their lantern light was a steep, wide, straight stair set off to the left. The two men looked up and saw that the cloaked figure was already at the top of the stairs.

The figure turned to the right, looking down at them, face obscured by the darkness well beyond their lanterns. Hermann and Géza charged up the stairs, taking them two at a time. Then the figure disappeared, not into more shadow, but into a blinding light that poured out around them and down the stairs into their painfully dilated pupils. Hermann and Géza were stunned for a moment, causing Géza to trip on a stair, falling hard onto his knee with a loud groan.

"Go on! Get him!" Géza commanded Hermann as the professor paused for an instant to check on him.

Hermann bounded up the stairs again, but the light went out suddenly and abruptly; fortunately, he could still see by his own lantern. As he reached the top of the stairs, he was confronted with a solid wooden wall. Géza began to regain his footing and climbed the stairs, relying mostly on the rickety wooden banister on the outer edge of the stairway. Hermann began feeling around the wall and the supporting framework of the stone around it. Desperately, he began clutching and pushing and searching for anything that might give. Then, at the bottom of the wall he found a lever and pulled it up. There was a click, and Hermann pushed against the wall, though it didn't fly open like when the figure had gone through. Instead, he heard something sliding and scraping on the other side of the door.

Hermann laid into the door with his weight. Once. Twice. And on the third time, the door swung wide as a loud crash of pottery resounded. He was thrown into bright light and onto a smooth, tiled floor. He looked around, first at the broken remnants of a toppled planter and then at the height and white color of the keep's interior. Géza stumbled up and through the doorway behind Hermann. The duo had come through a piece of wood paneling meant to look like the natural stone that supported the winding stairs above them to the mezzanine. The figure they had chased was nowhere in sight.

Tap. Tap. Tap. Tap.

A set of footsteps grew louder as they approached. Hermann rose to his feet, breathing heavily, and looked around the hall quickly, trying to catch a glimpse of the cloak or a footprint, but there was nothing. Géza followed, limping.

"Do you see him? Which way has he gone?" Géza asked.

"He's gone. By the time I made it through the wall, he'd escaped."

"Damn. Then it was all for—"

"What is the meaning of this?" Fürth had come around from the corridor, into the keep. "Do you find it amusing to destroy this house's prized possessions? That was a Ming vase brought by the special envoy of the Qing Emperor to Herr von Voitsberg. The pair was priceless." His blue-green eyes were set against bloodshot whites making him look on the verge of tears.

Hermann glanced over to the opposite stairway where there was a tall vase with an exotic looking plant. It's blue-and-white pattern matched the colors on the dozen or more pieces of its broken twin.

"We apologize Herr Fürth. Did you see anyone come through ahead of us?" Hermann asked.

"No. I only saw you and Inspector Orczy destroying this house. How could you be so careless?"

Géza interjected. "Now hold on one minute. You're out of breath and your eyes are bloodshot. Where were you just now?"

"What? I was here, doing my duty. I was clearing the dining room of the breakfast service."

Géza pressed on. "Can someone vouch for that?"

"I beg your pardon?"

Fürth may not have been anywhere near as tall as Géza, but the arrogance in his stance and the sneer on his face made the old man look like he was facing down the guardians of Hades. Hermann interceded before things got out of hand.

"Herr Fürth," he stepped between the space that was narrowing between Géza and the butler, "Inspector Orczy did not intend to imply anything."

"Oh really?" Fürth looked over Hermann's shoulder. "That's exactly what it sounded like."

"We were chasing a man who'd been spying on us. The inspector is merely trying to find the route he took through the house from out of the tunnels."

"Well, he didn't come past me." The old man backed up, relaxed his shoulders, and straightened his vest. "If you will excuse me, I must get back to my duties ... and find someone who can clean up this mess." He turned to walk down the hall from whence he'd come.

"Fürth?" Hermann said. "Funny that you're not surprised that two men stumbled out of a seemingly solid stone wall into the hall, from a secret passage."

The butler stopped and turned. His eyes were glassy and his expression void of substance. His eyes travelled to the faux wall and the darkness beyond, then to Géza, then they returned to Hermann.

"Oh, my goodness. What on earth is that? Was that there this whole time?" he said, his hand coming up to cup his cheek. "This is extraordinary. Though, this is ... none of my business, of course." Then he turned again and walked back down the hall.

Hermann raised his eyebrows and closed his eyes as he sighed. He rubbed his brow a bit before turning back to Géza who was desperately trying to shake the pain out of his leg. Hermann took Géza's lantern and set it and his own down near the remnants of the Ming vase.

"How's the leg, Inspector?"

"It hurts and it tore my trousers, but it is nothing serious. What matters is that the bastard got away and could be anywhere by now."

"More importantly is that whomever we were chasing knows those tunnels intimately and, more or less, has free reign of the house. They could be anywhere, or right behind a wall, and we wouldn't know it."

"That's not a thought that I'd like to dwell on. And what about the butler? He obviously knows about the passages. They probably all know about the passages. Could come in handy if you're a servant."

"Well, I'm not sure if he's more athletic than his age suggests, but I agree. He's not telling us everything."

Hermann pushed the panel to the understairs shut, noticing the click of the latch that held the façade. He couldn't see where the mechanism on this side of the door was, or if it even had one.

"We're outgunned here and we're not going to outwit the killer in their own maze," Hermann said. "We'll need another way. We need a map or a cartographer if we have any hope of navigating this house."

"Any idea where we get one? A map I mean."

"I saw a number of maps in the library's map room, spread out on the tables ... yesterday when I met with Herr Baum."

"Why am I not surprised?" said Géza.

Chapter 14

Géza returned quickly wearing a fresh pair of trousers, clean and devoid of holes. He found Hermann standing in the center of the keep under the blue ceiling of the arched rotunda, looking up, past the mezzanine. Two doors with large brass handles were visible over the top of the stone railing above.

"That's his study, right? Just up these stairs?" Hermann pointed in the direction of the set of doors.

"Yes, almost too convenient isn't it?" Géza walked to the center of the floor, limping slightly. He looked up, then followed the curvature of the staircase down to their level and squinted toward the hidden door. "Baum could have been the one we were chasing in the tunnels. He could have easily run up these stairs and locked himself in his study."

"I don't think so. I think we were chasing the same man who ran from me last night. And like I said this morning, Herr Baum's girth would make it difficult for him to keep up that level of activity. We need to know what he knows though. What everyone in this place knows, for that matter."

Hermann crossed his arms, thinking for a moment. His sleepless night and the recent level of intense activity left him looking more like an outdoor adventurer than a professor—but unlike most, the tussled hair, bright eyes, and high color suited him.

Géza, who didn't look quite as fetching for their morning activity, looked around the room with a deepening frown. "Right, the von Voitsberg era servants ... the housekeeper, Frau Schrode, the cook, Frau Kovács, Fürth, and Pavol likely know the house inside and out. Andrej too was a von Voitsberg era servant. Then there are the Baums, of course."

"I saw the deeply personal connection between Schrode and Kovács yesterday. I wanted to interview Frau Kovács, and Frau Schrode became protective of her. I'm sure one or both of them knows more than they are letting on about Andrej's character, and maybe what happened to him," Hermann said.

"There's a servants' stair near the dining room that will take us down to the kitchen. Herr Fürth should be nearby, we can start with him."

Hermann nodded. "Lead the way."

As they made their way through the hall to the dining room, Hermann was able to get a good look at the ornate ballroom. The floor was a dizzying pattern of herringbone made of lighter and darker wood, set into a checkerboard pattern, bordered by another, red-shaded wood. There were three brilliant, cut-crystal chandeliers which reflected the colors of the rainbow in jagged, mercurial patterns across the room as the bright glow of the midday sun radiated through the floor-length windows. Beyond the ballroom, they took the door into the dining room. The breakfast service had been cleared, tablecloth and silver stowed away until the evening. Géza headed in the direction of the butler's pantry on the far side, through the door the footmen had hustled in and out of during dinner the night before.

Herr Fürth was busy shelving and locking boxes of silver flatware. To the right were several built-in cabinets full of silver hollowware, china, glasses, goblets, napkin rings, and serving vessels of all kinds, stretching floor to ceiling.

"Herr Fürth. We need to ask you a few questions. Is there someplace we can talk?" said Géza.

The old butler turned, eyebrow raised. "Not now, Inspector. I have far too much to do today and I cannot leave it in the hands of those two baboons passing as footmen. You'll have to check with me later, or better yet, tomorrow." He gave a momentary look of enlightenment. "Ah. No, tomorrow doesn't work either, I have to set out the guns for the shooting party and clean up afterwards. We don't have any proper gamesmen, and with Andrej … *gone*, there's no one else I can assign to the task." He gritted his teeth. "It's beneath my dignity, but we each have to bear our crosses."

"Herr Fürth—," Hermann began.

Fürth interjected. "Herr, you are a guest in this house, invited by Frau Kam and retained at the will of Herr Baum. You don't need to address me as *herr*."

"All right, Fürth," Hermann continued, "All we need are a few minutes to find out a little more about the house and its history, especially after the late freiherr's death."

Fürth's face settled into a relaxed frown, leaving his light blue-green eyes fully illuminated.

"I apologize, herr, but I simply don't have the time. I must refuse."

"Damn it man, your responsibilities aren't any more important than a murder investigation," Géza retorted.

"They are when those responsibilities are my means of remaining employed, Inspector." He paused a moment. "And, it is *Herr Fürth* to you, a man of trade."

Géza's jaw tightened.

"Fürth," interjected Hermann, "Shall I clear some time for you with Herr Baum? He is most anxious to have the investigation wrapped up. We're on our way downstairs now to see Frau Schrode. It's most important that we speak with each of the senior staff. Perhaps you will be available afterwards?"

"I will try," Fürth replied.

Hermann looked to his left where an open stair was visible, stretching down to a landing. He extended his arm. "Shall we, Inspector?"

Géza led the way once more down the stair to the same green and grey hallways where they had started yesterday. Straight ahead and to the right was one of the entries into the kitchen, convenient for whisking the food up to the guests while it was still hot. A lady's maid in a plain black dress was walking hurriedly down the hall, carrying a pair of small shoes.

"Excuse me, fräulein. Do you know where we may find Frau Schrode?" asked Hermann as she approached.

"The last I saw, she was in her office. Down that way," she pointed, then half-smiled and continued on.

Hermann took the lead now, away from the kitchen toward the door that led out onto the work yard. The two walked to the end of the hall where on the upper levels the library tower would have been apparent. The walls and curve of the hallway gave the original stone away at its foundations, though all were painted grey and green. Once around the bend of the tower's base, they came upon an unexpected sight. Josef Baum was standing on a chair near the end of the hall with his back to the men as they came out from the shadowed curve. He was on his tiptoes in a pair of ankle-high boots and white socks that met his maroon breeches just below the knee. He was holding on to a small ledge that hosted a window, near the ceiling, to the room beyond. From his perch, he eavesdropped without being seen by those in the room.

Géza moved fast, grabbing the boy on the neck and arm, more or less plucking him out of his position and setting him down on the floor. Géza didn't release his grip as the boy began to call out.

"Unhand me you oaf! Get your hands off me. Do you know who I am?"

He was turning red, like a beetroot, to match his maroon breeches.

"I know well who you are. What do you think you were doing on that chair?"

"I don't have to answer to you. Unhand me or my father will hear of it," the boy continued to protest.

Hermann spoke up. "Josef, a young man like you shouldn't normally find himself in the downstairs. Were you looking for something?"

"When my father hears how you—"

The door from the room that Josef had been spying on opened, and Frau Schrode swept out into the hall. "What on earth is going on?"

"Good afternoon, Frau Schrode," said Hermann. "We just came on the young Herr Baum appraising his stately home through this window here."

Schrode's emotion softened from her initial surprise. "Inspector, thank you … for helping the boy to avoid a fall."

Géza looked between Hermann and the boy and let go of his arm. The boy began to straighten his jacket and pull on his sleeves.

"Meister Josef, you had best get along back to your tutor. You always have trouble focusing on your mathematics," said Schrode.

She approached him and began to fix his tie which had gone askew during the melee.

"Don't touch me with your boney old hands!" Josef said, slapping at the old woman.

She lowered her hands as a slight shudder registered through her black frock and white apron. Josef turned and stormed down the hall. The housekeeper regained her composure and addressed the men.

"We've often found him sneaking around. He's mostly harmless, apart from his attitude. I think he's bored and lonely out here with no other boys his age to play with."

"He should show more respect," said Géza.

Frau Schrode shrugged slightly and twisted her hands together. Hermann sensed her discomfort.

"We actually came to speak with you, Frau Schrode. Do you have a minute?" asked Hermann.

She nodded and beckoned them into her office, looking back into the hall before closing the door behind them. Her office was sparse, only furnished by a neat desk and a narrow table flanked by two armless chairs set against the wall opposite a small fireplace. There were cabinets arrayed behind the desk and a framed landscape print on the wall opposite. The walls were painted a warm cream rather than the gloomy grey and green of the rest of the level. Schrode made her way around to the desk chair where some papers were spread.

"Please sit, herren."

Géza and Hermann each took one of the side chairs and sat in front of the desk. Géza took out his notepad and pencil from his tab pocket and flipped it open to a clean page.

"Frau Schrode, I would like to begin by going over your statement about the night of Andrej's murder. You said that after the servants' dinner, you retired to your office." Géza used the tail end of his pencil to motion round the room. "You stayed here for a time before you went upstairs to bed, and on your way up you saw Herr Fürth in his office. Is that correct?"

"Yes, herr," she said. "It's just around the bend, inside the base of the library tower. You would have passed it on your way in."

Hermann nodded as he recalled a black door set off from a servants' stair.

"Did you notice anything that night?" Géza continued. "Anything that you may have remembered since the last time I asked?"

"No, herr. I believe I told you everything."

"Did you hear anything or see anything that struck you as odd or out of the ordinary?"

"No, I was asleep all night in my room, upstairs in the women's quarters."

"Thank you," said Géza.

"Frau Schrode," Hermann began, "is the work here difficult? For the staff and yourself?"

"Not particularly, herr. We're sailing a much smaller ship these days and the family doesn't entertain much, so we can keep to our schedules pretty well."

"This house is quite large. I've seen that myself since yesterday. Do the staff have a hard time doing their duty between all these rooms and floors?"

"Not so far as they've told me, or Herr Fürth. Many of the rooms are shuttered, so we can manage fine with the number of staff we have now."

"And how do they get around? I presume they don't use the main stairs and halls."

"They use the servants' stairs. They're located all around Schattenturm. There's one just outside that runs parallel to the library and western hall. There's one near the kitchen as well. We don't normally use the others except on laundry day or when we strip the beds after a guest has left."

"And you would say you know how to get around this house well?"

"Yes," she said with a smile. "I've worked here most of my life."

"Does Herr Fürth have the same knowledge?"

"Of course, herr, he has been here as long as I have and then some."

"So the two of you are the longest tenured staff members?"

"Frau Kovács has been here nearly as long as we have, and the next longest tenured staff member is ... was Andrej."

"What about any other ways to get around, Frau Schrode? Any ways that people wouldn't typically know about?"

She narrowed her eyes a bit. "I'm not sure what you mean," she answered.

Hermann sat back in his chair and crossed his leg. He analyzed Schrode in an instant. She kept her nails short and her deeply greyed hair pulled back tight into a bun. She obviously worked and was dedicated to it. She wore no powder or rouge to cover her wrinkles and no jewelry except for a small chain around her neck that may have been attached to a locket or a cross that he couldn't see. Her little office indicated a good deal of freedom, since it deviated strongly from the color and décor of the rest of the downstairs.

"What if I told you that there were secret passages and hidden entrances that led down to the foundations of the old castle ... would it surprise you to learn that there's an entire network of rooms and caverns just below us?"

She breathed in sharply and recoiled slightly in her seat. "I don't know anything about that, herr. Are you sure? It doesn't seem possible."

"Why is that, frau?"

"Because the freiherr told us that the old castle was torn apart and used to build this house as it is today. There are a few places that have the old buildings and walls, but not what you're describing."

"When did the late freiherr tell you this?"

"Well, it wasn't him exactly. When I started working here, Herr Fürth was already the butler and he told all the first staff about the construction. Oh, he was so young then. None of us ever expected a butler younger than forty." She smiled and looked toward the side table.

Hermann followed her gaze. There was a picture print photograph of three people in a frame, one man and two women. It was obvious that the man was Fürth, given his demeanor and rigid stance, though he was a good deal younger, mid-forties Hermann guessed. The next was Schrode when she was in her late thirties or early forties, though Hermann couldn't tell exactly from the angle of his seat. There was a young, plump woman furthest to the right. Hermann couldn't make out who she was, but she looked to be maybe eighteen or nineteen, and she was holding something in a bundle about her waist. The three were looking at the camera, posing, although the plump woman looked anxious in the photo.

"He was handsome then, all pride and pomp. He's always been good with those of us from the old days. Frau Kovács and me that is. God knows we had our good times and bad times over the years." Her smile waned. "I suppose now we're the old curmudgeons, the old guard so to speak."

"Is it possible that Herr Fürth would know about the passages? You said he started working here before the construction started?" asked Géza.

"I don't know if he knows, or even if these passages exist."

"They do very much exist, Frau Schrode. Inspector Orczy and I stumbled upon them today," said Hermann.

Schrode repositioned a loose strand of her hair back into her bun. "Herr Fürth began working here before Herr Georg von Voitsberg's father's death. Herr Georg was still young. When he inherited the house upon his father's death, he turned out most of the staff and hired his own. He made Herr Fürth the new butler. Fürth told us once that he was barely thirty-two when that happened. For years, the freiherr worked on renovating the old castle to what you see today. It never truly stopped until the crash of seventy-three, mind you, but it was fully finished enough to hire a full complement of staff after the first several years. I started here as a head parlor maid the year before Frau Kovács who was just a scullery maid at the time."

Her eyes moved over the picture again.

"I worked my way up over the years. Usually, it would be the senior lady's maid that would become housekeeper, but the freiherr never had the chance to marry, so we never had any ladies' maids besides for his brother's wife. Herr Fürth was always close with the freiherr, probably because they were almost the same age. He was very loyal to the freiherr, and he took his death hard." Her jaw tightened. "The freiherr had a lot of trust in Herr Fürth and relied on him to run the downstairs."

She seemed to notice that Géza was rapidly taking notes for the first time.

"But I'm certain he had nothing to do with Andrej's death if that's what this has all been leading up to. He couldn't hurt a soul."

"Not to worry Frau Schrode," said Hermann. "We just want to gather all the facts about this place. Do any of the Baum family know about the passages? From anything that you might be able to recall?"

"I'm sorry, Herr Horst, but not that I know. I don't interact much with Herr Baum or Frau Baum. My duties keep me to the maids and managing the stores and supplies. The closest that this house ever got to having a proper mistress was Frau Maria Theresa, the late freiherr's sister-in-law. We were all grieved when her husband, Herr Albert, died, leaving their children half-orphaned. I was sorry to hear she'd grown sick the last few years. She was a very noble woman and treated us with respect. Schattenturm was never the same after Herr Albert's death."

"Thank you for the information, Frau Schrode. We'll try to find out more from the von Voitsbergs when we can, and I'll pass along your sentiment. Just one more thing," said Hermann. "Could you tell us about Andrej's relationship with the staff? I noticed yesterday, shortly after my arrival, Frau Kovács was very upset by what had happened, more so than others it appeared."

Schrode stiffened in her seat and pressed her palms against the edge of her desk. "We all knew Andrej since he was a lad here. We had different levels of affection for him."

"What does that mean?" asked Géza.

"Frau Kovács is a tender soul, she feels very strongly about most things and tries to live her life as happily as she can. That extended to Andrej."

"But you had reason to feel otherwise about Andrej?" Géza furrowed his brow.

Schrode sighed and hung her head. She forcefully uncoupled her hands from the edge of the desk, before clasping them together on top of her notepad.

It doesn't bear hiding any longer. Anyone who would care, or who it would have bothered is dead or long gone from this house now."

Hermann looked again at the photo of Fürth, Schrode, and Kovács. "It's a baby. The bundle she's holding is a baby," he said.

She nodded. "It's not much of a secret that Andrej was Frau Kovács' ... son. I'd just ask that you don't spread the word around town ... if you would, please."

"You have our word, Frau Schrode. It must have been terrible for her to lose her only child. I presume she was unwed?" asked Hermann.

"Yes," said Schrode.

She rose and retrieved the small picture from the side table and handed it to Hermann.

"This was taken a few weeks after he was born, in Budapest. Fürth and I kept the secret, especially from the upstairs. A house like this couldn't be home to scandal, and Frau Kovács and her tiny son would have been put out on the street with no prospect of a reference. When she discovered she was with child she broke down, couldn't cope. Herr Fürth and I helped her. We made up a widow story for her and sent her back north to her family for a few months for *mourning*. She told her family she had eloped with a sweetheart who then died tragically, and a letter of approval from Fürth for the absence from work confirmed it for them. Herr Fürth and I took her to Budapest a few weeks after Andrej's birth. Herr Fürth found him a placement in an orphanage. Frau Kovács wrote to her family that the baby had died suddenly of fever one night and had been buried. The staff here never knew she ever had a child. One story for her family and one for this household. No one thought to ask much of a kitchen maid. It wasn't until he was about thirteen or fourteen that he came to work here."

"Why didn't you tell this to me earlier?" asked Géza.

"Because it wasn't anyone's business. It happened twenty-five years ago, and it wasn't my story to tell. I didn't want to bring Frau Kovács any shame."

"Was Frau Kovács aware of Andrej's reputation for being lazy, gambling his money away, and generally consorting with the wrong types of people?" asked Hermann.

"No. She turned a blind eye to anything she heard that maligned his reputation," said Schrode, shaking her head.

"And what about you and Herr Fürth? You were her friends. Did either of you try to straighten him out or help her see the reality?" asked Géza.

Schrode looked down at her hands and began to rub her veins with her bony fingers.

"Frau Schrode, we have it on good authority that Andrej was a card sharp, and perhaps even a thief. Can you corroborate that?" asked Hermann.

"Yes," she answered flatly. "Fruit from a bad seed. We saw it from the start and there was nothing any of us could do." She exhaled, before raising her eyes to meet those of Hermann and Géza. "He had a bad start, born out of wedlock, that's sure. But he was always a bit off. He took to con games in his teens. He always knew how to sweet talk the girls and corral some of the wayward lads to do what he wanted. I tried to address it early on with Herr Fürth, to have him act as a kind of father figure, but he wouldn't. Andrej had worked his way into the freiherr's good graces and Herr Fürth saw his own involvement with the boy as somehow disloyal. So, Andrej's antics went unchecked. After the freiherr's death, when the house all but shut down, he left the county. He'd been left a small allowance and a position here for life, like Fürth, Kovács, and myself. I thought he'd go off and live his life somewhere like Budapest or Preßburg, but just after Herr Baum bought the estate, he turned up again."

She paused for a minute, then shook her head.

"He was worse than ever. He'd taken up with a band of Gypsies nearby and would buy and trade things with them. Stolen things, I think. He got into bad card playing with the Slovak miners in town as well. More than once, a gang showed up at our door asking about him."

"And what was Frau Kovács' reaction to this behavior?" asked Géza.

"She could see and hear no evil from him, herr. He was her precious boy. You can't blame her for a mother's love."

"Of course," said Hermann. "Though, what did the others think of Andrej's behavior? Herr Fürth and Herr Baum couldn't have been happy at the negative attention on Schattenturm."

"Herr Fürth never said much about him, at least not to me. And like I said before, I don't have much interaction with Herr Baum besides work formalities, and he never brought up the issue but once as far as I know."

"When was that?"

"About a week before Andrej's death. He had words with him on the south terrace from what the valet and Herr Fürth told me. No one could hear what they said exactly beyond Herr Baum threatening to fire him for causing some kind of scandal. We all assumed it was hot air. They'd argued a few times before, to my knowledge, but nothing ever came of it over the last year."

"Are you sure you don't know what the argument was about, Frau Schrode? Any detail could be very important," Géza added.

"I'm sorry, Inspector, but no. I keep to myself and my work as I've always done. With a house like this, you don't have time for distraction and speculation. If Herr Baum had wanted to fire Andrej, I assumed he would've done so and that would've been that."

Hermann admired her directness and practicality. She was a survivor, not easily shaken. He needed to know more though.

"Can you tell us anything about the curse? Where did it come from and why has it had such an effect on everyone?"

"That I can't speak to. There have always been legends about this place. Stories of hauntings always accompany large old houses. There's no point in believing any of it. A curse, if you want to call it that, was around when I first started here, it was a way to scare the maids in their first days away from home. The first freiherr of this place, the one whose portrait is hanging in your room, is long dead and buried. He's not coming back. Everyone who has ever worked here has been at least a little superstitious, and some outright paranoid. They ought to put their faith in God and leave the rest out of it."

The intensity of the conversation was suddenly broken when the sharp cuckooing of the clock sounded. All three looked over to the fireplace where a dark wooden chalet cuckoo clock above the fireplace mantel was tolling in time with a miniature red bird bobbing back and forth. The artistry looked very familiar.

"That's noon, and my cue to meet the grocer. He's come up to replenish our stocks."

Géza and Hermann rose as Schrode stood.

"Thank you, Frau Schrode. Should we have any more questions, we'll know where to find you. Good afternoon," said Hermann.

At the twelfth toll, a faint melody began to play as one of the large pinecone weights sank down the wall toward the mantel while a trio of dancing pairs circled the chalet's balcony. One of the dancing pairs held a baby between them wrapped in a red cloth that matched the cuckoo.

The scene and the cuckoo reminded Hermann of home, the stories of Wechselbutte, which sent a shiver down his spine.

Chapter 15

Géza unlocked the door to the makeshift evidence room and stepped aside for Hermann to enter, then closed the door tightly behind them.

"So, the gardener was hated by a large portion of the town, argued with Herr Baum regularly, mistreated and took advantage of his assistant, Pavol, mistreated most everyone he dealt with, and … was protected by the late freiherr while he was alive," said Hermann.

"Yes, so it would seem. There's no shortage of people who have a motive to see him dead," Géza replied, shaking his head.

"I think we need to know more about Andrej's connection to the old freiherr, Georg von Voitsberg. It just doesn't make sense that he had gone unchecked for so long."

"Well, he was checked … with a hammer to the back of his head," said Géza.

"Right."

Hermann ran his fingers through his disheveled hair and rubbed his chin which was beginning to show a shadow of stubble. "Frau von Voitsberg, the widow that is, may have information regarding the connection between Andrej and the old freiherr, have you spoken with her?"

"Yes. I had a brief interview with her in the first week of the investigation. The widow is amenable enough, but unwell. Her health keeps her confined to the dowager cottage. She didn't have anything to say about who would have wanted Andrej dead."

"That fits with what Frau Astrid told me yesterday in the shop. If their interactions with Andrej weren't recent, they might not have had much to say. But knowing what we know now, I'd like another opportunity to see what Frau Astrid and her mother know," said Hermann. "I wonder if Frau Baum would be willing to invite them to dinner? If so, we could walk the invitation over to the dowager cottage. That would give us access to ask some questions now and to see how the dynamics play out over dinner."

"Frau Baum would be in her parlor at this hour," said Géza, looking at his pocket watch.

The men made their way through the main hall to Frau Baum's French Provincial parlor. All of the wilting greenery that had festooned numerous vases the day before was gone, leaving large empty spaces in their wake and a hint of decay in the air. Erzsébet Baum was seated at a secretary against the wall, wearing a yellow day dress with black floral lacing on the neck, down the center of her bodice, and across her bustle.

"Frau Baum, do you have a moment?" asked Hermann, entering the room.

She looked up from her correspondence at hearing his voice. Hermann caught a glimpse of the bruise along the base of her collarbone, now a faint yellow.

"Certainly, herren. Shall I call for some coffee or tea?"

"Oh no, we should only be a moment," Hermann responded.

She ushered them to the cream and gold furniture near the hearth where a low fire crackled.

"How are things coming along with the investigation? It seems like months since it began, though it's barely been two weeks," she said.

"I believe we've made some significant advancements," said Hermann. "We know what we're looking for in

Andrej's murderer, and there's more to it than just the actions of a troubled vagabond."

Géza gave Hermann a reproaching look, eyebrows scrunching.

"That's terrible, Professor. My husband and I had hoped that he'd just fallen victim to bad dealings with the wrong acquaintance or a robber. I suppose what you mean is that he must have known his killer." Her shoulders shuddered.

"It *is* terrible, frau, but Andrej's killer isn't what we've come to speak with you about. Not in a direct way, that is. Would you be amenable to having Frau Astrid von Voitsberg and her mother, Frau Maria Theresa as diner guests this evening ... if you have nothing against their attendance."

"It's late to be extending an invitation for dinner this evening, but I have no reservation against them, although I understand that Frau Maria Theresa is too ill to venture from her house. Why, may I ask, do you want them to come to dinner this evening?"

"Their knowledge of Andrej's tenure during the time of the late freiherr, as well as historical knowledge of his character, may be beneficial to the case. The opportunity to address the topic here, in the same setting where that history evolved could prove fruitful, from my understanding," said Hermann.

"I see. Yes ... his character." Erzsébet frowned and looked down at her lap for a moment.

"Frau?" said Géza. "Do you have something you'd like to add?"

Erzsébet looked between the two, sighed, and relaxed her shoulders. "It's no secret around the house that Andrej was disliked. He was manipulative and quite the scoundrel. After I found out what he was, I wanted to dismiss him."

"What was he, exactly?" asked Hermann.

"A loathsome wretch, terribly lazy. You know his assistant is the real brain behind these gardens? Andrej was just a middleman and a holdover from the time of the von Voitsbergs."

Hermann and Géza exchanged a quick glance, acknowledging they had recognized Erzsébet's change in tune regarding Andrej and Pavol since yesterday.

"I found out from Frau Schrode that he was notorious in town as a card sharp and that he had a way of … ill-treating the local girls."

"Forgive me, but yesterday it seemed as though you didn't know much about his character when I asked," said Hermann.

Frau Baum looked at her hands, folded serenely in her lap, but said nothing.

Hermann sensed Géza's impatience rising, even before he spoke. "Specifically, frau, what was it that made you want to dismiss Andrej and when?"

She shifted in her seat. "I learned that Andrej had made an improper advance on one of the kitchen maids here and left her in an unfortunate situation. This was several months ago. The girl gave her notice suddenly, then left for Budapest after telling Frau Kovács what had happened. Frau Kovács came to me with the story, not to condemn Andrej, but to beg that we allow the girl to stay on and have the child, here, right under our noses. But as it turned out, while the girl was in Budapest, she lost the child." Erzsébet looked down at her folded hands again. "Perhaps a roundabout blessing," she said softly.

"Anything else you'd like to share?" asked Géza.

"It seems the same sort of thing nearly happened again the week before Andrej died. I hadn't gotten around to acting on his dismissal, but I would have done so."

"Was there anything stopping you from dismissing him immediately after you first learned of his egregious behavior?" asked Hermann.

Frau Baum's facial muscles tensed. "Johan said we couldn't dismiss him. There was something about Andrej being retained at Schattenturm in the will of the old frei-herr."

Géza clasped his hands together and leaned forward, resting his elbows on his knees. "Frau Baum, surely with a husband as influential as yours, you wouldn't have hesitated to take your household in command and deal with a man like Andrej? Pardon my impertinence, but what was the real reason for the hesitation?"

"That is bold, Inspector." She was rigid in her seat, back taunt.

"I apologize, frau, but Inspector Orczy is right. There must have been a deeper reason for the hesitation."

She shook her head.

"I respect your pride, Frau Baum. But I must be frank with you. Before I introduced myself to you yesterday afternoon, Inspector Orczy and I overheard a conversation in the hall between you and Rachel. Suffice to say there was a heated disagreement between you regarding a scandal in which Rachel was involved, and ...," Hermann cleared his throat, "an accusation your daughter levied against you. Did either of these have to do with Andrej?"

She frowned and studied Hermann for a minute but did not answer immediately. Her thin alabaster skin was tinging blue.

Géza leaned back in his chair, hoping to ease the tension by relaxing his posture. "Frau, we only care about Andrej's murderer. I give you my word that your privacy will be respected. No report will reveal your confidence if it didn't lead immediately to his death."

"I'm certainly not his murderer," said Erzsébet. "My daughter is a handful as are many teenage girls. She doesn't understand the importance of boundaries and limits. I do ... that's the gift of age and experience."

"And did you adhere to your own understanding of boundaries and limits where it came to Andrej?" asked Hermann.

"I admit, I enjoyed his flattery, and perhaps encouraged it. But that was all. I would never risk what I have over something so trivial as false flattery from the gardener."

She scoffed and twisted in her seat to face away from the two men, looking out the window. She didn't realize her bruise had become visible. A faint purple oval, roughly the size of a quail's egg, surrounded by a ring of yellow.

"I convinced myself that he was an eccentric artist. That his character was other than it seemed. I sought to find something in his nature that I could admire. My husband is not an artistic soul as you might imagine. He has a gift for business and has tried to make us all happy, in his way. It hasn't been easy to move this far away from everyone and everything we've known ... everything that I've known. Budapest is such a vibrant, living city ... and this house, this county, isn't what it once was. In the beginning, I thought Andrej and I might form a friendship around the estate and a combined vision for what it could become. I wanted to create a myriad of beautiful gardens and a thriving forest environment that meshed into the man-made formality. Something to give light and warmth to this place which otherwise looks like a burnt cinder on a hill."

"But he disappointed you?" asked Géza.

She turned back to face Hermann and Géza. "But none of that is what he had intended. He was a scoundrel. I arranged a meeting with him, in the privacy of the maze, the day after I heard what he'd done to the second maid. I wanted to confront him and see what he had to say for himself. I hoped there was an explanation. Something to indicate I hadn't been so blind, so stupid. I had no idea, but Rachel watched me leave the house and spied on us from somewhere in the maze." She became quiet, looking again at her folded hands.

Hermann gently prodded. "What happened in the maze?"

"Andrej thought I had finally succumbed to his flirtations. He ... made an advance on me. I was horrified. I slapped his face. His mask was lifted. He made lewd insinuations, called me names, names I've never heard, much less had levied at my person. I retaliated with words and accusations of my own, namely regarding the maids."

"So, you confronted him about the maids. You wanted to see whether the accusation was accurate?" asked Géza.

"And it was. He didn't even try to deny it. He bragged about it. I raised my hand to slap him again, but he caught my arm and we fell. For reasons of her own, Rachel thought it was a lover's quarrel."

"Is that where you received the bruise?" asked Hermann.

She raised her thin, almost childlike hand to cover the base of her neck. "Bruise? Y-yes. Umm … I bruise easily and they take forever to fade. My health is often poor. That's part of the reason Johan brought us here. For the air, he said."

"What did Herr Baum have to say about this encounter, frau? Was he angry?" asked Géza.

Erzsébet turned to him with a relaxed expression. "He had no reaction because I didn't tell him."

"And Rachel? Has she told her father, or anyone else?" asked Hermann.

"No. And she won't. So you must keep this private between us."

"Frau, this may be a difficult question, but what was Rachel's relationship to Andrej? Did he … flirt with her as well?" asked Hermann.

"No. I would know if he had. Now herren, I must get word to the cook regarding dinner, and I have several letters I must have posted by this evening." She got up from the small sofa and strode to her secretary chair, laying a hand on its back.

"What about Andrej's assistant, Pavol?" asked Géza. "We know he and Rachel have a connection."

Erzsébet sighed. "She's been encouraging that boy. I don't think she really means anything by it, but you must understand that in our world these things just aren't done. Rachel needs to marry a wealthy husband to keep her in the status that she's accustomed to. A man who will tolerate her ... *independence* because of the benefits her name will afford him."

"And her father's business dealings," Géza said softly.

"Convincing her of how important her future is has not been easy."

"Do you think Rachel understood Andrej's character? Perhaps she learned of it from Pavol?" asked Hermann.

"No. She only talked to the boy to upset her father and me. That's quite finished now, I can assure you both."

She started to tap the top of the desk chair with her index finger.

"Teenagers can be difficult, I think we can all attest to that. I'm sure with some life experience she'll come around."

Hermann nodded to Géza before he rose. "We apologize for any discomfort this has caused you, frau."

"I will let the kitchen know that we will be expecting Frau Astrid for dinner ... if she can make it on such short notice. Her mother, I know, is not well enough to attend," she said coolly.

The two men each gave a shallow bow before departing, and once out of earshot stopped to plan their next course.

"Before we set off for Frau von Voitsberg's, I want to take a look inside the mausoleum. Knowing the approximate time of the murder, where Andrej's body fell, and the lack of defensive wounds, he likely didn't see his killer coming. That begs the question, why was he in the maze, in front of the mausoleum? I think that Andrej meant to go there, but never got the chance. I want to know why. You said you had a key?" asked Hermann.

"Yes, I've kept it with me since I took over the investigation and I've sealed the building," said Géza. "However, I'm not sure what you expect to find. My men and I checked it out thoroughly. There's nothing down there but tombs and cobwebs."

"Neither do I, really, but why else would Andrej have gone to the middle of the maze that night? He had a reason, and it's becoming ever more certain he was up to something nefarious."

———————◆———————

The two set out through the northeastern gatehouse, over the small bridge, and onto the highest terrace above the maze. Dark clouds were gathering on the edge of the far horizon above the treetops. The air was damp and a thin layer of mist had formed in the low-lying places around the castle. Géza cleared his throat as they began to descend the terraces toward the entrance to the maze.

"We've made more progress in two days than I made in nearly two weeks on the case," said Géza. "I have to compliment you, Professor. You have a gift for getting people to open up to you."

"That gift has been critical to my work in parapsychology. It's not really a gift, more like a well-honed skill that I've had to work for years to refine. I've learned how to press for the answers I need based on my read of the person I'm working with. I don't have indisputable proof that the paranormal, the spirits and presence of ghosts coming back to haunt us, is real. However, I do have research that supports the signals, signs, and activity may be manifested by those who do believe. In order to make the right inferences, I've had to learn the subtleties of emotional cues and the signs of a secret closely kept."

"Hmm. Subtlety wasn't in the training manual for the hussars. I shouldn't be surprised, really. I was taught first by my father then my commanders to go straight at a thing as quickly as possible."

The two passed through the entry of the maze. Immediately, the air around them changed.

"Conversation is as much a battle as everything else in life. Well ... not everything but the point remains, when you're speaking with someone, and more so if you need to pry something out of them, every word is like a direction on the field. You need to make yourself as similar to your counterpart as possible. If he or she likes the theater, ask them about their favorite shows. If they have a fondness for something you're familiar with, indulge them with a story about it. Set them at ease, make them feel like you're compatriots in a dissimilar world. Most people have an ego that likes to be tended."

"No offense, Professor, but I'm not sure that much detail and subtlety works on anyone outside the upper class. I tried the whole game when I was young and starting out, after I gained my lieutenancy. My parents taught me to work hard, stick to what you know, and you'll go far in life. That worked well enough until I discovered that without a title, you can only get so far, about as far as I've come now as a farmer's son."

"That's the reality of living in a bloated aristocracy. Too many nobles with too many children forces the rest of the population into stagnancy, despite their merit. In Vienna, the University is geared around who you know rather than what you know, per se. I don't have a patron yet like the senior staff and alumni, so I get the honor of the rearmost classrooms and the smallest funding for everything besides my direct coursework. It doesn't help that I'm not even thirty and delving into topics my social superiors would rather keep after hours, somewhere no one from society would see openly."

"Does it bother you, Professor?"

"The higher up the social ladder you go, the more important appearances and face become. Everything centers on your ability to appear superior to the masses in décor, manners, taste, and pleasures. The conversation is mostly shallow but easy to steer through. The bürgerlich are consumed by pathos, the emotions you have in response to everything and everyone. Your standing in their circles is based on your enthusiasm or your outrage about the subject de jour. The aristocracy are frankly easier to handle because once you impress them in some way, they open up and you can breeze through the rest of the social event. You gain a kind of emotional quarantine with them, and that's preferable in so many ways."

"I can see the truth in all that, for sure. Why would anyone prefer to live in an emotional quarantine though? That can't be very rewarding, personally."

Hermann stopped on the trail as he thought about Géza's statement and the extent of his answer. Géza had gained a few paces on him by the time he realized and turned back to see what was the matter.

"I prefer to be mostly apart, Inspector Orczy, because it's easier to keep myself in control of my own feelings and memories. They would consume me if I allowed it. I told you that I started into the study of the parapsychological because of the death of my parents and sister, but I never told you the extent of it. Needless to say, it was impactful."

Chapter 16

Géza was not without the ability to read people, albeit his talent was from the perspective of an investigator, searching for the proof that his subject was culpable in something. He liked Hermann, the young man's honesty, intelligence, and dedication to getting to the truth whether that be the existence of the afterlife, or the identity of a murderer. It was clear that Hermann was troubled.

"Professor, believe me when I say that I'm sorry for your loss. Would you tell me what happened? Why it sent you in this direction?" He smiled. "My fiancé, Kornelia, tells me I'm a good listener."

Hermann breathed in deeply, thinking about the ramifications of sharing the story. The inspector was not likely to come across his university colleagues anytime soon. Even his mentor and department head, Dr. Kießling, only knew the broad details and those only so much as Hermann could bring himself to tell. He stepped forward and motioned to Géza that they should continue their trek deeper into the maze.

"I was a bright student in my teenage years. I excelled in mathematics and architectural design. I applied and was accepted to the Academy of Fine Arts in Vienna at seventeen, where I planned to earn a degree and start a career with an architecture firm working with the Crown or private patrons. My father taught me to honor and love our nation's history, architecture, art, and culture. Naturally, I wanted to help in the Neo-Gothic movement or with the imperial style that's been coming up the last decade. While I was away from Salzburg, a wave of scarlet fever struck home. Both of my parents passed and my sister, Ingfrid, fell gravely ill. I returned as soon as I could and tended to her. She'd been weakened the doctors said by an infection of the blood that would forever make her vulnerable to fever. For a while after our parents' funeral, I stayed in Salzburg and watched as Ingfrid slowly regained her strength. I loved Salzburg, but any career I might have had was in Vienna. So, when she was recovered, I left her in charge of running the house and managing the household finances. Through my parents' inheritance, I was able to ensure Ingfrid was very financially comfortable. I went back to Vienna.

"You must have had a lot of confidence in your sister," said Géza.

"Ingfrid had a practical side. I was the dreamer, she was the doer. Growing up, our parents called us the perfect pair. But I didn't recognize how vulnerable a girl her age really is. I suppose I saw what I wanted to see. Her grief over the loss of our parents ran very deep, and unlike me, she didn't have the life of a student, studying at a large university, to distract her. In her letters she began to speak of contacting our parents, hearing our father in the silver basin that she would fill with water from the mountain streams and peer into for hours. I grew worried about her and kept in closer touch with our housekeeper, Frau Teicher. After a while, Ingfrid's letters became less and less frequent. Frau Teicher wrote to tell me that a man named Leopold Reiter, from Munich, had taken an interest in Ingfrid. I wrote to Ingfrid about him several times and she seemed to have fallen in love with the man. She knew little about his background, except that he was some kind of distant cousin to the Wittelsbachs on a female line. He took her to several balls and they went on excursions together, always chaperoned by Frau Teicher who reported back to me. Teicher liked the man, generally, but he didn't seem to have a profession or any land to support himself with, so she was wary, and I was too by extension. A few months after it began, Ingfrid wrote to me to ask my permission to marry Leopold.

"That was bold. And what was your response?"

"I withheld my approval, having never met the man, and I was more than a little perturbed that he did not write to me himself. I could hardly have been a secret to him and I was easily reachable by the post at the academy. My second-year finals were closing in and I couldn't go home to Salzburg without losing my place. I asked Frau Teicher to keep an eye on Ingfrid. I didn't think she would do something as foolish as elope, but it worried me. Then, there were no letters for three weeks. I was distraught and barely pulled through my finals. At the first opportunity I was on a train back to Salzburg. When I arrived, no one was at home. The cook told me that Frau Teicher had sent an emergency telegraph to me, but I must have left before I received it. Ingfrid had gone on holiday with friends of my parents and their daughter. It was only after Frau Teicher met the family's housekeeper at the market the next day that she learned the family was not on holiday. She set out at once to find Ingfrid. She had been seen with Leopold two nights before I arrived. Frau Teicher was pursuing them. They were headed in the direction of Munich by coach."

"The man should be brought up on charges," said Géza, shaking his head.

"I took a horse, rode fast through the night, and found them in a mountain village on the road. Frau Teicher, in our family's carriage, had also just found them. I could tell by the route they took that Leopold had kept them away from major towns."

"What happened when you confronted them?"

"Ingfrid, for her part, was half out of her mind with fairytale ideas and thought this was a grand excursion back to Bavaria to see Leopold's homeland and meet his family."

"My God. I don't know if I could have stopped myself from thrashing the man, were it me in your shoes."

"I sent Ingfrid and Frau Teicher home in the carriage that night and stayed behind to confront Leopold."

The two came around the final bend in the maze. The aisle of benches and pillars of trees was much the same as the previous day, but the absence of bright light caused the dark stone of the mausoleum to sink into a self-formed shadow. Hermann turned and looked up at the castle which exuded the same ominous effect. It felt sinister, shadows peeling down the exterior walls and bleeding into the greenery around its base. The windows had turned into black mirrors, save the very few that were backlit by gas lamps. One, to the left on the second floor, vaguely illuminated the figure of Frau Baum in her yellow dress behind a tinge of grey from the glare. She must have realized that Hermann was able to see her, because she quickly stepped away from the window and left the light to flicker in solitude. Hermann turned back and strode over to a bench and sat down.

"I've only spoken about the next part to a few people, Inspector," said Hermann.

"Take all the time you need. What you've told me thus far is that you did your duty by your sister," said Géza as he took a seat at the other end of the bench.

Hermann turned away and knitted his brows together before closing his eyes. He rubbed his temples, catching strands of sandy-blond hair around his fingertips. Then he opened his eyes and continued the story.

"That night at the inn, Leopold Reiter told me that he loved my sister. I pressed him on his unchivalrous behavior. He grew angry at my accusation that he was a cad. He told me that I was the one who should be ashamed, that I was trying to steal Ingfrid's inheritance. Leopold told me that he planned to live in Ingfrid's home, our parents' home, after their elopement and honeymoon. He said Ingfrid had only mentioned me as a brother who lived a separate life. I knew he was lying, but it was then that I realized how vulnerable Ingfrid truly was. Far from leaving her to blossom into a woman with the responsibility of the household, I had put her in a situation where she had no support system, was grief stricken and lonely, and completely vulnerable. Under the circumstances, her sanity had spiraled, hence why she tried to contact our late father from the beyond. I left her alone when she needed me most, and she'd fallen prey to the man's charms. I told Leopold Reiter the truth, that I was the sole inheritor by our father's will. If he loved her, understanding she had nothing of her own, and wished to marry her without a cent to her name, other than what I could allot for her modest dowry, I would approve the marriage after a reasonable period of formal engagement. Needless to say, his feelings of love for her vanished as quickly as he did. Before he left the inn I forced him, under threat of the law, to write her a letter explaining there could never be a future for them."

"The man was a fortune hunter," said Géza.

"The inheritance left by my father wasn't a treasure by any means, which Leopold didn't seem to have understood, and the largest portion of its value lay in the land we rented to tenant farmers in the mountains. I left the inn and caught up with the carriage to escort it back to Salzburg." Hermann paused.

"You did the right thing, to protect her," said Géza.

Hermann hung his head and clenched his hands into fists.

"I thought I'd done the best thing for her. Saved her from embarrassment. I was wrong. So wrong. I tried to explain to her what had happened, but Ingfrid had lost the ability to trust me, to understand. Far from the sharp, practical girl I'd once known, she'd regressed emotionally. After we returned to Salzburg, she was prone to fits of anger and depression. She barely ate and could hardly look at me. I eventually gave her Leopold's letter, hoping it would help her to move on. I'd held it, not sure what to do. I hadn't broken the seal so she would know it was his words. That was my mistake. Far from exposing his designs, he blamed me for forcing him to abandon her. He said he had no choice but to pursue his happiness elsewhere."

"Then he really was a cad. And what of your sister?"

"She entered a dark depression and began to seek our parents' spirits in all kinds of occult rituals and macabre activity. She re-entered mourning, for herself as much as our parents, she told me. The summer came to a close and I had to make a decision, to return to my studies and the promise of a position with the university after graduation or stay and tend to Ingfrid and her anger with me. I contracted a doctor to visit her daily and make a study of her mental condition, to try and improve her over time. She would sometimes have moments of clarity about her behavior, but these were infrequent, and I could tell that my presence seemed to aggravate her condition. Frau Teicher assured me that she, with the doctor's help, would look after Ingfrid. So, in the fall, I returned to Vienna. Things seemed to quiet for a time because neither Frau Teicher nor the doctor reported that her condition was doing anything other than becoming milder, despite her more frequent attempts to contact the dead which had become her only passion. I asked, and the doctor insisted that this was her way of working through her grief and that with enough time she would come out of it."

Géza let out with a deep sigh and ran his hand over his beard.

"Just before Christmas, I attended a ball in Vienna with a girl I had begun to court. While we were there, I saw Leopold Reiter once again, this time at a distance with a young woman who I learned would inherit a small fortune upon the death of her elderly father. I never told Ingfrid or Frau Teicher about this, but somehow Ingfrid discovered it. Teicher said a letter to me had come to the house and described the whole thing. Ingfrid's supposed progress was ruined. The night before Christmas I received an urgent telegram from the doctor saying that Ingfrid was in a raving state and couldn't be placated. He feared for her safety. I dropped everything and went back to Salzburg, but when I arrived, it was the undertaker, not my fair sister who I met."

Hermann wiped tears from his eye with the back of his hand.

"Ingfrid had left the house in the night and gone up to the mountains where our parents had often taken us. She didn't have a coat or gloves or boots and had trudged through the snow for miles. The undertaker said her fingers had shown the first signs of frostbite. She had reached the summit where we once looked over the Hohensalzburg. Her body was found the next morning at the base of the cliff."

"My God, man. I'm so sorry." Géza crossed himself.

Hermann looked skeptically on the motion and for a brief moment he envied Géza his faith in something higher, although after everything Géza had probably seen, it was remarkable his faith was intact.

"I didn't want to subject her to a demeaning sermon about how she had been possessed, had she been buried in a Lutheran cemetery. So, I set aside a plot on an old spot of land outside town that was too rough to be farmed. I think she would have liked to be in the foothills our parents loved so much. After that, I was too ashamed to stay or continue any part of our lives in Salzburg, not for what she had done, but for what I had done. I sold the house and the land and moved permanently to Vienna. I was troubled by dreams and what she'd been doing in the months before her death. She left a journal behind with descriptions of her visions and her attempts to speak not just with our parents, but with other entities that would reach out to her."

"So this is where the paranormal focus began for you?" asked Géza.

Hermann sat up straight and turned to face Géza.

"I felt compelled to understand why Ingfrid thought she had contacted ghosts or spirits. Why in her grief and her longing she sought the dead and felt she had real experiences. I was, and am, convinced that ghosts and spirits are in the mind of the person who wishes to experience such things, consciously or subconsciously. I transferred to the University of Vienna to pursue a degree, where I was able to start my study into the occult. After graduation, I had enough talent and standing with the university to be taken on as an assistant professor to Dr. Kießling in the Department of Philosophy, so that's what I did. It provided me stability and an income to research psychology and paranormal history. I formed a general school of thought around the two and wrote two tomes on the parapsychological. I hope to one day explain or come to the root of the belief in the paranormal, so that no one will suffer as Ingfrid did, nor fall prey to any charlatan selling a message from the dearly departed."

"I admire your perspective, Professor. I'd worried that behind the science, you might have been … less serious than you are. I see now that I was wrong. Forgive me if I doubted you."

Hermann chuckled softly. "Inspector, I've just told you how I study the unexplainable because of my own failure of care for my family, and your response is to apologize. You have to be the most human policeman I've ever met."

"That may be true, but don't let on to any of our suspects."

Hermann laughed, then rose and straightened his jacket. "We'd better get moving, Inspector. There's a crypt to explore and much more to be done before the day's out."

Géza got up as well and gave Hermann a pat on the back. "Well let's get on then. Though you've ferreted out nearly everyone's secrets and helped chase a murderer with me through the bowls of Hell, so please, just call me Géza."

Chapter 17

The anteroom of the mausoleum flickered into an orange, then yellow glow as Géza lit the two kerosine lamps that he'd left on the central stone table some days prior. Hermann took one and used it to scan the walls around the room, backlit by the soft grey light from outside. There were several inscriptions from poetry about the nature of life and death, the peace and serenity of the here-after. Hermann looked back toward the two large doors leading outside. Both had substantial plates of copper attached to their interiors.

"Seems like a waste of metal," said Géza.

"It's to keep any witches or spirits locked inside. They're supposedly repelled by copper."

Géza raised an eyebrow, and Hermann headed for the stairs opposite the doorway. Neither man was able to see very far in front of themselves, even with the lamps, so they made their way down carefully, one step at a time.

"You said there'd been no sign of forced entry when you first investigated?" asked Hermann.

"That's right. The doors were locked, and it didn't seem like anything was out of place, not that there's much to be out of place. These lanterns were over in an alcove, covered in dust."

Hermann noticed that a fine web of roots wound their way across the ceiling of the stairwell, which wasn't very wide. They increased in density the further down the men traversed until, at the end of the stairs, they encircled a key-stone archway which spanned a shallow landing. They had arrived at the mouth of the crypt. Hermann inspected the roots and the arch and saw that it was all made of stone; the roots were not living roots, they were very detailed artistry. Beyond the arch was a long hall, a little less than three meters high by Hermann's reckoning, with alcoves formed at regular intervals down each side. The alcoves were framed by thick-root stonework, descending from the ceiling to the floor. They passed by dozens of them, and Hermann noticed that most of the alcoves hosted a flat slab of stone of the same cutting and dimensions. They were without any writing or marking, though the further down the hall they went, some of the slabs began to show names, dates, and other information, presumably related to their occupants.

Beyond an intersection with further halls to the left and right, they stopped where two alcoves were missing their plaques. Instead, both sat facing out, leaning against the wall beneath each of the dark cavaties.

"Friederich Albert Freiherr von Voitsberg, born 1859, with no death date and space enough for an epigraph," Géza said as he stopped to examine the two. "That's the young freiherr, nephew of the late Georg Freiherr von Voitsberg. And this one reads, Astrid Maria von Voitsberg, born 1859, also without a death date."

"It's a bit macabre to have your tombstone carved before your death, isn't it?" said Hermann.

"This whole place is macabre."

"Frau Kam was right about the place being a confluence of energy," said Hermann.

"How's that?"

"Well, every time someone enters the maze above us, it becomes a kind of twisting path through the afterlife, all leading up to the mausoleum and this crypt. Each passage becomes like a transience of death itself."

The thought of that seemed not to sit well with Géza, considering his sudden frown and disquieted look.

They turned away from the not-as-yet late von Voitsbergs' crypts and continued through the hall. After a minute, they came to a thick archway flanked by stout Romanesque columns. Once they passed through, the style changed from the intricately carved roots of the previous hall to an arcade of Romanesque pilasters with floral designs on their crowns, each straddling alcoves for tombs on either side. All of these recorded names and dates from the recent past, stretching further back, and getting older, as the hall continued. There were more than a dozen von Voitsbergs entombed along each side, accompanied by some who didn't share the family name, presumably branching relations and female lineages. They passed through another intersection of halls where the dates passed between the 1750s to the 1740s.

"Where does this place end?" said Géza.

His question was answered after another minute of walking when the men came into view of the end of the hall.

"I wasn't exactly expecting that," said Hermann.

The men stopped at the edge of a large sarcophagus resting on a white-marble plinth, positioned horizontally to them. Hermann used his lantern to illuminate the monument which had an effigy atop a frieze of reliefs. The effigy was of a man in mail armor beneath plated grieves, gauntlets, bracers, and a semi-pointed helm with an exposed face and continuous nose guard. Long hair trailed under the edges of the helmet and lay over the figure's shoulders. Held in his stone fists were two real weapons, not carved replicas, but actual medieval style weapons. In his right, gripped at the hilt and held over his chest, was a longsword with a fine cross guard and pommel. His left fist crossed over the blade, and in it he held a medieval war hammer, its end rested on his shoulder. The weapon comprised a flat hammer head on one end with a small fist holding a blade on the other.

"Undoubtedly, Gustav Freiherr von Voitsberg," said Hermann. "I can't seem to avoid the gentleman."

"It's quite a coffin," said Géza. "I didn't think they still wore armor in the Great Turkish War."

"They didn't. This is a romanticization of his title and knighthood, presented in Gothic Revival glory as if he was from the twelfth or thirteenth century."

Gustav's name and dates were carved on the lid of the sarcophagus beside his ribcage. Hermann stepped back a pace and lowered the lantern to look at the frieze. There were multiple scenes arrayed lengthwise from left to right. Knights and ladies in medieval attire partaking in various activities, centered on a kind of procession. One figure seemed to be in pain and was carried on a litter while a younger figure was presented with a sword.

"I think this tells the story of Parzival, from the Grail Saga."

"The Holy Grail? As in, the cup Christ drank from at the Last Supper?"

"The very same," Hermann answered as he continued to peruse the scene that trailed around the edges of the sarcophagus.

On the rear side, Parzival was depicted opposite from Gringolet, the horse of Anfortas' Grail Castle who was festooned in drapery bearing the symbol of the Grail. Around them were other people, some singing, maids of the castle playing harps atop clouds, and the old magician, Trevrizent, observing it all as he leaned on a staff from the edge of the sarcophagus.

"Over here is the late freiherr, Georg Friederich Freiherr von Voitsberg, born 1815 and died in 1880," Géza said, facing the alcove behind the head of the sarcophagus.

Hermann went over to the plaque, searching for any outstanding information. There was nothing that differed from any of the others they'd passed on their way in. He made a scan of the area at the end of the hall. Around the sarcophagus there were more plaques in the alcoves opposite, but none of them looked any different. Behind Gustav's sarcophagus, however, was another arched tomb and plaque. Hermann approached it and read aloud.

"Albert Gustav von Voitsberg, born in 1817 and died in 1873." Hermann stooped to look closer, then rubbed his hand over a symbol beneath the engraving. "There's something here."

"What is it?"

"It's a chalice. I think it's the Grail." He inspected it, a lighter stone than that of the rest of the plaque. Hermann fondled the piece and pressed into its center, but nothing moved or could be pried away.

"It was worth a shot to see if there was another passage hidden away down here."

"I'm glad there wasn't," said Géza. "I have no desire to walk in on somebody's tomb."

Hermann smiled. Then, a thought occurred to him, and he crouched down behind Gustav's sarcophagus. He inspected the scene with the horse again and noticed more clearly that the Grail on Gringolet's flank was a lighter stone than the rest of the frieze. He rubbed it with the pad of his thumb, then pressed in, hard. A faint *tink* sounded from within the stone as something started to shift the sarcophagus. Hermann stood up quickly as Géza backed around to the other side. The whole effigy and plinth began to slide slowly to the front with a great amount of scraping and grinding.

"My god, is there no end to the ghastliness this place has to offer?" said Géza.

As the plinth ground to a stop, the men were presented with the secret it was designed to keep for those few who were privy to its existence. Revealed was a black void, cut from within the margins of the plinth that had rested over it.

"Remarkable," said Hermann.

"It's on some kind of cantilever," Géza said, examining the area closely. "They use them to shut down some of the ammunition depots when powder is stored near an armory."

Hermann lowered the lantern into the cavity. "I wonder where it leads? There's no ladder here. Could this be what Andrej had needed the rope and climbing gear for?"

"Listen. There's water down below."

Hermann braced a foot near the edge and cupped his ear. Sure enough, a faint tumbling of water was audible as an echo through the void. "I wonder if this is connected to the bathhouse?"

"There's only one way to find out. We'll have to get down there somehow. Especially if Andrej was planning on it as his last act."

"Géza, before we go rappelling into a dark hole, I think we might be able to learn a little more about this whole place and get an idea of what these passages are exactly."

"How's that?"

"By speaking with someone who lived here and who may have had access to design blueprints and building specifications. This passage was opened from a small button hidden in the frieze's scene, the Grail. The same symbol is here on Albert von Voitsberg's tomb, Georg's younger brother. That means Georg oversaw the inclusion of the passages when the castle was completely rebuilt a few decades ago."

"I see your point. I think we'd better get to Frau Maria Theresa's cottage." Géza shook his head a little, a smile forming on his face, "I'd much rather have a cup of tea and slice of cake with an old woman than jump down a dark hole under a creepy sarcophagus into god-knows-what."

Chapter 18

As the men stepped into the drive of the honey-colored, Baroque cottage, Hermann contemplated the fortune the von Voitsberg family must have possessed to afford the massive estate and the splendorous lifestyle that had accompanied it for centuries. For a cottage, as Astrid had described it, which she shared with her ailing mother, it looked more like a villa from the last century, one of the petite palaces built across the Habsburg domains. It stood two full stories with a shallow gable roof, punctuated by several small dormers. A classical portico covered a large entryway with a Palladian window for a transom light.

An elderly maid opened the door before Géza could knock.

"Who is calling, herren?"

"Inspector Orczy, and Professor Horst, to see Maria Theresa von Voitsberg," said Géza.

The maid looked rather dubiously at them, perhaps contemplating an excuse to shut the door.

"We wish to extend an invitation to her and Frau Astrid to dinner this evening at Schattenturm," Hermann quickly put in.

The maid's expression relaxed, and she pulled the door wide into the hall.

"My mistress is not well, herren. She has a sickness, but she's having one of her good days. I'll show you to the parlor where you can wait for her."

As she led them down the hall, past a great expanse of bare walls with a loosely strung piece of picture wire hanging on both sides, the faint sound of music being played on a pianoforte grew louder. On the left, past the staircase, she ushered them into a room with white molding and burgundy wallpaper beneath the chair rail. There was a very detailed classical mantlepiece of white marble on one side. A fine oriental rug lay over narrowly cut floorboards that hosted several pieces of furniture in a rich, dark stain. A violet chair of plush fabric stood apart from the others, set at an angle to afford a view of the garden beyond the large windows, and a pianoforte was situated in the corner where Astrid was playing. The maid announced them and showed them to two chairs then left the room.

Hermann noticed the music parlor looked out onto a dense Italian garden with a long aisle lined with old hollies of significant height and girth. Beyond the aisle was an open iron gate, supported by stone piers with round, cast-stone caps, through which Hermann spied an armillary and perhaps a stone grotto or other formation. The nearer end of the garden was host to a few geometrically designed beds with various flowers and boxwoods. Along the far wall, hemmed in by hollies, Hermann spotted a tall ginger figure who turned to retrieve some tools, revealing the face of Pavol Soták.

Looking up at their entrance, Astrid von Voitsberg moved in a smooth procession from the bench of the pianoforte to where they stood, to greet them. She was wearing a deep periwinkle dress with a frilled cravat about the collar. The ensemble's pleated skirt was cross-folded into a neat fan shape rising over her bustle. Her ashen-blond hair was piled into a swirled bun with two braided lengths looping down while her fringe had been tightly curled into ringlets that twined in and out of her hairline as they cascaded around her face. Her high cheekbones reflected the light from the garden window and showed off the shine in her silvery-grey eyes.

"Good afternoon, herren. I didn't expect to see you so soon after our last meeting, Herr Horst. Have you come to enquire about a particular piece down at the shop?" She held out her hand in greeting to Hermann.

Hermann crossed to her and lightly gripped her hand, giving a bow at the neck.

"No, frau, though I should like another pass through if you would allow. As a bachelor, I'm afraid I've terribly neglected the interior decorating at my apartment in Vienna. I welcome your thoughts on what I might do to furnish it comfortably."

Géza cleared his throat.

"However, at the moment, Inspector Orczy and I have come to speak with your mother, Frau Maria, and to extend to you both an invitation to dinner at Schattenturm this evening."

Astrid winced. "It's not every day that you're extended an invitation to dine at your own home, is it? Well, not my home anymore." She turned toward Géza. "Inspector, how do you do? It must be fairly serious, what you have to ask my mother, if the police are required."

"We only need to understand some of the particulars of the house's construction, frau. Your mother is the last family member in the county who would have had a hand in Schattenturm at that time," Géza said.

She smiled. "I should have thought you would ask one of my ancestors about the history of the castle."

"Frau?" For a brief moment Géza wondered if she knew they'd just come from examining the von Voitsberg crypt. His shoulder muscles tensed involuntary. Hermann hid an ever-so-slight smile as he looked away toward the view of the garden.

"I've heard that Herr Baum's mother-in-law is some kind of necromancer. Who better to answer your questions than the dead? I fear my mother will be a poor substitute for some of the stories they might tell you."

"As it happens," began Hermann, "there's only been one spirit willing to come forward so far. He's been rather hesitant. I think the von Voitsberg family secrets are still safe."

Astrid looked at Hermann for a moment, a faint look of annoyance playing across her sculpted features. "And who might this spirit have been, Professor?" She motioned for the men to sit across from her as she took her own spot.

"According to my séance companion, and her spirit guide, his name is Fridolin."

She replied with a slight crook of her head. "What's this about a spirit guide? Forgive me if I'm not up to date on the latest trends of modern spiritualists."

It was Géza's turn to stifle a smile.

"A spirit guide is a kind of conduit that a person's unconscious mind manifests ... in order to help their conscious mind make sense of information or memories that they might otherwise suppress. Some feel that the spirit guide, usually manifesting as a departed family member or close friend, can attune the mind to information that we knowingly, or most often unknowingly, dismiss in the waking world. Though, naturally, the whole concept is fraught with competing theories, and whether such things exist at all, even as inventions of the mind."

Astrid held his eye contact, nodding at intervals. "And can the person who believes they have a spirit guide reveal genuine information about the beyond?"

"More like they'll reveal details that they would've missed in their waking life, but which the mind made a record of nonetheless."

"Fascinating," she said, "to know something, but not know it until it's told to you by your own mind."

The door to the parlor opened again and the maid waited as a small woman in a light-brown dress with golden lacework entered, leaning heavily on a rosewood walking cane.

"Frau Maria Theresa von Voitsberg," the maid announced.

Her shock of white hair was loosely bound in a simple bun while her face hardly seemed to match the age her hair foretold. She had only faint wrinkles across her square-shaped face and deep smile lines. Her dark-blue eyes were obscured by her stature and her need of a handkerchief to cough into every so often as she made her way into the parlor. Both men rose to greet the woman who delicately folded her handkerchief and tucked it up her left sleeve as she neared them.

"Good afternoon, herren," she said, looking over both men for a moment before exhaling and moving to sit in what was obviously *her* chair. "My maid tells me that you're here to ask me a few questions?"

"And to invite us to dinner at the castle," Astrid put in, though she was looking at Hermann.

"Really? I think that will be quite impossible. The infirm rarely travel, lest they miss the ferryman." She gave a low chuckle that turned into a rasp.

Astrid looked away.

"We apologize for the inconvenience, frau," Géza began. "We wouldn't have troubled you had we known you weren't in a position to–"

"Oh nonsense. I might be half gone, but I can still walk and talk at least. The latter of which I already gather you wish to do a great deal of." Another cough. "It's been ages since anyone besides Astrid has wanted to talk to this old widow. Annika?" she said, holding up her hand in a bit of twirl. "Bring us a coffee service and some of that millirahm-strudel that Marta made."

"Yes, frau," said the maid before leaving the parlor.

"So, you two are—," she paused to let the men fill in the space.

"Professor Hermann Horst."

"Inspector Orczy Géza."

"And what do you want to ask me?"

Géza shifted and learned forward. "We want to ask you about the construction of Schattenturm. We thought you may know a great deal about it."

"Someone still alive to remember it you mean," she said with a smile. "Indeed, I am though. Oh, to remember back to those days, Astrid. When your father was so full of enthusiasm. I remember the way he looked at me as we danced together in the ballroom for the first time." She laughed. "There wasn't even any music, but the builders had just finished, and it was such a moment!"

A coughing fit caused her to nearly double over for a minute. Astrid clutched her mother's forearm until she regained her composure. She waved her handkerchief a little as she said she was fine.

"Frau Maria," said Hermann. "It seems that you and your husband were a part of the evolution of Schattenturm. Were you living in the castle at the time?"

"Of course they were," Astrid butted in. "My father's designs were hardly going to build themselves without his guidance."

Frau Maria nodded. "Frau Astrid is right. It was my husband's dream to turn that old fortress into something worthy of the age."

"Really. Herr *Albert's* dream? Not the freiherr's?" said Hermann.

"Dear oh dear, Herr Horst," said Frau Maria. "We'd better start at the beginning."

Hermann exchanged a look with Astrid. He could only describe her expression as one of pride—perhaps in what was about to be shared? He leaned forward to better hear Frau Maria.

"Schattenturm wasn't always the grand palace it is today. It started out as a castle that changed hands many times over the years, from one lord to another, Christian to Moslem, until Gustav Freiherr von Voitsberg gained his title at the end of the Great Turkish War, about 1700. The estate passed relatively unchanged down the generations, more decrepit with each, until it reached Georg and his younger brother Albert, my late husband. Albert was a brilliant student of architecture, mathematics, and literature. He studied at the University of Freiburg. He took what he had learned and, with the financial backing of the vast family fortune, started a grand renovation around 1850. It was a monumental effort, to be sure. Men worked night and day on the construction. The great keep alone took two years to complete, and the ballroom required a carpenter to be brought in from Brandenburg to supervise laying the flooring in the ballroom. Albert continuously worked on the designs, even heading his own engineering company for a time, to make it possible."

She paused to let another coughing fit pass. "I was able to see the last five or six years of work which mostly focused on the finer parts of the detailing like the paneling and acquiring the artwork. Fortunately, most of the artwork and objects d'art were in mine and my husband's names, so the bank didn't have purview over them in the sale of the estate."

Géza, stopping his note-taking briefly, asked, "And did his designs include hidden halls, passageways, to move about the castle unseen?"

"Oh yes, he was such a romantic. With the new parts of the castle merging with and encasing the old, it was practically impossible not to have hidden passageways."

"Are they recorded or mapped out?" asked Hermann.

"No, what fun would that be? Albert didn't even tell many people they existed. I knew of them, of course, and the twins when they were little loved to incorporate them into their playing."

Astrid shot her mother a sideways glance, but Frau Maria was already on to her next recollection.

"When I wasn't caring for the twins, Astrid and her brother Friederich, Albert and I took trips across the empire, Germany, the Low Countries, France, and Italy to acquire the collections of furniture, artwork, carpets ..."

She gave a little wave of her hand. "What a terrible shame that it's all lost to Schattenturm now."

Astrid looked down and to the side, brows knitted, a mix of disgust and sadness, Hermann supposed. Frau Maria just sighed with a rattle and shook her head.

Hermann took the opportunity to give the narrator a brief break from speaking. "Frau Astrid, I didn't realize you were a twin."

"Yes. I was born first, but of course Friederich inherited the title," she said with a faint smile. "He is at present part of the Landwehr, stationed somewhere near the border with Serbia, according to his last letter."

Géza noiselessly scrawled in his notebook.

"Forgive me, but is it not unusual that a younger brother would invest so much time and effort in a home that will be inherited away to his older brother's progeny?"

"Father had an understanding with Uncle Georg that my brother, Friederich, or me if something happened to Friederich, would inherit. Uncle Georg's lifestyle wasn't conducive to familial sustainability." The right side of Astrid's mouth drew in like a dimple and she shook her head slightly.

"He was a playboy, my brother-in-law," Frau Maria put in. "He enjoyed partying, to be the center of attention. Running an estate and managing finances never meshed with that reality. My Albert was the rock that held all of it … us … together, especially before the crash of '73."

"That was when things turned over?" asked Géza.

"When they started to," Frau Maria responded. "The brothers were opposites you see. Growing up, Albert was dutiful and stuck to his studies, learned what the household needed to stay in working order, and formed a good relationship with his father's agents. Being the oldest, Georg wasn't expected to have a career, you must understand, and so with lack of responsibility and endless money to entertain himself, he became a playboy. He used his allowance to travel, partying and gambling, while Albert went into the military and distinguished himself as an officer."

"The late Herr Georg matches the reputation I've read about Schattenturm, but he hardly seems the type to have cared about its reconstruction or to have spent resources on it," said Hermann.

"When their father died, Albert and Georg came to an arrangement. Georg knew he could never manage the estate or the money, and Albert was conveniently able and willing to do it all. This freed Georg to continue his lifestyle. The only involvement Georg insisted upon was completely overhauling the staff. He didn't like his father's core of servants. Georg placed his trusted and loyal valet, Fürth, in the supreme role of butler and gave Albert free rein to manage everything. Things went well from there. Albert began the renovations and Georg began to build his reputation as the biggest and most extravagant host in the empire. I was introduced to Albert at one of his brother's great parties, by a friend of mine who I was visiting after she'd gotten married. I was practically a spinster, over thirty, but Albert loved me all the same. He courted me and I visited Schattenturm often. Before long, we were married and settled in the eastern hall. Our rooms overlooked the maze that Albert had begun. He designed the whole network of intertwining walkways with the mausoleum at the center, a respectful acknowledgement of the generations of ancestors who were the genesis of the family."

Géza looked up from his note-taking. "He designed and built the mausoleum?"

"Yes."

"And the crypt underneath it?"

"Yes. I'm not sure how extensive it is, but he had all the family moved there, and I suspect, I'll be there too before long."

"Don't speak like that, mother. Your health will return, you're still young. Besides, those people might not even let us into the mausoleum, much less let us be buried there."

"Nonsense, Astrid. My cancer is terminal. There's no need to pretend otherwise. It's all right, dear. I've had a good life. And we *will* be buried there, it was a condition of the sale."

Astrid rose from her chair and went to stand near the window. Hermann noticed that she was watching something outside in the garden, perhaps Pavol, the gardening assistant.

The awkward tension was broken when the maid entered with a coffee set and portions of sliced millirahmstrudel on a serving plate. She laid out the setting on the low table, amongst the party, and poured each of the first cups. She carefully prepared Frau Maria's cup with cream and sugar before handing it to her.

"Frau Maria, may I ask what happened that caused Schattenturm to be turned over in sale?" Hermann asked.

Frau Maria sat back in her chair and let her saucer and cup rest on her lap. "What happened is what always happens when any spoiled child has unfettered control with no limits ... complete ruin. Georg was a moody and selfish man. As much as Georg loved his brother and respected him, after Albert died, no one else mattered but himself. He didn't care about loss of face, others' feelings, or what tomorrow would bring. Georg refused to let me manage the finances or hire an agent to do what Albert had done. He spent money right and left as fast as he could. After a while, I noticed that some of the art had started to thin out. Then, the staff dwindled ... not the core staff, but anyone that could be spared.

"Was Andrej a servant at that time?" asked Géza.

"Ah, yes, I'll get to that in a minute. Ultimately, I started to receive word from my friends at court who knew the true extent of what Georg had done. They were concerned for Friederich, Frau Astrid's brother. Unbeknownst to me, Georg was selling off the productive land that earned an income for the estate. His debts had grown beyond any hope of repayment. He'd been accustomed to throwing large sums from savings at the bankers after the crash of '73 and Albert's death, however, his ability to do that must have been substantially limited, along with most of his credit. Toward the end of his life he seemed to take on a different character entirely, and at some point I went away with the twins to live near my family. From his letters, and during the few occasions when we visited him, we saw things were very different at Schattenturm. Although most of the staff had gone, he'd taken on a new gardener and seemed quite pleased with the young man and his ideas. This was Andrej. I don't think there was any real money to implement any of those designs he talked about since the grounds have changed little since my husband's days."

"Could you speak about the will?" asked Hermann. "I've heard that some of the staff were kept on after Herr Georg's death, including Andrej. How was that possible if he was in debt?"

"I can answer that, Herr Horst," said Astrid as she turned away from the window. "Since it was Herr Friederich and I who executed the will and took inventory of Uncle Georg's estate and debts."

Frau Maria noticed that the maid had lingered. "Thank you, Annika, I shall ring if we need anything."

The maid gave a shallow curtsy and left the parlor.

"Herr Friederich and I were able to get some of the debts waved ... more or less. Uncle Georg had kept some records on what his guests had gotten up to at his parties over the years. Some of those guests were also his creditors, and they were willing to excuse the debts for ... old time's sake. Others weren't so generous. We also discovered an old investment my father had established and kept secret from my uncle, it had earned moderately well. Then, after a large sale of some of the furniture and art, we accumulated additional cash. All of this amounted to enough to keep on the three senior staff and the gardener, for a few years, at half rate, with enough left for minimal repairs to the house. None of us needed to live the way our uncle had, so we were able to use what remained more wisely. Unfortunately, it didn't matter in the end as there wasn't enough to cover the entire debt against the estate. We thought the bank would allow us to maintain possession and chip away at it, but they had a sudden turn of position and took possession of the estate to cancel out the debts. We were allowed to stay on in the dowager's cottage for the remainder of my mother's life and to keep a few family possessions for which we had provenance proving they were purchased by my father with his own money."

"Ah, the items in the antique's gallery," said Hermann.

Géza paused in his note-taking. "I didn't realize that Andrej had you to thank for preserving his position. He and the other staff must have been very grateful."

"Andrej was never grateful for anything," Astrid said, with a hint of a sneer. "Though Frauen Schrode and Kovács certainly were."

"And Herr Fürth?"

Astrid smiled faintly. "Fürth has always been loyal to the von Voitsberg family. He was honored to have been retained."

"Fürth lives for Schattenturm," said Frau Maria. "I'm not sure it's possible for him to leave now, even if he wanted to."

"When you say that Andrej was never grateful for anything, Frau Astrid, what do you mean?" Géza asked.

Astrid and Frau Maria passed a momentary look. Astrid pursed her lips, then looked like she was about to say something when her mother let out with a sudden, particularly bad coughing spell. The lady had doubled over with her handkerchief pressed tightly against her face as convulsive heaves shook her.

"Frau, are you alright? Should I send for a doctor?" asked Géza.

"No," Frau Maria choked out. "I'll be fine. I just need to catch my breath. Astrid, fetch me some water, please?" Frau

Maria regained her composure and sat up straight, smoothing the creases in her dress.

"Are you sure you're well enough to continue?" asked Hermann. He leaned back in his chair before taking a sip of coffee.

Frau Maria gave a smile and then a nod. "Andrej was brought on by Herr Georg a few years before his death. I had left by then with the twins. I'm not sure where he'd come from, but he made a positive impression on an old man nearing the end."

Frau Astrid returned with the water. "After we lost the estate, he worked here at the dowager's cottage in the garden on occasion, later his assistant took over," she said.

Frau Maria seemed restored somewhat after a sip of water and continued. "I remember when we visited that he always had a poor look about himself. It wasn't a surprise when I learned from some of the women in the county that he'd become notorious at cards and in the Gypsy camps. I asked Herr Fürth about that, but Fürth told me that Andrej had Herr Georg's ear and couldn't be gotten rid of." She chuffed. "Herr Friederich and Frau Astrid told me that his position was even mentioned in Herr Georg's will. It was sad to see my brother-in-law had been taken in by his false charm. You know the type, herren? Well, anyway, it's not for a lady to elaborate on such things." She smiled. "He was terribly arrogant, that much I will say. Though it's been the shock of the county for weeks now, I can't say Herr Fehér's death was out of character for his personality and his life-style."

"That's been the picture everyone has drawn of the man, frau. Though, even scoundrels should generally enjoy the freedom from being murdered." Hermann sighed. "Inspector Orczy, I think we've taken up enough of the frauen's time today. Did you have anything else?"

"No, Professor. That should cover it."

"Well then, let's be off."

The two rose, and Astrid followed to see them off.

"We'll see you at dinner then, Frau Astrid?" asked Hermann.

"I wouldn't miss it. Bis dann."

Hermann gave a short bow to both women.

Before they left the parlor, Géza stopped short and turned round. "Apologies, but just one more question. Frau Astrid, do you know what Herr Baum paid for Schattenturm? It must have been a very sizable amount, I would think."

"My brother and I were not privy to any of the details of the negotiation between the bank and Herr Baum. But yes, for the bank to succumb to Herr Baum's pressure and suddenly shift their course and throw us out on our ears, it must have been a vast sum."

Chapter 19

The men walked the short distance back to Schatten-turm beneath a thick stand of beeches before entering the clearing that lay in front of the castle's rise and the lake at its base. Upon close observation as they approached on foot, Hermann noted obvious signs of decay; the estate had fallen into disrepair. There were pinnacles missing on dormer points, patched slate on the roof's tiles, and more than a few places where vines and scrub had made a colony and begun to advance up the walls and out onto the lawn which was irregularly shorn, perhaps only tended to by rotating livestock. The lake was certainly pretty enough, though it was more like an irregular, crescent-shaped pond. The willow tree that Rachel had mentioned that morning stood near an outcropping of stone. It was easy to identify for the empty easel and chair underneath. A tendriled branch of the willow swayed back and forth in the wind. Hermann noticed that Rachel was nowhere in sight.

Before they reached the gatehouse, they stepped off the road suddenly, very close to the precipice of the hill above the maze three terraces below. A small black carriage dashed toward them from the castle, a coachman whipping his switch back and forth for the horse to keep up its speed, despite the turn. It was quickly beyond them. A few moments later they reached the door to the keep where Fürth appeared in the doorway to receive them.

Géza was first to address the old butler. "Who the devil was that? Their carriage nearly ran us over."

"That was Herr Baum on urgent business. He regrets to inform you both that he will not be at dinner this evening." Fürth had nearly slackened his entire lower face into a frown.

"A pity," said Hermann as he removed his gloves. "I would so like to have heard about Herr Baum and Frau Astrid's mutual interest in Schattenturm tonight when she comes for dinner."

Fürth's frown immediately shifted into a look of surprise as his mouth formed the shape of an 'O' and his bushy eyebrows parted like a perpendicular pair of doors above his blue-green eyes.

"Frau Astrid has been invited to dinner? Here?" he asked.

"Yes, an impromptu invitation from Frau Baum this morning, though I'm sure Frau Schrode has already been made aware. Inspector Orczy and I just came from Frau Maria's cottage to relay the invitation which was accepted … although sadly, Frau Maria is not able to attend with Frau Astrid. Fürth, is there a problem?"

The butler snapped out of his shock and resumed his bust-like pose.

"No, herr. The arrangements will be in order for this evening."

"What kind of business drew Baum away so suddenly, *Herr* Fürth?" asked Géza.

Fürth barely turned to address Géza, though he did squint slightly. "It is not my place to question Herr Baum about his affairs. Only to ask when he might return, which he couldn't say, and whether I should have a destination recorded if anything were amiss on his trip, which he declined. If I may," he said with a short bow at the neck before turning on his heel and marching back inside.

"I swear, every minute I spend with these people is like another meter trod toward Hell," Géza said, after Fürth had left.

"He's a bit tight collared, especially considering he serves Baum who isn't exactly from the gentleman class in the whole social hierarchy," said Hermann.

"Baum's sudden departure may be more fortunate than it appears," said Géza.

"Oh, how's that?"

Géza cast a look upward, beyond the mezzanine, to the double doors beyond. "What was it you said earlier, 'Sometimes men tell us the important things in what they don't say'?"

"Ah, I get your meaning."

———————————◆———————————

After a quick wait in the second story of the library, Géza met Hermann with a small canvas pack which he unrolled to reveal a set of picks and hooks.

"An inspector with a thief's lockpicks. You surprise me," Hermann said with a chuckle.

"You have to know both sides of the law sometimes. Come on, let's get this moving."

The two made their way back to the mezzanine outside the double doors. Hermann gave a look over the banister to see or hear if anyone was about.

"Have we tried the knob yet to see if it's actually locked?" asked Hermann.

Géza tried it. "Definitely locked."

He took two picks from his fold and began to insert and manipulate them at various angles to unlock the lever device within. Hermann couldn't help but feel uneasy with two long stretches of hall afore and behind them, with the keep echoing every little tinkering and scratch coming from the picks. At last, there was a satisfying, low *click* within the lock, and Géza was able to open the door. The two hurried inside, and Hermann shut the door behind them, careful not to make much noise.

Herr Baum's office was a long, rectangular room with a set of glass French doors on the opposite side, flanked by two large windows. The outline of a handrail beyond gave away the presence of a balcony facing south over the lake and the main drive. A large desk, with wide banks of internal drawers on the front and rear sides, loomed in the middle of the room. There was a gilded blotter, inkwell, and pen standing apart from the otherwise very disorganized stacks of files and papers littered around the edges of the desk. The rest of the office was in a similar state of chaos. A secretary's station on the wall had its doors hanging open with bits of paper and letters stuffed in cubbyholes and laying across the folded-down face. There were filing cabinets with more papers and some leather portfolios strewn on their tops next to a seating area. A coffee table that hosted a pot and cups for three hadn't been cleared in some time. The liquor stand in the far corner by the right window was conspicuously low on supply, indicating Herr Baum's consumption habit. A curious machine, in the opposite corner on a stand-alone table, began to whir and print out a line of morse code onto a reel that cascaded out of its endpiece with no one to catch it or tear it off. There was another machine, a box with wires and a little funnel-shaped piece hanging on a hook, positioned halfway up the wall with a cord connecting to the mechanism that fed the telegraph printer its orders.

"Good God," said Géza as he looked around. "The man's an utter slob. How can he run a business this way?" He strode over to the desk and began to pick through the documents on one of the corners. "Letters from a year ago. Bank notes that've been scrawled through." Géza moved to another pile. "What's this?"

He read silently to himself as Hermann poked through other piles.

"He's got blackmail on a peer. He's threatened him with exposure if he doesn't lobby for a new rail station that Baum is to build outside Preßburg. No wonder he never let me in here."

"That could explain his attitude," said Hermann. "Though it isn't what we're after. At least I don't think so. Géza, look for anything that doesn't fit the pattern of disorganized chaos."

The men stood and scanned the room.

"Everything is given to haphazardness," said Géza.

"Not everything," said Hermann. "Look at that shallow map dresser, near the seating arrangement. There's not so much as a speck of dust on it." When Hermann tried to open the drawers, he found that each of them were locked.

"Those are locked, and so is this drawer in his desk," said Géza. "The pattern you were looking for, Professor?"

"Do you think you can get them open with your kit?"

Géza took out some very small, brass hooks and picks and started to work on the bottom desk drawer first. It took a great deal of patience, but eventually a faint *click* signaled his success. Géza pulled out a small bunch of papers and gave half of them to Hermann. Then, he pulled out a revolver.

"Fully loaded," said Géza, after pressing the cylinder release.

"You think he's expecting trouble out here?"

"I don't know, but keeping it in a locked drawer in a locked room doesn't point to him feeling in danger."

Géza passed the gun to Hermann who noted that it was new, an import from America based on the brand, like the gun that Josef had described that morning at breakfast—an effective weapon. He put the gun down on the desk and spun the barrel away from them, then began scanning the papers Géza had handed him.

"February fourth," Géza read aloud. "Mine accident outside Deutschendorf-Poprád. Twelve dead. Ten injured. There seems to have been an investigation."

"This is much the same," Hermann said as he flipped through the stack, "but from three weeks ago, here in Salgótarján. Three dead and two injured. The stakeholders of Baum's company are demanding an inquest across all mines based on the next letter from his secretary in Budapest."

"I see. This one here talks about a Count someone or other, with a rival steel mill in Budapest and another in Vienna. Baum's secretary says he's been writing to parliament and spreading gossip about the mine accidents. That Baum's coal mines are a public health hazard."

"I wonder if this has anything to do with his sudden departure?" said Hermann.

"I'd bet on it. Something like this could ruin him or his company, if enough bad press spread about it."

"Let's try the map dresser. It may have more information about the whole business."

Géza restacked the papers and put them back the way he'd found them. He removed his lockpicks, and began work on the map dresser's drawers. After a few minutes, he had each of them opened and ready for inspection.

Most of the maps were of Baum's mines. However, the last document, in the last drawer, was a wrinkled, yellowed piece of paper. Just as Hermann pulled it out to examine it, the telegraph machine on the other side of the room began to whir away again and print off another message.

"I'll go see what that's all about," said Géza.

Hermann studied the document in his hand. It was a sort of informal receipt and status update on repairs to Schattenturm during Albert von Voitsberg's time. "What's this doing here with the mine maps?"

"What is it?" asked Géza.

"This document, it talks about the expansion of a vault here on the property. It's an update by the job foreman to Albert von Voitsberg. It reads, 'Herr Albert, Another four meters squared of floorspace has been cleared. Enough for a walk-in vault with shelving. As you instructed, the excavation dirt and debris have been discarded discreetly to avoid detection. The bill will be amended and passed on to your office in due time. My man and I are the only ones who are aware of this work.'" He lowered the paper. "Have you heard anything about a vault before?"

"Not at all. Though this," he held up the telegraph message, "brings up questions of its own. It's a message from Budapest I'd wager." He pulled the roll taunt. "'Have you left yet? Stop. Send word as soon as you reach the station. Stop.' He pulled through the roll to find more. 'Can't stop the story. Stop. Must have confirmation on information for our friend. Stop. Return to Budapest. Stop. Shareholders getting spooked. Stop.' Géza pulled through to another message. 'Account empty. Stop. Tried you on the tele-phone. Stop. Need an answer about revenue. Stop.'"

"Well," said Hermann, "we may have discovered why Baum wanted this house after all. This document is at least several decades old and was addressed to Herr Albert von Voitsberg during the renovations of the castle. If he had a vault built somewhere on the estate, to hide assets from his money-squandering brother, it could explain part of the family's downturn. A stash that Herr Albert took to the grave?"

"What? Oh, right. A supposed hidden treasure," said Géza.

"And if the builders knew about it, then maybe there was a rumor? Baum may have gotten wind of it."

"Well, if this telegraph message is any indication, an unknown stash would be very welcome right about now," said Géza.

"Exactly. It could explain his interest in the estate, and judging by the bank's sudden change in the debt management plan, it sounds like Baum applied a certain amount of pressure. Or, he may have heard about it after he bought the place ..."

"If these messages are to be believed, Baum is in serious financial difficulty." Géza's voice was elevating along with a look of evident satisfaction. "And if that hole under the sarcophagus is the entrance to the vault, it points to Baum killing Andrej before he could get to it! These telegrams and that piece of paper may be the very evidence I need to arrest him!"

"Hold on, Géza. We don't know that the space under the sarcophagus is the vault, or that it contains a stash of money or valuables. We have to explore the crypt. And that still doesn't give us a full motive."

"How can it not?" Géza said as his dark eyebrows started to knit together. "Pavol and Schrode both said Andrej and Baum argued, even the day of his death. Andrej was a known cheat and would have certainly been after any lost money in the house, and now we know that Baum would've been as well. Baum could have gone down the passage in the armory which is near enough to his bedroom, and headed off Andrej in the maze."

"We need more proof."

"Damnit ... You're right. But I'm sure it's Baum."

"It could be, but if the only motive is to get to a hidden vault first, a lot of people would have a motive. Including Pavol Soták. Don't forget the map I found in his sketch book. Is one of the *openings in the rock* the vault? I think he knows what Andrej was after that night when he went to the mausoleum with the climbing gear. Its time he tells us everything he knows, including what his relationship with Rachel Baum is all about. Will he be back at his cottage by now?"

Géza pulled out his pocket watch. "He should be, or soon enough. He's usually in by half past five."

"Then let's get down there."

They left Johan Baum's office the way they found it, minus a few key documents and headed for the groundskeeper's cottage.

The two walked downstairs, past the ornately carved paneling lining the first-floor halls, then down to the working level and out through the north end of the castle nearest the stables. With each step Hermann took through the grand house, he thought about Albert von Voitsberg and his romantic vision to create a modern, elegant home that celebrated the Teutonic history of his family and the castle itself. He was a man of deep feeling and passionate spirit. His wife and his children, Frau Astrid at any rate, reflected the same passionate sentiment for the home that they could now only watch deteriorate from a distance. What pain must Frau Astrid and her brother, Herr Friederich, suffer to have lost everything to a man like Baum, and to be reduced to such a state as they were now?

As the long rays of the deepening, spring afternoon light stretched through the trees, the path and woods were cast in an ominous coral luminescence with intensely contrasted shadows against the leafy floor beneath the oaks and beeches. The workers' cottages glowed against their black timbering. Only a few sounds could be heard from the vicinity of two or three that were occupied by temporary tenants who worked for Baum's business. They spotted Pavol Soták carrying a shovel and shears with a bag slung over his shoulder, heading up from a path between his cottage and the one next door. He saw the two men in turn and dropped his tools beside a small shed, along the side of his cottage, but kept hold of the bag which had a fresh, dark stain soaking through the bottom.

"Pavol, how are you? We need a minute to talk with you," Hermann announced when they were a few paces away.

The thin, ginger-haired youth just nodded, grimly.

"Pavol," Hermann began, "we need to know more about what you know of Andrej and who at the house he was connected to, and what he did on the grounds when he wasn't working. We've learned of some troubling information, including that he was involved in an improper relationship with Frau Baum. Did you know he assaulted her?"

Pavol's eyes grew wide and the muscles in his face and neck tensed.

"Come on, you shared a house with him. You must have known something about it," said Géza.

"I didn't know that he hurt her," he said, in his thick Slovak accent. "I knew that he was always giving her things. Some things she asked for and others that she didn't. She was always happy with them."

Hermann and Géza looked to each other for clarification, but there was obviously none to be had.

"What do you mean, that Andrej gave things to Frau Baum?" asked Géza.

"Strange things, herr. Old books that he bought in the traveling camps. Trinkets. Then, she started asking for game birds and rabbits. He thought that was funny."

"You mean for the cook?" said Géza.

"No, I don't think so, said Pavol, looking away.

"When did this begin, Pavol?" asked Hermann.

Pavol shifted uncomfortably before answering. "It started a few months after they all moved into the big house. The frau was out and Andrej met up with her. They started doing that a lot. The frau thought he was clever, and he thought he was clever for it too. He bragged to me once when he was drunk that he'd told her all about the big house. Where all of the secret fun places were. He also said he'd tell her ghost stories about the house and the family, the von Voitsbergs, that used to live there. He knew because the old freiherr told him things."

"What did she need with the books and the animals?" pressed Hermann.

"It wasn't right, I told her that. You're not supposed to play with things like that. There was an old woman near our village back home, but she got run off after she killed a woman with her magic."

"What on earth are you talking about, boy?" said Géza.

"One of the books, Andrej said it was full of spells, that'd it'd be fun for her to have with the old woman when they do … whatever it is they do up there. She told me that it was all for a joke, but I tried to warn her. Then, Andrej stopped giving her things, stopped talking to her so much, too. I don't know why, but Andrej said it was *to protect what's mine*. He never explained it. After that, she came to me, asking for things. It was simple enough at first, herbs and such, but after a while she wanted dead things. Birds, rabbits, and last she asked me for a deer's head. I never gave her any game animals after she asked for the deer's head. I've tried to warn her about this, but she's stubborn."

The lad looked down and kicked the dirt. He slouched, like he was trying to make himself small, despite his height.

"Pavol, I don't understand," said Hermann. "Did Erzsébet continue to receive these things from Andrej, or did the gifts stop before he died?"

"Frau Erzsébet?" The boy looked puzzled.

"Yes, Pavol," Géza interjected. "Did the frau continue to ask Andrej for dead animals and such until he died?"

Pavol began to kick the dirt again and refused to look up. To Hermann, he looked like a boy years younger, but he was outwardly a teenager. Half a lifetime of cruel treatment by Andrej and isolation from anyone with half a heart had worn the lad down into a mockery of a young man.

Hermann reached out and put a hand on his shoulder. "Pavol, I know that you've had a relationship ongoing with Fraulein Rachel."

Pavol looked up, his hazel eyes meeting Hermann's.

"Don't worry. You're not in any trouble and you're not going to be in any trouble. You needn't worry about protecting her reputation. We need to know the full truth. Was Frau Baum, Erzsébet, upset enough with Andrej to have wanted him harmed?"

"The frau was very upset, yes. Andrej told me a few weeks ago how she had screamed at him, calling him a bastard. The way he talked about it made it seem like he would have hurt her. I didn't want that, so I ... I warned him not to. He hit me for that, but not as hard as he could've done."

"Was that all Pavol?" asked Hermann.

"She told Andrej off for teasing her mother. I think she was a little jealous when Andrej started to give her mother flowers for her vases and show her around the gardens."

Hermann was taken aback for a moment, and judging by the look on Géza's face, so was he, with his thick brows practically joining into one black line.

At the end of the worker's village, just beyond the last cottage, Rachel Baum appeared from a side path that led through the woods. Sitting tall in the saddle, her horse held its head high and pawed the ground in fluid, dressage-like motions as it had been trained to do. Upon spotting the three men, standing close together talking, she stopped her horse but stayed at the edge of the clearing watching the men. Pavol looked past the professor to watch her.

"Are you saying that it was Frau Erzsébet that wanted the dark things from Andrej?" said Géza. "Or that it was Fraulein Rachel? And that one of them threatened Andrej after he stopped?"

Hermann followed Pavol's eye to where Rachel had appeared and lingered on her horse.

"Yes," he said.

"For god's sake man! Yes it was Frau Erzsébet or yes it was Fraulein Rachel?"

"It was the young frau that wanted the black magic things ..."

It was clear that an unspoken message had been transmitted to Pavol, and that it wasn't anything pleasant or benign. Rachel steered her horse sharply away. She glanced back over her shoulder briefly at Hermann, Géza, and Pavol, then she kicked her horse into a canter. Her dark riding habit flowed with the motion of the horse as they disappeared down the trail, back towards the castle.

———————————◆———————————

Hermann caught Géza by the arm as they began their return to the house. They had elected to avoid the same path they'd taken out to the cottages, near the stables, and instead went the long way round to the east, skirting the maze to come back through the gatehouse.

Géza vented as they walked along the trail. "I've suspected that Johan Baum was the murderer for the better part of two weeks and the evidence about his business and him knowing about a possible treasure in this place, plus his confrontations with Andrej, all seem to confirm it. However, now I have to consider that a teenage girl may have motive for the murder and that she might be a witch. A girl who might've killed Andrej for frustrating her efforts, whatever those might be. And that damned boy, Pavol, who knew it all along and said nothing. Is he playing us for fools? Is he still hiding something? He too has motive to have killed Andrej. How am I supposed to bring this to my commanding officer? I'm no further along than when I started, and now I've uncovered dangerous facts about the family of one of the most important men in Hungary. Facts which could get me sacked at best and disappeared into the prison system at worst should Baum have the political sway that his papers seem to suggest."

Hermann saw how tired he looked, shoulders slumped, deep frown lines, and circles appearing under his eyes. "Géza, we have a line of suspects, each of whom has withheld information to varying degrees, sometimes through purposeful omission if not actually lying. Of these, we have a pretty good idea which of them could have known about the secret passages and had the physical prowess to navigate them strategically, and in the middle of the night. We know the murderer accessed the hammer and immediately made their move on Andrej. And, the weapon of choice has symbolic meaning to the von Voitsberg legacy."

Hermann paused, thinking. They had wandered down a path through a beech wood that was late to leaf. Small, furry buds were visible all along the pale branches around them, letting in a good deal of the orange light of the burgeoning sunset. "Géza, I've told you that I study the psychology of people who claim to have experienced the supernatural. Well, the biggest part of that is studying their emotions, their expressions, the way they hold themselves, that slight twitch of the eye here or the nervous tap of a foot there. Tonight, only Herr Baum will be absent, so I'll have free reign to study everyone else and their reactions to what we've learned. I'll reveal small pieces of evidence to gauge what each already knows and how that relates to the murder."

"Do you think that's wise when the murderer, if he's not Baum, could be nearby?"

"I think it's the only path forward, Géza. By stressing the culprit, making them paranoid that we're getting close, they'll act rashly and hopefully make a mistake."

"Provided the murderer is in the dining room," said Géza.

Chapter 20

It had been a long day but Hermann knew the next act was critical to pushing the case towards completion, and anticipation energized him. He rubbed his clean-shaven jawline, donned his cufflinks, and smoothed his dinner jacket. He noticed Gustav, perched life-sized on the wall, watching his reflection in the mirror.

"Not now man, unless you're going to tell me why half the household keeps dark secrets, and who is running around under the floors and through the walls."

The portrait did not answer.

"Hmm, I didn't think so."

A deep breath. He began the trek to the Biedermeier parlor as he'd done on the previous evening. The gas lamps of his hall seemed to be particularly dim this evening, shrouding everything in a low veil of shadow, mixed with a sickly amber glow. Just as he was passing the door of the library tower, a raspy voice called out to him. "Professor, come in and look at what I've found."

Hermann entered the round room's second story which was decently lit by wall lamps that had evidently been turned up for Frau Kam's convenience. The old widow wore a pair of pocket spectacles on her aquiline nose that framed her bright amber eyes.

"How do you do, frau?"

"Fine, fine. Come here and look at this old book. I found it half out on the ledge over there in the antique book section. I don't know why I'd never noticed it before. Curiously, it was open to this bit about when the castle was sacked by that first von Voitsberg."

As he approached, Hermann saw a very large, weathered-looking tome containing yellowed velum, bound in leather, and secured with an intricate metal locking clasp.

"It says that Gustav Freiherr von Voitsberg sacked the castle in the night with a troop who'd climbed the walls and came upon the Turks without warning. They put everyone to the sword except the local commander who'd been posted there to defend the northern flank of the eyalet. The Turk was questioned, or tortured, and revealed a riddle before he died."

Hermann bent low, over the ancient text, to look at the words. He read aloud as he followed the verse with his index finger, careful not to actually touch the fragile vellum.

"Under stone and through the labyrinth of life,
The honourable come to their greatest
test of faith.
Over blind waters to the seat of their Lord's favour,
To earthly treasure by the cleansed soul
in secret waters."

"What do you make of it, Professor? Earthly treasure, that has to be what the spirits have been guarding. The text goes on to describe that there was no hoard found, despite a lengthy search."

Hermann looked up in time to see a puzzled smile discreetly manifesting across Frau Kam's face.

"You say you haven't seen this book before?" he asked.

"Well, I never looked for it before. I only noticed it because it was sitting out. I often come here to read. I've been collecting material on spiritualism and the knowledge of the ancients about such things. The treasure would belong now to the Baums. It's on my son-in-law's land after all."

"More likely there was no treasure, just a ploy by the Turk to keep his tormentors occupied from rejoining the war to retake Hungary. You'd have to ask a lawyer about it though, I'm only in the business of the mind and spirit, not the law. Would you mind saving this topic of conversation for after dinner? I'd like to think on it some. It may relate to the case."

"Oh my," she said. "Certainly. I'll help the case in whatever way I can. You know, I think the spirits wanted me to find the book, maybe they are leading me toward some conclusion, some unfinished business that must be resolved so that the spirit world can be at rest."

"Perhaps, we'll have to see. Shall we ask them at another séance?"

"Oh, yes," said Frau Kam as she clapped her hands.

"Ready to go down to dinner?"

Hermann held out his elbow and Frau Kam took it after repositing her spectacles into a pocket in her skirt. He was troubled in the journey through the hall and down the stairs of the keep, despite his pleasant demeanor with Frau Kam. Someone had been researching and studying the history of the castle and its acquisition by Gustav Freiherr von Voitsberg, and this had occurred since yesterday when he was in that area of the library. Things were definitely escalating.

Before they could turn the corner into the lower hall, the noise of an approaching carriage, echoing through the open door onto the bailey and back through the keep, caught his attention.

"Frau Kam, would you excuse me? I want to welcome Frau Astrid."

"Certainly. Such a resolute young woman."

A fine but minimalist black carriage with the top pulled up was being attended by a footman who lowered the step and opened the passenger door. The footman approached to give his hand to the occupant, but Fürth emerged from around the exterior edge of the door to shoo him away with a light wave then held out his own hand. Frau Astrid's small, silver-gloved hand extended from the carriage door, grasping Fürth's lightly, as she stepped down. She was wearing a dark-grey, silk-and-velvet evening gown, with puff sleeves to just below her elbows and a shallow collar. Her underskirt was a matte black, embroidered with silver thread in the design of a tree with branches snaking and twisting amongst each other, growing wider the further away from the base of the trunk they went. The pattern matched the embroidery along the cuffs of her sleeves. She wore the same simple amulet he'd noticed the morning he met her—a long, thin piece of metal with a floral design— but now it was strung on a black and silver ribbon to match her gown.

As she looked at Fürth, Hermann noted an easy familiarity between them. Born, he supposed, from having grown up at Schattenturm where Fürth had been the butler her whole life. Stepping forward, he noticed that her ash-blond hair had been pulled back into a loose braid and wound into a neat bun, fastened with a comb of small, intricate silver flowers. Though he couldn't hear what they said to each other from his position at the other end of the keep, Astrid and Fürth spoke for close to a minute before he bowed and led her inside.

Hermann approached, and Fürth gave way with a downcast look before assuming his usual judgmental posture of marble, heading toward the parlor. Astrid had paused to gaze up at the curved staircases and white marble columns holding up the golden starry sky on a rich blue background. The ringlets of her coiffure tilted back with her gaze. Her light-grey eyes caught and reflected the flickering brightness of the candelabra's tiny flames, giving the impression they were the same color as the silver embroidery adorning her dress.

Hermann bowed, "Good evening, Frau Astrid."

She lowered her gaze from the resplendent dome and smiled slightly in greeting. "Professor," she said as she held out a hand which Hermann grasped lightly in greeting.

"I must say, you look beautiful this evening."

"Thank you. This dress was a gift from my father. I'm sure it's out of fashion now, but it remains one of my favorites. He bought it as a present for me when he and Mama visited Vienna, just before he died. It seemed right to honor him tonight."

"Of course, this must be your first visit to Schattenturm as a guest. I'm sure the house welcomes your presence." Hermann didn't exactly intend to say what he had, but the house did actually feel different the moment she entered. There was the sense of a different energy. The lingering shadows receded, the air grew less heavy, and the very walls seemed to brighten and shake off their dark, sallow tone.

She caught her breath and looked down for a minute, before raising her gaze to give a half-hearted smile. "Yes ... as a guest. It feels strange, Herr Horst, to be welcomed back as an outsider when I was here for its rebirth. I will always love this house." She shook her head slightly with closed eyes. "However, I'm curious to see what's changed and how the Baums have improved upon it as the new owners."

"I'm sorry. Of course, I should have known how difficult it would be to return. Was I wrong to ask you to come?"

"No, no. Besides, I'm here now."

A coolness had crept into her tone and her emotions seemed to steady and solidify. She was now more like the cautious woman Hermann had met the day prior at her shop in town.

"Shall we?" she said as she took the first step, confident and commanding as though she was still mistress of the house.

They walked arm-in-arm through the hall, then into the parlor where Fürth announced them.

"Frau Astrid von Voitsberg," Fürth said, barely disguising his pride, momentarily letting down his marble exterior.

All eyes were on them as they entered, then solely on Astrid. Most were a mixture of apprehension, but Erzsébet looked duly impressed. She was dressed in a dark green evening gown with a spiral pattern around the hem and on the underskirt. Rachel was in cream with sapphire-colored detailing around the ruffled neckline and in the beadwork sewn about her underskirt. Mother and daughter had very similar hairstyles, with their dark strands bound in opposing folds that culminated in pyramidal pinning. Géza was in his formal dress uniform. He was standing with Frau Kam whose jet-black necklace and earrings caught the light in a reverse sparkle over her mourning dress, adorned with far too many tassels. Erzsébet approached Astrid, leaving Rachel to attend to Hermann.

"It's a pleasure to finally host you, Fraulein von Voitsberg."

Astrid raised her left eyebrow ever so slightly. Fürth coughed lightly into his fist before ducking into the hall.

Erzsébet quickly corrected, "Err ... *Frau Astrid*." Erzsébet's lack of aristocratic socialization had been laid bare.

"It's good to be back at Schattenturm, Frau Baum."

"May I introduce my daughter, Rachel, and this is my son, Josef."

Hermann turned away from the introductions to engage Géza, but was intercepted by Frau Kam. "Now I understand why you wanted to invite the fraulein, Professor," she said with an ivory-denture smile. "The two of you, entering the room side-by-side, what a lovely couple, how regal, how ... if only Josef was a bit older, I might live to enjoy some beautiful great-grandchildren. But alas, Josef is unfortunately—," she looked over to the teenager who had begun to stare at Astrid with his mouth half open, "—dull."

"I wish I was as clever as you make me out. No, Frau Kam, I needed another opportunity to gauge her character and her knowledge of the house. This investigation is still ongoing and our leads need fleshing out."

"Well, don't let a chance like this go to waste, Professor. You're likely to only find love once, and I can tell you that from experience." She laughed, then drifted over to the ladies' discussion.

"Do you think everything's in order?" Géza asked, in Frau Kam's wake.

"More or less, yes. Is there any word on Herr Baum?"

"None, he's still out. Frau Baum said as much as the telegram did, that he's at a shareholder's meeting in Budapest, but that he might make the evening train back to town."

Hermann nodded.

"There is something, though," said Géza. "Officer Erdei spent the last two days questioning townspeople throughout the village. The first day got him nothing, but on the second, everyone treated him like a prince. Whatever Frau Astrid did, it got them all cooperating. She seems to have the ability to control their fear of the curse."

"Old roots grow deep," Hermann said as he studied Astrid from afar. "Did Erdei turn up anything important?"

"Only that Andrej purchased his equipment from the general store a few weeks before his death. Wouldn't say what it was for, of course, even though the general manager asked him."

"It would have been convenient for the owner to have told us that yesterday morning when we were in there."

"Oh, and an old seamstress in town said she saw the freiherr get off at the train station in Salgótarján the morning before Andrej died."

"The freiherr?"

"I told Erdei it must have been one of your spirits." Géza chuckled.

Fürth reentered the parlor and cleared his throat. "Dinner is served."

Géza led Erzsébet, followed by Hermann with Astrid, then Frau Kam with Josef, which left Rachel on her own. Erzsébet was seated at the head, on the interior wall closest to the fire, with Josef to her left and Géza on her right. Hermann was positioned center opposite, with Frau Kam on his left and Astrid on his right. Rachel rounded the placement at the end between Géza and Frau Kam, the former of which brought a sly smile to her face.

A light consommé with pearls of sago was served for them beneath new, overly large bouquets in the silver vases. Erzsébet turned the conversation to her right during the soup which meant Hermann was paired with Astrid.

"Is it as you remember it?"

"Everything, actually. Although it's sad to see the halls so empty. I still have most of my parents' objects d'art and souvenirs, thankfully. I hope that Herr Baum simply shuffled the remaining portraits to another room, those which my uncle didn't sell, but he'd have no reason to save the portraits of my ancestors and their extended families."

"I understand. After my parents' and sister's deaths, I sold our home in Salzburg and moved to an apartment in Vienna to be closer to the University. It's large, but there really wasn't any room for my great-aunts and -uncles, and distant relatives to adorn the walls."

"I'm sorry. That's a shame, Professor. Why ever would you have sold your home? Surely you could have put the heirlooms into storage and let the house?"

"It seemed better at the time to have a clean break from it. There was too much leftover there for me to have ever felt real joy, and I had no indication that I'd even stay in Vienna if the time came."

"Really? Are there many opportunities open for a professor of the ... what do you call it?"

"The parapsychological, though I teach primarily history, mythology, and a kind of ethnic philosophy. I favor the Romantic school of thought. My studies elsewise are on the side, strictly speaking. I had thought about emigrating to

America at one point. There's a growing psychological movement in their academics and a large German-speaking population across the northern states. In many places, we outnumber the English."

Cod in a very salty sauce was served next, along with a thin paste of crushed capers, mustard seed, and dill.

"I admire your prospective tenacity, at least. Though, I don't think I could ever leave Schattenturm, not really." She looked down at the fish for a moment. "I suppose I already have, haven't I? I just haven't really let it set in."

"All things change in time, Frau Astrid. We can't always pick when or why, but we can move with the tide and keep the wind."

She smiled. "That was very poetic."

He shared her smile. "Well, I do teach antique prose as a profession."

Erzsébet shifted the conversation left once the rare lamb with mint glaze sauce was set down. She saved Astrid from an awkward few courses by overstepping Josef and speaking across the table while Hermann was occupied with Frau Kam, and Géza with Rachel and her increasing coquettishness. Frau Kam continued to expound on the supernatural, much as she had done the night before. Hermann thought she had an almost girlish giddiness about their recent shared secret as she kept alluding to *treasures of the beyond*. Géza focused intently on his food and made little effort to drink his wine while Rachel carried on a one-sided conversation with him, her dark eyes shifting from him, to Hermann, to Astrid, and her mother. Hermann was only able to catch a few bits of Astrid and Erzsébet's conversation, mostly having to do with a shared interest in gardening. Astrid had apparently been working with Pavol Soták for some months to clean up her Italian garden behind the widow's cottage.

"What are you talking about down there?" said Rachel, apparently bored by Géza's single-word responses and refusal to be taken in by her charms. "I heard you talking about gardening with the assistant? Though I guess he's the head gardener now that Andrej is dead."

Erzsébet scrutinized her daughter, trying to determine how much wine she'd drunken.

Astrid responded coolly. "I was telling your mother that Pavol has been working with me at the cottage and recently helped me reform the alley and beds off toward the woods."

"Well, Mama would know all about how important it is to keep a good groundsman close," she said with a smile. "Poor dead Andrej was so nice to take over the gardens here."

"I believe it was Pavol who came up with most of the new ideas," said Astrid. "Although, Andrej always took the credit."

"Is that right, Frau Astrid? So you must be on very close terms with … what's his name … Pavol?" said Rachel.

"Now, now, Rachel," said Erzsébet. "Why don't you tell us how your painting has been coming along?" She looked around the table at the guests. "She's really quite good for a girl her age."

Rachel slouched back into her chair. "Nothing inspired me, and I wasn't about to spend the day painting lily pads." She sent Hermann a sideways pouty look. "I went riding instead. Unlike Mama, I don't need to disappear outside for hours on end, skulking in some corner." She turned to face Hermann. "What do *you* think about riding, herr? She let out a sigh. "I think it's just exhilarating."

"Beyond my lessons as a boy, I haven't found much time for it."

"Pity. What about you, Frau Astrid? Do you ride?"

"I used to. We hosted many hunting parties here. It was one of my favorite events."

"And now? Not enough money to keep it up?"

Astrid settled into a smirk. "My mother needs my attention now more than my horses did. I take pride in my duty as a daughter."

"How convenient," said Rachel.

"Without our parents," Astrid continued, "we're just babes in the woods. If they've done well by us in our raising, we owe it to them to be there when they need us."

Rachel's dark eyes were staring unblinking at Astrid who, for her part, remained poised and unaffected."

"Rachel—," Erzsébet began, but her sentence was interrupted by the dining room door which suddenly swung open.

Johan Baum entered the room. He was still dressed in his traveling suit and looked agitated. Fürth's eyebrows nearly joined as he and the dinner party watched Baum walk toward the table.

"Fürth, bring me a place setting and some food. And you," he said to the footman, "bring that chair over here."

He ran a hand along the back of Erzsébet's shoulders. She looked terribly embarrassed. "We were just finishing, dear," said Erzsébet. "Perhaps you'll have a rest in here for a minute while the ladies go through?"

"And deprive myself of your great company?" he said. "And you, Inspector, did I miss any of your important investigation?" He half slurred, half sneered, in Géza's general direction. His eyes were bloodshot. His tie was pulled down and his first shirt button was undone. His stomach strained against his vest and he was clearly drunk.

"Who's this?" he said with a thumb jabbed toward Astrid, whose placid frown revealed her less than favorable impression of Schattenturm's new owner.

"Johan, this is Frau Astrid von Voitsberg," said Erzsébet.

Hermann quickly added, "I asked that an invitation be extended to her this evening."

Baum's mouth opened in realization of who was sitting at his dining room table, then closed suddenly into a grimace. Hermann thought he looked rather frog-like.

Baum sized up Astrid, his dark eyes narrowing in a mirror expression of his daughter's a moment earlier. "What the devil for?"

Astrid responded coolly, "To convene with old ghosts." Then she smiled.

Frau Baum set her napkin on the table as a footman pulled back her chair.

"Let's let the men enjoy a cigar. Frau Astrid, Mama, Rachel ... Josef, you too," she said as the boy inhaled the remnants of his dessert.

Fürth attended to Astrid's chair as she delicately folded over her napkin and departed silently.

A footman pulled back Frau Kam's chair. "All right, but I don't want to miss a minute of anything important. Smoke your cigars quickly," she said, rising reluctantly.

The footmen followed the ladies after clearing the plates. Fürth remained, presenting a box of cigars and the remnants in the decanters from the sideboard. Baum tapped insistently with his middle finger on the table in front of him until Fürth fetched a glass to pour the red.

"Von Voitsberg," Baum sneered. "That bastard still haunts me." He clipped the end of a cigar and lit it with a match. "She knows it too," he said through starting puffs.

Hermann refrained from smoking, but Géza took a cigar. He was watching Baum's movements carefully.

"How is that, Herr Baum?" asked Hermann.

Baum took a drag on the cigar. "When I buy something, I understand its value, what it'll do for me. This place—," he motioned with the cigar hand, "—was supposed to be handed over to me turnkey. But as it stands, empty, in disrepair, not enough servants to run it, it'll cost me more than it'll ever be worth again. You may not know it in Vienna, but men like me are the future of this country.

When time finally takes its toll on the aristocracy, the Germans, it'll be men like me that are left."

Géza tapped his ashes into a crystal tray.

"This place was supposed to be my crowning glory. Something my rivals could only dream of having. It should have put me at the front of the pack. But by the time the bank and what was left of the von Voitsbergs were done ... well, I was left with what you see. The bank had other priorities besides my rights in mind. That damned fool, Voitsberg, used this place like a pleasure palace. Year after year, parties, parades, shows, diplomatic gatherings, all of it. It built up a name, a reputation. Heh. This monstrosity and his playtime extravagances cost more than anything he could ever have come up with. He was a degenerate. A debtor in the end."

Géza exhaled and lifted his wine glass.

Fürth was the only one of the servants left in the room and his cheek was practically bulging from the tension in his jaw.

Baum chuckled. "But where'd he get the money to start all this in the first place? When he died, the bank took this estate to cover his debts. Then, when those two—," he motioned toward the door Frau Astrid had just vacated, "—couldn't pay. It was put up for sale, everything included. The art, the furniture, all of it. But when it came time for me to move in, most of it was gone. Pilfered it like thieves."

Géza listened, but Baum wasn't making much sense. Hermann was leading him, that much was certain, and Géza was just waiting for the moment when he would incriminate himself.

"So why buy the house, Herr Baum?" asked Hermann.

Baum curled his lip and took another drag. "You wouldn't understand it. You're just a teacher. Once you get to be a man like me, scrape it all up from nothing to become something, then you'll know why. You've got to let 'em know where you're at. Heh. Where you're at, better than them anyway. Ain't no way anyone'd *forget* to send an invitation after coming here."

He took a long drag as Hermann and Géza watched. The downward slide in vernacular was undeniable.

"That damned degenerate played it up with his women and his parties, taking out from more people than a starving man in a bakery. I even heard he'd gone beyond the parties and the debt. That he'd got up to worse than just a few whores in his day. Slime. Let him rot in Hell. He deserves it for what he's done to me. At least there he'll have a purpose."

Fürth's right hand was trembling and his eyes looked like they were boring through the back of Baum's skull, though he never turned his head. Géza snuffed out his cigar. Baum shifted his gaze to Géza and leaned over the table, pointing the stub of his own cigar at the inspector.

"You're shaping up to have no purpose here, Inspector. Have you found out anything at all? Got a killer in custody yet? Or are you just a prop?"

Géza's eyes narrowed and his jaw tightened. "As a matter of fact, we are very close. I think we'll have him soon enough."

"Well then, who is it? Spit it out." His small black eyes were fixed on Géza's.

"That is sensitive information about this investigation, Herr Baum. You'll find out in due course. Actually, you'll probably be the first to find out."

Baum slammed his fist down on the table, sending hot ashes from the cigar clenched tightly between his fingers, flying out over the cloth.

"Damn you! You know I've seen your superiors in Budapest? They tell me you haven't found a damn thing. Nothing, in two bloody weeks of crawling around my house, giving the papers troves to muck up about me. You're off this case, Orczy."

Baum pulled out an envelope with a broken seal from inside his suit jacket and flung it across the table at Géza.

"Your commander tells you to get on the first train out of here in the morning. You're finished! You'll be lucky to end up back in the stables where they found you."

Géza displayed no emotion, he didn't even blink. He stared through Baum across the table, his back perfectly straight, like a wound spring.

"That'll teach you to push in on your betters. I told you to quit asking about my business. My work isn't any business of yours, you up-jumped horse-shit-shoveler."

Géza was up from his seat in a flash. Hermann rose quickly as well. In a streak of green, Géza was practically on top of Baum. He gripped his hands over Baum's wrists, locking them onto the armrests of his chair. He leaned into Baum, his green eyes boring into the man, his nose inches from his face.

"I know what you've done, Baum. I know about the mines and why you bought this place. I know everything. You think you're safe behind your money?" He shook his head, eyes locked. "There's a cell with your name on it. Here and in Hell. You think you're going to be rid of me? No. When I return, it'll be with a warrant for your arrest, and a bullet if you resist."

Baum was leaning back as far as he could in his chair, mouth opening and closing quickly like a gasping fish. He tried to get free, but Géza's strength was immense, Baum's wrists remained locked on the armrests.

"And if you ever impugn me or my work for this country again, I'll put a cigar in your eye."

Hermann approached and put a hand on Géza's shoulder, gripping it for a minute.

"Now that we've all come to an understanding," said Hermann, "I'd like to ask Herr Baum one question and then I think we should discuss what we discovered today with the entire Baum family. Inspector?"

Géza released Baum's wrists and stood up. Baum's head was struggling to crane back to take in Géza's face at his full height. Géza relaxed somewhat and tugged at the end of his jacket to straighten it.

"Herr Baum," said Hermann. "How long have you been bankrupt?"

Géza looked to Hermann and back to Baum. Baum looked at Hermann as though he'd spoken in Chinese.

"You were asked a question," Géza growled.

"I wasn't bankrupt till today. I was struggling a bit because some of my miners got themselves killed and it spooked the shareholders. But today ... today they cut me out. Told me to liquidate everything I had, and if I could cover fifty percent, they'd let me stay on as owner. *Let me* stay on," he grumbled. "At my own company that I built from the ground up."

"That is helpful to explain your current state, but you must've had more trouble than that, and much earlier, for things here with Schattenturm to be what they are."

"This place was supposed to be security. Get the house, get the art, the furniture, and maybe ... well, anything else left over. Then I'd blow 'em all away with a bunch of parties. Make it look like I was flush so I could build confidence in the business and with the shareholders. Heh. That'd make Erzsébet feel good for once in those posh charities of hers. The value of the place would then go up and I'd make a profit when I sold it. Plus, I thought I'd get more business out this way."

"So, Schattenturm, it's all over for you now?" said Hermann.

"I've been down before, and I don't intend to just roll over."

"Thank you, Herr Baum," Hermann finished. "Please join us in the drawing room in your own time. It's important."

Géza and Hermann left Baum sitting at the table as they departed. Hermann cast a look at Fürth on his way out. He had returned to his marble demeanor, but with a slight smirk.

Chapter 21

Frau Kam and Astrid were locked in conversation when Hermann and Géza entered the drawing room. Erzsébet was near the piano speaking quietly to Rachel, who stood with her arms crossed, rolling her eyes, until she saw the two enter. "Fine," she said loudly to her mother, and slid onto the pianoforte bench.

"I could use a whiskey after that," said Géza.

"Me too. Was he right? Have you been recalled to Budapest?"

Géza pulled out the letter, addressed to him but obviously read by Baum, based on the broken seal. He looked over it quickly while Hermann poured them each a drink.

"It's not as bad as Baum made out, but it's not good," Géza whispered. "I've been called back to answer about the state of the investigation. I don't know what to tell my commander, though. We haven't arrested anyone yet, and now half the people in this room, and beyond, are suspects."

"Leave that to me. When you get to Budapest, tell them that we know who it is and we'll have them by tomorrow night, we just need a little more time ... a day."

"I wish I had your faith."

"The killer is going to reveal their identity, I have a plan for that. But now ... I'm going to intervene on Frau Astrid's behalf."

He headed toward the settee where Astrid was pinned by Frau Kam's overly enthusiastic discourse on the paranormal. Rachel was shuffling music sheets, her mother standing over her to supervise the selection.

"The house is clearly a focal point of great spiritual energy," said Frau Kam. "I hear them in the walls, the very air is alive with their energy. They're everywhere and nowhere within an instant. I've had so much success communing with them lately."

"We always joked in this house when I was a girl that you were probably never more than a meter or two from a ghost. A bit like spiders, so I'm told," said Astrid.

"Dear me, how extraordinary," said Frau Kam. "You know, just last night, the professor led a séance and we made contact with a very troubled spirit. Oh, what was his name?"

"Fridolin," said Hermann as he took a chair near the women.

"Yes, that's it! Do you recognize the name, Frau Astrid? Perhaps a relative you might remember from somewhere in the annals?" she asked.

Fürth arrived with a plate carrying a glass of a pale golden liquor that he bent and held out for Astrid.

"Thank you Fürth, you remembered!"

"How could I have forgotten?" he said with a faint smile.

She smiled as well, then turned back to Frau Kam and Hermann.

"And no, not particularly. We have a good many Friederichs throughout our history, but I don't recall a Fridolin."

Fürth stopped for a moment and looked over his shoulder at Astrid. Hermann caught the movement.

"Fürth, do you recognize the name Fridolin, by chance?" asked Hermann.

"Not at all, herr. I only thought I forgot something that needed done for a moment." He gave a short nod and then went back to his quiet post.

Rachel started suddenly, brilliantly, with Chopin's Piano Concerto No. 2 in F minor. Erzsébet drifted over to join the trio at the same time as Géza.

"Your daughter plays beautifully, Frau Baum," said Astrid. "She must have had a wonderful instructor."

"Thank you, Frau Astrid. Isn't it lovely when girls already have a skill at this age?"

"Professor," began Frau Kam, "do you think now we might talk about what the spirits have revealed?"

Hermann and Géza both caught Johan Baum's entrance to the drawing room and exchanged a look. He proceeded past the party to sit across from his son in the music room. He seemed within decent earshot, provided the pianoforte wasn't overwhelming.

"Professor?"

"Yes, now's as good a time as any."

"Well then," Frau Kam said, her voice more clear and commanding than usual, "you all should know that we've been blessed by the spirits ... or cursed roundabout ... I hadn't considered that till now."

All but Rachel became momentarily motionless, eyes on Frau Kam. In the stillness of the space, Chopin's concerto sent the piano keys flying, faster and faster, the notes reaching higher and higher tones before suddenly crashing to continue their previous delicate pace.

"There's a secret here in the house. A secret fiercely guarded by the spirits since the old Turks were banished. It's a treasure, waiting for us to find. Can you believe it?"

Baum turned to stare at his mother-in-law. Astrid's mouth and brows tensed. Erzsébet looked frightened. Fürth turned his head slightly and raised a bushy eyebrow. Géza had the slightest smirk on his face.

"A treasure, what do you mean?" said Josef, suddenly coming to life from his chair in the music room.

"Exactly what it sounds like. I discovered a very old book in the library. It contained history on the castle and documented when the castle was taken by the first von

Voitsberg. Most intriguing is that it tells how the Turks had left a hidden treasure here. A treasure that was never found."

"I wouldn't put much stock into that legend, Frau Kam," said Astrid. "It's been around as long as this house, at least. I think I remember the book you're talking about. I'm surprised it's still in the library after the … transfer."

"You'd know all about what's left in this house," Baum put in, between soft strikes on the pianoforte's keys.

"There's no truth to it, Herr Baum," she retorted. "I've been over every inch of this house since I was born, and I can assure you there's nothing like that hidden here."

Baum got up and came to stand behind his wife. "I've had it on good authority there *is* something here, and it'd be mine if it were."

Astrid pursed her lips. "What good authority might that have been?"

Hermann and Géza both watched carefully.

"A former member of staff who'd probably been into more places than you even know exist."

"I assume you mean Andrej, then. That man had a knack for tall tales and an over-inflated sense of his position. My uncle told him that story once and he never forgot it. If he'd ever found it, it would have been spent long ago."

"On drink and dice," grumbled Baum. "Good then that he's gone."

Géza stared at Baum who took a sip of the drink he'd carried in from the dining room before he moseyed back to his chair.

Had it not been for Rachel's piece winding down, Hermann might not have heard Astrid mumble beside him, "On that we can agree."

They all applauded Rachel, but before she could get up, her mother instructed her to play a Bach. Instead, she quickly jabbed out a ragged, folksy tune while her mother gave a beleaguered blink.

"There is another aspect to the legend," Hermann put in. He rose and proceeded to the liquor stand behind the sofa.

"Don't keep us in suspense," Frau Kam called out.

Hermann smiled and took another moment to pour his drink before rounding back and standing where he was able to see everyone in both rooms. Rachel's raucous piece thankfully ended.

"Frau Kam's legend has a grain of truth to it," Hermann said. "The house hides extraordinary details. Passageways, tunnels, chambers, all designed to allow one to travel throughout the house and grounds, undetected. Andrej's killer had an extreme amount of access to this house. More than what one could expect from an outsider."

Erzsébet covered her mouth with a gloved hand. "Are you saying that someone connected to the household was responsible?

"Yes, Frau Baum, I am."

Everyone looked between themselves, the professor, and especially the investigator.

"Herr Fürth," Hermann continued. "It's well known that you and Frau Schrode keep the downstairs entrances locked and under key, except for emergencies?"

The butler had a worried look for the first time that Hermann could remember. "That's right. There are two doors downstairs that are locked from the outside but can be opened from inside, in case of a fire."

"And the upstairs entrances are shut and locked at night, including the gatehouse entry, by you, on your evening round?"

"That's right, or by Frau Schrode if I'm occupied. We are the only ones with keys upstairs." He looked toward the Baums.

"What are you saying, Horst?" Baum put in, with a challenging tone.

"I'm saying that despite this house being locked up at night, and decently travelled by the staff in the daylight, there's another way to enter Schattenturm, probably multiple ways. Frau Astrid, as you know, this house was renovated by your late father, Herr Albert von Voitsberg, and his brother, the late freiherr."

"Yes. The renovations began before I was born and finished when my brother and I were four or five."

"Inspector Orczy and I discovered that everything is not as it appears with this house. The renovated sections were designed to disguise a network of secret passages hidden between the walls of the new and old, through alcoves, and in all manner of places."

Hermann closely observed the reactions of those in the room to this piece of information. Astrid maintained her cool demeanor and drew back as the Baum clan looked between each other. Rachel and Josef locked eyes in the music room.

"The killer used one of the passages to overtake Andrej in the maze and ambush him there. He watched Andrej from the window of the armory and took the hammer from its display case with the intent to kill him."

Johan Baum spoke first. "The murderer was in my house and you're saying nobody knew about it?"

"That's exactly what I'm saying. What's worse is that Andrej almost certainly knew about the passages too and used them regularly. He and his killer may have been searching for the rumored lost treasure. They may even have been collaborating."

Not a sound was made by any of them. Only the hissing and cracking of the fire could be heard.

"I don't believe it's an accident that the book you read this evening was left out, Frau Kam. I think that the killer has been back to Schattenturm, in the last 24 hours, and has consulted it for some clue that might bring them closer to the treasure ... if it exists."

"My God!" exclaimed Erzsébet. "How can we be sure none of us will be murdered in our sleep?"

Baum opened and closed his mouth a few times while his brows furrowed.

Hermann continued. "Inspector Orczy must return to Budapest in the morning. So, we won't have any round-the-clock police protection here besides Officer Erdei. However, when Inspector Orczy returns, it will be to arrest the killer."

Johan Baum tried to rub an ungraceful palm on his wife's shoulder, but she shrugged him off. Then she looked back to her children where Rachel seemed almost angry and Josef sat across from her in much the same state.

"Until I return," Géza put in, "I would suggest each of you take to your rooms, lock your doors, and check for any unnatural drafts coming from somewhere. If you find any, let me or Herr Horst know, so that we can be certain no entryway leads into your rooms."

Frau Kam leaned forward in her chair, twirling the end of a jet-black stone pendant around her fingers. "Can we be sure you will be back, Inspector Orczy? Who's to say it won't take you longer? What if one of us is killed in the interim? I don't want to end up trapped on the spirit side of this godforsaken place."

Astrid shot a contemptuous sideways look at Frau Kam.

"Try not to worry, any of you. The investigation will continue in my absence, and when I return, I'll be taking Andrej's murderer out in handcuffs. Preferably, to the gallows."

Erzsébet rose from her chair. "Thank you, herren, for warning us of the danger. I think we need to put ourselves in order now, and I need to see to my children."

"Of course, frau," said Hermann.

Erzsébet moved to speak with Fürth whose hand was trembling slightly.

"Please see to Frau Astrid's carriage. Let the staff downstairs know of the danger and try to make sure they're doubled up tonight in their rooms. Rachel will sleep in my dressing room and Josef in his father's."

"Oh Mama, we'll be fine," Rachel whined. "Besides, I can't sleep anywhere besides my own room. You know it has to be freezing for me, and you always keep your fire lit even in the summertime. I'll be a mess in the morning, and you know how I feel when I haven't slept."

"Fine, but I want your door locked and your window latched."

Fürth bowed and left to carry out his orders. The rest of the group filed out in a quiet solemnity. Astrid caught her carriage after a brief farewell from Erzsébet and Hermann. It was clear that none of them would sleep easily.

———————————◆———————————

Once the family had retreated to their hall to lock themselves in, and Fürth was off to organize the same for the staff, Hermann and Géza compared notes.

"Did you get what you needed?" asked Géza.

"It wasn't what I had expected," Hermann answered. "We knew from earlier today that Frau Astrid was aware of the passages and, based on his reaction to our sudden appearance from the wall in the keep, Fürth knew of them as well. The Baum children appeared to have come across at least some of them, judging by the sideways looks they shot one another. Erzsébet seemed almost too shocked and certainly wanted us all out of here quickly. But, I'm surprised that Johan Baum appeared ignorant of their existence."

"And you think he was genuine?" asked Géza.

"I do. The man was drunk and clearly emotionally unstable. If he were faking it, he would've done a much worse job than that."

"So, what does this mean? Do you believe it rules Baum out?"

Hermann rubbed his eyes. "He could have done it, for sure, but not by dashing from the gate house to the maze through an underground passage."

"If the killer was in the drawing room tonight, or was a servant and was close to someone here tonight, they'll know we're getting closer, since we already know their means in and out of the house," said Géza. "If they think something's hidden here, they'll be desperate to get to it now before they're caught."

"We need to go down the shaft in the mausoleum, tonight. We need to find out what Andrej was after," said Hermann.

"Agreed. And with the servants and family locked in their rooms, anyone we run into is up to no good."

"I'll go and change and meet you down by the maze entrance."

"I'll get some rope and lanterns and meet you out there."

"And Géza, stay out of sight if you can."

Chapter 22

Just after ten, Hermann left his room and locked the door behind him. He made his way through the second story of the house, looking and listening for anything out of place besides himself. The library had been darkened and shut, Baum's office was locked just as Hermann and Géza had left it earlier, and no light or noise came from Herr or Frau Baum's rooms around the turn of the corridor toward the east. A light came from one of the rooms in the east hall which he assumed belonged to one of the Baum children, still up.

Stopping at the entrance of the chapel, he opened the door slightly to peer inside. It was dark and silent, save for the ambient light that barely illuminated the center aisle and white marble altar. Hermann shut the door and made his way down the circular stair beside the chapel to the first floor. A draft coming in from somewhere sent the temperature down several degrees. Since he couldn't feel any airflow, he assumed it must be due to the fires having been extinguished in the main rooms. There was little need to heat the whole house, or even attempt to do so, not that Baum could really afford to anyway.

He briefly checked in on the parlor, the drawing room, the dining room, and finally the ballroom. Even in the dark, the ballroom's grandeur was stunning. The coffered ceilings reflected the minimal light from their gilded hexagons, and the patterned floor cast a kaleidoscope of color in the otherwise grey-blue aura. None of the paintings that must have hung on the walls, save for some oversized land-scapes, remained. The Murano chandeliers, all three of them, still hung on long chains, with more than a dozen swan-necked arms on each, waiting to illuminate the floor for forgotten waltzes. Hermann turned toward the center of the far wall of the ballroom where an apse lined with triple-hung windows and a large glass door looked out onto the terrace outside. To avoid being seen, he slipped out this door to the terrace and around the eastern side of the house, made his way down to the dry moat, and followed its path under the bridge and around the rise, to come around onto the terraces leading to the maze. He was able to see Géza at the maze's entrance, barely visible.

"I brought the rope from the evidence room," Géza said as Hermann approached.

"Good, let's get down there before it gets any later. We might get lucky and catch the murderer if he's looking to get to the treasure he thinks he'll find."

"Hopefully in time to save my head," Géza said with a soft chuckle.

They felt their way through the maze, made more difficult because they wanted to keep the lanterns dark in case they were being watched, and to avoid spooking their quarry. Eventually, they reached the mausoleum which looked craggy and sinister in the dark, as did Schattenturm looming over them from its perch, all dark, pointed win-dows and indefinable shapes along the rooves and battle-ments. Once they were inside, Géza shut the door firmly to keep any light from being seen from outside while Her-mann fumbled for the matches and got the two lanterns lit, momentarily blinding them.

Hermann studied the disturbances in the dust on the floor. "No one's passed through here since our explorations earlier today."

"Was that just earlier today?"

They retraced their steps through the subterranean colonnade of crypts to the end of the passage. The mechanism that held open the entry to the shaft below Gustav Freiherr von Voitsberg's sarcophagus was still active, leaving the gaping, black-square pit ready for them. Géza roped the line around the plinth of the sarcophagus and again on the columns nearby, before tossing the remnant down the hole.

"I'll go first," Géza offered.

"Though I appreciate your bravery, it might be better if you stayed back as a counterweight should anything go wrong."

Géza nodded in response. "Plus, you're the only mountaineer between the two of us."

"And someone will still need to arrest the murderer, should Andrej's dead man's rope give out."

"I'm not superstitious, Hermann, but try not to tempt fate."

Hermann smiled, then wound part of the rope around his waist and his wrist, tugged on the line to test its surety, then slowly backed himself over the edge. The only thing that kept an overwhelming sense of dread from crawling up his spine, was the light from the lantern he'd hooked to his belt. That way, he told himself, he wouldn't fall into Hades in darkness. The walls of the shaft were cold and faintly moist but absent of any earth. He slowly maneuvered down the line of the rope, meter after meter, before he saw that several pairs of perforations in the stone had hosted iron ladder rungs. After another meter, the first intact and sturdy rungs appeared, enough for him to get a grip.

"Géza," he called up. "There's a ladder here about four meters down."

"Be careful that they don't pop out of their tethers from rust."

Hermann used the rungs to continue down. One, then another, then another. After four or five meters, he discovered the smooth stone floor below.

"The shaft's about ten or so meters deep. It looks like there's a passage down here as well, and I think there's an underground stream beyond it, based on the noise. Can you make it down?"

"If my knots hold out, yes. Give me a minute."

Géza wound himself up in the rope and back walked carefully down the wall as Hermann had done until he reached the rungs of the ladder. Once they were both on solid ground, they proceeded through the passage toward the sound of running water. They came to a T-shaped intersection where a stream was running in a cut channel with two walkways on either side.

"Come on, let's see if this empties out. There may be another entrance downstream," said Hermann.

They followed the stream for several minutes until they came out at an obscure opening in a rock outcropping. The water continued to flow in the open air over a series of boulders. At the end of the shallow drop was a very large pond with a thickly wooded islet in the middle.

"I think I recognize this location from the map I took from Pavol's cottage," said Hermann. "I think we're somewhere far east of the castle."

"It looks like the pond I saw during the early days of the investigation. It's at least a twenty-minute walk, overground, from Schattenturm."

"There's a way down to the pond over there." Hermann followed the path of the running water to a narrow set of rock-hewn stairs, barely different from the natural crags. They led downward to the edge of the pond where Hermann began to follow the shore, studying the islet.

"I think there's something out on the little island, Géza. It's reflecting the moonlight. Do you see it?"

"Is it a rock?"

"I'm not sure, but—" He stuck his boot into the water, then took another step which was no deeper. "—There's a sunken path here."

He pushed through the pond to reach the islet, from where he was able to pull back some brambles carefully to peer through a dark patch of overgrowth.

"It's some kind of statue or little monument," he called back softly.

He continued pulling away brambles, untangling himself as he went, until he reached the object. It was a kind of rounded obelisk on a plinth; it bore no inscription. He tapped his boot on the ground around it and studied the base with the light of his lantern.

"The base is the same stone as the crypt. Like a slab, and it's plain like the monument, except the monument has a small hole in the center, like a keyhole."

"A keyhole?"

"I can't tell for sure, but it hasn't been disturbed in quite a while."

He made his way back across the submerged path to the shore after pushing the brambles back where they'd been before, hiding the object.

"There's no sign of any activity here, so we'd better get back to where we started and follow the water and the tunnel in the other direction," pressed Hermann.

"Let's see where it leads us," said Géza.

The tunnel was more eerie going uphill than it was going down. There was no light at the end, simply a black square equal to the dimensions of the space which could only be pierced by the approach of the lantern light. They walked past the T-shaped intersection for several minutes, each step much like the last with no real change in scenery, giving the effect of a liminal space in either direction.

Eventually, they came upon the end of the tunnel. A large wooden door, its girth wide enough to encompass the channel of water plus the two walkways on either side. The metal grate set into its base allowed the water free passage.

Hermann raised his lantern to study the door and saw that there was an iron-ring handle. "I think this is the same door I looked through from the other side, in the bath-house. Let's see if we can get it open."

Géza reached for the ring, and with a firm pull the door gave way, scraping over the stone before swinging loose over the stream. "It's the bathhouse from yesterday," Géza said as he stepped into the room. "There's the mosaic and the hallway out into the undercroft. We're back at the castle."

"And someone's been through here, because the door is no longer locked," said Hermann.

They passed through the hallway where they'd chased the cloaked figure. Then they were in the open, cavernous space beneath the courtyard. Hermann lowered the flame of his light to catch anything emanating from the myriad of alcoves and dark doorways, but nothing seemed amiss.

"Do you want to split up? We could cover more ground that way," Hermann offered.

"There's a killer out there somewhere and one or both of us could be ambushed. I'd prefer to stick together."

The two pressed on, skirting the edge of the rocky out-croppings and rough masonry below the castle courtyard. Hermann ducked into the first passageway after the one that lead to the armory, but it was a dead end, so they continued. They traipsed through two side passageways and briefly up a stone stair and then around the pillared under-croft again. They passed the square room beneath the keep, and a passage that led on straight, beyond their sight.

Just before they were about to start down that path, muffled noises echoing off the rock caught their attention. They dimmed their lamps, and each used a hand to keep near the outer wall of the undercroft. The noises grew louder around a doorway with a shallow, pointed arch. Hermann peaked around the corner, careful to keep his lantern away from the entry, and saw faint light and notice-able voices beyond. He turned out the gas on his lamp and motioned for Géza to do the same. Géza nodded and snuffed his light before following Hermann through the doorway.

They crept into the space, a large chamber with oriental columns in red and white hues, dulled and chipped. Hermann and Géza advanced to two columns and peered carefully around the sides. At an angle, they observed two figures in hooded cloaks standing around a half dozen or so candles arrayed in a geometric pattern.

"From my flesh, I perceive the divine," came the low voice of a female. "Out of my expression is the will of creation, and in its opposite is the un-created."

The figure bent down to read from a large, antiquated book on the floor, surrounded by some objects. She turned the page and used a finger to trace the text. Then she rose with a triangular object in her left hand, a knife in a sheath based on the antler-handle sticking out of the scabbard. She threw back her hood, and so did the figure across from her, revealing Rachel and Josef Baum.

"Witness me, spirits of un-creation, of the antonym of bliss. Witness me now. I call upon you to accept the offering laid before you, slain in your honor."

Josef held up a dead rabbit from its rear legs, dangling the body over the center of the space outlined by the candlesticks. Rachel grabbed the thing by its ears, pulling the body taunt, then she slit its throat, sending a gush of clumped, ruby blood down over its head and into a bronze bowl beneath. Some dripped sloppily onto the floor around the bowl as Josef's grip caused the carcass to sway.

"Hold it steady, stupid," Rachel growled.

Once the blood had mostly stopped, Josef slapped the body down onto the floor and Rachel retrieved the bowl, setting the knife aside. She turned in the direction of Hermann and Géza who slipped their heads back around their respective columns and listened.

"Watchers of the gates of the west, hear my call. Awaken with the blood offering and heed my will as I have heeded yours."

She dipped her right hand's fingers into the bowl and then flicked the blood out in the direction she faced. Then she turned to another cardinal point.

"Watchers of the gates of the south, hear my call. Awaken with the blood offering and witness my deeds as I have witnessed yours."

She repeated the motion with the blood, then turned again. Hermann and Géza resumed their watch.

"Watchers of the gates of the east, hear my call. Awaken with the blood offering and listen to my chorus as I have listened to yours."

She repeated the process.

"Watchers of the gates of the north, hear my call. Awaken with the blood offering and watch my hand become yours as yours have become mine."

Josef retreated into the shadows, then returned a moment later with a large iron brazier which he sat near the carcass, the bowl, and the knife in the center of the space. Rachel retrieved a candle from its stick near where the old book still lay open. She brought it close to the brazier and then spoke an incantation that sounded familiar, yet terribly foreign, like something the Moslems say during their prayers but more distinct. Then she lit the brazier's charcoal with the candle and a fire leapt to life.

"Josef, get their things," Rachel ordered.

Josef pulled around a bag, and handed first a small metal item to Rachel. She peered at it, then smiled.

"Entities below, beyond, without, heed me. Do unto my enemy all that thou will. Take their name into your book and out of the book of life. Extinguish his line and wither his roots. Burn his fruit and spoil all seed. Let his scream be your music and his torment your pleasure."

Hermann and Géza passed a very concerned look in the shadows.

"I speak his name so that you may know your prize, your sacrifice. Reap unto Orczy Géza your utmost vile, your greatest treachery, and take the air from his lungs and the breath from his voice."

As she scooped a handful of blood and tossed it on the fire with the little piece of metal, Géza reached for his service revolver and slowly released it, without making a sound, from its holster inside his jacket. He had a very determined look in his eye, the same look he'd had when he pinned Johan Baum to his chair in the dining room.

Hermann snuck a glance around the column at Rachel who'd turned to get the next thing from her brother, and jumped to Géza's column. "Wait!" he mouthed silently.

He was met by Géza's angry look.

"Let them expose themselves." Hermann whispered, eyebrows arched.

Géza thought for a moment, gave a curt nod, and eased the revolver slowly back into its holster. Hermann breathed a silent sigh of relief as the ritual continued.

"Entities below, beyond, without, heed me," Rachel's voice echoed over the stones. "Do unto my enemy all that thou will. Take their name into your book and out of the book of life. Extinguish his line and wither his roots. Burn his fruit and spoil all seed. Let his scream be your music and his torment your pleasure. I speak his name so that you may know your prize, your sacrifice. Reap unto Hermann Horst your utmost vile, your greatest treachery, and take the air from his lungs and the breath from his voice."

Géza looked at Hermann. "Still want me to wait?" he whispered.

Hermann smiled.

Rachel tossed two little objects onto the fire, followed by another handful of the rabbit's blood.

"So let it be," said Josef.

"Not yet," Rachel shot. "There's something else. We're going to need more than bunny blood to make this work."

She bent down and pulled up the bloodied knife.

"You of the foul, the low, the wicked, the wretched, the vile, the un-born, the never-dead, witness me! I know your power and you know mine. I call upon you now as I did then, to make your will and power manifest. My family is at threat from these two whose names I have offered in sacrifice. Their potential is great, but yours is greater. Destroy Orczy Géza and Hermann Horst as you destroyed Andrej Fehér. I give to you my bond, my will, my power in service for this act. Witness me and do as I command!"

She raised her bloodied hand and slashed it with the blade, letting the blood from her palm mingle with the animal's as it fell onto the fire.

"My blood for their blood. Erase them from the book of life."

She was smiling grotesquely, a mixture of ecstasy and vitriol in equal measures.

"Rachel," Josef said, more than a little worry in his tone. "You shouldn't have done that. You know what Grandmama said about human blood. You'll bring it back on us."

"Shut up. You want them to take Father away? Over some stupid hedge trimmer? Because that's what they'll do. The spirits ripped that bastard apart when I asked them to. They'll do it again now."

"But what about the rules? The book says we can't do this."

"Then why's it in the book? Power is power. I swear if I weren't a girl, I'd be the man Father always wanted you to become. Besides, how can we not curse them? Andrej betrayed us and he started after Mama, not that she didn't want it. Now these two are going to arrest Father for giving Andrej what he deserved, and we'll all be left with nothing. Do you understand what that means?"

Josef looked on, mouth half open.

"Of course not. You can't even think a step ahead your own feet. Come on. Help me clean this up before someone notices we're out of bed."

The two men ducked back behind the column while Rachel put the rabbit on the brazier, followed by what was left of the blood. She wrapped her hand in a cloth she pulled from a pocket. Then the two blew out the candles, save for one which they used to light a lamp. Rachel closed the old book and fastened a little latch on its front. She put it in an open slot between other tomes on a low stand against the far back wall. She cleaned the knife on another piece of cloth and re-sheathed it and put it beside the books. Then they both disappeared over and up a narrow set of stairs on the back wall. Near the top, Rachel pushed on the stone of the ceiling, and it parted to the side above them, revealing a shaft of blue light that vanished after the siblings had gone through and closed the entry behind them. Only then did Hermann and Géza come out from behind the column and relight their lanterns.

"Why on earth didn't you let me arrest them?"

"On what charges, exactly?"

"Witchcraft for a start. Conspiracy to commit murder, and maybe abetting murder as well."

Hermann approached the ritual space and raised his lantern to give the most light. A six-pointed star had been drawn in chalk, with salt laid over it. Candlesticks were positioned in each of the triangles created by the intersections of the overlapping shapes, leaving the central hexagram open where the brazier had been lit and the rabbit still burned. He looked closer and discovered that Rachel or Josef had apparently stolen a pair of his cufflinks from his room, despite keeping it locked the last two days, and had done the same to Géza to get hold of some small medals, probably to his dinner jacket.

"Hermann?"

"They think their father is the murderer. If one of them had murdered Andrej, we'd have heard a different conversation."

Géza chuffed. "I'd still like to arrest them."

Hermann walked through the ritual shape and over to the shelf where the books and the knife were placed. He pulled out the black book that Rachel had been reading from and carefully leafed through the pages. Some were written in German, others in Latin, Greek, and even Hebrew, the last of which he couldn't read. It was handwritten and drawn, with no title. He shut it and put it back on the shelf. He pulled out another, a leather-bound journal and opened it.

"Géza, I think this belonged to Andrej." He flipped through several pages.

Géza looked at the journal beside Hermann. "I wouldn't have taken him for a man who kept a journal. He didn't seem the type."

"This explains where all the ink he ordered went." Hermann leafed through the pages. Every entry was written in a large, clumsy hand. He flipped to the front. "Look at this, the first entry."

Géza bent over the page and read the words aloud.

My lawyer, Dobay, told me to keep a journal of anything important during my time at Schattenturm. I'm to write down my interactions with the Baums and the von Voitsbergs so there's a record of what they say and do toward me and about my inheritance.

"His lawyer ... and his inheritance? Hmm," said Géza.

"It starts up again on the next page." Hermann read the entry.

I've been a groundskeeper and chief gardener at Schattenturm since 1874. I was given to an orphanage in Budapest when I was a baby, but I was never adopted. When I was twelve, I was told who my mother was, and I wrote to her. She visited me and said she was the cook at Schattenturm, up in the country. The orphanage refused to keep me after I turned thirteen and could start working, so my mother found me a position as a groundskeeper where she worked. She told me to keep our rela-tionship a secret, so I did. I wanted to know who my father was, but she wouldn't tell me for years. When I turned twenty, she told me the herr, Georg von Voitsberg was my father. I had known him for a while and he was always nice enough to me. He let me borrow books from the library so I could learn more about gardening. I took books on cards and gambling instead which helped me better. I confronted Herr von Voitsberg about being my father, from the story that my mother told me. He said it was true. He increased my salary after that.

Hermann flipped through to another entry.

I confronted Herr von Voitsberg about my inheritance. He's getting old and sick. I don't think he'll live more than a year. I wanted to know what I could expect, since I'm his only son. The codger told me that the house and everything in it would go to his brat nephew, Friederich. The land and the title were tied together. He told me I'd gotten as good as I could hope to get, since I'm bastard-born. I was angry and cursed him.

Further on there was another entry.

Georg von Voitsberg died last night. I spoke to him the day before and I pushed him again about my rights, what I'm due as his son. He couldn't speak very good, but he told me that the trea-sure was mine and had me look at the riddle in the old book about when the castle was taken from the Turks a long time ago. He said he couldn't remember where it was, but it belonged to me since I'm the heir. I'll find it, no matter what it takes.

"Well, now we have confirmation Andrej was seeking the treasure the night he was killed," Géza commented. "What's that afterwards?"

The bank men came with the police and ordered the house be closed. Herr von Voitsberg had been in a lot of debt, and that

brat Friederich couldn't pay it, so they took the house. My house!
They told Fürth, Schrode, my mother, and me that our salaries
were protected as separate payments from the debts, but that
we're only to keep the place standing and to let no one live in it.
I'm not allowed into the house by Fürth, and he knows all the
passages in and out. I can't sneak past him to look for my trea-
sure, he's found me three times already and told me he'd have me
locked up if I kept at it.

Another entry picked up what happened later.

Fürth must have told the bank I'd been inside the house
because now they'll only issue my salary from Budapest, with a
portion going to Fürth to provide for Pavol. I guess the runt is
supposed to replace me. I won't give up. I'll be back. Dobay says
I should bide my time and enjoy my salary. Try to find some
other work before it runs out. I'm owed more than that. What
does a toff like him know, anyway?

"Based on the next entry, it looks like he didn't write
again until just about a year ago," said Hermann as he
scanned ahead. "He received word from his mother that
the house had been bought by the Baums, so he came back
just after they started to move in."

"Anything of note?" asked Géza.

"Only that Andrej seems to have charmed Frau Baum
with his knowledge of the house and the grounds, and she
was responsible for his continued position here. He brags a
great deal about it." Hermann flipped through more pages.
"He discusses the various places that he's searched for the
treasure. Hidden rooms, secret passages, the extensive
undercroft. He found nothing though. Here's the last
entry."

Gustav's old legend may as well be worthless. I can't find
anything in the lower levels and I've tried all the passageways.
There's nothing up any of the towers either, besides the observa-

tory. The sluice only leads back into the bathing room and an alcove with a broken ladder. Baum won't give me a key to the mausoleum. Is he hiding something in there? He won't keep me from what's mine. He probably pulled out the ladder rungs. I told him his pretty wife wasn't worth the trouble of bedding after he accused me of seducing her. Bastard would've hit me if I didn't have my shovel in my hand. Rich bastard. Have to try something else.

That bitch Astrid thinks she's better than me. Even now. She's got nothing besides a half-dead old bat and a bunch of junk. Thought she'd tell me what was my business and what wasn't. Well, I got her key and I'm going down into the mausoleum tonight. I'll be damned if she'll keep me from my inheritance. They're all hiding it in there. Astrid and Baum are probably in on it together. Wouldn't want a good working man to get what's coming to him.

"Andrej confronted Frau Astrid? She never mentioned that to us," said Géza.

"No ... she didn't. Nor did she say he'd stolen one of her keys. Or even that she had keys to the property at all. I'll speak to her tomorrow and see about it. Géza, I'm going to keep this journal on me. It may be the only solid proof we can get without a confession."

Géza nodded, then looked around the ritual space again with a slight shudder. "What do you want to do about all this? We can't let her keep putting hexes, or curses, or whatever she's doing on everyone."

"Hmm? Oh ... this?" Hermann said with a wave. "It's just a pastime for them. None of this can affect you unless you believe in it, Géza. Your own mind will often warp reality around what you think your fate is supposed to be. Just ignore their antics and you'll be fine."

Géza winced, but said no more. "Alright, well let's get out of here then. I've got an early train, and everyone seems to have gone back to their beds now."

Hermann kept hold of the journal in one hand as he followed Géza up the stair and into the ceiling stone which the inspector pushed to reveal an entry under the altar in the chapel. The chalice that had been toppled on their first incursion through, now sat tucked amongst some hay in a nearby crate where it couldn't serve as an alarm system to the unwary ritual-makers.

Chapter 23

For the second night in a row, restful sleep eluded Hermann. He tossed and turned and had fitful dreams. Whether it was his worry that Andrej's killer might get away, the reality that Géza might not return from Budapest, or the fact that even in the darkness of his room Gustav von Voitsberg stared at him with luminescent silver eyes, he couldn't manage a state of deep sleep. After waking before the end of a troublesome dream reached its conclusion, he rose to the first glimmers of the sunrise starting to radiate blue over the sky outside. He dressed himself and fit Andrej's shabby journal inside the pocket of his black suit jacket, then slipped out into the hall. He wandered back to the second floor of the northern hall and found it the same as he had the first night, with the séance room's door locked once more. He took a stairway down to the first floor and circled back toward the south, past unused and unlocked rooms and beyond the first floor of the library. He was glad of the opportunity to think clearly about the last two days and nights and what he'd read in Andrej's journal. He couldn't shake the feeling that after what he'd heard, it was no wonder that Andrej's death was a welcome state for most who knew him. His demise ended the disruption and inflammation of the lives of everyone he came into contact with during his life, and whom he continued to irritate in death.

He circled the main hall, ducking into each room briefly for a look around. He entered the billiards and smoking room which, based on the lack of smell, hadn't been used in some time. Something made him stop in his tracks. It was the sound of a low, singular tone or the semblance of one, but he couldn't place its origin. Unlike the buzzing tone that permeated his bedroom the first night, this was more melodic in nature. The room was finely decorated with a colorful scarlet rug beneath the billiards table that matched the upholstery on the chairs set around the rail of the fireplace. More landscapes like those in the dining room were dotted sparsely around the walls on picture line. Two suits of armor, which must have stayed with the house, stood mounted on the wall opposite the fireplace. Hermann moved around the room slowly, listening for the sound.

After a while of trial and error to locate its strongest point, he gravitated to the wall between the suits of armor which gave a clearer and louder tone when he pressed his ear against the wood paneling. He searched around for something out of place nearby, a sconce or different colored material. He found his mark in a stretch of the floor molding that was a darker stain than the rest. He pushed on it, and sure enough the section of wall he'd focused on gave way with a faint *click*. He pressed on the paneling, and it swung inward on a hinge to reveal a set of stone stairs leading up around a center column. The sound was clearly music as it echoed off the stone and down the stairs, a kind of plucking and strumming combination. Thin streams of light danced on the stairs through narrow arrow slits as he climbed up toward the sound of the music. He peered through one and glimpsed a mirrored staircase on the other side with larger windows in the space beyond, allowing in the light from the leavening sunrise.

Once Hermann had nearly reached the top, he slowed his pace in order to make as little noise as possible while the chords echoed around him. The stairs led to an open doorframe in a brighter room. He peaked over the lip and saw a man sitting on an Empire Style bench with his back to the doorway. Hermann recognized Fürth's shock of white hair and the weathered skin on his neck. The room had four large windows set into shallow dormers and looked out in various directions over the tops of the roofs of the castle. There was some other furniture scattered about with a large brass telescope on a tripod, positioned at a window. Fürth's music continued for another few moments before coming to a gentle conclusion.

Fürth sighed, then turned his head slightly to the right to speak over his shoulder. "Come in, there's no sense in hiding on the stairs. I'd recognize the sound of that old latch anywhere."

Hermann obliged and stepped into the room. "You play the lute well. Did you teach yourself?"

Fürth smiled. "No, it was a gift from an old friend. He had a flair for history."

"You mean Herr Georg von Voitsberg." Hermann sat opposite the butler.

"Yes. He and I knew each other from boyhood in this house. I was the only other boy his age and he never had a problem with ignoring protocol if he felt like it." He chuckled. "His father was another matter. Mean as nails and a stickler for tradition. We used to come up to the top of the old minaret before the renovations. No one but us would dare to make the climb. He honored that by building us this observatory. It sits on top of the old room just below us. I come here when I can't sleep. It's still the only part of this house with a degree of privacy."

"It does grant perspective," Hermann said as he glanced to the east and the red aura. "Did you stay close with the freiherr beyond boyhood?"

"Herr von Voitsberg wasn't one for close connections. I don't flatter myself by saying I was the only one who really knew him."

"More than his own brother?"

266

"There were aspects to him. Layers that he didn't reveal, even to his family. I honored his discretion and returned it with my own." He paused. "I know what kind of reputation he has now. The great playboy and partier extraordinaire. That was only half of him. The half he wanted seen. The Georg that I knew was quiet and thoughtful."

"Herr Fürth—"

"Just Fürth, Herr Horst.

"I believe that there was more to Andrej than is readily apparent."

Fürth frowned.

Hermann continued. "He was Herr von Voitsberg's son, wasn't he?"

"Yes," he answered with a sigh. "That was the freiherr's other half. The half he wasn't when he was with me. The half that Andrej inherited."

"Why the secrecy? The freiherr is dead and so is Andrej. Why keep the secret?"

"A family doesn't die with one individual, Herr Horst. Nor does its honor. Andrej was a black mark on this house and everyone associated with it. His heredity should be forgotten. He was never able to live up to his legacy, despite our attempts."

"Tell me, Fürth."

The old man raised his eyebrows and laid a heavy elbow against the arm of the bench to rub and support his temple.

"The other half of Georg von Voitsberg was a terrible thing to behold. An appetite in all things. Drinking, gambling, and women. It had happened a few times before Frau Kovács came to work here as a kitchen maid. More than once, I'd had to escort a lady out of the house in the early hours or tend to her in the night when she'd come across the freiherr badly. Herr Albert and I managed to orchestrate a discreet payment or a court favor for them here and there. The staff were another matter. He'd ... *taken* ... two in the years since his father had died, and Herr Albert managed the house. Both were given a reference and sent far away: Zagreb and Brno. Frau Kovács was then, as she is now, sweet but incredibly simple-minded. When he took advantage of her, she convinced herself that he'd fallen in love with her. Far from assaulted, she felt somehow recognized. Frau Schrode defended her and pressed Herr Albert and I to keep her on, and to prevent the freiherr from continuing his behavior. It was set in stone when Frau Kovács revealed she was pregnant. It was all Herr Albert could do to convince her to give the child up for adoption when the time came. Only the worst realities imaginable prevailed when she understood what his life as a bastard would mean and ... how she would be put into the pauper's house with him. Forever a leper from decent work, should she tell her story. I'm not proud of my part. Time went by and Herr Albert passed, much of the staff turned over, and the freiherr's personality changed. His brother had had a hand in that, from grief and dishonor. He confided in me more and more, and the parties toned down. When Frau Kovács told us that Andrej and she had been in communication, and that he was to be turned out of the orphanage he'd lived in his whole life, I spoke to the freiherr and convinced him to bring him here to work. Guilt weighed on Georg, and he gave the boy unnatural advantages for his rank and position. He showed too much trust in him, affording him favors and privileges to the house."

"Did no one ask about this boy that Herr von Voitsberg had taken a liking to?"

"I suspect Frau Maria knew, of course, but it was only later that Herr Friederich and Frau Astrid understood. As the freiherr sickened, he acknowledged Andrej, though never legally. This wondered and aggrandized Andrej. He wasn't grateful in the least for knowing his father and the privilege of living here with security. Instead, he started demanding that Herr von Voitsberg write him into an inheritance as payment for his situation and the freiherr's past indiscretion with his mother. It grew worse toward the end. He started demanding legitimacy, that as his son, Andrej should be the heir, not Friederich, much less Astrid. He wouldn't understand, no matter what I or the freiherr told him. There was no money by then to quiet him either."

Fürth shook his head.

"He tried to impose himself on the funeral. There was barely enough to afford it as it was, and only the family's true friends and those who knew Herr von Voitsberg from the county came here to the chapel for the service. Andrej tried to sit in the front row. It took Herr Friederich threatening him with a duel to quiet him and force him downstairs where I sequestered him. God, he was too bold. I wrote to the freiherr's executor in the capitol to have Andrej's pension payments solely transferable in Budapest. It kept him away for years while Schattenturm was shut up by the banks, decaying in neglect and stale air."

"Why would you do so much for them? For the von Voitsbergs? You said yourself that this house had fallen from grandeur and renown. I can imagine your pension payments didn't match your earlier salary. So why spend your time and energy keeping up and protecting them?"

"It wasn't about them. Herr Horst, when you devote so much of yourself for so long to a thing, it becomes a part of you. This house and I, we're one and the same. Leaving it would be like tearing down a wing and pulverizing the stone to dust. The ... *connection* I shared with Georg lives on here. How could I leave a part of myself behind? Practically all of myself that I've ever known, to see it come to harm?"

"And your honor? How did that factor with Andrej? Wasn't he a part of this house as its son, and as the son of its herr? How could you lie and cover up Georg von Voitsberg's sins?"

"I would've done anything for Georg." He paused, eyes reddening. "Andrej was a product of the worst parts of a man you can sum up. A rudderless ship left at sea. The half of Georg that was responsible for Andrej was the opposite of everything he was when he was with me. Georg's rot was the product of what came from his father's cruelty and neglect. Andrej was Georg's son, and he never would have thought much of it if his mother, and his low self-worth, didn't fill his head with visions of a righted wrong he never truly knew."

"Friederich von Voitsberg? Once Andrej returned with his dreams of inheritance and a scheme to work under the Baums, what did the true heir of Schattenturm think?"

"Friederich had taken his position in the military by then and Frau Astrid ... she ..." He paused. "Frau Astrid dismissed him for what he was, a scoundrel and a thief. Beyond that, I don't know and it's not my business to know."

"Surely you must think they felt threatened by his appearance. She lost this house, nearly everything in it, and her dowry. Her brother left with an empty title."

"Frau Astrid is a noble woman with a difficult path ahead of her. She could no more have helped Andrej than she could have hurt him. She's not to blame if Andrej's schemes turned folly again. The man couldn't realize his own position and what good to make of it."

Hermann leaned forward. "By scheme, you mean his search for the Turkish gold."

Fürth scoffed. "I have lived in this house for over fifty years, Herr Horst. I have seen it taken apart and rebuilt. Walked every inch of its halls and grounds, the ones you can see and the ones you can't. There is no treasure hidden here and there never was. The freiherr was open with me about his plans with Herr Albert. They used their father's savings to start the renovations and pay for the parties. The fact that the money ran out is evidenced by the fact that the family now sits destitute. The treasure is a fable, something to ponder while fluffing the pillows and dusting the furniture, nothing more. Andrej's interest in it was just another bad path he led himself down that would turn up nothing but wasted time and disappointment."

"Then how did he die? You must have some theory about his murder."

"I really can't say, Herr Horst." He pursed his lips and turned to face the rays of sunrise piercing through the glass to the east, radiating over the mist settled in the low places of the grounds out beyond the castle. "It's not my place to speculate on things beyond my understanding. All I know is that Andrej doomed himself, with his own actions and his behavior. Doing what he did, despite knowing what had happened to his mother … knowing what produced him …" He shook his head. "What happened to him was always going to be his end. It was clear from the start."

"You think he was always going to be murdered?"

"I think the boy couldn't walk a straight path. He only saw the narrative he'd created to call his life a tragedy, and he ultimately made it his reality, with himself as the perpetual victim, no matter what he may have done in service or sin to others."

Fürth rose, straightened his vest, and brushed his jacket sleeves.

"Herr Horst, we can't always help the people we love, we can only mitigate the harm they do to themselves when we can. Now, if you will excuse me, I must begin my duties. Dawn waits for no man."

Hermann rose to meet him. "Thank you, Fürth. For better or ill, I hope this turns out for the best in the end."

Fürth's marble demeanor had awakened and come to rest over his expression before he gave Hermann a short bow and departed.

Chapter 24

Hermann managed to catch Géza on his way to the carriage when they passed going through the main floor of the keep. Géza had a forlorn look on his face and seemed not to have slept much either, given the dark circles under his eyes. He wore a long green coat with his black dress boots and kepi.

"Géza, I know it'll be hard, but you have to convince your commander to keep the investigation open, at least until tonight. I've just spoken to Fürth. I can't say for certain, but I believe he knows the details of Andrej's death."

"I'll do my best, Hermann, but it's not just this investigation that's in question. It's my whole position with the Gendarme. Pointing the finger at Baum may have cost me more than I realized."

"Well then, tell your commander you've narrowed the possibilities, and by this evening one of the last two primary suspects will be revealed as the killer. And Géza, it's critical you return immediately."

"How can you be so sure?"

"I'm going to use a parlor trick, so to speak, to bring the truth out."

"There's a little Gypsy in you after all, Professor." Géza said, slapping him on the shoulder.

Hermann smiled. "We do what we have to do. But seriously, let your commander know that you have Andrej's personal journal and it strongly implicates the killer. And that since you've been pulled away, I'm carrying out our plan for this evening. I'll send you a wire before the evening train departs, telling you that I've discovered the identity of the killer but that I don't trust the security of the telegraph operator not to tip them off."

"That would give me enough leverage to get a blanket arrest warrant from the court. I hope you're right, Hermann. Now, I've got to get going or I'll miss the train. Good luck and try not to get yourself killed."

The morning quickly lit the castle grounds with intense white-yellow rays, highlighting the foliage of every treetop and the dew on every blade of grass. Hermann took the rear path to the groundskeepers' cottages, past the stables which already appeared active, given the open door and wafting odor of warm manure. Pavol was nowhere to be found around his cottage or the surrounding hamlet, and his tools were missing from the unlocked shed. Hermann decided to trek east in the direction of Frau Maria's cottage, in hope the boy's duties had taken him to that side of the estate.

The walk gave him space to think about the dream he'd had just before waking. It consisted of visions of what Rachel and Josef had been doing at their unholy sacrifice. That was followed by images of his sister, Ingfrid. It had been years since he'd pictured Ingfrid's face so clearly, though the dream had brought with it a fresh wave of torment. Had he failed in his duty by not remaining in Salzburg and taking up his father's mantle as the head of the household, and in the process doomed Ingfrid's future? What else was he to do though, but continue his education in Vienna? He couldn't very well have resigned himself to the life of a gentleman farmer, the world his parents and grandparents had known was eroding as the world grew smaller. He'd planned on elevating his family's standing through education, not land holdings, but he'd caused their ruin instead. He had attained a professorship, but was that all he could hope for? That, and the publication of his niche books on the parapsychological, which few enough had a passing interest in. He had lost his family's estate, the respect of his family's long-standing friends in Salzburg, and his actual family—his sister who was all he had had in the world. How couldn't he have foreseen that she was too young, too naïve, and too grief stricken to manage her heart as well as her head? He wondered at why she would appear to his subconscious now, in the midst of the investigation. And the cliff? Why did the cliff manifest in his dream? Looming, beckoning, taunting him to go there, the site where they'd found her broken body.

He was shaken from his morose thoughts at the sight of the beech and oak woods, with their lush undergrowth of ferns and brambles that gave way to thick detritus and open views beneath the boughs. The chill of the morning air was lifting as the sun continued to rise and send a warm southernly breeze. Rustles in the underbrush revealed a squirrel and the faint outline of a deer leaping out of sight. After a few more minutes hiking through a narrow path, he slowed. He could hear voices ahead. He stopped on the path to listen when the tone of one of the speakers rose in intensity.

"I only ever asked you to do me a few favors. Go here, get this, bring me that. How was that so hard to do?"

"It was more than that and you know it. What you're doing ... it's wicked. I can't help you anymore. I won't."

"Then I can't do anything for you."

Hermann carefully stepped further down the path. He spied Rachel in a dark riding habit, and beside her was Pavol, looking very grim.

"All those things I promised ... *sweet things*. You'll never know them if you don't stay loyal to me. I can make you very happy. My family has money, and we've never been cheap. Do you really want to work as a laborer for the rest of your life? You could be important Pavol, but not if you don't do what I want."

She glided over to him, her riding skirt making it look as though she levitated above the fallen leaves. She placed her two gloved hands on his chest and stretched up to kiss his mouth. Then she whispered something in his ear and smiled. Pavol closed his eyes tightly for a moment; a low, intense groan could be heard before he opened his eyes suddenly. He grabbed hold of her hands and pushed her away, hard enough that she lost her balance and almost fell. She let out with an exaggerated yelp, then straightened herself, a look of surprise on her face.

"Well, maybe you're more of a man than I thought you were," she said and made to come toward him again.

Pavol stepped away. "You need help, Rachel. Your mother is right, listen to her. I don't need this ... to be your aide in hurting them, and I'll never trade favors with you and ignore doing what's right just to make you happy. You need to confess, and then you need to pray."

This finally appeared to have broken her resolve. She stepped back and looked as though she'd been struck.

"Don't talk to me about Mama. You know nothing. She knows nothing. Just wait, I'll have you sacked, Pavol. You'll be right back in the dung heap of some scratch-hole village in rags where you belong." She stood up straighter. "That's if I don't tell them what you did to me. How you tried to force yourself on me, just like Andrej tried to do with Mama."

"You're a liar. That's not true and you know it. We never did anything like that."

"Who's going to believe you? I'm the daughter of one of the richest men in the country. An archduchess to the likes of you. Hah, they'll never even bother to hear what you have to say."

Panic seemed to creep over Pavol as his eyes darted back and forth over Rachel's face, processing what she was saying.

"None of it has to happen though, just do as I said."

Hermann picked that moment to stroll loudly down the remainder of the path toward the pair. They both noticed him immediately. Pavol looked at him with confusion. Rachel shut her mouth tightly and relaxed her posture to attempt something like indifference.

"Good morning, Fraulein Baum. How do you do, Pavol?"

Neither answered.

"You're out for a very early ride, fraulein. Any reason?" Before she could answer, Hermann continued. "In my case, the early morning helps me clear my head. I barely slept, and I had the most peculiar dream. I was a tree and my roots were withering and dying, and I'd lost my voice. Some kind of eerie apparition in black was trying to steal the very air from my lungs. Fortunately, I was able to manifest a lady's fan and shoo the apparition away with a little flutter. I ended up fanning it right out the door and back to wherever it came from, with surprisingly little effort in the end. What do you make of that?"

Rachel didn't respond. She spun on her heel and trod away at a fast pace down a narrow game trail in the woods, leaving Pavol and Hermann behind.

Hermann shrugged. "Pavol, walk with me, would you? I'm headed down to Frau Maria's cottage and I'd like to speak with you."

Pavol nodded and took a few long strides to join him. Hermann said nothing for a few paces, putting further distance between Rachel and them. Pavol was furiously kneading his cap in his hands.

"Pavol, I heard the entire conversation between you and Rachel. Don't worry about her threats. Her mother understands her better than she understands herself, and as to the last thing she said, I know the context and I'll stand for your innocence should her threat come to pass."

The ginger-haired lad breathed a deep sigh of relief and dropped his arms to his side. "Thank you, herr. But I wish you wouldn't have heard all that stuff."

"I already know about her dalliances with witchcraft. I've seen her black book, and I watched her try to cast a spell on *me* last night."

Pavol quickly crossed himself and kissed the cross hanging on a leather strip about his neck.

"I told her she needs to confess to the Father and to pray. That what she is doing is evil. I swear the devil's in her."

"No, my boy. Just teenage antics. Rachel feels she needs to rebel against her mother and test the boundaries of her privileged world. None of that stuff, the spells or the spirits, can have any effect on you if you don't believe they can."

"But the Bible says that witchcraft is real. It can turn the crops bad and make you sick. Do you think that's what's wrong with old Frau von Voitsberg? Why she don't get better?"

"Pavol, Rachel used a half dozen different methods, incantations, languages, and techniques in her silliness. If the Devil were trying to work through her, he'd be more confused than pleased at what she has tried to accomplish. As for Frau von Voitsberg, I've heard from her that her doctors have diagnosed her with cancer. A very real, very medical condition that affects the body and which can be brought on by a number of different lifestyle and hereditary factors. It's nothing to do with the Devil. Which brings me to why I want to speak with you."

He stopped them on the path, at the head of a small clearing of wildflowers. "What did Rachel want you to do for her? I know a good deal already, so don't bother trying to protect any secret by concealing any part of the truth. And I want clear answers, not that nonsense you gave the inspector and me yesterday when we questioned you about Andrej and Frau Baum. Do we understand one another?"

Pavol hung his head, wringing his hat in his hands again. "I'm sorry about that. But things with Rachel ... well, it started out simple enough. She made friends with Andrej almost as soon as he came back to Schattenturm. They was like two peas in a pod at first. He told her about what the Gypsies get up to with their cards and their spells. He used to bring her things and she liked that. She was doing her rituals with her grandmother and her brother, so I didn't think it was all bad. But something happened between her and Andrej after a while. He stopped being so nice to her and getting her things. That's when she started coming to me instead of Andrej. She wanted things ..."

"What kinds of things did she want?"

"She wanted things for her rituals. A hawk's beak once. Fleece from a lamb. Then she asked for things from the staff's rooms. I didn't want to, but she um ... she kissed me a few times ... and, um ... I couldn't ..."

"Yes Pavol, I understand. Go on."

"Well, I took a watch from Herr Fürth. A piece of hair on a ribbon from Frau Schrode. One of Frau Kovács's aprons. And a pair of gloves from the groom. Plus, some other things. It took a long time to get them all. Then she wanted more. She kept wanting more and the things got more strange."

"Animals? ... Worse?"

"She started asking me to get her blood. I asked why, but she wouldn't tell me. I didn't know what to say, so I did it. I trap rabbits and hunt birds for the estate kitchen, so I got her blood from the rabbits or from some birds. I never killed a hawk. The beak I gave her was from a pigeon that the cook used in a pie."

"I'm glad. Hawks are courageous, noble hunters."

"Just before Andrej was ... um dead, she had a big fight with him. I overheard it and he called her all kinds of nasty things. That night she asked me for sow's blood. I told her I could buy it from the butcher, but she'd have to wait until the cook sent me there on an errand. She said no. Said it had to be fresh. She said she needed me to kill it myself. I didn't ... um ... I didn't know how to say no."

Pavol looked away from Hermann, he didn't seem to be able to face what he was about to say.

"How did you get the blood, Pavol?"

"I killed the neighbor's pig and did like she told me. Herr Horst, it made me feel so bad, but I wanted to make her happy. My mother told me animals don't have souls or nothing, so it wouldn't have really mattered, but it still felt bad to hit it with the hammer while it was looking at me."

Hermann was momentarily stunned. "You killed the pig with a ... hammer?"

"I took the sledgehammer and hit it right on the head between the eyes. I'd seen it done once before back home. The poor thing kept looking at me while I did it, but it died quick. Andrej was mighty mad when I told him what I'd done. He smacked me around a little like he does ... did. Then I slept over in the barn that night. I couldn't look at him after that. I kept seeing the pig's eyes when I looked at him. He looked a lot like that pig to me." He sighed. "Anyway, that was the night Andrej got murdered, so I never got to tell how sorry I was again."

Hermann crossed his arms behind his back and rubbed his middle knuckle as he took it all in.

"The night Andrej was killed, you slept in the barn?'

"Yeah, that's why I didn't know that he never came home."

"Pavol, it must have been very difficult for you, living under Andrej's rule. Did Andrej often hit you?"

"Only when I did something wrong or looked at him the way he didn't like. Sometimes he'd say I was thinking bad about him, but I wasn't"

"So, in the couple of weeks since Andrej's death, have Rachel's requests continued?"

"Oh yes. It got worse. She must have been fine with the pig's blood I gave her. There was a lot of it, and I don't know how she kept it hidden in her room or wherever, but she didn't ask for anything but small animals for a while."

"Have you participated in the rituals with her? Tell me the truth."

"No, never. I was too afraid, and besides, she never wanted me to."

"Did she or Andrej show you the tunnels and hidden passageways around the castle?"

"No. But I knew about some of them. I found a map in one of Andrej's books. I asked him if there were tunnels and such and he lied to me and said I was daft for thinking that. But I knew he was using them and looking for the treasure."

"Was anyone else looking for it, Pavol?"

"No, Andrej was real secretive about it."

"Is Rachel interested in the treasure?"

"No. She's only interested in her black magic stuff."

"What was her most recent request?"

"Um … day before yesterday she came to me."

"More pig's blood?"

"No." There was a long pause as Pavol seemed to contemplate what he was about to say next. "She said she had to have … human blood. I asked her what she meant, like a pinprick? She said no. She wanted liters of it. I told her that was impossible. You'd have to kill someone to get that much blood. Then she asked me if I'd get her bone dust instead. I didn't know what that was. She said it's when you grind up a body and scoop up all the bits. She said I could get loads of it from the old crypt, in the maze where the von Voitsbergs are buried. I told her that was sacrilege, that you can go to hell for that. She didn't care. She said she could pay me. And if I didn't do it, she'd she put a curse on me like she did Andrej."

"Had she previously asked Andrej for bones from the von Voitsberg crypt?"

"Yeah, and she said he told her no and to keep away from there."

"And did you get her the bone dust?"

"No! Never. I told her then that I wouldn't do it. That the angels would come down and punish me, that she'd never get judged good after she died. She was mad at that. Then she asked me again this morning, and you said you heard all that."

"Indeed. Was there anything else about Rachel or anyone else that you haven't told me yet?"

"Not that I can think of … no. I don't like to keep secrets, Herr Horst. The father in town says bodies aren't designed to keep secrets, like the gates of heaven aren't meant to open for donkeys."

"That's quite the metaphor. Can you tell me who else Andrej knew around the estate in more than just his role as gardener? Did Frau Astrid von Voitsberg and Andrej know each other well? I understand you've been tending her gardens for quite some time and I wondered how that came to be."

"Well, Andrej gave me that duty after I learned how to do things. Before that, it was his job to work at the widow's house. I don't know if they spoke a lot, but he told me once that Frau Astrid thought she was higher and mightier than what she was. I never knew what to make of that."

"And that was all?"

"As far as I can remember, yes. Andrej complained about almost everyone he met. It's hard to remember why for all of them."

Hermann nodded. His clarity on Rachel had been helpful, but his statement about the pig's eyes was unsettling.

A faint rustle in the brush at the tree line, amid the pause in conversation, caught Hermann and Pavol's attention. When they turned to look, a good-sized stag was stepping out carefully into the small meadow. It had noticed the two men and appraised them, but it seemed content enough to start grazing, not seeing them as a threat. It was quite a sight and Hermann thought again of how Schattenturm was as conflicted as the troubled souls who occupied it. The serenity was broken by a reverberating *crack* and a whistle passing very near their heads. A half a heartbeat later, the bullet struck the stag which let out with a confused garble and dropped to the ground.

"I did it, Father! Nearly a hundred meters, too."

The rotund figure of Josef Baum popped up from behind a low bit of brush on the other side of the meadow. Soon after, his father appeared alongside him.

"That you did, boy. Go and see where you hit it."

"Did you not see us standing here in the broad daylight?" Hermann questioned, barely containing his anger as the Baums came near.

"We saw you. You weren't in any danger, not with Josef's shot. Now, if you'd jumped a bit to the right, well ..." Baum let out with a chuckle.

Josef glared at Hermann as he passed. Then he bent down to inspect the deer.

"I got him right in the cheek!"

"Josef," Hermann said forcefully. "Do you know what the first rule of stalking and shooting is?"

"Line up the shot?"

"No, It's to never take the shot if there's a risk to someone else."

"Enough of that, Horst. Don't be a tiresome fool about it. My boy's an ace." Baum curled his mouth as though he were chewing cud for a moment. "You there, gardener boy. Get over there and dress that thing. I want it ready by tonight. You know how to butcher it, right?"

Pavol dropped his gaze and nodded, then put his hat back on and unslung his tool bag by the carcass.

"Father, I want him to take it back whole so he can get all the blood out. He'll ruin it if dresses it here."

"What the devil are you talking about? Field dressing is the first step. Why do you want the blood?"

Hermann raised an eyebrow in Josef's direction, knowing perfectly well the reason.

"For ... um, my black sausages. I want to have black sausages made from it."

Baum shook his head a little. "Fine. Boy, drag that back up to the gamesman's shed. It's only about a mile."

None of the party stayed around after the pronouncement. Pavol used some rope to bind the stag's hooves together so it could be pulled over the leaf litter back to the house. The Baums walked off up the path, rifle butts resting on their shoulders. Though, Hermann couldn't help but notice Josef's wicked eye as the boy glanced over his shoulder to have another look at him before they passed out of sight.

Chapter 25

As Hermann approached the Baroque cottage from the back, he spotted a wooden gate into the cottage's gardens through the thick exterior hedge wall. As he neared the gate, he saw the armillary he'd noticed the day prior and a rock outcropping beyond, shaded by a large yew tree towering above. Before he reached the gate, Astrid strode into view from the direction of the house. She seemed not to notice Hermann as she passed towards the yew tree and out of sight around another wall of hedging. He opened the gate and stepped inside.

"Frau Astrid? It's Hermann Horst."

"I didn't expect to see you here." Her voice came from beside him.

She was sitting on a stone bench under a bough of the yew, wearing a simple white tea gown with wide cuffs and delicate floral embroidery. She rose slowly, barely disturbing the mixture of short grass and needles beneath her cream-colored shoes.

Hermann bowed in greeting. "I apologize if I startled you."

"You didn't, I don't startle easily."

"I'm afraid I've come to ask you a few more questions ... if now is a good time?"

"I don't know what else there is to tell you. I think you understand my position, especially regarding the Baums after that display last night."

"Indeed. Johan Baum's feelings about nearly everyone are not long suppressed it seems."

He looked around the garden room, at the thick, gnarled, twisting trunk of the yew and its splayed branches that swept over the space like a wind-bent screen. The rocky outcropping wasn't entirely natural. A faint bass relief of a female figure with closed eyes and long, flowing hair was central. A small candle was lit beside her, wax dripping down the face of the rock below it.

"Was this more work by your father?" he asked.

"No, the lady and the yew were both here long before this garden. Even before this house and Schattenturm." She stepped under the shade of the yew to the relief. "I don't know who she is, nor did my father, but we both thought her grove beautiful, so we designed the garden around it. He thought she was an elf or a goddess. Her name and her story are lost to us, but when I come here, I feel a sense of calm. A connectedness to something."

"A communion with the timeless. The yew was a symbol of everlasting life to our ancestors, before Christianity and its promise of everlasting life through a messiah. For thousands of years we knew the world through the spirits in everything, even stone." He reached out and touched the face with his fingertips.

"Do you think of her often?" asked Astrid.

"Her?"

"The woman you've lost. The lady of the stone doesn't draw on those who haven't lost someone. And it's clear you have, Herr Horst."

"Yes ... Ingfrid haunts me in a way." He dropped his hand, but the smooth stone had left a residual coolness.

"After my father died, I often thought I had seen him in the castle or on the grounds. I wanted to speak with him, ask him why he'd left us, but I never got the chance."

Hermann smiled softly. "You are kind to tell me."

"Come, Professor. Let's see the rest of the gardens." Her tone was cheerful, her smile soothing. "They're nothing compared to those at Schattenturm, but they have their own simple beauty."

Astrid led Hermann past the armillary, away from the secret grove and the lady in stone, just as a faint breeze extinguished the candle.

"I am very sorry to do it, Frau Astrid, but I must press you on something related to Andrej."

They walked along slowly beside each other for another few steps toward the rear of the house.

"I am sorry too. I would have preferred if we just had a friendly moment together. It's been too long since I met someone who shared my same interests and take on life. Andrej in death is as destructive as he was in life."

"Unfortunately, yes … I found his journal last night. It seems he'd been keeping it on the behest of a lawyer who he hired to contest the inheritance left by the late Freiherr von Voitsberg. He claimed that he was Herr Georg's natural son by Frau Kovács."

Astrid's long, ash-blond hair was unbound and flowed airily as she walked, though it did little to hide her frown.

"It's true. We in the family knew of my uncle's indiscretion. He was not a respectable man for much of his youth and middle age, despite his rank. He became more genteel, wiser, late in his life, around the time he descended into comparative poverty. Shortly before my uncle died, things with Andrej started to spiral out of control. I'm sure the journal you found can provide seedier details than I can."

"Andrej wrote that after he learned of his parentage, he pressed the freiherr. Money as restitution for his bastardy, and a share, or the entirety if possible, of Schattenturm's value upon the freiherr's death."

"As far as I know from my uncle, and from the reading of the will with my brother, Andrej was given a generous pension as a senior member of the staff. As I've mentioned already, my brother forfeited some of his ability to repay my uncle's debts to honor the promises made to the staff, but we agreed it was the right thing to do. Though Andrej hardly deserved it."

"There was mention of an incident at the freiherr's funeral."

They entered the main garden behind the house. A small table had been set up between the Italian-style beds. Astrid motioned for them to sit.

"Andrej pressed himself on our family attorney and attempted to open a civil case in the county once my uncle had died. The legitimacy of his birth to Frau Kovács wasn't in question, but there was never anything in writing that said my uncle acknowledged Andrej as his son. Besides that, the freiherrschaft and Schattenturm were entailed together centuries ago along agnatic primogeniture. Only the firstborn son of a marriage recognized by the Crown and the Church could inherit. The lawyer and my brother both explained this to him, but he could not, or would not, accept it."

"That does not surprise me," said Hermann.

"On the day of the funeral, he bypassed the staff's seating area in the chapel and moved straight to the front pew to sit with the family. He wasn't even properly dressed. Everyone started to murmur and ask about who he was. We tried not to make a scene at first, hoping that sitting with us would be the end of it. It wasn't. Once the Father had delivered the homily and eulogy, and as the congregation stood, preparing to take part in the Holy Communion, Andrej announced that he had prepared, and would be delivering, a final commendation. It had already been arranged that my brother would do this, but Andrej thought he could charge up to the pulpit and make a spectacle of us all. I don't know what he planned to say, but it would have been disastrous. My brother actually threatened him with a dual should he continue. That worked and Fürth came forward to lead him out of the chapel, and out of our lives after that."

"An incredible show of loyalty."

"Fürth always was loyal to us, to the memory of my uncle. We've been lucky to be served by him." A distant look crossed her face.

"Frau Astrid, did you have contact with Andrej once he returned to Schattenturm?"

"He rather imposed himself on the Baums from what I could gather. Frau Schrode mentioned when I saw her in town one day that he had turned up in the village and impressed Frau Baum with his knowledge of the estate and his former position. Frau Baum offered him his place back on staff and Andrej made no small show of his return below stairs, causing trouble with the maids and making life difficult for Frau Schrode. Shortly thereafter, he began showing up here to work in the gardens until I requested he not. Pavol came back after that."

"When he came here, did he address you?"

"It was clear he harbored a grudge. The first time he spoke to me, he let me know that he'd *come home* as it were."

"That must have been unsettling."

"Very."

"Did he threaten you?"

"Not in a direct way, no, but I knew he was up to something. Based on what you've told me about his journal, I suppose it was something to do with his wish for more money from the inheritance. Lord knows he never actually cared for Schattenturm."

"Why do you say that?"

"He said it ... a few times over the years, during his more unhinged moments. Though it didn't fit with his new role as the Baums' creature as far as I knew."

"As their creature?"

"Andrej cornered me once in town. He must have been watching when I came and went from my shop. He tried to upset me by saying some cruel things, and he added that the Baums had been removing everything to do with my family history that remained in the castle. He said they had tasked him with clearing out the family crypt, removing the bodies. I found that impossible to believe. I was relieved to see, last night, that what remained in the house when we left appeared to still be there."

"He really wanted to see the remaining von Voitsberg family laid low. But your brother, Herr Friederich, is doing well, is he not?"

"Yes, once he received his commission he enjoyed some success in his career. I've had word recently about some good luck, but these are early days yet, and I don't want to be overly optimistic with things being as they are at present."

"I'm glad to hear it." Hermann smiled. "Regarding Andrej's return, did Frau Schrode indicate if there was anything she could do once Andrej had returned and was causing trouble below stairs? That is, what role did she play, since manservants are under the domain of the butler, usually?"

"I'm not entirely sure. Frau Schrode is a force to be reckoned with when she wants to be. She follows a strong personal moral code and isn't likely to look aside if she feels strongly about righting a wrong."

Hermann nodded. "There is one more question, Frau Astrid. When was the last time you spoke with Andrej?"

She cocked her head slightly. "It must have been some weeks ago now. He tried to tell me of some sort of sordid gossip about me in town that I knew to be untrue. I went inside and that was the end of that. The first tulips hadn't emerged, so it must have been … ten or twelve days before he died?"

Hermann thought for a moment and studied her. "I think that must be right, based on an entry in his journal. May I ask what the gossip was?"

"He said that a witch was known to be practicing in the town and that everyone suspected me and my mother. He used language that I will not repeat. I may not be very active in the Church, Professor, but I can assure you that witchcraft is far from anything I care to concern myself with."

"Nothing tangible then, fortunately. I doubt anyone would seriously consider that rumor."

"I'm sorry I couldn't be of more help," she said as they both rose from the tiny table. "Let me walk you out."

"I have one more request of you. I'm afraid it's quite an imposition, but I wouldn't ask if it wasn't extremely important."

Astrid looked Hermann squarely in the face but said nothing.

"I would ask that you come again tonight to Schattenturm."

"Herr Horst, I couldn't possibly do that. My presence last night was strained, and I barely got out of there before ... well, before it got worse than it was. I doubt Herr Baum would allow me through the door. Not to mention, it's very unpleasant for me to be a guest in what was once my home."

"It's critically important to the investigation which, if all goes well, will be concluded this evening."

"How so, Professor?"

"You must trust me when I say the evening will end in the murderer being revealed."

"And I'm needed for this revelation to come to pass? Why?"

"I have arranged for all of us to participate in a séance. As you know, my theories on the parapsychological purport that the subconscious will allow truth to manifest through one's beliefs in the supernatural. There are many who believe the castle's ghosts are all-seeing and all-knowing. The inspector and I know who the killer is, however, the séance is necessary to provide the backdrop for unveiling his identity. Your presence, as the only von Voitsberg in the party, is therefore necessary to the outcome."

"Oh for heaven's sake."

A faint glisten of sweat had formed on Astrid's brow.

"Unless, of course, you are afraid the evening will reveal you to be the murderer."

"Are you serious?"

"Forgive me, that was an awkward attempt at humor. Please understand, I'm desperate that my scheme go according to plan. You needn't do much but attend."

"Very well. If it's that important."

Hermann expressed his thanks as Astrid walked him to the lane. "Until this evening then," he said, but Astrid had already turned away. She was walking slowly toward the cottage, deep in thought, hugging herself as though she suffered a chill.

Chapter 26

Fastening a borrowed pair of cufflinks, which Fürth had procured from somewhere, Hermann watched the last shards of the day's light slip beneath the horizon. It hadn't been easy to convince Fürth and Schrode to help him assemble the ballroom, but he had eventually prevailed upon their sense of duty to the household. To prepare, he had sat for hours in the library, going over Andrej's journal and the many complexly interconnected details that had emerged during the course of the investigation. He returned time and again to the one theory that provided motive, opportunity, and a satisfactory outcome from Andrej's death.

He turned to face the portrait of Gustav Freiherr von Voitsberg above the bed. "Well old friend ..."

Every time Hermann faced his chamber-mate, the subject's features seemed to grow coarser and more intent. There was a cool fire in the silver-grey eyes that his descendant shared, in her own remarkable way.

"Tonight is the night. I can't say I'll miss you, but I'm sorry your destiny has come to no more than an out-of-the-way guest bedroom. You deserve better, I suppose. But look at it this way, you could be across the Atlantic in America ... the central curiosity hanging on the dining room wall of a Newport mansion."

Was it his imagination or did the man in the portrait squint his eyes and frown ever so slightly?

Stepping into the dim hall, the house oozed a certain spirit of ferocity. Every nook, every detailed feature was the essence of the von Voitsberg family, borne out. He wondered if the personality traits that had long fermented in Andrej, leading ultimately to his own doom, was a flawed characteristic carried through the generations of the von Voitsberg line. Most of the aristocracy had been ruthless at some point before the refined manners, luxurious balls, decadent meals, and aversion to all things humble and mean had taken root. How else had their names ever been etched above the beam of any nation, but by the point of their swords? Perhaps Baum and his ilk would be the spiritual inheritors of that legacy.

The family was already gathered when he entered the parlor. Erzsébet and Rachel were both staring into the fire from opposite sides of the seating area. Mother and daughter were dressed similarly in shades of pearl and green, almost mirroring the inverse of each other's detailing. Johan Baum rubbed his left brow, already nursing a drink as he sat near his son.

"Good Evening." Hermann addressed the members of the family.

Erzsébet was the first to respond, "Good Evening, Herr Horst."

"Since you are all here, I want to let you know this will be my final dinner with you. I plan on taking the morning train back to Vienna."

"That can't be so," said Frau Kam. "You've only been here a few days and I've hardly had a chance to speak with you about your book or have any other communions with the spirits."

"Alas, Frau Kam, I can't remain at Schattenturm forever. My professorship requires my presence. However, tonight, I've devised a way to settle the nerves and restore the general tenor of the castle to peace and calm. If you would all entertain a bit of theatricality."

Only Frau Kam looked pleased. The rest looked anything but and wore worried expressions, except for Rachel who cast a lazy look in Hermann's direction with what he interpreted to be contempt.

Erzsébet passed a concerned look toward her husband. "Can you tell us, Professor, what you have planned?"

"I'm afraid that would spoil it, Frau Baum. Both for the research aspect and the psychological objective," said Hermann.

"So we're to be your rats in a cage," came Johan's sticky voice.

"Not in the poking and prodding sense. Think of it as a kind of party game that will help our understanding of the psyche."

"Will we discover the depths of the spirit world?" Frau Kam piped in.

"In a sense, but if I say any more, it will be ruined." He smiled.

"We shall wait with bated breath then," said Erzsébet, frowning. "Ah, Fürth. Is that dinner?"

The butler bowed and they filed into the dining room. Hermann took the opportunity to glance at his pocket watch; he hoped that the night train transporting Géza wouldn't be delayed, tonight of all nights.

They sat much as they had the night before. The conversation, however, was stilted and the soup course resulted mostly in the sound of the diners sipping from the sides of their spoons.

"Do you know if Inspector Orczy will be back?" Erzsébet asked over the next course.

"I'm afraid he was recalled to Budapest by his commanding officer. I expect that he'll return only to dispose of some of the items in the evidence room," Hermann replied.

"It's a relief that this will all be over, but I can't help feeling uneasy that there's a killer out there somewhere."

"Don't fret, Erzsébet," said Baum. "Andrej got himself killed for his own reasons and everyone can see that. It's nothing to do with us."

"But still, he was murdered right here. What if one of the children had been out, or one of us? Who's to say we wouldn't have been killed too?"

"You'll get yourself worked up if you keep on like that."

The entrée was served as Hermann picked up. "Herr Baum is right about Andrej's character," he said. "I learned that he had begun to involve himself in some very dark pursuits toward the end of his life."

"What kind of dark pursuits?" asked Frau Kam.

"From what I can tell, based on a personal journal he kept—"

Rachel's disinterest evaporated instantaneously.

"—Andrej was involved in a scheme to extort Schattenturm's lost treasure. He believed it had been secreted away. He had reason to believe that the treasure lay somewhere within Schattenturm, waiting to be found by him."

There wasn't an immediate reply from any of the Baums, and Fürth who stood diagonal from Johan's back made no sign of acknowledgement other than to slightly raise one eyebrow. Baum was staring curiously at Hermann, mouth firmly closed.

Frau Kam clapped her hands together, causing Erzsébet to jump. "How marvelous, Professor," she said. "So did the spirits kill him, to keep him away from the treasure?"

"There is reason to believe that another person whom he had dealings with believed as much." Hermann looked at Rachel. "Andrej was supplying some grisly articles to a confidant of his, to conduct a form of black magic at Schattenturm."

Frau Kam nodded, but didn't seem to understand. Rachel was clenching her jaw and Josef was staring at his sister with his mouth open. Johan and Erzsébet shared equally squinted eyes.

"What do you mean by black magic, Herr Horst?" asked Erzsébet.

"I mean that in the old room under the chapel where the Turkish prayer hall once was, Inspector Orczy and I found what appeared to be a ritual space. I'm afraid to say that it appears something, or someone, had their blood regularly let there."

"Dear God!" Erzsébet said as she covered her mouth, her earrings bobbling as she looked around the table.

"Do you know who's been doing it?" said Johan.

"It was an obvious amateur enthusiast. Someone with little training and understanding of what they were doing. In my experience, those who partake in such acts are largely ignorant, narrow-sighted, and of low social standing. Provided you lock the doors and continue to seal a few entry points around the sub-floors, I think you should be safe from the sad, mad fool who has been at work."

"How did you come to that conclusion, Herr Horst," asked Rachel, with a sneer. "Surely this person must have had a good education if they knew how to conduct an esoteric ritual. What traditions were they following? How long did they have to study the lore? Wouldn't a simpleton have been intimidated by the act of invoking any strong dark powers?"

Hermann turned in his seat to more properly address her, but Erzsébet cut in.

"Is this old Turkish prayer hall linked to the passages you told us about last night?"

"Yes, it is. There are several ways in and out using the passages, with a few tunnels leading quite a distance away from the house."

Erzsébet was obviously uneasy, given her shifting glance and retracted posture.

"You still haven't answered my questions, Herr Horst," said Rachel. "How can you be so sure that this person was, as you say, a fool?"

"While it's true that it takes a higher order of miscreant to get involved in the esoteric and occult, it has often been the case that many adherents are just lost on their journey to either a universalist truth, which is fleeting, or else they're rebel reactionaries trying to tear down what they feel has been the established order of tradition and etiquette. They combine two, three, even half a dozen different cultures' snippets of practice to form their amalgamation. It points to a chaos of the mind as much as the spirit. Such a person would be low indeed."

Rachel was rigid in her chair, color rising, turning her pale complexion a blotchy red. She leaned slightly forward with her hands on the table. "Then I say again, how could a simpleton have come to such a practice if they weren't intelligent in their own right? It's nonsensical."

"Rachel," Erzsébet said softly, scrutinizing her daughter.

"Perhaps they read a book?" Frau Kam said with a very odd expression on her face.

Rachel continued. "What genius it must actually be to see truth in many traditions and put their common elements together to reach the best powers. When they call on them and the results are achieved, how then aren't they proven right? When their enemies are killed and their position strengthened, their family safe? How then, Professor Horst? I think you must hardly know at all. What secrets have been passed down to you, through generations of hidden memory in secret languages few can begin to understand?"

"Shut up, girl!" Johan said.

Everyone at the table was staring at Rachel, as were the footmen. Only then did the teenager begin to understand. Fürth motioned for the two footmen to depart, following on their heels out into the hall, then he shut the door softly.

Once they had gone, it was Frau Kam who broke the silence. "Rachel, what have you been up to?"

"Only what you've led me to, Grandmama."

"I told you never to use the black book. It's only meant for healing, never for harm. I thought that the spirits had taken it when it went missing weeks ago, but now I see that you stole it."

"You can't steal what already belongs you. You're the one who told me it was full of family knowledge from centuries of our ancestors' work. Why shouldn't I have used the grimoire?"

"Mama, you knew about this ... this, this, *witchcraft*?" Erzsébet was as white as the tablecloth.

"It's not witchcraft," said grandmother and granddaughter in unison.

"Erzsébet, it's a book of potions, spells ... prayers to God really. You were raised wholeheartedly in the Church as your father wanted, rest his soul, so I knew I couldn't involve you. But Rachel, she was never pushed into the pews as you were. I knew she could carry on our legacy."

"But she's been ... my God, Herr Horst, what has she been doing?"

"She butchered a rabbit and a pig in sacrifice and used the blood to enact vengeance on her enemies."

"She didn't butcher them," blurted Josef. "Pavol killed them for her. She just used the blood."

In a single fluid movement, Johan swigged the contents of his wine glass. Before another comment could be made, he confronted Hermann. "What hogwash!" he blurted out. "I'll tell you what I told that fool Orczy." He pointed a meaty finger at Hermann. "Watch who you accuse or I'll see you done for."

"I don't think so. Witchcraft is not taken lightly by the authorities, and I saw the ritual with my own eyes, Herr Baum, as did Inspector Orczy. Rachel offered up mine and the inspector's souls so that we'd stop haranguing her family, you actually. More important to the investigation, she had been working with Andrej, before his death, to retrieve articles she wanted for her rituals. He encouraged her at the start, but shortly before his murder her demands became more bizarre, and he had begun refusing her. He didn't choose to continue being her supplier."

"Rituals ... there was more than one?" Erzsébet said shakily. "And Josef ... Josef was involved too?"

"I'm afraid so. Rachel made sacrifices on several occasions. She was facilitated first by Andrej who would bring her animal carcasses and blood stock, not to mention some Gypsy paraphernalia, then by Pavol."

Erzsébet crossed herself. Frau Kam shook her head, looking down at her bony fingers which were gripping the table edge. Johan Baum looked like he'd just been dealt a blow to the head.

"What the hell did you think you were doing?" said Johan. "Are you mad?"

"No, I'm not mad, dearest Father. I'm the only one with any sense in this family. I did what I had to do to protect us, to protect you, from the police. How else do you think it was that they couldn't come up with any evidence to arrest you for Andrej's murder?"

Johan opened and closed his mouth once with great consternation. "Rachel, there was no evidence because I didn't do it, girl. Andrej got himself killed, probably by some of the bad lot he had dealings with, and that's that. I insisted the police investigate to put an end to the gossip circulating amongst my competitors and spooking my shareholders, but after weeks of investigating with no results, I just wanted them out of here. They were making it worse for me, not better."

Rachel shook her head, a smug look on her face. "You don't get it, do you? This place is a conduit of energy, powerful energy. There's blood in these walls, tons of it, over centuries. This place is a monument to killing and you think I'm in the wrong for using it to our own advantage?"

There was a swift knock. Fürth didn't wait for a response before opening the door. "I apologize, but Inspector Orczy has arrived and asks to speak with Herr Horst ... immediately."

"What?" Johan blurted out. Then he looked from Fürth to Hermann.

"Ah, well, thank you Fürth. I'll be right out." Hermann rose and proceeded around the table as Johan and the others watched in confusion. He found Géza back in the main hall of the keep. He was wearing his officer's uniform of green and red, though his kepi and long coat had obviously already been taken away.

"Good to see you made it," said Hermann. "Another few minutes and it could have gone off the rails in there."

"It was all I could do to convince my commander to let me come at all. I've brought three men with me, plus Erdei, they're waiting in the ballroom. So, what's the plan, exactly? Have you gotten Baum to confess yet?"

"Not quite. It's a little more complicated than that. I'm taking everyone into the ballroom to get them to reveal themselves and how each, whether knowingly or not, played a role in Andrej's death. As each reveals their part, the killer will be trapped."

"My god, Hermann. You'd better be sure."

"I am, trust me. Now, come into the dining room so we can gather the others."

Géza nodded.

Hermann approached Fürth outside the dining room door. "Has Frau Astrid arrived?"

"She has. She is waiting in the ballroom as you requested."

"Very good. Now I'm going to need you to fetch Frauen Schrode and Kovács, and Pavol, who I summoned shortly before dinner. He should be waiting in the kitchens. Bring them into the ballroom, along with yourself, of course."

"Bring them to the ballroom? Why? That's not acceptable. I don't understand."

"It's the last part of the investigation, and I'll need everyone involved."

Fürth raised both of his bushy eyebrows and looked down the length of his nose. "This will have to be cleared by

Herr Baum. It is inappropriate for servants to converge with the family, in of all places, the ballroom." He appeared immovable.

"Not this time, Fürth. It's on the orders of the police if that helps to settle you. Now, please, do as Herr Horst requested." Géza added.

Fürth pursed his lips. He stood immobile for a brief moment while what Géza said seemed to register, then he gave a curt nod and left for the servants' stair down the hall.

Hermann reentered the dining room with Géza. Baum was downing a glass of red that he'd refilled at the sidebar while Erzsébet and Frau Kam were huddled around a sullen Rachel.

"If you will join me now in the ballroom, please," said Hermann.

"I'm in no mood for parlor games, Horst," said Baum.

"It's important that you participate, Herr Baum. We will learn the truth once and for all regarding Schatten-turm's mysteries: the location of the treasury, the validity of the curse, who murdered Andrej, and why he was murdered. All of those beckoned to the ballroom have some involvement and, therefore, your attendance is required."

"Shall we?" said Géza. He motioned them toward the ballroom.

Chapter 27

Hermann followed Géza through the door at the end of the dining room which he had opened wide onto the ballroom. A large circular table had been set up in the center of the room, directly under the central chandelier, one of the three glittering glass masterpieces imported from Venetia. The space was lit only by several candles in wall sconces around the room. Through the expansive floor-to-ceiling windows, the cloudless night sky framed the nascent crescent moon. Twelve chairs had been arranged around the table with handwritten place cards bearing the names of their intended occupants, save for four. Hermann pulled the four remaining place cards from his dinner jacket's pocket and began to arrange them in specific locations while the dinner party and servants filed into the room.

The group immediately noticed the policemen in their green uniforms beside the entry into the hall and the door onto the outer terrace. Géza took his position behind his placement at the table, watching each of the assemblage funnel in. Astrid, who looked calm but curious, was standing in shadow near the inner wall. The others didn't seem to notice her at first. Hermann walked around to his placement, opposite Géza, and signaled for him to begin. Géza took a breath, releasing it slowly. His deep, steady voice soon drew their attention.

"In a moment, you will find your spot based on the cards placed around the table and take your seat. Your participation tonight is necessary to the investigation of Andrej Fehér's murder, which I have led these last two weeks on behalf of His Majesty's Budapest Gendarme Police Force, and for which Herr Horst, professor of history and mythologies at the esteemed University of Vienna, has assisted. Professor Horst is an expert in parapsychology and the history of the occult. His work in this field has provided the investigation a scientific approach to uncovering the murderer's profile and motive."

The group gathered in the ballroom looked from Géza to Hermann and back again, like so many sheep standing in an open field, about to be descended upon by an invisible predator.

Géza continued. "What you will learn tonight, sitting around this table, is that Andrej was not killed by chance or based on a random offense. He was murdered by a member of this household, someone who now stands beside you. Each of you had motive and opportunity, and each of you had something to gain by Andrej's death. Professor Horst and I are aware of them all."

Hermann observed each face, the body language, and the movements of the people in the room. They in turn scanned the room, eyes darting left and right, looking nervously around the space and at each other. Hermann could guess some of the thoughts passing behind their eyes, each wondering at the fact that one man had caused such hatred amongst so many, and was still disrupting their lives, despite his ghastly death.

The uneasy silence across the room was abruptly broken by Johan Baum. "Enough of this, Orczy," Johan said as he stepped forward. "You don't know any of this. I wrote to your commander, you're off this case."

"Not so quick, Herr Baum." He pulled a piece of paper from his jacket and unfolded it, revealing the official red stamp of the Crown of Saint Stephen. "I carry with me, from Budapest, a warrant for the arrest of the murderer of Andrej Fehér. The officers I've brought with me will ensure this warrant is carried out and the murderer taken into custody. Should you, or anyone else in the room attempt to flee, my officers are authorized to use deadly force if necessary."

Hermann broke the tension. "Now, will each of you please step forward and find your name on the place card in front of your chair."

Frau Astrid was the first to step forward. As she strode from the shadows, her grey eyes caught the light of the flickering candles and gleamed with an almost unnatural brightness. Next were the Baum family members. Frau Kam was delighted to see she was seated next to Professor Horst, a deep smile causing her skin to crease in wrinkles over her cheekbones. Rachel, with an air of contempt glared at Hermann and stood near her place at the table, arms crossed. Erzsébet put her gaunt hands on her husband's elbow and latched on. He all but dragged her around to find her place card, then his own. Josef seemed caught between wanting to please his father and sister, and run for the nearest door, which was guarded by one of the inspector's officers.

Next, the servants began to circle the table, searching for their names. Frau Kovács prayed continuously, whispering over and again a verse under her breath, and wrung her hands nervously. Pavol stared at the floor behind his chair. Frau Schrode and Fürth locked eyes, but kept their expressions neutral. Once they were all standing at their places around the table, Hermann addressed them.

"I have arranged your positions in the circle to generate the best flow of energy as we commune with the spirit world tonight."

Frau Kam clapped her hands. "A séance. Wonderful!"

Rachel sneered while Pavol, Kovács, and Schrode all crossed themselves.

Hermann continued. "Frau Kam, you are on my right as you will be our medium. Your connection to the spirit world is strong and will help us to avoid the dark force's attempts to break through and mislead us. Will you please sit down?"

The old widow slowly settled into her chair and edged it forward. "I hope that I can help. I can't believe any of these people would actually be murderers. Nor any of my family. This darkness must be dispelled. It's a demon that did this awful thing. I will prepare myself," she said before closing her eyes and concentrating on her breathing.

"Herr Soták." The boy startled, looking up from his intent focus on the floor's inlaid-wood pattern. "Pavol. You are to the right of Frau Kam. You were closest to Andrej and will be the most suited to channel his energy and memory to Frau Kam for her spirit walking." Hermann motioned for him to sit. Pavol quietly slipped into his chair, casting a nervous glance at the police officers and their sidearms.

"Frau Astrid, as the only member of the von Voitsberg family, it will be important that your energy is close at hand to myself and the medium. Your ancestors may give us the valuable knowledge we need to understand and dispel the dark force that has been summoned. Please take your chair here on my left, if you will."

Astrid pulled out her chair and gracefully swept her skirts to one side before perching on the chair's edge. "I've never been involved in any dark arts or anything of the kind, Herr Horst, but for the sake of putting this chapter behind us, I will try to be helpful."

"I trust that's true, frau. Though the only path to truth tonight is to lay bare the forces that have wreaked havoc and brought us to this place."

Astrid raised an eyebrow. "Do try not to malign my ancestors too much with this. Our name still means something."

Hermann nodded slightly, then continued. "The rest of you may now take your seats. Rank and history are to be forgotten this evening. Each of you has a particular spiritual cadence that requires your designated position in the circle."

Hermann watched each of them as they took their seats, clockwise from Frau Astrid. Frau Schrode inhaled deeply before sliding into her chair. Baum sat in his chair and with a pained expression looked over toward his wife who appeared resolute, but was stifling emotion, apparent from the tremble of her lip.

"Frau Kovács," said Hermann, "please sit down now."

"What?" said the plump cook, still in her apron. "I'm to sit next to the meister? I can't do that."

It was Fürth who intervened. "Please, Frau Kovács. Don't be upset. You see Frau Schrode there is between Frau Astrid and Herr Baum. Just breathe and try not to worry."

The cook nodded and sat down in her chair, with several subsequent sidelong glances at her employer.

"Rachel," Hermann pressed.

The black-haired teen slid into her seat with a scowl.

"Beyond Géza will be Josef. Please sit down Josef."

The boy eyed Géza suspiciously and with a decided lack of delicacy, plunked into his chair.

"Then Herr Fürth and Frau Baum, please take your seats," said Hermann.

Fürth pulled out the chair for Frau Baum before taking his own seat.

Hermann, still standing, motioned for the officers to step outside of the ballroom and stand guard at the closed doors.

"Oh my, what is that!" exclaimed Frau Baum from her position between Fürth and Pavol.

She was pointing to a chair placed next to a side table along the wall. Everyone followed her directional, some squinting to see in the now very dimly lit room. Frau Kovács shuddered, Pavol crossed himself yet again, and Rachel smirked.

"How wonderful," said Frau Kam. "Odette has joined us. The spirits are indeed strong tonight."

"What the hell is that dreadful thing?" said Johan, looking intently at the white-rabbit doll in the flowing red-velvet dress.

Its stitched smile and grey-glass eyes stared across the room at the group at the table. Géza shot Hermann a quizzical look. Hermann shrugged slightly and raised an eyebrow.

"Oh, for heaven's sake," said Astrid. "That's Bonnie Bunny. She went everywhere with me until I lost her in the maze when I was about eight years old."

No one seemed relieved by this bit of history.

"Shall we begin?" said Hermann. "I will be here," he grabbed the back of his chair "in order to conduct the séance and maintain a connection of energy directly with our medium.

He and Géza extinguished the candles in the few wall sconces that were lit. The ballroom's size fell in on itself. Hermann took his seat, then he pulled a small box of matches from his pocket to light the short candle in front of him. He slid the candle forward to the center of the table. Each of the participant's faces shone clearly in the light—all their uneasiness, or annoyance, laid bare.

"To channel our energy and begin the journey, we must each lock hands with the people next to us. You must forget your misgivings in rank tonight, for on the spirit journey, we will face each other without position. Please, take the hand of the person sitting to your left and right."

After some hesitation and murmuring, all but Frau Kovács did as they were instructed. She sat wringing her hands and staring down at the table.

"Oh for God's sake woman, give me your hand," said Herr Baum. "The sooner we get this over with the sooner you can go back to the kitchen and I can down a whiskey."

"It is vitally important that once the séance begins, none of you breaks the circle. Else, the spirits that have been called forth will be released and energized to do whatever they may. Now, I want each of you to close your eyes. You will concentrate on your inner being, the quiet place within your minds. We will achieve balance before communing with the spirits. Everyone, breathe in and out. Breathe in ... and breathe out. Breathe in ... and ... breathe out. In ... and ... out. In ... and ... out. Now, think of Andrej as you knew him. The good and the bad. Form an image of Andrej and work to keep it solid, like a fixed point in your internal vision. Don't forget to continue to breathe deeply."

After a minute or two, he continued.

"Frau Kam, do you feel that you have attuned yourself to the spirit world?"

"Yes, Professor."

"And have you summoned your spirit guide? The same from the last séance would be good."

"Yes ... I see him now."

"Very good. Frau Kam, I want you to focus on your guide with your eyes closed. Stay concentrated. Now, the spirit that we contacted the other night, I want you to use your energy to summon him forth. Your guide will take you to him. All of our combined energies, in this circle of twelve, will prevent you from weakening and will keep the spirit close. Can you do that?"

The widow kept her head down, eyes firmly shut. "Yes, I can do that. I see ... a dark hallway. My guide is leading me to a room. We're going inside. Oh, there he is. I can see his face much clearer now."

"Very good. You are in the heart of Schattenturm, Frau Kam. Please, describe to us the man in the room."

"He's standing. He's about one hundred seventy-five centimeters tall, I'd say. Very well dressed, a gentleman. He's wearing a large, jeweled brooch on his lapel."

Hermann felt a twitch in Astrid's fingertips.

"He has a short white beard and he's balding, but not much. I think ... yes, he's some sort of lord."

Hermann noticed Fürth and Schrode shoot one another a quick look before closing their eyes again. Géza was watching each in the circle as well.

"Very good. Now, is this man willing to help us find and dispel the darkness?"

"Yes … He says that it doesn't belong here."

"Frau Kam, I want you to bring the spirit forth to us here at the circle. Imagine you're stepping through a door with your spirit guide who holds this spirit's hand. You can see yourself here, though your own spirit is in the other realm."

"Ah, it's incredible. I can see myself. We're all here at the circle, I'm walking around us."

A few in the circle glanced with one eye over their shoulders, into the dim space.

"Good, but make sure you keep your eyes closed. Is the spirit here in the room?"

"Yes. He's here next to my body."

"I will address the spirit directly now, Frau Kam, but relay his responses so that we may hear him."

"I will."

"Spirit, I want you to commune with the young man next to Frau Kam. His name is Pavol, you may know him. Please move close to him and touch his shoulder so that you may know his spirit."

"Ah!" Pavol yelped. "Something cold brushed against me."

"Don't be afraid, Pavol. The spirit will not harm you. The energy of this circle is positive and powerful, and the spirit only seeks to help us. Spirit, focus on Pavol and his connection to Andrej. Learn of his struggles, his anger, and his apprehension."

"Herr Horst, the spirit says that he knows that Andrej was difficult with the boy, that he upset the boy."

"Spirit, do you see how Andrej took Pavol in and put him to work on the grounds?"

"Yes," Frau Kam answered.

"Look at the memory of those gardens and the grounds, they are critical for us to understand what happened here. Look into the pain that was felt here by Pavol. The turmoil." Hermann turned to the young gardener. "Pavol, tell us your feelings. Do you sense that the spirit is imparting his understanding onto you?"

"I feel funny, herr. Like I want to go home, but I can't."

"Tell me why you feel that way. The spirit will remove all doubt from you, all fear will be gone when you speak without reservation."

Pavol swallowed. "I can't help but think how Andrej used to ... hit me after he'd been drinking or just if he'd been upset at something. I wanted to write to my mother about it, but I knew she couldn't do nothing anyway."

"Hmm. What was it about Andrej that made him violent?"

"Well, he lost a lot of his money at cards when he'd play in town or with the Gypsies when they'd come through. He said none of it was fair. That he had to be poor, I mean. Said he was owed more than his lot."

"Did Andrej know anyone that could help him?"

"No. He always said no one ever cared about him or would help him when he needed it. That's when he'd take out his anger on me."

"He was desperate as a man, wasn't he?"

"I guess he was, yes."

"Tell me, did Andrej ever know love? Did he ever try to marry?"

"Oh no, he never did anything like that. He said the girls wouldn't talk to him, except when he'd give them drink. My mother and father told me never to be too near a girl before we was married, and I have tried that, herr."

A muffled scoff came from the direction of Rachel.

"But Andrej," said Pavol, "I don't think he cared about what you should do and shouldn't do. He used to tell me sometimes about the girls that he'd ... um ... that he'd ... been with."

"I understand, Pavol. Feel the spirit's hand on your shoulder, Pavol. He's giving to you nothing but truth. Clarity about everything. He wants to help you see. Do you feel it?"

"Yes. I think I do."

"Tell me, did you confront Andrej about his behavior? Did you ever tell him it was wrong?"

"I tried to, I did, but he wouldn't hear none of it. He'd hit me if I talked to him too disrespectfully."

"Hmm. Thank you, Pavol. I want you to stay focused on the spirit as he moves around the circle. Try to focus on him. Frau Kam, do you sense that a fog is moving in? I feel something in this room."

"Yes, I do. A black mist spreading out. It's coiling up around us now."

"Your spirit guide will protect you from it, if you keep him close to you. The spirit that is here, can you see him moving around behind us?"

"Yes, he's coming around, oh, he's behind—"

"Frau Schrode?"

"Yes. I see him there."

"Good. Spirit, place your hand on Frau Schrode's shoulder and begin to feel her energy and her knowledge of Andrej."

Frau Schrode shuddered as she looked sidelong for anything that might be touching her.

"Frau Schrode, please, feel the spirit's grip. He will help you to see clearly. Tell us of Andrej's character. Did he seek out courtship from a girl here?"

The wrinkled corners of her mouth pursed before she spoke. "No, not in a way that one should."

"Tell me what Andrej did. The spirit will give you strength."

"Andrej ... Andrej was dishonorable. That is the sad truth and there's no escaping it. He tried to assault more than one of the kitchen maids here. Would force himself violently on the ones that he couldn't sweet talk."

A muffled moan came from Frau Kovács.

"I saw it with my own eyes. I tried to protect the girls, get them away from him. I'd confront him about it, but he had no remorse. Acted like it was a game to him or something. Oh, it was awful, and more so considering the circumstances of his own birth."

"Why did you keep his behavior a secret?"

"Only a few of us knew about it, sure, but that's the way things are, isn't it? It shouldn't be. If I'd tried to have him fired, Andrej would've denied it and ruined the girls in the process. That would've been that. I had to protect them. They weren't to blame." She began to tear up as she opened her eyes and looked at Frau Kovács. "I'm sorry, but it wasn't right. I did what I could."

Hermann looked around the circle, at their emotions. Then, he appeared to be tracking something they couldn't see, an invisible force. "Frau Kam, is the mist growing thicker? It feels quite strange, like something is approaching."

"Yes, I see it. There's a huge stream of it, pouring in through the hall. It's very deep around us now. Up to my calves. Oh this is very strange, Herr Horst."

"And the spirit, I sense he's approaching someone that Andrej was very close to, is that right?"

"Yes, I think so, he's moving around again, past Johan."

"To Frau Kovács?"

"Yes. Yes, he's behind her now. He's putting out his hand to touch her shoulder."

"Oh Lord God!" the cook shrieked.

"Don't be afraid, Frau Kovács," Hermann urged. "The spirit, I sense he's someone you knew. Not in a loving way, but in a close way. Tell me that you feel it."

"Herr, I don't right know what I feel."

"That's all right. Just focus on Andrej. All the illusions are lifted. You can see him clearly now. Tell me about him."

"Andrej was a good boy, he never did any wrong. I don't know what Frau Schrode saw, but she couldn't have seen that from Andrej."

"Frau Kovács, I sense a darkness around you. The spirit, he's behind your shoulder. He will help you to see everything clearly, despite the darkness. Frau Kam, what can you see from the other side?"

"Oh, Professor," said Frau Kam. "There's a shape coming forth. It's in darkness, shrouded by the mist."

"Where is the shape?"

"It's in the archway of the door to the hall ... I think it's coming closer, like it's being drawn in." There was a slight catch in her voice.

"Frau Kovács, the darkness is manifesting, it feeds on untruths ... on lies. There is an untrue energy in this circle. As our own darkness wells up, so does this demon's power. To fight the demon, we'll have to be honest like we're standing before our maker. The spirit behind you, I sense that he was close to you, maybe only once, but you must have felt strongly about him. Tell me how that connects to Andrej."

"Oh Lord." She began to cry softly. "Andrej ... was my son. Mine and the freiherr's. He took me when I was a girl, a maid here in the kitchens. I never knew what happened really. My mother hadn't told me properly about what married women and men are supposed to do. It happened so fast and then later ... I knew I was going to have a baby."

Fürth and Erzsébet both looked pained. At the same time, Astrid's grip seemed to tighten in step with her jaw.

"I went away for a while and left my boy in an orphanage." She started to sob. "I shouldn't have, but there wasn't any other choice. I couldn't work with a baby and no husband. I never told anyone but Frau Schrode and Herr Fürth. They never did say nothing bad about it. I thought the freiherr must've loved me, in his own way, because I wasn't fired. After a time, I got Andrej to live here. I never told his secret, but I think he did." Another sob. "He got into trouble as a boy with cards and drink, but I thought that he'd get over it. He always said nice things to me, except when he was angry, but I knew he didn't mean nothing by it ..." More sobbing. "I didn't think that he could be like that. Not when he knew that's what'd been done to me." Tears were streaming down her face. "I wanted him to be good, but no matter what I said he was like his father. He was like his father was that night. There was a darkness in him. A cruel streak. I didn't want him to do those cruel things." She let out with convulsing sobs, hands still locked between a wincing Rachel and Johan. "No, no. Please, herr. No more. I can't do it no more."

"It's alright Frau Kovács. You must keep your hands locked in the circle. Your friends know that you loved your son as every good mother should. You tried to see the best in him, but even you couldn't be blind forever."

Hermann paused while Frau Kovács collected herself. He scanned the space, seeing things none of the others did, through the veil.

"Spirit, I sense that you wish to speak to someone. A man. You knew him well in life, and he's here now. You were friends, I feel. Closer than was to be expected. Frau Kam, tell me, where is the spirit moving to?"

"He's ... he's moving on past the inspector."

"To Herr Fürth?"

"Yes, that's where he is. He's happy to see the butler, but sad too."

Fürth looked annoyed at the situation. He hardly moved.

"Spirit," said Hermann. "I sense you want to tell us something. A name that you shared with Herr Fürth. Is that right?"

"Yes," Frau Kam answered. "He says his name is Fridolin."

Fürth's face dropped. "What? What did you say?"

"Frau Kam said that the spirit's name is Fridolin. Tell us Fürth, who is Fridolin to you?"

Fürth opened his eyes and shook his head, just once, before responding.

"Fridolin ... was the name that he wanted me to call him ... when we were together."

"That seems strange, Herr Fürth. This spirit is of Schattenturm. Why did you need to have a different name for him than the one he used otherwise? Hmm, I sense he's very drawn to your combined history. Am I right, Frau Kam?"

"Yes, he has both hands on Fürth's shoulders."

"Who was this Fridolin, Herr Fürth?"

The butler sighed deeply. "Fridolin was Herr Georg Friederich von Voitsberg."

Every face at the table was locked on Fürth. All eyes open now. Not a sound could be heard. The participants were motionless.

"Fridolin was the medieval form of his middle name which he asked me to call him when we were young together."

"Ah, so you shared more than age with the young Herr Georg before he became the freiherr. You must have been in quite a confidential friendship with him."

"I was. I knew the best part of him, that few others did."

"And you were deeply loyal to him in life, and to his memory after he was gone, is that right?"

"Yes."

"What did you do when you learned that your friend had raped Frau Kovács? You were the butler, even then, in charge of the household and all the staff in it."

"I ...," his shoulders slumped, "I helped to suppress it. I had helped him to cover up affairs with women before, but this was different. Frau Kovács is a sweet woman, so I convinced the freiherr, with the help of his brother, to keep her on, and I found an orphanage for the child, for Andrej."

The women at the table were grimacing and Astrid's fingers were stiff in Hermann's grasp.

"What did you do when Andrej came back to Schattenturm? Certainly, he must have felt entitled as the freiherr's son?"

"Andrej didn't know for a while, but the freiherr took an interest in him and allowed him access to the house. Showed him around too. I think Andrej figured out who he was after a while and then he got it out of his mother entirely. He wanted money from the freiherr, to be written into his will if he couldn't get it from him directly. He may have wanted the house. I did what I could to explain why that wasn't possible for him, but he wouldn't hear it."

"Fridolin, the spirit of the freiherr, I sense that there's more he wants you to tell. What did you do when you learned that Andrej had some of the same tendencies for assault as his father?"

"I tried to keep him as far away from the house as much as I could. When he crossed the final line in the sand, at the freiherr's funeral, I forced him away, back to Budapest, where he stayed until last year."

"Did you not feel compelled to warn the Baums of Andrej's character when he turned up again? Surely you couldn't neglect your duty to the household."

"What could I say? I told Frau Baum that he wasn't suitable, but I couldn't say why."

"And why was that?"

"Because I swore an oath on my life to the freiherr. To look after Andrej's interests as best I could. To do everything to keep him safe and see him turn out better than he really was."

"But you failed in that respect?"

"Yes, he got worse with time. He became a threat to everyone around him. I helped create the monster you see."

"I sense that there is more there than we know. Frau Kam, tell me what you see from the spirit world. I sense the other presence, the dark one."

"Yes, Herr Horst. It's the figure. He's here with us. Oh, it's so dark, I can't see his face."

Hermann spoke, "He's being drawn in by the dark force that sits within our circle. Only when all of the secrets are revealed and the truth is out will we be free of it. Tell me, I sense that Fridolin has shifted, though not far at all, to someone new."

"Um ... he's with—"

"Frau Baum?"

"Y-yes."

"Frau Baum, tell me. Andrej was a scoundrel, yet you developed a relationship with him. How did that happen?"

Erzsébet shifted uncomfortably. "He seemed like a decent man at first. Deferential, complimentary. He was very knowledgeable about the grounds and the house. It was nice to have someone friendly here. Lord knows there was no one else to talk to."

"Did you realize that he was trying to seduce you? He couldn't have been very subtle, a man of his nature."

"I suspected it, yes. Though truth be told, I enjoyed the flattery. I felt so alone here, with Johan busy with his work. I never let it go beyond his superficial compliments though. Never."

Erzsébet was looking across the table at her husband.

"Are you sure about that? There seems to be a strong belief otherwise. By someone at this table."

Erzsébet shifted her gaze to Rachel. "There was never anything between Andrej and me. He forgot his position and made a highly inappropriate advance toward me. When I refused him he became very ugly, very abusive. Like a rabid dog."

Frau Kam, tell me what you see. Is the darkness boiling around us?"

"There are shadows around the table now. The figure, he's a man. He's circling us all."

"Tell me Rachel, what did you think of Andrej? He was your coconspirator, your enabler on your travels into darkness with your spells. You and your brother, Josef, have been involved in dark sorcery here, beneath the holy altar of the chapel."

Hermann looked across the table, addressing the group. "They conjured evil forces to do their bidding and enact terrible doom on their enemies."

Rachel sneered.

"Is that not so, fraulein?"

"It's true that I cursed him, and he got what he deserved, but I didn't kill him. He was above himself and I told him as much. He thought he ought to have gone higher."

"Was this after he discovered your own false flirtations toward him? Your attempts to use him to aide you in the dark arts?"

"Ha. He thought he could fawn on me like he did Mama. I knew what he was from the start. I just entertained him so he'd be useful."

"And after that he was a hinderance, wasn't he?"

"I didn't need him."

"Because you had ensnared Pavol with the same guile, hadn't you? And you had your brother do other dirty work, like with the blood you wanted. But what of Andrej himself? The spirit, Fridolin, knows what you summoned, what dark forces you sought to compel. What could have made you offer up a man's soul to devils like that?"

"I only did what was needed."

"The darkness is thick around you, fraulein. It will swallow you forever if you're not careful. Is that what happened that night? You did what you needed to do?"

"Josef and I didn't have to do anything. The spirits killed him, and that's that."

"But that isn't the whole of the dark force at work at this table, is it? No, the darkness you empowered, it lived in the hearts of others before it was born onto this estate."

Hermann closed his eyes and swayed his head a little.

"Herr Baum, I sense the darkness around you. You must tell me why you brought your family here, so far from all they knew, to this castle. Why did Schattenturm call you?"

"I came here for the mines and because this was once a grand home. I've told you this already."

"No, there's more. You've kept something back. I sense that Fridolin knows what you've been after. Remember what I said about the darkness. You came here for a very specific reason, didn't you? What is it?"

"I knew that the von Voitsbergs were in serious debt. It seemed a good opportunity to have a country house."

Astrid's hand twitched.

"Herr, you did more than learn of the debt. You manipulated the debt, didn't you? You used your powerful connections to pressure the bank into taking a hard line against the von Voitsbergs. Because of you, the bank reneged on their previously established agreement allowing the family to stay on the estate and work slowly at paying off the debts."

"I was just doing what any smart businessman in my position would do."

"But your motives went beyond those of an opportunistic businessman, didn't they? You didn't buy the house. In fact, you didn't pay a single forint for it. You got it for the same deal the bank had arranged with the von Voitsbergs, with the exception that you would pay off the debts within five years. You did this thinking you could cash in on the hidden treasure, the vast art and antiques, and then the property itself. You planned to sell the estate, pay the debt you assumed the day you acquired it, and pocket the rest. Your motives were pure greed."

"Johan, is that true? You brought us here for that?" Erzsébet asked over the table.

Baum sighed. "Yes, it's true. I'm not going to lie. I'd seen the bills on the old freiherr's accounts, from his lifestyle, and I knew they were less than it would've cost me to build and furnish a place like this from scratch. You'd have needed more than three times what he owed, and then some. I also knew the income from his investments, holdings, and title would never have let him build up the kind of resources he'd have needed to live the lifestyle he'd enjoyed. So, I concluded that he, like many wealthy men, had a secret stash. That's why he could spend so freely and keep the bankers at bay, by throwing some cash at them when he needed to. His bills were a fraction of what I suspected he must've had squirreled away. When I heard the rumor of the treasure, I knew I was right. This was an opportunity I couldn't pass up."

"But you didn't just hear the rumor, did you? Your lawyer, Dobay, told you all about it. The same lawyer that Andrej hired to contest the freiherr's will."

"Yes. It's true. He's well-known for challenging nobility in court."

"Though, you hadn't anticipated Andrej would return to look for the treasure you sought as well."

"No. I wasn't expecting any competition in seeking the treasure. That damn fool got in my way at every turn."

"Until you realized, in his own way, he served your purpose. If he found the treasure, you knew legally he couldn't keep it. So you let him look. You encouraged him even. And, you let him stay on, despite his character."

"Yes."

"Though you couldn't contain your anger when you found out he'd been after your wife. Right under your nose, he'd been doing what you couldn't, making her happy even for a while. What about your rage, Herr Baum? Your wife didn't have bruises on her neck for two weeks because of Andrej, did she?"

Baum looked to his wife, but couldn't meet her eyes.

"Did you defend her honor, later that night in the maze?"

"No!"

"Tell us why finding the treasure was so important that you allowed a man like Andrej to stay on here, be in contact with your family. Even after you knew what he'd done."

"What are you talking about?"

"You have no fortune at all do you? It's gone. Finding the von Voitsberg stash was your last hope."

"What!" Rachel said as she and her mother both stared at Johan.

"Your mines have been underfunded and so have become unsafe. You've had two accidents with deaths this year and your shareholders called you down to Budapest urgently just last night. Did more of them pull their funding from your company? Leave you bankrupt?"

"Yes," Baum said in little more than a whisper, his face turned down. His eyes were red like his fleshy face. "There isn't much I can do but force cutbacks on my company and sell my mines and factories." He looked to his wife. "I should have told you. If I sell, there might be enough left to start over with."

Hermann looked around the table, following the path the spirit took, watching it move through the air and circle the candle. "I sense that the dark one within our circle did not kill Andrej merely for banal desire. Frau Astrid, tell us what Andrej did after the late freiherr's death."

She grimaced and her pulse intensified, Hermann could feel it in her grasp.

"You already know what he did, Herr Horst. I told you earlier today."

"Frau Astrid, this isn't about me or my knowledge. Herr von Voitsberg, Georg, is present with us. He needs to understand what happened as a result of his decisions so long ago, and who they've hurt. Frau Kam, tell me what the spirits are doing."

"Oh, Herr Horst, the dark one is taking shape I can see he's wearing dark, shabby clothes, but I can't see his face. It's a swirling dark cloud. The other one, Fridolin, he's there behind Frau Astrid. I can see him rubbing her shoulder and nodding. He says that it's all right."

"How dare you use this charade to air my family's secrets." Astrid glared at Frau Kam, then Hermann.

Géza watched intently, not entirely certain where Hermann was leading the group. He sensed that unlike the others, Hermann hesitated when he reached Astrid. Was he questioning his approach, or was it something more personal?

"We deserved better. Andrej was a cruel man, we all know that. After my uncle's funeral, he tried to contest my brother's inheritance. No one gave him any credit though, being bastard-born. How could we? He was too stubborn or too stupid to see it though, and tried his best to humiliate my family. Fortunately, he failed, but his brutishness never diminished. After he returned to Schattenturm, he wasted no time in tormenting me and the rest of the staff with his presence."

"That wasn't all of it though," said Hermann. "He told you of his exploits with Rachel Baum. How she had begun to cast dark spells in the castle and profane your father's intent for this house. He told you that he'd shown them the passages, or some of them at any rate. That secret you thought only you and your family had shared."

"Yes. He thought it would unhinge me, but I'm made of sterner stuff."

"You are. That's why you formulated a plan after he told you that both he and Baum were searching for the treasure. You decided to play the part of the ghosts that everyone feared already haunted this house. That's why you spied on the séance Frau Kam and the Baum children held the first night I arrived. Why you played the pianoforte in the old music room at night. Why you whispered through the walls, and used tuning forks to send strange vibrations. You thought you could make life uncomfortable for everyone. You even spread the rumor of the curse after the murder. Do you deny it?"

"I don't deny it. I know this house, and its unsettling qualities. I thought I could roam the passageways at night, appear out of nowhere as a specter, be the wraith that haunted them in their dreams. It was to scare and unsettle them ... to get them to return the deed to the bank and move on, so I might have a chance to save it ... to win it back for my family."

"Save it? With what money, Frau Astrid? The money is what you were really after, wasn't it?"

"That's not true. There is no treasure here. There never was. I've lived in this castle since I was a girl. I've been down every passage and inside every secret cavity. Every one of them. Neither my father nor my uncle ever told me about it and I never stumbled upon it. Sadly, there is no treasure, only my father and uncle's debts. They created beauty beyond imagining, but they didn't plan far enough ahead. Especially not my uncle. You can't live like a prince when you're only a knight."

"What did Andrej think when you told him the money wasn't to be found? Did he grow angry?"

"He thought I was lying as you did, but there's nothing to lie about."

"Did he try to upset you? As retribution? Did he tell you what the Baum children were planning? What Rachel had asked him for?"

"I don't know what you mean."

"I think you do. Andrej told you that he was going into the crypts to desecrate the bodies of your ancestors, of his own father, perhaps of your father too. He was seeking the treasure but he also thought to gather their bones so Rachel and Josef could sprinkle their dust around and play with their skulls as they cast spells. You had seen them in the old prayer room under the vault."

Astrid shuddered, but kept her gaze steady, focused on the candle in the center of the table.

"That night, you waited for Andrej, hidden in the dark of the maze, and you confronted him. He laughed at you, insulted you, and was even bold enough to assault you. You scratched his face when he came at you. Isn't that what happened?"

"You have it wrong, Professor." Astrid said softly, looking down at her hands, now folded in front of her, no longer completing the circle of energy.

"When he turned his back on you, and continued toward the mausoleum, you struck. You were compelled by the need to save your family's honor."

"Please, stop this!" Fürth exploded. "She doesn't deserve this." His face was turning a deep red and he started to stand.

"Sit down, Herr Fürth," ordered Hermann. "Is that what happened that night, Frau Astrid?" he asked, softly.

Astrid silently shook her head, first at Hermann, then across the table.

"That amulet you wear, it may not look it, but it's a key, isn't it?"

"Yes. It was a gift from my father. That's why I know there's no treasure."

"Andrej didn't know that though. He stole your key from you earlier in the day, the day he died. He said so in his journal."

Fürth spoke again, "Leave her alone, Herr Horst."

"Or was it your brother who went to the maze that night?" Hermann said, more forcefully.

"What? No." said Astrid.

"Your brother, Friederich Albert, the current Freiherr von Voitsberg. You said he was away near the border with Serbia, but he was seen in Salgótarján the day before Andrej's death. Did he stay over? Was it he who drove the war hammer into Andrej's skull, a message to Andrej and everyone else about the strength of the von Voitsberg spirit?"

"Look … I won't lie," she said. "I knew what Andrej was capable of. He did everything you said, but I got to the mausoleum ahead of him that night. I meant to confront him, warn him off. He couldn't get away with breaking into the mausoleum if there was a witness. And he knew I'd turn him into the police." She shook her head, tears welling up, but she strengthened her resolve. "But he didn't care. He told me he'd do whatever he wanted to. That this was his opportunity to be free. To be free of poverty, of being cheated out of his inheritance, to be free of all of us. He grabbed me and hit me hard across the cheek, he raised his fist to hit me again and I tore into his face with my nails. I began screaming for help and he knocked me to the ground. He began kicking me on the ground and when I tried to crawl away he grabbed my ankle and dragged me back. He was on top of me with his hands around my throat and I thought for certain he was going to kill me."

Astrid's eyes were liquid silver; tears ran down her cheeks. She looked across the table at Fürth. His face was red, sweat had formed on his brow. He was holding his head in his hands.

"I started to black out when I heard Fürth's voice. He was screaming for Andrej to get off me. He was running toward us through the alley. Andrej turned to look and I scrambled away and got to my feet. I was holding onto the side of the bench, doubled over … trying to breathe when Fürth swung the hammer at Andrej. He missed, but it was enough to stop Andrej from coming after me again.

"Frau Astrid, don't!" said Fürth. He was struggling to stand and his face was dripping with sweat. He'd gone from red to an unnatural shade of grey. "I murdered Andrej Fehér," said Fürth, gasping for air.

A stunned silence filled the room. The candle burned brightly in the dark, the one ray of light through the darkness that had nearly consumed them all. Frau Kovács began to sob softly.

The old white-haired butler made it to his feet and grabbed his chest as he fell backwards to the floor moaning with pain.

Géza yelled for his officers. "We need light, and open all the doors. Get some air in here."

Hermann and one of the officers rushed around the table to Fürth's crumpled form. Hermann flung the man's chair out of the way and pulled him away from the table to give him more room to breathe. Astrid ran too. In a swirl of black and gold, and ashen-blond hair, she came around the table to Fürth, collapsing onto the floor beside him.

"Fürth! Fürth! God, someone, do something. He's having a heart attack!" she pleaded.

"Give him some room. You all, come away," Géza told the others.

Astrid was crying while Fürth gasped and gnashed his teeth through the pain. One of the officers approached Astrid to remove her, but Hermann waved him off. Fürth raised a hand and Astrid clasped hold of it, fear and sorrow erupting.

He managed to shake his head. Then he turned to face Hermann. "It was … me. I killed Andrej. I took the hammer from the armory that night … I saw them in the center of the maze. I dashed through the tunnels to get to the maze before he could kill her. I was afraid I'd get there too late."

Another wave of pain hit him. For a minute, all Fürth could do was stare upward. He pushed himself beyond it.

"I failed once. I failed him. I couldn't do it again."

Hermann looked to Astrid. She was crying and holding Fürth's hand in both of her own. "No Fürth, No."

Géza had approached, searching for Hermann's reaction. Hermann nodded, "Send for a doctor, quickly. We have our killer, but there won't be an arrest."

The light returned to the room as one of the footmen lit the gas in the chandeliers. Fürth was quickly turning from grey to bluish purple, his pupils dilated.

Hermann watched as Astrid lowered her face to Fürth's. She whispered into his ear, "Dear man, you have now saved my life twice."

He attempted a faint smile. "I swore to him, Astrid. I swore to Georg ... on my life and ... love for him that I would help Andrej. I failed. I failed so often ... as I failed with Georg and Kovács. I couldn't do what I should have done back then. I'm not going to fail you too."

"You didn't fail him."

"I broke my oath. This is my ... punishment."

"You did more than you ever should have done, more than even my father did. You have more honor than most who've walked these halls. You've proved that."

Pain mingled with tears in his blue-green eyes as he raised his hand from her grasp to cup Astrid's cheek.

"I see him, Astrid." He smiled. "I see—"

The candle on the table blew out with a soft breeze as Fürth's focus turned inward, out of sight of the living.

Chapter 28

It took hours to get everyone's statements with the officers that Géza had brought from Budapest. They wanted to be sure that every piece of the story of Andrej Fehér's life and death was fully recorded, to leave no room for doubt. Fürth's body had been taken below stairs to wait for the undertaker. The footmen and kitchen maids stayed up through the night to keep the coffee going, leaving everyone in a dazed state by the early hours of the morning. No one was allowed to leave the ballroom, so the classes and cliques had split to their separate corners.

Johan and Erzsébet seemed to be locked in a low, but heated discussion with their children for much of the time.

When an opening appeared with the patriarch, Hermann approached.

"Herr Horst, the great spirit psychologist," Johan said, as he filled a cup of coffee from the setting placed on the center table. "It was quite a trick you pulled tonight. I thought you meant to frame me with all that talk of the darkness and what have you."

"People are more inclined to be honest with each other, and themselves, when placed in stressful situations. I never meant to frame you for Andrej's death. Yes, there was a lot of evidence that implicated you. However, once I began to piece the other parts together, your motive just wasn't complete."

"Well, there's that then."

"What did you plan to do with Andrej, given his hold over you and your family?"

Herr Baum sighed and put his cup on his saucer. "Truth be told, I don't know what I would have ended up doing with him. I wanted him fired, sure. I knew he would never follow orders or fall into line, a man like him rarely does. I'm glad it never came to another end. That day, I confronted Erzsébet and she told me that nothing happened between them. I didn't know if I could believe her because I don't know that I would believe myself if I were in the same position. I was … wrong to treat her the way I did."

"Not many men would have the dignity to admit they're wrong in that way. I'm glad you do. Though, I think the more important and immediate task at hand will be Rachel and Josef. What they did was extreme. Not just morally, but psychologically too."

"Her phase, if you want to call it that, is at an end. She was retaliating against me and her mother for taking her away from Budapest and the life she'd known. That standard isn't coming back for some time. So, we've decided to move everyone into Erzsébet's hereditary family home east of old Pest. We'll be keeping a tight eye on them both and we'll do what we can to straighten her out."

Hermann nodded. "You might do well to make a habit of speaking privately, but openly and honestly with her every day. She's looking to complete her vision of herself, but that vision, at the moment, is self-destructive. Hearing her feelings without judgement and meeting them with practical reality will help her start to see the world as you two have."

"It'll be a journey to just hear her, for myself more than Erzsébet. But I'll do whatever it takes to get her back to normal."

"Herr Baum, if you plan on leaving, moving back towards Budapest, what will you do with Schattenturm?"

"We can't stay here, that's certain. I should be able to transfer the lease back to the bank. My lawyer had a

twenty-four-month release clause built into the arrangement I made, and nothing's damaged. Erzsébet's home is
too small for most of what we brought with us, so whatever
price the bank can sell our furniture for should sweeten the
deal for them. The mines in Salgótarján are another
matter, along with my company. Getting back most of what
I sunk into this place will help us to stay afloat, but without
a restructuring, I don't know how long that'll last. I'm just
glad to have Erzsébet with me, no matter what happens."

"You know, there's a concept of karma in the Orient.
That whatever one does, good or bad, is returned to them
in kind. Doing what's right may help you more than you yet
realize. I wish you luck, Herr Baum."

"Likewise, Professor."

"There is one thing I would ask."

"Yes?"

"When you release the house back to the bank, indicate that you'd like for Herr Friederich von Voitsberg and
Frau Astrid to be considered under special circumstances
to regain the estate. Her reputation is strong, and she's liked
by many of the bankers, it's how she held onto the estate in
the first place. If you suggest this, it may get you what you
need."

Baum chuffed, but nodded.

They did not shake, nor could Hermann say they
parted as friends. However, despite all that had happened
to him, a change for the better had come over Johan Baum.
A softness, or perhaps a realization of humility in the face
of fate.

———————————◆———————————

Astrid stared out of the south-facing windows that overlooked the drive to the castle. Beyond the ramparts, the
blue hue of the tinges of morning were beginning to illuminate the details of trees and the far-off town of Salgótarján.
In a few minutes, the whole room would be bathed in pure
morning light.

"It will be quite the sight," Hermann said as he neared her. "The dawn."

"It will. Though, not one like to ever belong to the von Voitsbergs again."

"That's not yet set in stone."

She turned. "It may as well be, Herr Horst. Nothing's changed for me because of ... this."

"Herr Baum is leaving Schattenturm. He's returning the deed to the bank in exchange for absolution of his obligations. Things will be as they were a year ago when you were negotiating with the bank to pay off the debts and keep Schattenturm. It may not be deeded to you, but you may have a chance with the bank."

She gasped. "Can that be true? Then it means ... no, I won't spoil it."

"What is it?"

"My brother visited, brining good news, the day before Andrej died. Friederich had helped the Serbs in their fight against the Turks. It was a covert action, apparently. The empire couldn't get involved directly. For his service, he's been extended a new title and the income attached to it. He told me that they were still early days to celebrate. But with this news and his newly landed income, there may be just enough to cover a mortgage on the estate."

She was smiling, but still looked worried.

"That's wonderful news. I wish you both the best, and your mother also."

"Thank you, Professor."

A pause filled the space, like the edge of a precipice.

"Frau Astrid, what really happened in the maze?"

She studied his face for a moment, contemplating whether she should follow her instincts, whether she should trust him. She shook her head and looked toward the rising rays of morning sunlight. "He laughed when Fürth missed him with the hammer. He called him a pathetic old fool, a sorry excuse for a man. He grabbed the hammer from Fürth and pretended like he was going to hit him with it, swinging it at Fürth's face. Fürth didn't flinch. I don't think he even blinked. I had regained my breath by then and I told him to leave us alone. He laughed and tossed the hammer on the bench. He said 'If you ever get in my way again, I'll kill you and see that your skull is placed alongside your father's at the point of the Devil's star. Now I'm going to finally get what's rightfully mine.' He picked up his gear and turned toward the mausoleum."

Astrid became quiet, so still that she appeared to have stopped breathing.

Hermann watched her profile, "What happed next?"

"I picked up the hammer, and as he took a step forward ... I buried it in the back of his head." She turned and met his eyes, unflinching.

"Hmm, I thought so."

"Are you going to have me arrested, Professor?"

"No. I live in a world that is not so right and wrong, so black and white. I used to, but not anymore. Because of your actions, the world is less one man who hurt many people and showed no remorse, or aptitude for rehabilitation. How he left this life to enter the next is not so much my concern."

"Do you think he'll return from the afterlife, Professor, like the subjects of your studies?"

"Ah, now that is something to consider. Certainly his transition was not a peaceful one."

"No. No indeed."

"Take care, frau. It is my experience that when we ourselves are uncomfortable with our actions, a channel to a shadow realm may open."

"I've spent my life in service to my family ...," she looked out toward the sunrise. "I fear no dark shadows." She smiled. "How could I have lived and loved Schattenturm all these years if I wasn't comfortable with shadows? And you? What will you do now, Professor? Will this experience color your research?"

"Oh, undoubtedly. And you, what will you do now?"

"Once my brother can come away, I'll explain everything to him and try to work on Schattenturm. It'll be for him that I do it, and his children eventually. And, if I should ever find love for myself, like that which my parents shared, it would be a blessing I would cherish forever."

He smiled. "That reminds me, your amulet, the key, you've tried it everywhere inside. Every hall and passage?"

"Yes, that's right. There's nothing to be found in Schattenturm besides history."

"Well, I don't think you've explored quite enough outside of Schattenturm. You know the island in the pond by the end of the sluice, from the spring's old bathing room?"

"Yes. My father and I used to walk there when I was a girl. He called it our own little holy isle. A reference to the Grail stories he loved."

"Well, you'll find a little monument hidden in the brush at its center. You'd hardly see it except by moonlight. On it is a keyhole. I think your father meant for you to have not just the key to Schattenturm, but a key to something else as well."

She looked quizzically at him.

He smiled and bowed, then turned and walked away.

"Leaving so soon?" Géza said as he walked through the keep's door onto the pea gravel of the courtyard.

"It seems my work here is finished, Inspector," Hermann replied. "Do you think you have enough to close the case?"

"Thanks to you, yes. Though, I'm not sure my commander will be as happy as if we had someone to bring in, for the newspapers you know. But in a way, I'm glad Fürth didn't have to go through all that."

"Would you have really taken him in? It seemed like self-defense to me."

"You know I live by a rigid code. It's not for me to render judgement, that's the responsibility of the court system. I don't always agree but ... I'm duty bound."

"Yes, I knew that. I'd be disappointed if you were anything else." Hermann smiled at his friend.

"I can't thank you enough for your help," said Géza. "Without you, I would've gotten nowhere. Worse, I probably would've accused Baum openly and lost my job as a result." He traced the edges of his beard. "Though, I can't say it wouldn't have been nice to give that man a good punch."

They both laughed.

"How did you know it was Frau Astrid that gave us a run for our money through the house?"

"I knew that she was involved in some way. It was her ethos about this place. She cared deeply about it and wanted to preserve its memory, even at her own expense. She had unfettered knowledge of the passages and access to the house as well. What would you do, what could you do, if you wanted your home back?"

"She's gutsy. I'll give her that." Géza laughed and shook his head. "And how did you know it wasn't Baum?"

"It came to me after Baum's drunken outburst in the dining room. If he'd killed Andrej, he wouldn't have covered it up. Being who he is, he wouldn't have needed to. He would have claimed the man suddenly attacked him and that he was forced to defend himself. No one would have questioned it. Plus, he couldn't have navigated the passageways even if he knew they existed."

"And the others? How'd you rule them out?"

"Pavol slept in the barn that night because he didn't want to face Andrej. He assumed Andrej was back in the cottage. The Baum siblings thought their father was guilty as we heard. Erzsébet didn't have a strong enough motive, he hadn't harmed her really. I believe Frau Schrode might have had the fortitude to do it, but she'd already taken care of the last maid he tried to ruin and I don't believe she was aware of the tunnels. His mother, poor Frau Kovács couldn't have done it, but she needed to come clean for the sake of her own conscience, which is why I had her attend the séance. Really, that's in part why I had all of them attend. From a psychological perspective, they needed to air their years of dark secrets and be free of the power those secrets held over them."

"That's the *darkness* you kept mentioning. I wondered about that."

"But what threw me off was the hammer. I was wrong when I thought the hammer had been used to send a message about the von Voitsberg sigil. If anything, Fürth would have wanted to do the opposite. He grabbed it because it was a convenient weapon."

"Frau Astrid could still have grabbed the hammer in the night and taken it down to the maze, no?"

"Not the way she had to come. It would have been extremely far out of her way to try and get ahold of the hammer and get ahead of Andrej before he made it to the crypts that night. And why that hammer? If she wanted a weapon, she could have taken one from the cottage."

"So, then you suspected Fürth. The last man with access to the hammer, the tunnels, and who had no alibi for his whereabouts that night."

"What I was lacking was a strong motive for him," said Hermann. The séance provided that. But what really gave it all away was the fact that Andrej's journal said he had a key that night, but no key was found on his body. Frau Astrid constantly checked and held her amulet during the last few days, almost as a subconscious means of ensuring it wasn't stolen again. I could tell it was important to her, and the shape of it does remind one of a large key, so long as you look at it correctly."

A footman brought out Hermann's cases and strapped them to the back of the hearse-like carriage waiting for him.

"Well, I'll say it again. Thank you for everything, Hermann." Géza extended his hand which Hermann shook in kind.

"Don't hesitate to call me again should you ever need a parapsychologist."

"Take care of yourself. And know that if you ever need an investigator, you've got one."

Hermann smiled, then climbed into the carriage. With a nod and a short wave from Géza, the carriage turned and rolled through the gatehouse of Schattenturm.

Hermann slid to the other side to watch the diminishing view of the castle from the window. The dawn was truly beautiful, illuminating the stonework and the layers of history that the castle had been built upon, Medieval ramparts and Neo-Gothic detailing. The glare was not so intense as to obscure Astrid, still in the window of the ballroom looking out. She raised a hand and waved at Hermann. He gave a wave back through the window of the coach.

There was something else, above the ballroom, on the next floor. Hermann only caught it out of the corner of his eye for a moment. A half-visible outline of a man with long blond hair and the same bright silver-grey eyes as Astrid. He had watched Hermann's carriage drive away from Schattenturm, though instead of his usual scowl, he bore a smile.

About The Author

Ingram Hargrave is an author of historical mystery and speculative fiction. His love of history, particularly antiquity and the late nineteenth century, propelled him to pick up the pen and give life to new stories. He is excited to probe the depths of rich European history and excite readers with new settings and enigmatic characters rooted in classical literature. Ingram believes in the value of folk tradition and the legacy of high culture in all things.

A native of Virginia, Ingram lives just outside of Washington, D.C. He graduated from the University of Mary Washington with a B.A. in political science, and from Tulane University School of Law with a Master of Jurisprudence. When he is not touring historic homes and gardens around Virginia, or hiking and canoeing in the Blue Ridge Mountains, you can find him buried in his home library with his standard poodle, Ashby, nearby.

Connect Online

———————————————

Author Website: IngramHargrave.com

Instagram: @IngramHargrave

Twitter: @IngramHargrave

Printed in the USA
CPSIA information can be obtained
at www.ICGtesting.com
LVHW021443011024
792647LV00003B/419